Praise for Kristy Woods

"A major new voice in Southern fiction."
—Elin Hilderbrand, *New York*

"Harvey pulls the reader into the hearts and souls of her characters."
—Heather Gudenkauf, *New York Times* bestselling author

"Southern fiction at its best. . . . Beautifully written."
—Eileen Goudge, *New York Times* bestselling author

"Sweet as sweet tea on the outside and strong as steel on the inside. . . .
Kristy Woodson Harvey is a natural."
—Ann Garvin, author of *On Maggie's Watch* and *The Dog Year*

Praise for *The Secret to Southern Charm*

"*The Secret to Southern Charm* is a compelling, beautifully drawn tale
of love, hope, and small-town secrets. The richly detailed backdrop of
a charming coastal town and the struggles and joys of four genera-
tions of women solidifies Kristy Woodson Harvey's spot as a rising
star of Southern fiction."
—Mary Alice Monroe, *New York Times* bestselling
author of *Beach House for Rent*

"The characters will leap off the page and into your heart, and you'll
find yourself rooting for them so fervently, you'll forget they're not
actually real. Kristy Woodson Harvey has delivered another master-
piece. . . . Let's just say that this one had better have a sequel too, because I'm not ready to leave these charming ladies behind."
—Kristin Harmel, international bestselling
author of *The Room on Rue Amélie*

"An engrossing contemporary tale that readers of Southern fiction
will enjoy. . . . Harvey is proving herself to be an author to look out for
in Southern fiction."
—RT Book Reviews

"Harvey's growing fan base will find another great beach read in this second novel in her Peachtree Bluff trilogy. . . . Harvey is an up-and-coming Southern writer with staying power."

—*Booklist*

"Looking for a perfect romancey-angsty read? Then look no further. . . . Harvey's exploration of infidelity and the challenges of being a military wife add wonderful layers to an already great read."

—*USA Today*'s *Happy Ever After*

"Harvey . . . infuses plenty of woman power in this story of juggling the highs and lows of life."

—*Raleigh News & Observer*

Praise for *Slightly South of Simple*

"Kristy Woodson Harvey really knows how to tell a Southern tale. Every single time her stories unwind gently, like a soft wind in Georgia, then that wind catches you off guard and throws you into her characters' tumultuous lives. I loved it."

—Cathy Lamb, *New York Times* bestselling author

"Kristy Woodson Harvey cuts to the heart of what it means to be a born-and-bred Southerner, complete with the unique responsibilities, secrets, and privileges that conveys. . . . It's easy to see why everyone is buzzing about *Slightly South of Simple*."

—Cassandra King, author of
The Sunday Wife and *The Same Sweet Girls*

"Harvey's devotion to realistic character development pays off by the end of the novel, which provides clear resolutions to some plots and leaves others hanging in a way that practically begs for a sequel. . . . *Slightly South of Simple* is so warm, inviting, and real . . ."

—*BookPage*

"My prediction is that writers come and writers go, but Kristy Woodson Harvey is here to stay. The warmth, wit, and wisdom of this novel pave her way into the exclusive sisterhood of Southern writers."

—*Huffington Post*

"Full of heart, emotion, and Southern charm . . ."

—*PopSugar*

"With a charming, coastal Southern setting, *Slightly South of Simple* is a heartfelt story about the universal themes of love, loss, forgiveness, and family. I'm thrilled to hear that this book is part of a series and look forward to getting to know this cast of strong Southern women even better."

—*Deep South Magazine*

the southern side *of* paradise

ALSO FROM KRISTY WOODSON HARVEY
AND GALLERY BOOKS

The Secret to Southern Charm
Slightly South of Simple

the southern side *of* paradise

A NOVEL

Kristy Woodson Harvey

GALLERY BOOKS

New York   London   Toronto   Sydney   New Delhi

G

Gallery Books
An Imprint of Simon & Schuster, Inc.
1230 Avenue of the Americas
New York, NY 10020

First Gallery Books trade paperback edition May 2019

GALLERY BOOKS and colophon are registered trademarks of Simon & Schuster, Inc.

For information about special discounts for bulk purchases, please contact Simon & Schuster Special Sales at 1-866-506-1949 or business@simonandschuster.com.

The Simon & Schuster Speakers Bureau can bring authors to your live event. For more information or to book an event, contact the Simon & Schuster Speakers Bureau at 1-866-248-3049 or visit our website at www.simonspeakers.com.

Manufactured in the United States of America

10 9 8 7 6 5

Library of Congress Cataloging-in-Publication Data is available.

ISBN 978-1-9821-1662-0
ISBN 978-1-9821-1663-7 (ebook)

To my mom, Beth Woodson,
and my aunts, Cathy Singer, Anne O'Berry, and Nancy Sanders,
who taught me what it means to be a sister

ONE

ansley: the best friend a girl can have

Growing up, I didn't like surprises. Not surprise parties, not presents. Even losing a tooth was steeped in horror, as I couldn't stand the idea of some tiny Tinker Bell sneaking under my pillow unannounced.

My grandmother, the one who lived her entire life in what was now my white clapboard house on the waterfront in Peachtree Bluff, Georgia's historic downtown, used to say, "Honey, you better get used to that, because life is nothing but one big surprise after another. You can plot and you can plan, but God will always have the last word."

As I sat in the porch swing beside Jack, my first love, the one I'd met right here in Peachtree Bluff the summer I turned fifteen, I realized that my grandmother was right. I never would have imagined that our lives would weave and cross and intersect down any path that would lead us back to each other.

Yet here we were, not on my front porch but on the front porch of the house next door, the one I had wanted to decorate for decades, the one that Jack had bought. It was right beside my grandmother's house, the one she left me in her will. She didn't leave it to my mom, my brothers, or my cousins. Just me. None of us found out until her will was read. Surprise.

My husband, Carter, being killed in the second tower during the 9/11 attacks? Surprise. Having to leave New York and come back to raise my three girls in the town where I had spent my childhood summers? Surprise. My daughter Caroline's husband cheating on her with a supermodel whom my daughter Emerson then played in a movie? Surprise. And my daughter Sloane's husband missing in action in Iraq? Yup. Another surprise.

So, obviously, surprises had been a mixed bag at best for me. But as I held the hand of the man I first held hands with, his brown eyes as bright and youthful as the day we met, I realized that I'd developed a newfound respect for surprises. That my brother Scott, a travel writer, helped find and rescue Sloane's husband floored me in a way nothing else ever had. My feisty, beautiful, and ferociously bold Caroline giving her husband, James, a second chance was the shock of my life, and, of course, Jack and me finding our way back to each other, finding this love in a new way, a bigger and better one, was nothing short of a miracle. So I had to consider that this latest surprise—the one that included a diamond on the left hand of my youngest daughter, a diamond that I assumed would bring her back to Peachtree Bluff and remove her from Hollywood, where she had spent the last eight years pursuing her acting—might work out OK.

I looked across the water toward Starlite Island, my family's home away from home, the place where I had so many of my best memories. My grandparents' ashes were there, and now, after a painful but beautiful few months of caring for my mother at the end of her life, my parents' ashes were there, too. I had to consider that one day, Jack and I would also become a part of the island that had defined our childhoods and, to a large extent, our adulthoods, too.

The swing rocked rhythmically, facing into the most beautiful sunset in the world, the view almost completely unobstructed. But I had to admit that I loved the view down the street, of a dozen more white clapboard houses of various shapes and sizes, almost as much. It wasn't only the houses that I loved (or, maybe, that the decorator in me loved) but the people, too, the ones who had wrapped their arms around my family and refused to let go, the ones who had loved us back to life after it felt like tragedy would define us forever.

As if he were reading my mind, Jack's voice broke into my thoughts as he said, "Ansley, I have honestly never felt this happy. Getting you back is the biggest surprise of my life."

There it was again, that word: *surprise*. I leaned my head on his shoulder. "You know, Jack, after a lifetime of hating surprises, I think you might have taught me to love them."

He kissed my hand and whispered, "I hope I never stop surprising you."

It said a lot about Jack—about us, about our relationship,

about how, though I longed for the slow and steady, the comfort and rhythm that I had come to rely on in my marriage to Carter, Jack still relished the unknown. And I was OK with that.

As long as I had this front porch and this sunset, I would be OK. I could roll with the punches and face the surprises head-on, with an open heart. It was a happy thought, a good one. And unbeknownst to me, it was one I would need over the next few months when the surprises—good and bad—just kept coming. I spent a lifetime thinking that surprises were the enemy. These next few months, I would learn that wasn't true at all. Surprises, if you take them for what they are, can be the very best friend a girl can have.

emerson: the middle

Peachtree Bluff is one of those places that everyone can't wait to grow up and leave. Only no one ever does. Not really. Because they get out in the real world and realize that regular cities, normal places, they don't care about you like your hometown. They don't love you no matter what, don't say hey to you in the grocery store or remember your favorite lunch order. Because to the people in the real world, you won't always be the head cheerleader.

So maybe that's why, even though my plan had been to go back to LA and continue to chase my acting dreams, my boyfriend Mark's marriage proposal was tempting. Marrying Mark would remove the stress, take the unknown out of the equation. I would come home to Peachtree. Coffee Kyle would bring me my favorite latte every morning. I would have babies and stroll them down to Sloane Emerson, Mom's store named after yours truly, in the afternoons. Everyone would know my name.

And that's what I wanted, right? Everyone to know my name? Wasn't that why I had gotten into acting in the first place? It was so hazy now. I'd like to think that I loved my craft, that becoming famous—or a little famous, like I currently was—was the by-product of that. But I was twenty-six years old. If that fame I had longed for hadn't happened yet, would it ever? And if I wasn't ever going to get to the top, did I want to keep clawing and scratching to keep myself in the middle?

But I didn't think about any of that in the moment Mark proposed. I'd only been back in Peachtree Bluff for six months, had only been back with Mark for five. But I'd dated him for three years before, so it wasn't like we were starting from scratch. It was more like hitting the refresh button.

We'd been sitting at the end of Kimmy's dock, on her farm outside of town, resting after picking early summer's blueberries and tomatoes. It was a decrepit, rambling dock with uneven boards and nails sticking up, the kind of dock that some people would think needed to be repaired. It would never have flown in the historic district where Mom and Mark lived, where tourists paced and the Historical Association inspected with a disapproving eye, where appearances needed to be kept. But Kimmy, Peachtree Bluff's produce girl, didn't care about appearances. In fact, she was probably the only person in the whole town who didn't care what anyone thought. I loved that about her. But it kind of scared me, too. People caring what other people thought was the basis of our society. It was what allowed people like me to be famous.

"Can you even imagine?" I asked Mark that day. We had slipped out of our flip-flops, skimming our toes across the water. Had some schoolkids not been roaming around, I would have peeled my clothes off, jumped in, and made Mark do the same. But they were. They were too little to really know what was what, but my mom would hear about it, and she would be mad. It was a battle I didn't feel like fighting that day.

I rested my head on Mark's shoulder, and he laced his fingers through mine. "Imagine what, babe?"

"Being Sloane right now." I paused. "Or Adam, for that matter." My older sister's husband had been MIA in Iraq for months, and, against all odds, our uncle had done the unthinkable. He had found Sloane's husband. Or at least helped find him, anyway. It was one of those things that made you believe in miracles, that made you know that there are so many things in life that can't be explained.

What Mark said next was one of them. "Don't go back, Em."

"What?" I said, my feet still lazily trailing in the water.

"Don't go back to LA," he whispered.

I had been in Georgia for the past six months, filming a movie about a model named Edie Fitzgerald. It had been a dream job—until the news broke that my oldest sister Caroline's husband was having an affair with the real-life Edie Fitzgerald. That had not gone over well, as you can imagine. I would be finished filming at the end of the month, and then it would be time to go back home.

Home.

It was funny, after being back in teeny-tiny Peachtree Bluff for so long, to think of sprawling LA as home.

I kissed Mark's cheek and yawned, not wanting to have this conversation now, not wanting to disturb the feeling of the sunshine on my face and the soft breeze in my long blond hair.

"Do you remember the night Peachtree High won state?" he whispered.

I laughed, my head still on his shoulder. "You mean the night *you* won state?"

His turn to laugh. "Well, I mean, I didn't want to say that . . . but if that's how you remember it."

Mark had been the star of the Peachtree Bluff basketball team all four years, had been recruited by several wonderful colleges, and had gone to UGA on a full scholarship. He probably could have gone pro if he wanted to, but that wasn't Mark. After he graduated, he'd been ready to come home, take over the family shipping business, take over the care of his mother, who, I'll be honest, was the only black mark on the man's record. Thank the Lord for me that crazy bat had moved to Florida for more sun and fewer taxes.

Everyone had been jealous of Mark and me, Peachtree High's version of a power couple. He would play in the NBA, and I would be the basketball mogul's trophy. Only, I didn't want to be a trophy. I wanted to be a star. And that was all on me.

"Do you remember how that felt, Emerson?" Mark asked now. "All those fans cheering in the stands, that anticipation of those final moments, feeling like your entire life hung on that shot, knowing that, win or lose, you would never be the same?"

I smiled. "I couldn't ever forget it, Mark." Those nights became a part of us. A piece of me would always be the flyer, the top of the pyramid. Sometimes I longed for the simplicity of those days, for the feeling that life would never get better, I would never get better. Sometimes it scared me that maybe I had been right.

"That's exactly how I feel right now," Mark said.

I laughed and sat up, looking at him. "What do you mean, that's how you feel right now?"

He cleared his throat. "You know, Em, this wasn't really how I was planning to do this, but I can't wait anymore."

I could feel my brow furrowing. "Do what? What are you talking about?" My pulse quickened, but I had no idea what was coming next, no inkling of how my life was getting ready to change.

"Emerson, I used to look at you when I was standing on the free-throw line, when you were jumping up and down in that crop top and car-wash skirt, and I knew even then that everything I would ever do for the rest of my life would be for you. I wasn't only making those free throws for you. I was making a future for you. For us."

Now my heart was beating really fast. Part of me thought this was just a typical Mark confession of undying love. The other part of me thought that maybe this was something more. "Mark, I—"

He cut me off. "I tried to move on, Em. I swear I did. But

no one else is you, and it is so abundantly clear to me that you are the one true love of my life. No one is ever going to make me feel the way you did." He took a deep breath. "The way you *do*."

I was having a hard time swallowing or breathing or any of the other things that are supposed to be automatic biological functions, because he was pulling his feet out of the water and shifting onto his knee.

I wanted to stop him, say something, do something. But before I could, Mark reached into his pocket and pulled out a ring box.

"Oh, my God," I said, my hand over my mouth. "You have a ring."

When they have a ring, it's not a spur-of-the-moment thing. It's a real thing.

"Emerson Murphy," Mark said with a huge grin on his face, "will you marry me? Please?"

I gasped, and I could see the hope written all over his face. Did he seriously think that I would say yes? That a big, sparkly ring could counteract all the conversations we'd had about our future? I couldn't count the number of times over the past few months we had talked about the impracticality of this. I wouldn't, couldn't, stay in Peachtree. He'd contended that he couldn't leave his business behind and run off to LA. I was willing to commute, to fly back and forth, to live a life between two places. But Mark wasn't. And that was the sticking point for us every time. That was where we always ended the conversation, where it got too hard.

I couldn't bear to say no to his proposal. I loved Mark with all my heart. And maybe this proposal meant he would change his mind, he would be willing to compromise. But I couldn't quite say yes, either. I wanted to marry Mark. I even wanted to have his babies, which was a big damn deal, considering how important looking flawless in a swimsuit was to my career. But I also wanted to go back to my old life. No, I wasn't wild about the traffic or the high rent, but I was wild about the thrill of being in front of a camera, of becoming someone else. It was an incredible feeling.

But this was an incredible feeling, too. Thinking about spending my life with Mark, waking up with him every morning and going to sleep with him every night. It was all I had wanted as a girl.

"Mark, I . . ." I started, but I didn't know how to finish.

He was looking at me now, his green eyes so full of anticipation and hope, his hair mussed from the day on the farm. He was so handsome, but he didn't know it, preppy in that good Southern way where he could put on a tux and take you to the ballet, pull on a pair of work boots and plow a field, or don camo all day in a deer stand and bring home dinner. My heart swelled so full of love for him that I leaned over and kissed him.

"Is that a yes?" he said, pulling back from me.

Damn. I knew I shouldn't have kissed him.

I bit the inside of my cheek. "It's a let me think about it for a minute."

"A minute?"

I shrugged. "A day?"

"Oh," he said sadly, looking down at his feet.

I had ruined everything. Again. I had ruined it when I left for LA and Mark left for college, when he had pursued the plan, taken the basketball scholarship, and I, instead of choosing electives and picking out a roommate, had hopped on an airplane, found a waitressing job and an agent. And now I had done it again. Tears of guilt puddled in my eyes as Mark stood up, looking so forlorn that I wanted to pull him back down and say, *Just kidding! Of course I'll marry you!* Then we could revisit the skinny-dipping plan I had formulated earlier.

But he was already walking away. If I had to guess, I would bet tears were puddling in his eyes, too, and he didn't want me to see.

The moments that followed felt like something out of one of the movies I'd shot. With the sun high in the sky over the water and the farm grass up well past my ankles, this place seemed so foreign yet so familiar, this landscape such a piece of my past yet so unimaginable in my future. I could hear children's laughter reverberating across the acres. I couldn't help but smile, despite the tears coming down my cheeks.

I thought back to earlier that week, when my sisters and I had been talking about my future with Mark. I'd been sitting quietly with them on Caroline's front lawn, arms wrapped around my bent knees, neither of them saying anything. That's the thing about my sisters. Caroline has a big, giant mouth, and sometimes you think she'll never shut up, but she also knows when to just sit with you and rub your back. In the world's grandest ironies, she's quite nurturing.

With tears coming down my cheeks, I choked out, "I don't know what to do. Whatever choice I make, I'm giving up something I love." I had thought I was upset then, and the proposal hadn't even happened yet. It wasn't even real.

"I just don't understand." Sloane had finally piped up. "This isn't the 1950s. Relationships aren't cookie-cutter. If Mark doesn't want to live in LA, then fine, but I feel like there has to be some way to travel back and forth and work this whole thing out."

Caroline slid her arm through mine and rested her head on my shoulder. "Mark wants a really traditional relationship. If you don't, that's fine, but pretending you can gloss over that is kind of naive and silly."

I thought of my sisters that day as I trailed behind a very upset Mark, the wildflowers almost up to my knees. Life holds no guarantees, as my sister Sloane well knew after the hell she had been through these past few months.

Love was rarely easy, and sometimes it meant sacrificing something, even a piece of yourself. My sister Caroline could tell you that after the months she had spent trying to repair her relationship with her cheating husband. As the sun hit my eyes, making me squint, I realized that life was never going to be perfect. Not even mine.

I thought of my mom, of Jack, the man she had loved so much but given up in favor of my father, of us, really, since Jack never wanted children. I wondered if she regretted that decision, if she wished she had chosen him first instead, if she wished she had compromised more for love.

I thought of Mark, of how wonderful he had been these past few weeks as I dealt with doctor appointments and blood work to figure out why I was so tired and dizzy and why I seemed to bruise like a peach. He knew I might have aplastic anemia, that bone-marrow transplants and blood transfusions might be a reality of my future, and that children—as much as it broke my heart to think so—might not. I thought of how he'd stood by my side through all of that, how he'd come through for me while Grammy was dying.

And as if the breeze had carried in my answer on its wings, I knew exactly what I had to do.

"Mark!" I called, running behind him, the grass and dirt on my bare feet cool and soothing. He didn't turn. "Mark!" I called, feeling myself get out of breath, reminding me that just because we hadn't named it, that didn't mean I wasn't sick.

He finally stopped and turned to look at me, and I could see the pain in his face. But even still, when I reached him, he couldn't help but wrap his arms around my waist.

"Mark," I said softly, smiling up at him. "I think I've had enough time."

"What if I've changed my mind now?" he asked, grinning boyishly down at me.

"You can't change your mind." I shook my head. "There's no turning back now."

"There's not?"

I shook my head again, trying to be myself, trying not to slip into the character of a bride saying yes. I kissed him softly. "Mark, I love you. And I know you love me, too. And there are some things—some big things—for us to work out. But I believe that the two of us can get through whatever life throws at us."

Mark picked me up and spun me around in the air and kissed me again. "We can make it through anything," he said, setting me down and sliding the ring onto my finger.

I nodded and grinned. And I hoped like hell that it was true.

ansley: chopped liver

Thirty seconds earlier, all I had been able to think about was the email I found when I inadvertently opened my daughter Emerson's MacBook Pro instead of mine. The email on the screen from Park Avenue Hematology and Oncology that said my daughter's test results were back. It had made my blood run cold. Something might be wrong with my daughter. I stared at the screen. I tried to convince myself that it was nothing more than run-of-the-mill anemia like I had in my twenties. But as a mother, I'd become an expert at having thoughts that spiraled completely out of control. That part of me was certain it was terminal cancer.

Moments later, when I heard Emerson calling "Mom!" from the front porch, I ran out to confront her, to find out what she had been keeping from me, with my little dog, Biscuit, in my arms. But when I saw the look on her face and

Mark standing beside her, when I heard her calling her sisters, too, I realized this was not my moment.

When she squealed, "We're engaged!," her blue eyes flashing, an entirely new set of worries flooded in.

Now, twenty minutes later, I sat stock-still while Jack paced nervously around the living room. I wasn't sure exactly why he was nervous. It was sweet that he was so concerned for Emerson even though, unlike Caroline and Sloane, she wasn't even biologically his. But this reaction seemed disproportionate. If someone was going to be nervous, shouldn't it be me, the mother of the bride?

I took a sip of the champagne that Caroline had poured for all of us before my girls left to tell their friends the good news.

I sighed. "He didn't ask me for permission, Jack. What does that say about him? I mean, sure, he couldn't ask Carter. But what am I? Chopped liver?"

Jack stopped pacing. "I thought you loved Mark. I thought he was your dream husband for Emerson."

"Well, he is," I said, setting my glass on the marble-top coffee table. "But my concern is that he's *my* dream for Emerson, not Emerson's dream for Emerson."

I started crying, realizing that my child might be sick, that all her dreams might be put on hold. "Whether she decides to marry Mark might be the least of our worries," I said, wiping my eyes and clearing my throat.

"Why?" Jack asked, jerking his head in my direction, a look of terror on his face.

"Jack, what is going on with you?" The Emerson situation

was worrisome, sure. But I couldn't help but think Jack's nerves were coming from another place.

He shook his head and sat down beside me on the couch, squeezing my knee. "I'm sorry," he said. "I'm just anxious."

"I can see that. But why?"

He didn't say anything, and it hit me. I laughed out loud. "Oh, Jack, I know," I said.

"Know what?" he asked, a little too quickly.

The poor man. "You're afraid that Emerson getting married means it will be a terribly long time before we can."

He leaned back against the couch and exhaled, long and slow. "Oh, um, right," he fumbled. "You know me too well. Does that make me selfish?"

I squeezed his hand. We had talked about getting married, eventually. I could see now that Jack's eventually was sooner than mine. "It makes both of us selfish, because I'm thinking the same thing."

This would be Emerson's first and—I hoped—only marriage. I didn't want anything to steal her thunder.

"I'm sorry, sweetheart," I said.

He shrugged again. "It's OK. I just want her to be happy."

I leaned over and kissed him. He was the best man in the entire world. He was the one who got away, the one who came back, the one who had given me so many of the things I had wanted for my life. He had never asked me for anything in return. And now I got to have this man who had sacrificed so much for me, forever and for always.

Jack took my hand in his. "Let's pretend, just for a minute, that we were the engaged ones. What would we want for our wedding?"

I looked into his handsome face, the lines around his eyes that made him seem kinder yet also more distinguished, the gray around his temples where time had replaced the brown hair that the sun used to bleach lighter in the summer. "I want what you want," I said, smiling.

"I have an idea," Jack said, "but it might be crazy. In fact, I'm positive it's crazy. But I want to do it anyway."

I laughed at his enthusiasm. It was like we had switched roles: he was the effusive bride; I was the apathetic groom. "Then please, by all means, let me in on the idea."

"Well, I've been thinking about this a lot, of course." He cleared his throat. "In fact, I've been thinking about it for thirty years or so."

I wanted to say, *Spit it out, Jack. For heaven's sake.* But I didn't, of course. What I said was, "Right. So have I."

"So I'm thinking we should do it on the sandbar."

I almost spit out my champagne. The sandbar was a special spot for us. It was where Jack and I first met, where we shared our first kiss, where we danced as teenagers until the tide rose to our knees, and maybe most important of all, the place where we were forced to realize that all these years later, maybe nothing had changed, not really.

"So is that a no?" he asked.

I laughed. The sandbar came and went with the tide. It wasn't a permanent fixture. "Jack, it's preposterous. How would that even work?"

He put his arm around me and pulled me in close. "It will be exactly like the sandbar parties we had as kids. We'll time it with the tide and go from there."

I laughed. "But Jack, that was a few cases of beer and some chips. This is our wedding."

He put his hand up, painting the picture for me. "Moon tide, stars glowing, breeze blowing, bare feet in the sand, all our friends gathered around as the priest pronounces us husband and wife. Then we can move over to a real venue for the reception."

Now I was getting into the spirit. "Forget a real venue," I said. "Let's do the reception on Starlite Island."

He shook his head and kissed me. "Now you're getting the picture."

"Totally unique." I smiled. "Totally us."

"Exactly."

"So it's settled. We'll get married on the sandbar and have our reception on Starlite Island." I sighed. "Someday."

He nodded and smiled at me. "Someday, Ans."

I kissed Jack again, this time deeper, this time letting myself really feel it, that overwhelming joy that here was this man I had loved for a lifetime who would be my happily ever after. He pulled me closer, and it was only then that I felt it in the very marrow of my being, knew once and for all that his nerves and his jumpiness weren't about the timing of our wedding. I had known this man since I was fifteen years old, and I could tell he was keeping something from me.

I knew all about keeping secrets, had kept the secret that

Jack was the biological father of my eldest two daughters since the day they were born. When we discovered my husband Carter's infertility, when a rare infection from a routine intrauterine insemination had almost killed me, when Carter and I made the life-altering pact to get these children in a very unconventional way, and when I promised him that he would never have to know who the real father was, I had known about keeping secrets then, too.

Carter had eventually discovered that Jack, my first love, was the father of our first two girls. It had broken something inside him, made the pain run deeper, despite the fact that it had soothed me for my babies to be made out of love. I had wondered ever since if the truth had set either of us free. It had felt, instead, like the truth only complicated things, only put a gray haze over our marriage during one of its best times, when Carter and I had conceived our miracle baby, Emerson, all on our own.

Part of me wanted to press Jack now, to push him further into telling me what was on his mind. But the part of me that knew that sometimes the truth does more harm than good just leaned into him, sighed, and remembered that even though I might want to, I would never truly know all of another person. Not my daughters. Not even Jack.

To this day, Jack and I shared a monumental reality, the deep, dark truth that he was the father of my eldest two girls, who knew they were from a sperm donor but had no idea that their sperm donor was the man I almost married before their father. They had no idea that the sperm was donated not through a test tube but through real, true love, the kind that never ends. With that huge thing between us, I always felt I could tell Jack anything, that he could do the same.

As he cleared his throat for no reason, always a dead give-away that he was hiding something, it scared me to wonder what he felt he had to keep from me. It terrified me to think what in our present could possibly be bigger than the behemoth of our past.

FOUR

emerson: the indomitable murphy women

After about twenty phone calls to Mark's parents and our best friends and a feverish lovemaking session on the kitchen island, where I tried to ignore the fact that because of whatever mystery illness was haunting me, I would certainly have bruises the next day as a souvenir, I realized I had a wedding to plan. So I walked to my mother's house, pushing away the doubts I'd had previously, flung the door open dramatically—I mean, I was an actress, after all—and exclaimed, "Get out Grammy's veil!"

If you ever need to know for sure how you are feeling, just look at your mother's face. It's like a mirror. Her mouth said, "Oh, yay! Honey, you are going to look gorgeous." Her blue eyes, the ones that matched mine perfectly, said, *Are you sure this is a good idea?*

She shot me the tight-lipped smile I knew well from days of bombed performances that she tried to put a positive spin on.

"I am so happy for you, sweetheart, but I know you've had your concerns about Mark and the logistics of this relationship. Are you sure about this? Because you don't have to rush into anything." She ran her fingers through her layered, shoulder-length hair, and it occurred to me that it was significantly lighter than its usual chestnut. I wondered if it was summer sun or great highlights.

"Really, really sure?" Jack reiterated.

I rolled my eyes. Great. Just because I didn't have a dad, that didn't mean I needed *Jack* interfering in my affairs. I felt guilty almost immediately. Jack was a very nice man. But I kind of wanted him to leave, and I didn't really want his opinion.

Before I could answer, my sister Sloane's voice traveled from the kitchen and into the living room, calling, "Mom, do you have any mayonnaise?"

As if my oldest sister, Caroline, could detect someone talking about a fat other than avocado and had to come save the day, she walked through the front door in a maxi dress cinched at her tiny waist, looking as if she'd stepped off the pages of a magazine. "I should certainly *hope* not," she said by way of greeting. Her long hair was lighter, too, the exact same brown-but-sunkissed shade as Mom's. That's when I knew they had gotten their hair done together. I felt a little pang of jealousy that they hadn't invited me.

Caroline looked at Mom accusatorily. "Why would you have mayonnaise, Mom? Surely you know better than to have that artery-clogging excuse for a condiment."

Sloane, in a pair of faded sweatpants and one of Adam's old

T-shirts, her noncolored, regular brown hair in a messy bun on top of her head, crossed her arms. She had put back on a little bit of the weight she had lost while Adam was missing in action, and her face had regained that natural, Neutrogena glow it had always had. Having Adam back home had made her look so much healthier. It had also made her brave. Very brave. Brave enough that sometimes she even stood up to Caroline. "Adam and I have started buying the organic kind made with sunflower oil, and I think it's a healthy fat that way, actually."

Caroline nodded knowingly, and for a second, I thought she was agreeing with Sloane. Instead, she said, "Ah, yes." She gestured at Sloane. "I've found the person who actually started buying doughnuts when they"—she paused to make air quotes—"took out the trans fat."

This was totally beside the point, and I knew I shouldn't say anything. But I couldn't help myself. "Wait," I said. "Who was it again who took us all to McDonald's a couple of months ago?"

Jack was looking helplessly at Mom now, and I wondered if he was rethinking this quest he had undertaken to be with her. I didn't doubt he loved her, but was she worth all of this? All of *us*?

"No, no, you're right," Caroline said. "I tell you what: why don't you get married and have Mark go on a reality show with some slut and then give me a call and let me know how you react. 'K?"

I smirked at her and told myself the lie that every bride has to in order to fling herself down that aisle. *My marriage will be different.* But I said, "Mark doesn't even want *me* to be on TV."

Mom stood up now, too, the four of us in a circle.

"I love Mark," Caroline said, "and I love you, and I love you two together. But we all know you've had your doubts about this relationship . . ."

"Actually," I said, "I thought about what my brilliant sister Sloane said the other day at your house, and Mark and I don't have to have a cookie-cutter marriage. I can be in LA some and here some, and even though he doesn't want to move, that doesn't mean he can't travel back and forth every couple of months for a week or so. I mean, we'll work it out."

I could see the worried look on Sloane's face, those double wrinkles she got between her eyebrows. But she didn't say anything, so I ignored them.

Then Caroline started singing. "Goin' to the chapel and we're . . ."

Mom chimed in, "Gonna get ma-a-arried . . ."

Sloane started on the verse, "Spring is here, the-e-e sky is blue, whoa-oh-oh . . ."

Then they were all in full song, and for the first time but not the last, I realized it: I was going to be a bride. I was going to walk down the aisle and wear a white dress and get married. It was then I realized I didn't have anyone to walk me down said aisle. I decided immediately I would get Adam to do it. If he was walking right by then. He had sustained multiple injuries in the helicopter crash that led to his capture and even more during the months he was MIA. But the man was a soldier. He knew all about fighting a hard battle and coming out the other side.

A few minutes later, when the squealing and singing and

general noise had stopped, I noticed Jack still sitting on the couch, looking something between amused and terrified. You couldn't blame the man. I would wonder what I had gotten myself into, too. I also noticed that Kyle was now leaning on the open front door, admiring all of us. Well, maybe not all of us. Maybe just me. Either way, my heart skipped a beat. But I got myself back together. It had been one night. Just one night. It had meant nothing.

"What are you doing here?" I asked.

He shrugged. "Stopping in to say hi on my way home from work."

I kept meaning to ask my mom if Kyle always stopped by on his way home from work or if it was only when I was around.

I felt suddenly tongue-tied, and instead of responding, I said, "You know what would be so great? I'm totally in the mood for some green juice."

Mom and Sloane groaned, while Caroline said, "Oh, yes, yes, yes!"

Mom sighed. "I love you, Em, and I'm glad you're being healthy, but the mess in the kitchen after you juice is too much."

"I can see there's a lot happening here tonight, so I'll come back in the morning," Kyle said, laughing. Then he added, "Congrats, Em. You're going to be a beautiful bride." The words seemed to taste bad in his mouth.

"Please," Jack pleaded. "Please, Kyle. Take me with you."

Kyle put his hand to his heart, as if it genuinely pained him to say what was coming next. "If only I could, my good friend. But you know as well as I do that when it comes to the indomitable Murphy women, it's every man for himself."

Maybe it was only in my mind, but I felt like he looked at me a beat too long when he said it. And it made me wonder if Kyle thought about that night every now and then, too.

ansley: a nice gesture

I had known Kyle for seven years. I had drunk his coffee every day. And for the entire time I had known him, I had begged him to do just one thing. Last week, he had finally agreed.

My assistant, Leah, had taken over a lot of the ins and outs of my daily design business, but this was something I knew I had to do myself. I made my way to Kyle's shop, Peachtree Perk, with a bag full of samples I planned to drop off: black and white tile for the floor, wood choices for the booths that would be handmade at Peachtree Furniture, leather for the cell-phone pouches that would hang on the walls to encourage people to disconnect so they could reconnect. I had pictures of industrial barstools and renderings of a sophisticated, modern white quartz bar with metal trim that we would install in the center of the café.

When I walked in, Kyle was rushing around behind the

counter as two women old enough to know better—or at least hide it better—admired his chiseled jawline. "So what's the damage?" he asked, never stopping his movement.

I slid a piece of paper across the counter with the quote. My time would be free, obviously. Kyle was like one of my children.

Glancing at the paper as he walked by, he said, "Solid. Let me know when I need to close for the installation."

I held up my bag. "Don't you want to see some samples? Choose some things?"

He finally stopped moving, his hand on the steamer as he prepared a latte, and looked up at me. "Ans, you don't tell me what to put in your coffee. I don't tell you what to put on my floors. We're artists. I trust you."

I smiled. "You're going to love it."

"No doubt." He started moving again, and as I walked back out onto the sidewalk—wedding planning with the girls called—I got lost in my thoughts.

I wanted to ignore it, tried to ignore it, hoped it would go away. But there were no two ways around the fact that Jack was acting very oddly toward me, skittish, almost. We had made a pact not to eat any sugar the entire week—a real feat for both of us—and when I was making dinner at his house the night before, I had found a Snickers bar in the pantry. I turned to him, arms crossed, and said teasingly, "Jack, do you have something you need to tell me?"

He went completely white and stammered, "Oh, um . . ."

I pulled the Snickers out from behind my back, laughing,

and he visibly relaxed, his shoulders going soft. I wanted to ask what was going on, but I couldn't quite bring myself to. I got the feeling it was news I wasn't going to like.

And while I was mostly wrapped up in the Emerson wedding-planning fest, it was hard to ignore that Caroline and Sloane were also acting strangely. It wasn't unusual for Caroline to be a touch chilly toward me, but Sloane? When she snapped at me about letting the boys have cookies after school, I wrote it off as stress over Adam's difficult physical therapy that day. But when she didn't call me or drop by a single time for three days, I had to think it was me.

I wasn't that worried about my daughters being upset, because I only assumed I had done something inadvertently to offend them. It wouldn't be the first time, and it wouldn't be the last. But the Jack part worried me.

Being back together with your first love is one of those things that sounds sweet and romantic, but all the craziness of the past few days must have been eye-opening, to say the least. I couldn't help but worry that the magic was wearing off and Jack was changing his mind.

Caroline was supposed to be heading back to New York, to her permanent home, but she had decided (and rightly so) that she couldn't possibly leave all of us alone in charge of the wedding planning. I didn't doubt that she wanted to be here to micromanage every detail of Emerson's wedding, but I also felt there was something more, something she wasn't saying, underneath her gesture. I was sure she would miss us, of course, but I also wondered if thinking about being back in the city with James was becoming harder than she'd imagined now that it was almost here, if it made her rethink taking him back. But you couldn't ask Caroline things like that. She was very defensive when she felt her decisions were being questioned.

Caroline was the first to arrive at my dining-room table, with a huge white binder in her hand. I mean *huge* huge; I'd never seen anything quite like it. She was wearing a pair of white jeans and an off-the-shoulder top. It wasn't anything special, but she looked unfathomably glamorous even so. Sloane walked in behind her, still in her flannel pajamas.

"Sloane," Caroline scolded, "did you seriously walk down the street in those?"

She shrugged. "It's two doors down, Caroline. Honestly."

Caroline sighed. "Where is Kyle?"

I smiled. Coffee Kyle delivered us our favorite beverages every morning, as he did to the rest of the locals. He usually brought mine to Sloane Emerson—my waterfront design store a couple of blocks away—but he knew I'd be home with all the girls.

"The coffee shop was slammed this morning," I said. "Plus, it's a nice gesture that he delivers to us, Caroline. We're not on a schedule or anything."

She rolled her eyes and sighed. "I see those bills you get from him every month. You should be on a schedule, for what you pay."

Sloane and I shared a glance. It seemed like scary, controlling Caroline had come to our wedding-planning meeting today, which worried me. Whatever Caroline acted upset about was usually a deflection from her true pain. In that way, she was masterful at hiding her emotions.

She looked at her watch, a diamond-encrusted Cartier piece that James had recently surprised her with, which sat inches below the massive apology diamond ring he had given her a few months before. I could have told him that my baby couldn't be bought. But if she was going to stay with him despite his idiocy, she at least deserved some nice gifts.

"Where *is* the happy couple?" Caroline asked.

"They stayed out way too late last night celebrating," I said. "I heard Emerson come in after two. I'm shocked she's already out and about this morning."

But Emerson rarely missed her morning run, no matter what was going on. Sure, she was an actress and had to keep her figure, but Emerson said running was more than that for her. It was her therapy. It was my torture, so I couldn't really relate, but whatever made her happy. Plus, if she was running, she couldn't be sick. Right? I was bursting to ask her what was going on with her health, but I hadn't found the right moment.

"That's sweet," Sloane said. "I'm happy she's so happy."

I felt Caroline's mood shift from foul to pleasant as she said, "I want her to have everything she has ever dreamed of."

I knew that was true. Caroline was the one who had encouraged Emerson to follow her acting passion—in fact, she had been the one who had persuaded me to allow Emerson to act when she was younger. I didn't want her in the spotlight

35

and had been worried about what that life might be like for her. But you can't deny your children their passions. I got that uneasy feeling again, as I hoped that Mark was her true passion. I had always believed that work was important, but it was nothing compared to finding your life partner.

Mark and Emerson burst through the door, giggling, breaking my thoughts. You couldn't help but smile. They were both in black running shorts, Mark in a T-shirt and Emerson in a form-fitting jogging top. And they were both really, really sweaty.

"Gross," Caroline said under her breath.

No one exercised more than Caroline, but she always showered immediately afterward.

"I'm sorry if our love is gross to you, Car," Emerson said.

"I love your love, Em. I just don't love your sweat."

"I love your sweat," Mark said, kissing Emerson's nose.

"I love your sweat, too," she said back adoringly.

"Sorry in advance about the soon-to-be-sweaty dining-room chairs, Mom," Emerson said, sitting down.

Mark sat down beside her, but instead of facing the rest of us on the other side of the table, he sat sideways, staring at Emerson, rubbing her antique-diamond-clad hand with his. His expression said it all: he couldn't believe she'd said yes. He couldn't believe that he would get to spend the rest of his life with this woman, who had been a fantasy for him for so many years. The rest of us couldn't believe it, either.

She'd only been engaged for a day, so we hadn't bugged Emerson yet with the finer points of the relationship, but we'd get our answers soon. Caroline and I had been up late—we were the night owls of the bunch—debating whether Emerson was making the right decision. I had gotten the nerve up to ask Caroline, "Does Emerson seem OK to you? I mean, does she seem well? She hasn't mentioned to you being sick or anything, has she?"

Caroline had looked at me like I was crazy and said, "No. She seems great to me."

That eased my fears. If something serious was going on with Emerson, she would have told her sister.

I loved that Caroline and James were letting Sloane and Adam live in their house while they got back on their feet. I loved that my grandsons were right down the street. I loved that Caroline, Vivi, and Preston had to stay with me because their house was occupied. And I would love it if Emerson stayed in Peachtree, too. But I wanted her to put her happiness first.

"OK," Caroline said, opening her massive book. "Let's get down to it. I think the first thing we need to pick is the venue. Then we can nail down a date."

"Actually," Emerson said, "we've decided we want to get married Labor Day weekend. All of our friends will be down here already, and . . ." She paused dramatically. "I have to be back in LA the next Tuesday."

She cut herself off, but we could all tell there was more to that story.

"Why do you have to be back in LA the next Tuesday?" Sloane took the bait first.

"Well," Emerson crooned, looking ecstatic. Mark looked

less ecstatic. "I just found out that I am playing Sissy in the new film version of *A Tree Grows in Brooklyn*."

I heard my gasp before I felt it in my chest.

Sloane jumped up from her seat and ran around the table to hug Emerson. "I don't even care that you're sweaty!" Sloane exclaimed.

"Wait just a minute," Caroline said. "You mean to tell me that they hired you to play Sissy? The one with all the cleavage?"

Looking at Emerson, who had a body more like Twiggy than Marilyn, I had to admit it was a fair question.

Emerson crossed her arms and rolled her eyes. "That's what push-up bras are for, Caroline." We all laughed.

"Em," I said, "this is unbelievable." I could feel tears in my eyes. I was so proud of her. She had worked so hard for every role, big or small, that she had gotten.

"It really is unbelievable," Mark said under his breath. I didn't love the way he said it, as if what was *really* unbelievable was that someone would leave him. But acting was Emerson's first love. Anyone who was with her would have to understand that.

Caroline glanced at me across the table. This was exactly what we'd talked about last night: Mark wanted Emerson all to himself.

Sloane, oblivious to our silent discussion, was crying. "You're going to win an Academy Award. I'm going to have a sister who's an Oscar winner!"

Emerson laughed. "OK, OK. Let's not get ahead of ourselves. It's an amazing part, but an Academy Award?"

You could almost see her goose bumps as she said it.

"I wanted to complain about having to plan your wedding in two months," Caroline said with a smile, "but now that I know you're getting ready for the role of a lifetime, I'm going to be OK about it." She opened her binder again. "Labor Day will be absolutely glorious anywhere in Peachtree Bluff." She paused. "I'm assuming you want to have it in Peachtree? I mean, I have an entire section of destination-wedding locales if you'd like to look at those."

I looked at Caroline in astonishment as Emerson said what I was thinking: "When did you have time to put this all together?"

"She's a vampire," Sloane said. "She doesn't need sleep."

"Exactly," Caroline agreed. "But I do need coffee. I'm going to kill Kyle if he doesn't get here soon."

"We'd like to get married in Peachtree," Mark said, chuckling. "But thank you for your thorough research, Caroline. It is much appreciated."

"In that case," Caroline said, "I have several options, but the one I think you'll like the best is getting married at St. James's and then having the reception at the Yacht House."

The Yacht House was a beautiful old shingled building with twenty-foot ceilings whose entire back wall opened onto the water. It had a huge deck and the prettiest view of the sunset. I could get on board with that.

"I love the Yacht House," Mark said enthusiastically.

Emerson scrunched her nose. "Why don't we do the rehearsal dinner there?"

"OK," Caroline said, jotting it down in her notebook. "Do you still want to do the ceremony at the church?"

Jack walked in from the kitchen, sat down beside me, and squeezed my shoulder, seeming like his usual self today. He kissed my cheek, and I smiled, but neither of us said a word. This was wedding planning. It was serious.

Emerson shrugged. "I want something kind of different."

Caroline ran her hand through her hair. "You could do the Bluefish Club, or the Sea Oats."

Emerson looked bored. "That's definitely not different."

"What about the Historic Site?" Sloane asked, referring to the beautiful green space in the midst of Peachtree Bluff's oldest part of town, which included a historic jail, an apothecary, a schoolhouse, and a beautiful home complete with a full catering kitchen.

Caroline nodded. "We could tent the whole thing and have Peachtree Grocery cater."

"That might be cool," Mark said.

"Maybe," Emerson said unenthusiastically.

Caroline looked at Jack, and he looked at her, and there was something unsettling in that look, but I couldn't put my finger on what. I could tell Caroline was getting a little desperate now, because there were only so many venues that could hold 150-plus people in the Peachtree area. And knowing Emerson, she was going to have a big wedding.

"You could do it here," I said, wondering if that was the right offer.

"Or at my house," Jack chimed in.

Emerson nodded. "That would be better, but . . ."

"I know!" Caroline exclaimed. "I've got it. It's perfect. You can get married on the sandbar."

Emerson gasped, and Mark laughed.

"Yes!" she squealed. "Yes, yes!"

I felt my heart drop into my stomach. I looked at Jack, and he smiled sadly. There went our wedding. At least we still had Starlite Island.

"But there's no way the sandbar will stay out long enough for us to do a reception there, too."

"Oh, my gosh!" Sloane exclaimed. "We could do the reception at Starlite Island."

"Yes!" Emerson said.

Never mind.

"We could transport all the guests on Jack's boat," Caroline enthused. She paused. "I mean, if it's OK with Jack, of course."

He nodded and smiled, but I could see the disappointment in his expression. This was our wedding. I think this might have been his first lesson in parenthood: your children's happiness is more important than your own.

"Whatever the girls want," he said. "I'm here to serve."

I was about to finally add something to the conversation when I heard, "Hello, hello, Murphy girls," from the entrance hall.

"Kyle!" Emerson trilled, running to meet him. Caroline was right behind her. "Thank goodness the coffee is here. My brain will begin functioning."

Emerson gave Kyle a side hug as he balanced the Coke crate he had converted to a drink carrier around his neck.

I didn't think anything of it. Emerson was a hugger. But

Mark rolled his eyes and looked out the window, shaking his head. That was another thing he was going to have to get over. Emerson's basic personality was affectionate and borderline flirty. It was who she was. Always had been.

Caroline grabbed two cups and walked back to the table, handing mine to me.

"Not so fast, Car," Kyle said, handing her another cup. She raised her eyebrow suspiciously.

He handed a fourth cup to Emerson. "Sip, please," he said.

"What is it?" Emerson asked.

"Surprise," Kyle said.

Mark's countenance darkened.

Caroline and Emerson sipped, and both squealed simultaneously.

"Kyle, you are a god," Caroline said.

"I can't believe you did this!" Emerson said.

"Green juice," Caroline said, giving me a look that said, *He sure as hell didn't start making green juice for me.*

We had both long suspected that Kyle had a bit of a crush on Emerson.

"Ask and you shall receive," Sloane said.

Emerson put her hand to her heart. "Kyle, thank you."

"I figured if you were going to be living here, you couldn't be without your favorite green juice." He shrugged as if it were nothing. But the look he gave her when he said it told me absolutely everything.

SIX

emerson: limelight

I'd be lying if I said I didn't think about it every now and then. Not every single time I saw Kyle, but occasionally. And obviously, when he was the first person I saw when I arrived back in Peachtree Bluff last January, I had to question whether that was some sort of sign. But then Mark and I fell into our old routine at rocket speed. And I knew then that Mark was the one for me. That one night I'd shared with Kyle all those years ago had been just that: a night. One single night that didn't mean much of anything.

I had been in LA almost a year when I met Kyle for the first time. I'd been starting to get small roles here and there, and I had that feeling, that glorious, golden feeling. Getting what you want is fabulous, attaining the goal, crossing the finish line. But the feeling you get when you know that you're *almost* there, that you're on your way to your dreams, that you

43

might be getting everything you ever wanted in short order . . . that feeling is almost better.

I thought of that feeling, that same feeling I had now, whenever I was with Kyle.

When I saw Kyle that first morning at the LA coffee house I frequented, I noticed him. Who wouldn't? He was devastatingly handsome. I knew right away that he must be an actor or, like me, a wannabe actor. He smiled at me, and I smiled at him, and that was it. Insignificant.

But when he walked into the restaurant where I was waitressing that night, I recognized him immediately. And I gave my friend Ellen five bucks to switch tables with me. I had seen him twice in one day. That had to mean something.

When I went over to Kyle's table, he cocked his head to the side. "I know you . . ." he said, like he couldn't quite place me.

"Maybe," I said. "You look kind of familiar." He didn't say anything, so I added, "Maybe we've run into each other at a casting call or something?"

Kyle and all his friends had burst out laughing, but I sensed it wasn't at my expense. I could tell already that there was something completely genuine about Kyle that you couldn't find much in this town, where everyone spent most of their time trying to be someone else.

"What?" I had asked, amused by the fun they were having.

One of Kyle's friends smacked him on the back and said, "This guy is about as far from Hollywood as you can imagine."

Kyle shook his head. "Yeah. No offense—I think what you do is awesome—but I'm not into all that."

"It's a shame," I said. "With that face?"

"You should see his abs," another of his friends chimed in, making him groan.

I still don't know why I said what I said next. It was totally unlike me. Much too forward. But with no permission from my brain, my mouth said, "I would really like that."

I immediately put my hand to my mouth, blushing. "I am so sorry." I cleared my throat and smiled, recovering. "I'm kidding, of course."

"No, you're not," another friend said.

Kyle was clearly uncomfortable.

"I'm so sorry," I repeated. "I'll get your waters, and then your waitress will be right over."

I grabbed Ellen and said, "You have to switch back with me."

She shook her head and looked at me like I was crazy. "What? Why? No."

"I just made a huge ass out of myself, and I need you. Please."

Ellen sighed. She was a nice girl. I went over to my new table and tried to forget how embarrassed I was.

An hour later, I felt someone behind me. When I turned, I almost bumped right into Kyle.

"Hey," he said.

Now I was nervous. I didn't want him to think that I was some slutty waitress he could pick up and take home. "I'm going to Limelight to get a drink," he'd said. "Just me. I'd love it if I saw you there. If not, I understand."

I shook my head. "I'm so embarrassed. I'm not like that at all."

He smiled at me warmly. "Like I said, I'll be there. If you want to come, I'd really like to get to know you."

It was a tempting offer, but I already knew I wouldn't go. Two hours later, though, as I was walking home, I realized that I was passing right by Limelight. I could just stop in.

I could use a drink, I told myself. With what I was living off of, I could also use someone to buy it for me.

Plus, a little voice inside my head said, *you never know when you might meet someone who could help your love life or your career.*

I smiled to myself, thinking about the call I had gotten from my agent earlier. My agent! I had an agent! I had gotten a callback. I felt it again, the sense that this was my moment, that I would look back on this time and realize that everything in my life that mattered was happening right here, right now. I had left Mark behind months earlier, and although it had broken something inside me to let him go, I knew I'd never be whole if I didn't pursue my dream. And I was doing it.

That gave me the courage to open the door to Limelight and walk through it. True to his word, Kyle was sitting alone at the bar, his back to me, sipping something from a rocks glass. When he turned to look toward the front door and smiled at me, I knew it wasn't the first time he had checked to see if I was coming in. It made me feel warm and fuzzy inside, which was ridiculous. He didn't even know my name.

"You made it," he said.

I decided to get it out in the open, erase the embarrassment. "But you have your shirt on, so I'm leaving." We both laughed.

He patted the stool beside him, and I slid onto it. He looked into my eyes and stared at me long and hard. Then he turned back to the bartender and said, "Champagne with a splash of bourbon, muddled mint, and one sugar cube for my friend." Then he looked back at me, smiled, turned to the bartender, and said, "And two strawberries, please."

I laughed. "That's not what I order."

Kyle smiled confidently. "It's what you'll order from now on," he said. "Trust me. It will change your life." I smiled back at him. "I'm Kyle, by the way." He held his hand out to me, and I shook it, holding it longer than necessary.

"Emerson Murphy," I said as the bartender set the drink down in front of me.

I took a sip.

"Well?" Kyle asked.

I smiled. "It's fabulous."

"Perfect drink for a starlet."

I could feel my eyes widening, that familiar sense of pride I got when thinking of my hometown welling up in me.

"What did you say?"

"Perfect drink for a starlet?"

I laughed. "Oh! I thought you said Starlite. It's this little island across from my house where I grew up. My sisters and I spent our summers playing there every day. It's kind of . . . heaven on earth."

Kyle smiled. "Then that's your drink. The Starlite Starlet."

The bartender came over. "Anybody need another?"

"We'll have another Starlite Starlet," Kyle said.

The bartender laughed. "I like that. Can I add that to the cocktail menu, man?"

When the bartender was gone, Kyle said, "I hear having a drink named after you is the first step to getting a star on the Hollywood Walk of Fame."

It felt significant, having my drink on the menu, having the island where I had grown up associated with me, associated with LA in any way. In that moment, my two worlds converged. Sitting with Kyle that night was the first time I'd even felt like that was possible.

Two hours later, I asked Kyle to walk me home. I should have been bone-tired from the day of auditions, the evening of waitressing, and the night of drinking. But I felt alive, on fire, like anything could happen. Kyle's confidence was rubbing off on me already.

"I never asked you what you do," I said, as we were walking.

Kyle took my hand. "Oh," he said, "a little of this, a little of that."

I felt my warning bells go off. I stopped walking. "Please tell me you aren't a drug dealer or the head of a prostitution ring."

Kyle dropped my hand and laughed so hard I was afraid he had quit breathing. "No, no. I own that coffee shop you were in this morning."

I looked at him, wide-eyed. "You knew I was in the coffee

shop this morning? I thought you weren't sure where you'd seen me."

He took my hand again. "When Emerson Murphy walks into your coffee shop, you don't forget."

He was cute.

"So why coffee, Kyle?"

"Just a hunch. I think coffee is going to be really big."

"If your coffee skills are anything like your cocktail skills, then I think you have a bright future."

When we got to my building, he insisted on walking me to my door. I slid the key into the lock and bit my lip. I had turned over a new leaf, and I had promised myself no more sleeping with virtual strangers. If I invited him in, was that what he would expect?

As I opened the door, Kyle said, "It was really nice to meet you, Emerson Murphy, Starlite starlet."

He didn't so much as lean in to kiss me. As he turned to leave, a strangled "Wait" escaped my throat.

He turned and smiled at me again, those rows of teeth so perfect. His hands were in his shorts pockets, making him seem like a little boy. I bet he wore shorts even when it was cold outside. He was one of those guys.

I smiled coyly. "Do you want to come in?"

He exhaled like his life was hinging on that question. "Thank goodness," he said. "I really need to use the bath-room."

We both laughed, and I pointed toward the bathroom door.

When Kyle reemerged, I was sitting on the couch and had poured us each a glass of the cheap white wine I had in my fridge. I was really lucky I didn't have a roommate. I would never admit it to anyone, not even my mom, but the reason I didn't have a roommate was that Caroline paid half my rent. She was a good sister. I'd promised to pay her back one day, and she had said, "I think of it as a nondeductible charitable expense. I'm a patron of the arts."

"I'll warn you, this is not quite as good as the Starlite Starlet."

Kyle sat down close to me, angling his body so he could see me, and took the glass of wine. "I like the quote on your mirror," he said.

I took a sip of wine and smiled. "I like it, too. I thought about getting a tattoo of it, but I couldn't decide where." I shrugged. "Having a decal made and sticking it to my mirror seemed like less of a commitment."

"Less painful, too," Kyle said. He turned my wrist over and pretended to write on my forearm with the tip of his finger, *Though she be but little, she is fierce.*

Every letter caused a trail of goose bumps to break out. When he was finished, he raised the inside of my wrist to his mouth and kissed it gently. "That would have been the perfect spot for it," he whispered.

I felt my cheeks flush. There was something about this guy. I was always chasing men who could help my career, give me a leg up. It wasn't like I was sleeping with directors in exchange for parts or anything, but the people from the world I was beginning to break into were so potently attractive to me.

When I was with them, I felt more glamorous, more "in." I loved feeling that way.

So much so that it caught me off guard how quickly I had taken to Kyle. He was different from the men I normally dated. Gorgeous, yes. But also soft-spoken. He wasn't overtly powerful, yet he had some sort of power over me. I felt like simply being beside him opened up something inside me, something I had never really felt before.

I had to remind myself that I had only just met the man, for heaven's sake.

I swallowed and nodded. "It sure would have."

He laughed.

"What?"

"Nothing. I just love that Southern accent."

I gasped. "I do *not* have a Southern accent." I had lived in Manhattan for the first ten years of my life, until my dad died, so I had convinced myself that I had the neutral accent that was perfect for an actress. Yet I had to admit that Southern roles were awfully easy for me to get.

He smiled. "No, no. I love it. I'm actually getting ready to move to Georgia. I'm opening another coffee shop there. Giving this one to my cousin Keith."

I thought about telling him that I had lived in Georgia for most of my life, that my mom was still there. But then I would have to go to the trouble of explaining where Peachtree Bluff was, and it wasn't worth it. I knew I'd never see him again anyway.

"Good peaches," I said, leaning forward the slightest bit,

indicating to him that he could kiss me but not wanting to be so forward as to kiss him.

He took my cue, putting his hand on my cheek, stroking my chin with his thumb. His lips met mine in a way that was soft and warm and good. It felt almost familiar, like coming home. It was the sweetest kiss I had had in quite some time. It was the first kiss, in fact, that made me wonder if maybe I had been right to leave Mark—and the life we could have had— behind.

Now, all these years later, the script had flipped. It was Kyle I had left behind. It was Mark I had come back to. As I took the last sip of green juice Kyle had made for me and threw the cup into Mom's bathroom trash can, taking her concealer out of her makeup bag and piling on yet more so she wouldn't notice the deep purple circles under my eyes, the ones that were a visible sign on my face that something wasn't right inside my body, I had to admit to myself that the Kyle in the here and now had continued to impress me just as much as the Kyle of all those years ago.

He was different now, of course. He had grown up, become even more sure of himself, a man in every sense of the word. As I added concealer to the deep red bruise above my elbow, the one I had gotten from merely bumping the chair this morning, I had the disturbing thought that Kyle might always be the one who got away. And that, worse still, we would both be right here to remember it every day.

ansley: grack

I had made a fledgling attempt at Instagram in the past few years to share photos of my design work. But I was less than consistent and mostly just enjoyed looking at pictures of my friends' grandchildren. As I scrolled through my feed, enjoying the noises of my girls drying and fixing one another's hair upstairs as they got ready for their night out, a new story popped up on Caroline's profile, a video of the three of them singing into hairbrushes in the mirror, just like the old days. I clicked on the icon by her name to see if she had posted any pictures of Preston lately that I had missed. And I almost dropped the phone. "Caroline!" I called, running up the stairs.

Emerson was applying blush to Sloane's cheeks, and Caroline was holding a round brush in one hand and a blow-dryer in the other. She turned it off when she saw me in the mirror.

"Oh, my gosh!" I said. "Caroline! You have almost a million Instagram followers!"

"What?" Emerson said. "That's more than *I* have."

Caroline shrugged. "James having the public affair of the decade really upped my social-media game."

"Do you have any idea what you could do with all those followers?" Emerson asked.

"I know exactly what," Caroline said, holding up the hair dryer. "Do you know how much Dyson just paid me for that post?"

An hour later, I was calling, "Don't drink too much!" as Emerson, Sloane, and Caroline walked out my front door. I was shocked, actually, that Sloane was finally leaving. She had been glued to Adam's side since he got home. But according to Sloane, he had insisted she take Emerson out to celebrate her engagement, saying, "Just because I'm home now doesn't mean I'm the only person in your world. You can't stop your entire life for me."

As I poured myself a glass of wine and got ready for an evening alone, I wondered where they were off to. Probably walking downtown to our favorite restaurant, Sharpie's, which was perfectly safe and filled with locals who would watch out for them. Still, when I saw all three of them walk away together, panic welled up in my throat that I might never see them again. What if they were all hit by a car? What if a shooter came into their restaurant? I knew it was silly, but after Carter had been killed on an ordinary day in an extraordinary way, I was all too aware that every time the people I loved walked out the door, I was in danger of never seeing them again. Thinking that Emerson might be sick had intensified the anxious feelings that always seemed to ebb and flow a bit.

I jumped when I felt a pair of arms wrap around me from behind. "Alone at last," Jack whispered.

I smiled and turned to kiss him. I knew that kiss would turn into something more.

"Want to go back to my house?" Jack asked.

I smiled. I would always, *always*, want to go back to Jack's house.

An hour and a half later, I was sitting in Jack's backyard sipping sweet tea while steaks sizzled on the grill. Every time Jack grilled steaks, it reminded me of the day I'd gone to his house in Atlanta, the day I'd seen him for the first time since I'd told him I was pregnant with Caroline, the day I'd made love to him right there on his back patio until the steak turned to absolute charcoal.

We never really talked about it now, about our past. But I couldn't let the moment go. He might not even remember. "Try not to burn these," I said, testing the waters.

"That was the best worst steak of my life."

I smiled wistfully, knowing exactly what he meant, knowing that he felt such pure relief at my return to Atlanta, to him, all those years ago, that it was scarcely something he could verbalize. But we both also knew what we were getting back into. My getting pregnant with Caroline, Carter's knowing—but never saying—that another man must have been a part of that, had shifted something in our relationship. Still, we both wanted a sibling for Caroline.

I had come to Jack once to ask him this unaskable favor. So when I came to him a second time, we both knew what that meant. We both knew that indescribably wonderful night on his back patio would mean another few months down the rabbit hole, another beginning of something that would have to end when I got pregnant, when I went back to my husband, my family, and my life, for good.

I felt I should say something else, but I wasn't sure what, so I sipped my tea and stayed quiet, still in that moment so many years ago.

"Sometimes it doesn't seem real," Jack said, saying what I felt.

I nodded. "I know. I look back and think, *No, no. I would never have done that. That must have been someone else.*"

"I'm so glad that this is now and not then," Jack said.

I nodded in agreement, staying silent.

"So," he finally ventured, "I'm thrilled that Emerson is having our dream wedding."

"I don't even know what to say about that. Do you think Caroline heard us or something?"

Jack shrugged.

"But even if she did," I added, "it's not like she would want to punish us in any way. It's not like she would want to ruin our special day for any reason."

Jack, who was in mid-gulp of a beer, choked.

"Are you OK?"

He gave me a thumbs-up but kept coughing. There it was again. That odd behavior that disturbed me so much. Sure, it could have been a random choke on a beer. But it seemed like something more to me. He walked inside, and when he came back out, he was sipping a glass of water.

I studied his face. "Jack," I said casually, "is there anything you need to tell me?"

He peered at the steak on the grill like it was his most important life's work. "Nope," he said, equally as casually but with a strain that shouldn't have been there. "Not a thing."

Maybe it was my paranoia kicking in, but things had been off with him for days, and I couldn't stand it for a second longer. "If you don't want to be with me, just say it. Don't make me wait until I'm even more in love with you to break my heart."

Jack looked at me incredulously.

I threw my arms up in the air. "What?" I asked. "Is it someone else? Do you miss Lauren? Because something is going on with you." Neither of us had ever so much as uttered his ex-wife's name. We hadn't even mentioned her since the night more than six months ago when Jack had walked back into Peachtree Bluff and back into my life. But I couldn't help but feel lately that his odd behavior meant a secret. And it terrified me deep down to my core that a secret meant another woman.

He walked over, pulled me up off the chair, sat down, and pulled me onto his lap. "Ansley, all I have wanted for forty years is you. You are the absolute love of my life, and I will probably die if you ever say that again."

"The steaks," I whispered. I could smell them starting to burn.

"I don't give a damn about the steaks. Not then, not now. I don't care if the whole house burns down. I want you to hear me when I say this: you are oxygen. I cannot live without you, not really, and I refuse to do so for another single day in my life."

The steak was tough and overcooked. But Jack loved me. If I had to choose one or the other, it sure wouldn't be the steak.

Three hours later, I was about to call it a night when I heard shouts and laughter from the end of the street. "No," I said. "No, no, no, no, no."

Then someone screeched, "Mom! You waited up."

And someone else screeched, "That's not even our porch, you drunk dumb-ass."

And I knew for sure that no one had listened to my sage advice not to drink too much. Sober Caroline, Sloane, and Emerson were a lot. Drunk Caroline, Sloane, and Emerson should be locked up. I hated drunk people. They were my pet peeve. And it seemed my next few hours were going to be peevish.

"Mom, Mom!" Emerson called as she fiddled with the gate. "Tom at the tavern is adding a new martini list to the menu."

"Mom," Sloane chimed in, "he made one of every martini on the menu for us to share."

I grimaced. "Yes, Sloane. I can see that."

"Mom, look what Sloane and I got you and Emerson." Caroline stumbled up the walk and pulled a lacy thong out of her purse. It had "bride" in rhinestones on the front, and a veil attached with a blue bow on the back.

She burst out laughing, and Emerson and Sloane joined her, falling down in the front yard. "It can be your something new and your something blue," Caroline cackled.

For heaven's sake. They were grown women. Mostly, practically grown women. I hadn't seen them like this since college. "Girls," I scolded, "this is not ladylike behavior. And besides, I'm not the one getting married."

"Oh, Mom," Emerson trilled. "Lighten up."

Then Caroline got up and said something that made every hair on my body stand on end. She sat down beside Jack on his outdoor sofa, wrapped her arms around his neck, and said, "I bet Daddy dearest thinks we're charming even when we've had too many martinis."

I wouldn't swear to it, but I thought the color in Jack's face changed.

Sloane said, "Can we call you that? I mean, come on, you two are going to get married eventually. You're going to be our stepdad. It's happening."

Emerson giggled. "What a treat. Going from the single life to three girls calling you Daddy."

I looked at Jack, but I could tell he was trying not to catch my eye. What wasn't he telling me?

Jack said, "Girls, you can call me anything you want."

Sloane sat down on the steps, teetering. For heaven's sake. I could usually at least count on her to behave. "What are our kids going to call you? That's a big deal."

"Oh, oh!" Caroline said. "I know!"

Emerson interrupted her. "Well, Mom is Gransley, so he should be Grack."

They all keeled over with laughter and were in a pile on the front porch.

"Grack!" Sloane wailed, holding her stomach.

"It sounds like crack," Caroline said seriously, which set them all off again.

Honestly. I looked out over the water and thought, *Mother, I promise you I did my best with them.*

"That's enough out of all of you. Go home and get into bed right this minute."

"Young lady," Sloane hissed, wagging her finger.

That's fine. She could mock me all she wanted. If they were going to behave like teenagers, then I would treat them like children.

"I'm extremely sorry," I said to Jack. "When they come home, they revert back to being teenagers. I've never seen anything like it."

"Caroline's right," he whispered. "I think they're sort of funny."

I sighed. Great. That was all I needed, another father who, like Carter, would be the fun parent, the lax parent, the parent who was always saying, "Just don't tell your mother." I didn't *want* to be the fuddy-duddy; I wanted to be like the mother of Sloane's college suitemate, who was always taking shots at whatever bar we went to after their sorority's Parents' Cocktail. But that wasn't me. I was always going to be the parent who wanted them to stay on the straight and narrow, even when they were older.

I never wanted them to lose control. If they lost control, then I could lose them.

I was relieved to see that Emerson and Sloane acquiesced, leaving the gate and walking to my house, arm in arm.

"Oh, Mom," Caroline said. "The night is young. Carpe diem." She paused. "Actually, carpe nightem." She snickered.

"Caroline, you are making a fool of yourself."

She looked at me seriously. "Mother, trust me, this is far, *far* from the most foolish I've looked this year. When your husband has an affair on national television, that's about the dumbest you can possibly look. This is *nothing* compared to that."

I thought she might cry, but she didn't. Her face was stoic yet resigned.

"Caroline, I'm so sorry," Jack said.

Caroline smiled and patted his hand. "You really did choose the best daddy for us, Mom. Sloane and I love him."

She kissed Jack's cheek, kissed mine, and then teetered off in the direction of the house, trailing after her sisters.

I could feel that all the color had drained from my face. My limbs felt horribly cold, even though it was warm outside. The way she said it, *Sloane and I love him . . .*

I looked at Jack's face, which was probably as pale as mine. They knew.

Caroline and Sloane knew that Jack was their biological father. And he knew they knew it, too. It explained all his behavior. How jittery he had been acting, how withdrawn. It wasn't the wedding he cared about, as I had guessed. It was keeping this big secret from me.

After decades of hiding and scheming, of plotting and planning and worrying. After decades of close calls and sleepless nights, my worst nightmare had come true. My secret was out. And there was nothing I could ever do to bring it back in.

EIGHT

⤜❦⤛

emerson: the starlite starlet

My head was throbbing in time with my thoughts. *No, no, no, no, no.* Why had I done this? Why? Don't get me wrong. I could drink. But not the entire martini menu at Sharpie's. All that sugar. All those carbs.

I didn't want to open my eyes. They were painful and puffy, and I was quite certain they were as bloodshot as they had ever been. Yuck. But I had to open them eventually. No time like the present. When I did, I realized Caroline was beside me. Sloane must have discovered in the middle of the night that, no, this was not her house anymore and that, yes, it might be a good idea to go home and get into bed with her husband. My sisters had given me a memorable evening, that was for sure. I mean, I didn't remember any of it, per se, but I remembered we had fun. Our Instagram pictures looked really fun, anyway.

My phone dinged, and Caroline groaned as she cracked one eye open to look at me.

Ready, ready, ready, ready, ready to run, the text said. Mark had taken me to a Dixie Chicks concert our sophomore year of high school, so he must have thought this was funny. Well, I mean, his mom had taken us, that lunatic. We couldn't drive yet. My heart raced just thinking of Mark's mother—and not in a good way. If Mark was the prize, she was whatever the opposite was. I couldn't think of anything now because I was so hungover.

"Why?" Caroline asked. "Why would Tom do this to us?"

"He hates us," I groaned. "That's the only explanation."

"Rise and shine, ladybugs," I heard a voice bellow through the hallway.

"No, no," Caroline whispered. "Get up and lock the door before she can get in here."

"You get up and lock the door," I said. "I can't move."

"No one will be locking any doors," Mom said, stepping into the bedroom. "I suggest you get showered, because you two are going to work with me today."

"No, Mom," I said. "I can't." A wave of nausea washed over me, and I was on the verge of actual tears.

"Mom, we have the flu," Caroline said. "It is very bad, and we can't be around people."

"Yeah," Mom said, "the tequila flu. I was mortified by the way you were acting in front of Jack last night. Just mortified. You will make it up to me by taking inventory."

"Jack?" I asked. "We saw Jack?"

Caroline whimpered. "Mom, we hate inventory."

"I hate drunk grown women making fools of themselves, so maybe now we'll be even."

I turned my head toward Caroline. "Do you remember seeing Jack and Mom last night?" I whispered.

"I do not," she said. "I think she's making it up to test us."

"Do you think that?" Mom asked. "Really? Does 'Grack' ring a bell?"

As hungover and close to death as I felt, I chuckled. "Oh, yeah, 'Grack.' That's funny."

With that, Mom reared back and shot something into our bed. Caroline picked it up, looking confused, before we both dissolved into hysterics. It was the thong with the veil.

"No, no, Mom," Caroline said, gasping for breath through her laughter. "You keep that. It's a gift."

She shot it back to Mom, who rolled her eyes. "You two are both grounded," she said, setting us off again. Poor Mom. It wasn't fair. There were three of us and only one of her. Sometimes she was one of us, but really, it was usually her against the sisterly trifecta.

Caroline groaned again. "Mommy dearest, we love you. Mommy, we need coffee."

"Ohhhhh," I groaned. "I need Kyle."

"You need *Kyle*?"

Shit. I shot up in bed to see Mark standing in the doorway. This was impressive. My makeup from last night must have been everywhere, my mascara caked under my eyes. "I mean, you know, I need coffee from Kyle."

Mark eyed me warily, but he didn't say anything else. "When you didn't meet me for our run, I got worried."

"Sorry," I said, smoothing my hair out of my face. I was trying to be charming as I said, "I was not, in fact, ready, ready, ready, ready, ready to run."

Caroline sort of rolled off the bed and onto the floor. I wasn't sure she was going to get up, but then I saw the crown of her head appear over the top of the mattress. "This is so bad," she groaned. "Why did you make me drink so much, Emerson?"

"Should I come back?" Mark asked.

"No," I said, patting the space beside me on the bed. "I need you to hold me."

Mark loved to cuddle. But I was usually wiggly and had a lot of energy, so mostly I didn't feel like it. Today was his lucky day. He climbed into my bed and wrapped his arms around me. "My poor girl," he said, kissing the top of my head. "Those big, bad sisters made you drink too much."

"I heard that," Caroline shot back as she crawled across the floor. "I might not be able to walk, but my ears are half functioning."

"Mark, it's so bad," I said. "I mean, I've never been this hungover. I will never recover."

He kissed my head again. "You smell like the bathroom at a bar."

"Oh, no," I groaned, trying to pull away from him.

"It's OK," he whispered. "I'd rather be with you when you smell like a bar bathroom than with anyone else freshly showered."

I sighed, letting my head sink onto his chest. This was why I loved him. It wasn't only that he worshipped me and made me feel like I was the head cheerleader again. Actually, maybe it *was* only that.

"Em, baby," he said, stroking my hair. "Do you love me no matter what?"

I yawned and looked up at him adoringly, looking down before I spoke so as to spare him my dragon breath. "Of course I do, sweetheart. I love you more than anything in the whole wide world."

"I have something to tell you," he said.

The normal Emerson, the one whose senses were not dulled by obscene amounts of alcohol, whose head was not pounding, stomach not churning, whose mouth did not feel like the Sahara, would have jumped out of bed, put her hands on her hips, and said, *What do you* mean *you have something to tell me?*

Hungover Emerson didn't have the energy. "If you slept with someone else, I'll kill you," I said lazily. I knew he hadn't slept with someone else. Mark had worked really hard to get me back. I was pretty sure he wouldn't jeopardize our relationship now.

"I didn't," he said slowly, "but you're going to wish I had. It would be easier to forgive. And far less permanent."

OK. Now old Emerson was coming back. My heart started to pound, which was not a positive addition to the list of symptoms. I needed less pounding and more water in my life. *Easier to forgive and far less permanent.*

"Oh, God. Did you get a bad tattoo?" I gasped. "Or an STD?"

He rolled his eyes. "I'm terrified of needles, and I practically put a condom on before I'll kiss *you*."

Both things were true. I was out of guesses. Again, normal Emerson would have been bubbling over with them like a fresh bottle of champagne. Hungover Emerson felt like she had an anvil on her brain.

He cleared his throat. "My mother is coming to Peachtree."

"Of course your mother is coming," I said, attempting a laugh but falling short due to the pain in all my extremities. "We're getting married, for heaven's sake. She'll want to be here to plan the rehearsal dinner." I snickered at the thought. "She will absolutely hate that we're getting married on the sandbar."

Mark shook his head and smiled. "Yeah, I thought of that. I'm not thrilled that I'll have to hear about it from here to eternity, but I am thrilled that she will be so irritated." He cleared his throat. "We're getting off track. I meant she's coming back to Peachtree Bluff for good."

Now I shot up in bed, pounding head be damned. "What do you mean, 'for good'? What about Florida? What about the sun and the tax rate and the single men?" I leaned over and put my head in my hands. "Oh, God," I groaned. "This is the worst morning of my life. That settles it. We'll move to LA. We have to move to LA permanently. I know you have a business here, but you're smart and capable, and people have to import and export there, too." I could feel myself getting hysterical.

"Emerson," Mark said, now getting kind of hysterical, too, "we've been through this. I'm not moving to LA. My business here supports my mom and me, and I can't take that kind of gamble with her future."

"Can't you just sell the company?"

Now I'd made him mad. I knew I would, but I couldn't help myself. He got out of the bed and crossed his arms. "For the thousandth time, I'm not selling my company. I'm not moving away from Peachtree Bluff. My mother coming here doesn't change that."

I shook my head, incredulous. "Do you see this?" I asked, holding up my left hand. "This means that you have to learn to compromise a little. This means that sometimes you do what I want to do."

"Moving to LA is not 'sometimes doing what you want to do,'" Mark said, making air quotes.

I could feel fury rising in me. It was a familiar fury, one that I had felt with Mark since I was fifteen years old. It was hard to explain how angry he could make me one minute and how the next minute I felt like I couldn't live without him. "My giving up my entire career that I have worked my ass off for is not 'sometimes doing what *you* want to do,' either."

"I don't get it," Mark said for probably the ten millionth time. "I make plenty of money. Why can't you be happy here? Why can't we just stay here?"

Wow. We were so far off track now that this wasn't even remotely about his mother anymore. That scared me a little. Because this was *the* fight. This was the reason I hadn't said yes right away. He'd said that we would work it out, that when you loved someone, you found a way to make it work. But he clearly wasn't willing to give an inch, and let's face it, neither was I. We had two months to figure it out, so we had to find a solution quickly.

"I just don't get," I said, for what was probably also the ten millionth time, "why you don't get that I don't want to be an actress because of the money. I want to act because it fulfills me, Mark. It gives me purpose and strength. It's who I am. And I can't do it here. I need to be in LA."

"What about our kids?" he asked. "That's why my mother's coming back. She said that if you were always going to be flitting off to LA or making some movie, someone had to be here to take care of our children."

That cut right to the heart of me, to my fear that maybe I was selfish. Maybe this dream of mine had clouded my vision to the point where I couldn't see anything else. Maybe I was giving away too much of myself in exchange for reaching a level and attaining a life that, to be honest, I wasn't even really sure how to know I had reached in the first place. But that dream was mine. And I was getting there. I wasn't going to give it up now. I might not give it up ever.

"Hey, Mark," I said, eerily calm. Then I yelled, "We don't have kids! I might not be able to have kids at all!"

I turned my head to see a terrified-looking Kyle stop dead in his tracks in my doorway, his mouth open. "So sorry," he said, getting ready to turn to go back downstairs. He held his hands up, each with a cup in it. "Ansley told me you were up here, and I, um . . ."

He gestured toward the stairs, but Mark brushed by him

and said, "Don't leave on account of me." He looked back at me and said pointedly, "*Her fiancé.* You were the one she wanted anyway."

Then he was gone, and I felt absolutely awful. Not hangover bad but existential-life-crisis bad.

I could feel myself blushing. "I'm so sorry," I said. "That was awful."

Kyle walked toward me and said, "What did he mean, I was the one you wanted anyway?"

I could have been reading into it, adding something that wasn't really there, maybe even projecting a bit, but I could have sworn that he seemed almost hopeful when he said it.

I shook my head. "Oh, he meant because I was dying for a cup of coffee for this gosh-awful hangover."

Kyle and I had never talked about that night in LA, never acknowledged it in any way. Of course, we recognized each other when I arrived in Peachtree Bluff and he was standing at my mom's back door. But we never talked about the night we met, the kiss we shared, the secrets we swapped, the way we stayed up all night talking about our hopes and dreams. Nothing had ever passed between us that indicated to me that he considered that night remotely special.

He handed me the first cup. "Hangover cure," he said. "Green juice with tons of lemon and cayenne."

Then he handed me the second. "Black coffee. Hangover helper *número dos.*"

"Thank you," I squeaked out. "Hey, I'm really embarrassed that you saw that."

Kyle sat down on the bed beside me. "Em, are you all right? Because you don't have to do this, you know." He paused. "I mean, I don't want to overstep, but you are . . ." He looked down at the duvet cover, running his finger down my forearm just like he had the night we met. He looked me straight in the eye. "You are everything, Emerson. Don't give away any of that to make anyone else happy. Ever."

I couldn't say why, but I knew it was the best compliment I had ever received, that contained within it was a meaning that I couldn't comprehend any more than Kyle could verbalize.

I wanted to compliment him back, but I knew I couldn't. Well, I shouldn't. And I didn't know what I would say. *You are the weirdest, most wonderful man I know? You have always made me feel like I'm more than just what everyone else sees?* None of that made sense. And were those even real feelings?

I knew I should defend Mark. It wasn't his fault that he was in love with a hotheaded blonde who wanted her own way or that I was in love with a temperamental brunet who wanted his own way. We seemed to egg each other on, which sometimes seemed like a negative, but when it was for something positive, it was the very best part about our relationship. It made me know that we wouldn't be bored. But I couldn't explain all that to Kyle.

Instead, I sipped the hangover cure he had handed me and smiled at the way it burned when it went down. I noticed he had shaved this morning, which made him look younger. Before I could stop myself, I put my hand up and rubbed his smooth cheek. When I realized what I'd done, I blushed.

"A new Starlite Starlet?" I asked, looking down into my

cup. I knew I was opening a door that had been locked tight between us, one that had been barricaded since I first saw Kyle back in Peachtree Bluff. I knew it, but I did it anyway. Impulse control has never been my strong suit.

The look that passed over Kyle's face said, *You remember,* even though he hadn't said a word. But he smiled at me and leaned a little closer. "You know the thing about the Starlite Starlet?" he asked.

I shook my head. "Please enlighten me."

It nearly took my breath away when he said, "Its roots will always be in Peachtree. But the Starlite Starlet belongs in LA."

THE THING ABOUT MARK, the thing that kept us together, was that we might have fought, but we were always quick to make up. We had an unofficial system. One time I would apologize first, the next time he would.

Today it was my turn, I realized with disdain as I swigged my second cup of coffee, unpacking boxes in the back of Mom's store. At least I had Caroline to commiserate with. It made me a little bit happy that this was the first time in, well, twenty-six years that I had seen her looking something less than perfect. I mean, she was still gorgeous. But the lack of sleep was written all over her face.

I let out a low, frustrated groan as I slid the box cutter over a container of candles.

"Do you want to talk about it?" Caroline asked, raising an eyebrow.

"No." I paused. "I don't *want* to talk about it, but he's such a nightmare. Why does he act like this? I mean, his mother has to move here because I'm going to be an unfit mother traveling around? No one calls Angelina Jolie an unfit mother. No one shames Sandra Bullock. Actresses have been mothering and working since the beginning of time." I looked around to make sure no one could hear me and whispered, "And he knows how scared I am that I may not be able to have children. So that was the lowest blow I could think of."

Caroline shot me that look I hated, the one that questioned whether I was doing the right thing. "Look," she whispered, "I'm not kidding you. If you don't call and get those test results, I will pretend I'm you, and I will do it myself. Do you hear me?"

I did hear her, but I wanted to pretend I didn't. I wanted to pretend none of this was happening to me, that I was fine and dandy. If I called, they might say I was OK. But they also might say that I did have aplastic anemia as they feared—or potentially something even worse. And then I'd have to face it. I'd have to deal with it. I'd have to tell Mom.

"I mean, I don't understand why he's so unflinching on the move," I said, changing the subject. "He is filthy, dirty rich. He could sell that business and be even filthier, dirtier richer. I just don't understand why he won't."

"I think that's the root of your problem," Caroline finally said.

"That Mark is rich?"

"No," she said, setting her box on the floor and leaning

back on her hands. "The fact that once you marry him, you don't *have* to work, because you don't have to make money. I think when men have money, they assume their wives will jump at the opportunity to stay home. But you want your own identity, and I think that scares him. Or at least threatens the picture he sees of his future."

That kind of made sense. But when had I not been Mark's future? We'd been together all of high school, he had barely dated when he was in college, and now here we were again. Surely he recognized that I was never, ever going to be a stay-at-home mom or wife. But maybe that was the problem. I was the woman he wanted, and he was the man I wanted. But what we wanted out of life were two very different things.

"You don't need to work, and you don't need money, but James is thrilled that you're working for Mom," I said.

"Honey," Caroline said, rolling her eyes, "James left me for Edie Fitzgerald, shamed the hell out of me, and then came crawling back. If I decided to shave my head and join the Peace Corps, he would act thrilled. He is on really, really thin ice."

I nodded. My head was pounding again. This was supposed to be *my* therapy session, but the exhaustion and severe hangover had made Caroline somewhat vulnerable. She never wanted to talk about herself, but I felt like it was now or never.

"Car, are you happy?"

She shrugged. "What's happy, really? I mean, I love my job, I adore my children, my family is together." She paused. "I *was* happy. I was so, so happy. I can only hope that I can get back to that."

"And if you don't . . ."

She looked at me sadly. "If I don't, then I will have to make some changes."

"You'll leave him?" I whispered.

Caroline cocked her head to the side. "I won't spend my life miserable." She smiled at me. "I have a lot to offer, and I won't be taken for granted again."

I smiled back at her. No one wanted her sister to deal with the hell of a divorce. But I also couldn't stand the thought of my sister, my strong, brave, stand-on-her-own-two-feet sister, living a life where she felt trapped.

"Good. I can't stand the thought of you being miserable."

"Hey, Em, back at you." She raised her eyebrows.

"I'm not miserable," I protested. I mean, at least I thought I wasn't miserable. I loved Mark. That was all that mattered. Wasn't it?

"I know I'm extra-sensitive right now because of what I'm dealing with, but please don't lose yourself, Emerson. If you want a different life, then by all means, have a different life. Plunge into it headfirst. Sit on the deck and eat bonbons. I don't care what you do. I just don't want you to be unhappy. It's not worth it." Then she groaned. "Just like all those martinis last night. I am never drinking again. Ever."

I would remind her of that when she was popping champagne on Friday night.

I thought about what Caroline said as I left the store and walked to Mark's house. He was standing on the porch when I got there. Neither of us spoke. Instead, Mark swept me up in his arms and kissed me with so much passion that I couldn't imagine how I could live without him, how I could possibly be happy without him in my life. All of the worries I'd shared with my sister earlier melted away.

An hour later, lying in his bed, catching my breath, I finally said, "I'm sorry, Mark." I wasn't sure if I was actually sorry, but it was my turn. I mean, he had basically told me I was an unfit mother, and I had taken it like a chump. Should I have to be defending myself to my fiancé? I wasn't sure. But there in Mark's arms, I felt like I was where I was supposed to be, like he had loved all the fight right out of me. That moment with Kyle, when I wondered if we had let something special slip by us, suddenly seemed irrelevant. This, Mark, was my life, my future.

"So when does the princess arrive?" I asked.

"Oh, right," Mark said. "She's actually asking everyone to call her Duchess now."

"You're joking."

"I wish I were."

I didn't know how he'd lived an entire childhood with that nut and turned out even remotely normal. Mark rolled over and pulled me closer to him, kissing my forehead.

"That woman cannot keep our children," I said lightly, not wanting to start another argument over our nonexistent kids.

"Oh, God, no," Mark said. "Not happening. I wouldn't even let her babysit for like an hour." He kissed my lips softly. "Your sisters already said they would have kids for us if we needed them to," he whispered. "Or we could adopt. Or we don't even have to have kids." His eyes welled up. "I'm sorry, Em. I don't know why I do that, try to hurt you when I love you so much." He kissed me again. "I can't live without you. I've tried before, and I couldn't do it. Without you, life isn't life at all."

I kissed him now. "I agree," I said. "And I don't want to fight with you. We have to figure out a way to get past this issue before we ruin this amazing thing between us."

Mark nodded. "I know that. I do. And I'm going to try to be better. We're not going to be that conventional couple. We'll travel a lot. We'll go back and forth to LA. I think I can come at least every other week or so while you're there or wherever you're on location."

"Really?" I asked.

"Sure," he said.

"And I'll only take parts if they are really important. I don't want to be away from you if it's going to be for some sucky role that won't get me anywhere."

Mark kissed my nose. "Deal," he whispered.

I felt so at peace and so right in that moment. I kissed him again. Then kissed him longer. "Hey," I whispered. "When do you have to get back to work?"

He pulled me on top of him. "You mean I have a job?" he asked.

I giggled and was lost in him again, in that feeling of being so connected to another human being that you don't ever want to be away from him, that the real world completely slips away. I briefly thought of poor Caroline unpacking boxes at Mom's store, taking our punishment while I was over here having the time of my life.

But then again, I thought, as I kissed Mark deeper, Caroline had made me her servant on the regular when we were kids. It wouldn't hurt her to have a little payback now. I closed my eyes and savored this moment with the man I loved. With my future husband. And I knew that I would sacrifice anything, be a different person, in exchange for getting to spend the rest of my life with him.

ansley: the first rule of parenting

I hadn't been able to face Jack for two days after I became pretty sure Caroline and Sloane knew he was their father—and I was pretty sure he knew they knew. Once Caroline had called him "Daddy dearest" that night, it all started making sense— why Jack had been acting so jumpy around me, why Caroline and Sloane had been the tiniest bit distant.

The mere idea of it made me feel sick. What would I say to the girls? Why hadn't they come to me? But most of all, how could the man who claimed to love me more than life itself have hidden something so important?

After two days of avoiding Jack, not sleeping, and barely eating, I was at the point we all inevitably reach, where the knowing seems easier than the not knowing.

I knocked on Jack's door, which was strange. I hadn't

knocked on his door ever. Since he'd moved next door and we'd gotten back together, I walked in and out as I pleased.

Confusion was written all over Jack's face as he opened the door. "Did you forget your key or something?" he asked. I shook my head.

Even in my anger and sorrow, I couldn't help but admire the entrance hall as I walked inside. I had designed this house for us, created a place where our children and grandchildren could come, where Jack and I could start the life together that we had always wanted. The marble floors, which had been there for more than a century of this home's century-and-a-half life span, had been beautifully restored and honed. A large oyster-shell chandelier hung every six feet down the hall's long path. It was perfect. And knowing that the life we were supposed to share might never come to fruition broke something inside me.

Whereas I had carried nothing but my righteous indignation over here, I was now handing Jack my tears.

"Babe, come here," he said soothingly.

He pulled me to him, but I pushed him away.

He bent down to look in my face. "What's wrong with my girl?"

I shook my head. "How could you keep this from me?"

For a second, he looked genuinely mystified. Then, as if the fog was lifting, recognition crossed his face. Still, the man was cautious. "Keep what from you, Ans?"

"How could you know that my daughters knew you were their father and not tell me? How could you live with a lie like that?"

Jack shook his head, and I could tell he was trying not to laugh, which brought the anger back. "How could I live with a lie like that? Ansley, are you serious? I'm pretty sure the lie I lived with for thirty-five years, the one where I was the father of two of your children, is the issue here. Remember that one? I feel like maybe that was the big lie. That they know feels like a relief."

I pushed past him into the living room. "So, what, you got tired of the lie and told them? Told *my* children a secret that, quite frankly, wasn't yours to tell?"

I sat down on the couch, and he stood up straighter. "For one, it wasn't only your secret, Ansley. I have lived with this earthshaking other life that I couldn't tell anyone about. Not my family, not my friends. I have lived a lifetime trying to protect you, so let's get that straight right now."

Jack wasn't explosive like the rest of my family; he was calmer and steadier, better at controlling his emotions. But his darkened eyes and shaking voice were a dead giveaway that he was very upset. Despite that, he sat down beside me on the couch.

I shook my head. "So tell me. I want to know how they found out."

He shrugged and sighed. "First of all, I think you know that I would never, ever go behind your back. I would never tell them our secret without your permission." He paused. "I honestly don't even know if they know for sure."

I shook my head in confusion. "What?"

Jack took a deep breath and swallowed. "Sloane and Caro-

83

line were putting the furniture back after the painters had come. I walked in, and they were standing by my antique secretary. They didn't say anything, but I could feel that something was off. They looked up at me with . . ." He trailed off. "I don't know. Disbelief and understanding. I knew they knew. I can't explain it, but I did."

I felt as breathless as if I had been there in that moment. "So what did you say?" I whispered.

He reached over and took my hand. "Ans, I didn't say anything. I couldn't. And neither could they. And then Emerson called for them to tell them she was engaged, so we never got a chance to speak." He sighed. "That secretary, the one they were standing by, is where I keep all the pictures you sent me while they were growing up." He paused like he was weighing his options. "And their fairy stones."

Now I was confused. "Their fairy stones?"

Jack nodded, looking sheepish. "That day on Starlite Island, the day I came to you . . ."

I had rushed my little girls into the boat so quickly that they had left their stones. We had gone back to the island to look for them, but we never found them. Now I finally knew why.

Jack sighed again, and I could feel the emotion welling up in him. "After everything that happened that day, I needed a piece of them." His voice cracked. "I knew I would never see them again, and I wanted a piece of my children."

I wanted to keep being angry. I wanted to keep feeling my pain and humiliation, but sitting here with this raw wound of a man, it hit me what I had actually put him through all those years ago. I had gotten these beautiful girls. And he had gotten nothing. Not his children, not me. Not a single memory. While I wanted to chide him for being so careless as to keep those pictures and stones where people might easily find them, I had to realize what that had cost him.

"I didn't know what to say. I didn't want to confirm their suspicions—if they even had any—but what would the explanation be for why I had years of photos with notes from you written on the back of them?"

"Do you know if they saw the notes?" I asked, clarifying.

Jack shook his head. "I don't know. But also, I kind of do." He continued. "I just stood there. I couldn't say anything. Sloane and Caroline turned to walk out the door. Sloane was gone, but then Caroline came back and whispered to me, 'She does have your eyes.'"

"What?" I asked.

"I know. I was confused, too. But then I opened the top drawer of the secretary, and Sloane's baby photo was on top. You had written a note on the back that said, *Thank you so much, Jack. She's perfect. She has your eyes.*"

I grimaced. That was pretty damning evidence. I had only myself to blame, really. Why would I have done that? Why did I write him those notes on the photos? How could I have been so careless? I guess at the time, I couldn't have predicted how this would turn out. At the time, I believed with all my heart that I would be with Carter until my dying breath and that Jack would always remain a part of my memory but never a part of my life—and certainly not a part of Caroline, Sloane, and Emerson's lives. It boggled the mind. Defied all logic and reason.

He shook his head. "I just stood there like an idiot. I was so stunned. And then Caroline gave me this look. It was just a look, and she didn't say anything, but I knew it meant *Don't tell Mom*. So I didn't say anything to you, because I didn't want to break their trust when this was my very first move as their father as they knew it." He paused. "Or as they *maybe* knew it. Again, I still don't know what they really think."

I actually laughed now, because it was clear that he didn't have the first clue about being a parent. And how would he? He had never had a single day's practice. Talk about on-the-job training.

"Honey," I said, "here's the first rule of parenting. If your kids tell you not to tell Mom something, that means you run, don't walk, to tell Mom."

He put his head in his hands. "I'm sorry, Ansley. This has been impossible for me. I didn't want to lie to you, but I didn't know what to do. I mean, how do we even navigate this? I'm their father, and I'm dating their mother. Last week, I was a test tube. Today I'm living next door. It's so big."

I smiled, all the anger gone now. "It's big for you, too, Jack. I know it is. And no one expects you to be perfect at this on the first day. I've been doing it for thirty-five years, and I still mess up more often than not."

Then he asked me the question I had asked him all those years ago on Starlite Island: "What about Emerson?"

It broke my heart. Caroline and Sloane got a brand-new dad—their real dad, one who was living, breathing—but Emerson didn't. Although Jack could be a wonderful father figure, I knew it wasn't the same thing, which seemed unfair. But she was grown; she was getting married. I figured she would take the news in stride.

I didn't realize yet, after twenty-six years of being that girl's mother, just how wrong I could still be.

IN ADDITION TO TAKING inventory at my store all day, the second punishment I had in mind for my girls was making them go to the monthly town meeting. I loved town meetings, seeing all my friends and neighbors in one place. Compared with the hate and terror happening in the rest of the world, the "serious problems" in Peachtree Bluff seemed comical.

Tonight's meeting was going to be a doozy.

"I don't understand why Sloane doesn't have to come," Caroline whined as we walked down the street toward Paradise Pub, where tonight's meeting would be held. It was the dividing line between historic Old Town, which was established before the Revolution, and New Town, which was settled in 1776. You either lived on the northern side of Paradise or the southern side of Paradise. We were on the southern side, naturally.

"Yeah," Emerson chimed in, "why *doesn't* Sloane have to come? She was just as drunk as we were."

"Drunker," Caroline said. "And she was the one who decided it would be a good idea to order every martini on the menu."

"Yeah," Emerson said again. "If anything, Caroline and I are the victims here."

Jack winked at me and took my hand. I wasn't ready yet to sit the girls down and talk this out. I hadn't decided if I should talk to Sloane and Caroline without Emerson or approach them all at the same time. Then there was that tiny two percent of me that hoped that if we never talked about it, it would all go away.

So to the girls, I just said, "Sloane is at home with her wounded national hero of a husband and her two children. She gets a pass tonight."

"Did you forget *I* have two children?" Caroline asked.

"I did not," I said. "Did you?" I turned back to where she was on the sidewalk and gave her the eye. James had taken the kids to visit his mother, and Caroline had begged off the trip, saying she had to work. Perhaps James had forgotten that her pushover of a mother was her boss. I wondered how long it would be until he finally started standing up to her again. "Your children won't be here for two more days. Until then, you live under my roof."

"Hooray!" Emerson and Caroline shouted at the same time, nearly making me jump out of my skin.

Jack smiled at me, and I shook my head.

The meetings at the pub were my favorites. It had a huge patio with dozens of strands of bubble string lights, plenty of places for us all to sit, and, of course, cocktails. I had a feeling that I was going to need one, as my daughters had turned back into whining teenagers.

But perhaps my favorite thing about the pub was its stage. It was really for bands, but Mayor Bob, who had been the mayor of Peachtree for as long as I could remember, stood up there to act as a moderator while his citizens aired their grievances. It could turn into quite the performance, considering that this was a town of artists, actors, musicians, and otherwise free-spirited people. It was organized chaos, with more emphasis on the chaos.

"Did Mark not want to come?" Caroline asked Emerson.

Emerson pointed at me. "Someone wouldn't let him."

"When you're grounded, you don't get to see your boyfriend," I said with my most serious face. As I'd said since the beginning of time, if they were going to act like children, I would treat them like children. "This isn't supposed to be fun."

Only, it was a little fun.

Hippie Hal sauntered over, and I jumped up to hug him. "How was India?" I asked, noticing that the rope Hal usually wore to hold up his pants had been replaced by a woven belt.

Hal hugged Emerson and Caroline as he said, "It was great. But I missed my Murphy girls."

He grinned at us. He didn't even seem stoned, which was a little off-putting. As if he could read my mind, Hal said, "I have to have my full faculties tonight. I have something to present, and I know Mrs. McClasky isn't going to like it. Not one bit." He grinned conspiratorially. Hippie Hal and Mrs. McClasky had been feuding since 1995. She hated that he kept refurbished bikes on his lawn, and she hated even more that she couldn't make him move them because there was no bike ordinance in New Town, where Hal lived, in a home built in 1789.

I was tired, frankly, of hearing them argue about it at every town meeting. So I hoped this was something different.

.Emerson went to look for Jack and, I could only assume, flirt her way to the beginning of the bar line. It was amazing how a two-day hiatus had cured her proclamation to "never drink again." I leaned over and whispered to Caroline, "Have Emerson and Mark made up?"

She nodded.

I shook my head.

"I feel like I'm not the person to give marriage advice," she said. "Maybe you should say something."

I put up my hands. "I'm not touching that with a ten-foot pole." I had heard snippets of the fight between Mark and Emerson, and I didn't have the stamina to have all that fire directed toward me if I meddled. I was too old for it. Plus, I knew Emerson. She'd do whatever she wanted no matter what I said.

Everyone quieted as Mayor Bob called the meeting to order. First on the docket was Paula Jones and mail carrier Roger Smith's spat. Roger would win this one. He was our beloved mail carrier, the man who brought us our *Town & Country* magazines and packages even in the rain. Who could possibly turn against him?

Paula Jones, on the other hand, yelled at children for walking on the edge of her grass on the way to the park. The woman didn't stand a chance. Unless she had stacked the audience with members of First Methodist's parish—where she was the largest tither—she didn't have a prayer, pun intended.

Paula took the stage, wearing a pale-blue short-sleeved

skirt suit with a pillbox hat that would have been more appropriate for a British wedding than the Peachtree Bluff equivalent of a deposition. She had a tiny, upturned nose, and beady eyes. Her usual bright red lipstick had been replaced by pink. I'd hand it to the woman. She looked very innocent.

"I took the mailbox off the front porch for one day to have the porch painted. *One day*," Paula began, as though she was on the verge of tears, "and now *Roger* says he will only deliver mail if I put a mailbox on my fence, that he won't come up to the porch anymore."

As she continued with her diatribe of how this had horribly impacted her life, taking full advantage of her three minutes, Caroline whispered to Emerson and me, "Mom, I'm texting you a pic of your mother-of-the-bride dress."

"What?" I whispered back. "I thought maybe *I* would pick that out."

Caroline shook her head. "No. My friend Ramon is a huge up-and-coming designer in Manhattan, and he had this vision for your dress. It's flawless." Then she whispered to Emerson, "He's making the bridesmaids' dresses, too."

Emerson rolled her eyes at me. Both our phones vibrated. I gasped when I saw the picture. The gown was the palest blue floor-length lace with straps about three fingers wide that came slightly off the shoulder. It was fitted at the waist and flared out the tiniest bit, my favorite style, except that I usually wore something with a sleeve. I thought it was more appropriate at my age.

"Car, this looks like a wedding gown," I said.

"Oh, Mom," Emerson said, "you have to wear this. It's perfection. You will look gorgeous."

Caroline looked at the picture and then back at me. "Yeah," she whispered. She looked me up and down disdainfully. "But, Mom, you really need to lose some weight in your shoulders."

I rolled my eyes.

Jack, who was back now and passing out rosé, said, "How does one lose weight in her shoulders?"

Roger was having his moment now. I thought it was a smart move for him to wear his uniform. It made him seem professional and knowledgeable right off the bat. Probably, though, he hadn't put the thought into his outfit that Paula had. He had simply come straight from work. "It clearly states in the Peachtree Bluff Mailbox Statute of 1962 that existing front-porch mailboxes have a right to stay, but if that front-porch box is moved at any time for any reason, it must be replaced by a street-accessible box," he was saying.

"But I moved it for *one day*," Paula protested.

Mayor Bob interrupted. "Paula, you've had your time."

I waved at Kimmy as she passed around photocopies of the Mailbox Statute. Word around town was that she and Roger had something going on. Kimmy denied it, but when you're passing around a man's flyers at the town meeting, you're sleeping with him. No two ways about it.

As Roger continued, giving his full three minutes its due, my phone beeped with another text from Caroline that said, *Bridesmaids*. The bridesmaids' dresses were the same shade of pale blue as my mother-of-the-bride dress, but instead of lace, they were made of a thick raw silk. They were strapless and floor-length, with huge white grosgrain ribbons tied around the waist. They were simple, elegant, a little bit Southern, and perfect for a beach wedding.

I returned my attention to the matter at hand. "All right, ladies and gentlemen," Mayor Bob began. "You have heard both sides of the case. It's time to make a decision. All in favor of Ms. Paula Jones, raise your hand." Yup. She'd done it. She'd stacked the audience. This was going to be a close one. "All in favor of Mr. Roger Smith?" My hand shot up, because, as I said, Roger delivered the world to my front porch.

The mayor started counting, and my arm started losing feeling as I waited for him to finish. "All right, ladies and gentlemen." He smiled. "It was close, but Roger Smith wins by three votes."

Cheers rang out from my section of the pub, while Paula shouted, "I demand a recount!"

But Hippie Hal was already shooing her off the stage. It was his moment in the spotlight. I had butterflies at the thought of what he was going to present. But this was even better than my wildest dreams.

"As most of you know," Hal began, "I recently returned from a three-week stay in India. While my eyes were opened to many things there, I had a wonderful idea that I think could be of benefit to the town."

"And what is that?" Mayor Bob asked.

"Goats," Hal replied simply.

Caroline and Emerson grinned at me so widely I thought

their faces were going to fall off. And they had complained the whole way here.

"Please explain," Mayor Bob said.

"We all have our lawns cut each week, creating a noise problem and polluting our environment. Of course, I'm not suggesting that every person put a goat in his or her yard. That would put my friend Billy Washington out of a job. But I think some of us could replace our traditional mowing with goats, and then that could become another tourist attraction in town."

There was a wave of muffled laughter through the audience.

I couldn't believe it when Caroline very solemnly rose and said, "As owner of one of the largest lots in downtown Peachtree Bluff, I think this is a wonderful idea. I would love to have a goat in my yard."

Jack burst out laughing, and I couldn't help but chuckle. The mere idea of Caroline with a goat was too much to take.

Emerson said, "If this gets passed, you are so screwed. You're going to have to get a goat."

Caroline scoffed. "Please. There is no way this is going to get passed."

A few more people stood up and voiced their concerns for the goat movement. Mayor Bob said, "We have time for one more comment."

That was when Mrs. McClasky, Hippie Hal's nemesis, made her move. She and her hot-pink crop pants and white Keds climbed up onto that stage, and she wagged her finger.

"There is a reason we have a no-livestock ordinance in

Peachtree Bluff. Not only does livestock spread disease, but it also creates a noise problem." She paused to put her hands over her ears. "All that infernal bleating—and the feces smell? Why spend all this time, energy, and money preserving our town's homes and keeping our downtown beautiful only to have it smell like goat waste as you drive in?"

"Why is she so unpleasant?" Jack whispered to me.

"I don't know. Maybe she has had a hard life."

I handed my phone to Jack. He put his hand over his heart. "Oh, Ansley, I want to see you walking down the aisle in this."

I smiled ironically. "No such luck. This is my mother-of-the-bride dress."

"You're joking."

Mrs. McClasky sighed and looked over at Hal. "Why can't you just let yards be yards? With grass and flowers. No bikes. No goats. Just grass like God intended."

And this is where I felt it all go south for her. She had made great points. She was right. But Hal was popular, and she had made it personal.

Mayor Bob asked, "All in favor of having goats downtown?"

I raised my hand as a pity gesture. Almost all the hands in the room went up.

"All opposed?"

Only nine hands.

"Oh, my God." Emerson was hysterical. "Caroline!" She was laughing so hard she could hardly breathe. "Now you have to get a . . . a . . ."

Now Jack and I were laughing, too, as Emerson finished, "Goat."

I thought she was going to fall off her chair.

Caroline looked at me in shock. "What is wrong with these people? Who would agree to goats in people's yards in downtown Peachtree?"

Hal came over, a surprised look on his face. "Caroline, I'll let you know when your goat comes in."

"Oh, well—actually—" Caroline stammered, but Hal was already gone. That set us all off again.

"James is going to be furious," Emerson said, still laughing.

Now Caroline smiled. "He is, isn't he?" She nodded. "Well, silver lining."

Twenty minutes later, after talking to everyone who wanted to congratulate Caroline on a successful goat campaign, we were leaving the pub. We usually walked down Main Street to get home, but tonight Jack said, "Let's take the alley." He raised his eyebrows. "I hear it's haunted at night."

I smiled. Caroline and Emerson were a few steps in front of us, and when I heard their piercing screams, I thought maybe they had seen a ghost.

I looked ahead of them to see Hippie Hal's back . . . and Mrs. McClasky leaned against the brick wall, her hair disheveled. They pulled away quickly, but it was too late.

"Hippie Hal, you dirty dog," Jack said.

"Oh, my God," Caroline wailed.

"I can never ever unsee that," Emerson chimed in.

I stood, gaping in amazement, until Jack pulled my hand. I

knew it was terribly rude, but come on. Hippie Hal and Mrs. McClasky. Mortal enemies and . . . lovers?

It just goes to show that even in a small Southern town you know is full of secrets, there's still one that can shock you every now and then.

emerson: the dark side

The first two years I was in LA flew by. It was all a blur, really. Between auditioning and filming the small roles I was getting here and there during the day and waitressing at night, intermixed with the professional partying we were all doing, let's just say there wasn't much sleep. It was a good thing my twenty-year-old skin could take it like a champ and never show my exhaustion.

Two weeks after my twentieth birthday, I got a call that I knew had the potential to change everything. A new network was looking for an actress to star in four of its movies. It wasn't big-budget, and it wouldn't make me rich or famous. But a well-known director was backing it, and it would give me the thing I needed the very most: real, true experience.

When I answered the phone that morning, Morris Stevenson, the director, was on the other line. "Emerson, I need you to meet me for dinner tonight. I think you have great potential, and I'd like to talk about the possibility of you starring in these films for me. I think we could work really well together."

I almost dropped the phone. "Wow," I said, so flattered. "Tell me when and where, and I'll be there."

"Don't worry about it," he said. "Just give me your address."

When Morris picked me up in his Bentley the next night, I have to admit I was impressed.

"Pretty nice building you have here," he said, winking at me.

I felt so proud in that moment. I was happy that I had agreed to let Caroline help pay for my apartment, because maybe it would give Morris the impression that I was success-ful, that I was, indeed, the girl he should take a chance on.

Over caviar and champagne, we talked for hours about my career. I wanted to remember everything about this night, freeze it for the future. He was so polished and handsome. A real director who really knew what he was doing, who could give me feedback and help me grow. And he wanted me. Me! It was a dream come true.

When dinner was over, he asked, "Do you want to come back to my house and check out the new scripts I'm consider-ing?"

I wasn't stupid, and every girl I knew had a story with a question just like this, so it put me the tiniest bit on edge. But I didn't want this night to end. So I said, "Sure. And I'd love to meet your wife."

He looked a little surprised, but come on. Of course, I had googled him. I knew he was married.

I was pleased when we got to his palatial home and, instead of offering me another drink, Morris handed me a Perrier. That he wasn't trying to get me drunk made me feel a little more comfortable.

Morris showed me his awards and his office. We were sitting side by side on his white banquette, which I was sure his wife had had custom-made for him, admiring the view of the Hollywood hills, when he leaned over and kissed my neck.

Honestly, it wasn't a bad feeling. He was handsome and attentive, and he smelled nice. But he was married. So I pulled my neck away and reminded him of that. I'll never forget what he said next.

"Honey, you're beautiful, but you're not that talented. You have one thing to offer directors like me, and if you can't figure out what that one thing is, you're never going to make it in this town."

His words cut deep, because he had verbalized my biggest fear at that time: maybe I wasn't good enough. I'm embarrassed to say that his proposition gave me pause. I had been working myself to the bone for the past two years, and I hadn't really gotten anywhere. He held the keys to a door that I really, really wanted opened for me. For a moment, I pictured myself doing what he wanted me to. I would be his mistress. I would be his star. And, really, hadn't this been happening since the beginning of acting itself?

But then I looked down at his left hand, which was conspicuously devoid of a ring. And I remembered that Morris had a wife. A real woman with real feelings who didn't deserve any of this. And, God, it pained me to realize what doing the right thing was going to cost me. At the time, it felt like it was potentially costing me the one thing I wanted most, that another opportunity might never come along. I loved those days when I got to become someone else, but I knew I couldn't slip into character here. I had to stay true to myself.

So I got up off the beautiful couch that I was certain had cost more than my last six months of rent and said, "Morris, I want this role more than I have ever wanted anything. But I'm not willing to disregard your wife, a woman who is worthy of my respect and yours, in order to get that."

I wish I could use this as some anecdote of how doing the right thing gets you what you want. I wish it had been some triumphant story where Morris shook my hand and said, "Emerson, you're right. A young lady with your morals deserves this opportunity. See you on set on Monday."

But that didn't happen. Morris just snickered at me and said, "You might as well pack your bags now. You'll never make it in this town."

I wish I could say that I walked out of Morris's beautiful home feeling determined to prove him wrong, that I walked out with my head held high, confident in my decision, and knowing for sure that I had done the right thing. But that wasn't what happened. I walked out of his house feeling defeated. I knew that some other girl would accept his proposition and that she would make those movies, have that experience, get bigger roles, and be on the way to the career that I wanted, that a million girls wanted.

That was the first night since I'd arrived in LA that I had called Mark. I had given him his space, had let him have his freedom. I didn't want to lead him on, because I knew that, just like Morris, I wouldn't ultimately give him what he wanted. I expected Mark to tell me to come home, and, as ripped open as I felt that night, I might have said OK. But he didn't.

Instead, he said, "Emerson, there is always going to be some asshole out there who will tell you that you aren't good enough, who is going to make you believe that you aren't worth it. But he will be wrong. Because you deserve everything you want. I believe in you. I believe that you'll make it. That's why it was so hard for me to let you go, because I knew that you would be the biggest star out there and that I'd never get you back."

Maybe I knew then that one day, I'd end up with Mark.

And now, all these years later, it was crazy to think that it was finally happening.

After our makeup session, Mark and I were sailing as smoothly toward the Labor Day wedding as the slick, waveless sea beyond Mom's porch. On the bright side, Mark and I couldn't get enough of each other, and I was more convinced than ever that this was the right decision. On the dark side— the very, very dark side—Mark's mother would be arriving soon. And she would be living with Mark until she found a new place. Poor Mark. He was a saint. I wouldn't have lasted an hour and a half.

On the other dark side, the extreme fatigue, dizziness, loss of energy, and bruising that I was hoping would go away if I ignored it hard enough were still constant companions. But I kept rationalizing that with all I had going on, I didn't have time to deal with that, too.

Vivi, Preston, and James had already arrived, and Caroline's entire family was piled into Mom's guesthouse. Sloane had suggested that her family take Mom's guesthouse and let Caroline and James back in their house, but Caroline had insisted—very unselfishly, if you ask me—that Sloane stay. Adam was recovering quickly and had graduated from a walker to a cane, but it had become clear that he would never be back in the field again. I was sure that inside he was devastated, but outwardly he was taking it very well. He said that this was a new chapter for him, that he had made a deal with God that if he could survive his capture, if he ever got back home with his family, he would never ask for another thing. I'm sure nearly dying put it all into perspective for him. Despite his progress, it was still very challenging for him to climb stairs, and you couldn't get to the guesthouse without climbing a flight.

With all that settled, we had something even more potentially thrilling than my wedding to look forward to. Today, I was pretty sure, was going to be the best day of my life. We were all sitting on Caroline's front steps: Mom, Jack, Mark, Sloane, Adam, Taylor, AJ, James, Caroline, Preston, Vivi, and me.

"Hey," Mom said casually, "I was thinking . . . could we have a sister-and-mom dinner tonight? Just Caroline, Sloane, Emerson, and me at my house?"

"Nope," Mark said. "She's all mine."

"She's not all yours until Labor Day weekend," Caroline said. "You have to share between now and then."

"Speaking of . . ." I said. I had purposely been waiting to drop this bomb on Mark until we were in public and he couldn't get too mad at me. I smiled at him enthusiastically. "*Us Weekly* wants to do an exclusive on the wedding!"

Mom cut her eyes at me, and Mark sighed. But it was Caroline who spoke first. "That's really tacky, Emerson. You do not want your private wedding splashed all over the press."

I looked pleadingly at Mark. "This is a big deal for me. It could be a big opportunity."

He took my hand, and I could tell he was trying to be sweet. "Honey, I want our day to be about us. That seems so intrusive."

Great. I could only imagine how many hours I had paid my publicist to orchestrate that kind of incredible press. These people didn't understand. Weddings were the perfect time to get your name out there. I rolled my eyes.

"So, dinner?" Mom asked, as if we had put the *Us Weekly* issue to rest.

"I don't know, Mom," Sloane said. "I feel like I need to be here. Adam had a particularly rough day at PT."

"You know I can hear you, right?" he said, laughing. Adam was sitting on the step above Sloane, and she was leaning back onto him. He leaned down and kissed the top of her head. "I'm fine, babe." He paused. "Men," he said to AJ and Taylor, "with Mommy out of the house tonight, I say we order pizza and have . . ."

They all flexed their muscles and said simultaneously, "Dudes' night!"

They were cute. I knew that Mark would be a really good dad one day, too. I couldn't wait to see him with our own kids. The thought made my stomach sink for the second time in as many hours. I had to get those test results. I leaned in closer to him and kissed him to distract myself from the bad feelings.

"I'm cooking tonight," Vivi said.

"You are?" James asked, surprised.

She nodded enthusiastically. "Yup. I'm cooking like Mommy. I'll make reservations at Full Moon."

We all laughed as Kimmy's truck pulled up with a small trailer. Kimmy jumped out of the driver's side, Hal jumped out of the passenger's seat, and we got up and scattered around the yard. We had been plotting all morning about how we were going to grill Hal about the torrid McClasky affair. But Mom had said we needed to give Hal his privacy and had sworn us to secrecy. All that meant was that she knew what was really going on and didn't want to share the juicy gossip with us.

"She's here, she's here!" Vivi yelled.

AJ and Taylor ran ahead. They were the first ones to the trailer, and Kimmy handed AJ a leash.

Caroline and I stood in the yard while everyone else made a fuss. "How did I let them talk me into this?"

"To piss James off, remember?"

She crossed her arms as we heard the first ear-shattering "Bleeeeeaaaatttt." Caroline groaned. "It was so not worth it."

"You don't have to get anyone to cut the yard now," I said optimistically.

"What do I care about having someone cut the lawn? James deals with all that and pays for it. It affects me in no way."

"Oh, Mom, she is so, so cute," Vivi said to Caroline, hugging the little white goat with brown spots. She nuzzled into Vivi with a brown ear. "Let's call her Ellie Mae."

"Ellie Mae?" I asked. "Wow. A few months in the South, and you are really owning it."

Vivi was leading her new pet/lawn mower into the yard, pausing to pat her head. Ellie Mae jumped in the air like she was just so excited. She really was adorable. But as soon as she entered the gate, the goat simultaneously ate one of Caroline's prized roses and pooped.

"Swell," Caroline said. "The house is yours now, Sloane, as long as you keep the goat."

We all laughed. Five hours later, we were all laughing again, this time around Mom's dining-room table. She had made Grammy's favorite dinner: tea service. We had cucumber, egg salad, and tomato sandwiches, brownies, lemon squares, and, of course, tea. Mom said it was all gluten-free for Caroline, but quite frankly, I had my doubts. Still, it was a perfect summer supper, light and easy and reminiscent of a simpler time.

We talked—deliciously, gloriously—about absolutely nothing of importance. None of the major issues we were tackling in our lives was at this dinner with us. I knew in the back of my mind that it would be a good time to share with my mom what was going on with my health while my sisters were there to soften the blow. But I didn't want to ruin our drama-free event.

Mom took a deep breath, and we all leaned in, somehow sensing that what she was about to say was going to be important.

But before she could speak, Caroline interjected, "I'm packing up, Mom. The guesthouse is officially all yours again."

The way she said it felt abrupt, even for Caroline. I got the distinct impression that she was trying to change the subject, despite the fact that a subject hadn't even been broached.

"No!" Mom said. "I don't want the guesthouse to be all mine again. You can't leave!"

"Mom!" Caroline was incredulous. "Surely you didn't think we were going to stay here forever?"

"No. Not forever. But it's still summer. There's still a wedding to plan."

"I'm only going back for two weeks. Then I'll be back here for a bit. But the last time I came, I moved. I have parkas crammed in the closet. It's time to get out of here and reboot."

Now Mom was crying in earnest. "But when you come back, you'll be staying at *your* house, and it won't be the same."

I think we were all a bit surprised by the display of emotion. You didn't have to be a rocket scientist to figure out that Mom had been thrown by the idea that we would all be coming home to live with her, all at once. I didn't blame her, really. When you were by yourself, it was easy to get into your routine, become set in your ways. Seven of us suddenly living under her roof and James down the street had to have come as quite the shock. I'd assumed she would be relieved to see that her nest was shrinking.

I was crying now, too, because if anyone cries, I cry with them. That had been a big hurdle for me to overcome as an actress, because I even responded compassionately to fellow actors' fake tears.

"This really has been the best few months," I said, sobbing, which was totally ridiculous, because Adam had been missing and James had cheated and Grammy had died and I had been sick that whole time.

I looked over and was surprised to see that Sloane was crying now, too.

"Here's the deal, though. I have a surprise for all of you, and I need you to come to Manhattan on July 29 to get it."

"What kind of surprise?" Sloane asked warily, drying her tears with her napkin.

"It's a good one, I promise," Caroline said. "I've been working really hard on it, and I think you're all going to love it."

Sloane crossed her arms, and I expected an argument from her, but none came. It had taken everything we had to get her to New York a few months ago. Before that trip, she hadn't been on a plane or in the city since Dad was killed in the 9/11 attacks. But now she seemed resigned. With Caroline, it was just easier that way.

I was excited about going to New York and excited about a surprise of any kind. But I was not excited about my sister leaving. I started sobbing again.

"You guys," Caroline said, "I'm not dying. Let's get it together."

More sobbing.

We heard heavy footsteps on the front stairs. James appeared in the doorway, in a suit as always, looking—I had to admit—irresistibly handsome. He looked at Caroline, then me, then Sloane, then Mom. He inhaled as though he were going to say something and then turned and bolted back down the steps.

It was the best thing that could have possibly happened, because just like that, we all burst out laughing.

Mom stood up and motioned for us all to come to her. I wrapped one arm around her and one around Caroline, resting my head on my mom's shoulder. Even though I hadn't told her about any of the things that were bothering me, still, at twenty-six years old, there was nothing more soothing than my mother's hug.

There we were: one mother, three daughters, a lot of tears, a lot of laughter. I knew then that no matter where life took us next, no matter what the future held, these women and this hug would always, always be worth coming home to.

ELEVEN

ansley: forever and always

I try not to consciously think about that night. So maybe that's why I dreamed of it so often, why I woke up in a cold sweat that I did the wrong thing, made the wrong decision, picked the life behind door number two instead of door number one.

Carter and I married in late December, after Christmas and before New Year's, giving everyone something to look forward to during that dark and gloomy time when it feels like there's really nothing to celebrate. It would have made sense for us to marry in Peachtree Bluff, the place we had met. It would have made sense for us to get married in Athens, in my home church, and have the reception in my own backyard. But Carter and I decided to get married in Manhattan, at a chapel we had stumbled upon while we were spending a lazy afternoon meandering through the city.

Our wedding was an affair to remember, to be sure. But

in a lot of ways, that day was tainted for me. I spent years lamenting how unfair that was. I spent years lamenting it, that is, until I went to Jack to ask him for the most unthinkable thing I could imagine. Then I realized that life happens as it should, always, even the less desirable parts. Once I asked Jack to father not one but two of my children, the fact that he had almost broken up my wedding was put very much into perspective. And I knew for sure that had he not come to me that night, had we not made the promises we made, I never would have gone to him when it seemed like I was running out of options.

I was staying at the Plaza that night, a wedding gift from Carter. We had lied to our parents that my apartment had been sublet quickly, so it wouldn't appear that Carter and I had been living together for months. They would have had a stroke.

The night before the wedding, everyone was already asleep, and I felt anxious. I was thrilled to marry Carter. I knew we loved each other. I knew the life we would have together would be as perfect as a life could be. But I had so much nervous energy all the same. It was a cold night in New York, and I watched the snow falling from my window, congregating in slow circles around the streetlights and melting as it hit the sidewalk. Suddenly, I had the strongest urge to be outside in it. So I bundled myself up in my grandmother's fur, the one she had loaned me for my wedding day, and made my way down to the now-quiet lobby. The street outside, which was normally bustling, was calm. No well-heeled women rushing in and out of Bergdorf Goodman. No tired parents corralling screaming children out of FAO Schwarz. No cabs honking and screeching their way down the street.

It was an enchanted night, one from a fairy tale, so much so that when I looked down the street and saw him, I wasn't even surprised. Head down, hands in his pockets, Jack looked at me. When my eyes met his, he lit up like the tree in Rockefeller Center. I didn't bother to move, just stood there in front of the steps, the revolving doors with the *P* on them quiet for the moment, taking time off from the relentless *swish-swish-swish* they made all day long.

I should have put my hands up to stop him, because I knew what was coming. I could tell by the look in his eyes, by the way he walked toward me steadily, with such intention. Maybe it was that I wasn't prepared. Maybe it was that I didn't want to stop him. Maybe it was that I wanted to pretend, at least to myself, that what was happening wasn't something of my doing.

He looked so handsome that night, the way the streetlights cast a glow on his face, the snowflakes collecting in his eyelashes. When he scooped me up in his arms and kissed me, I didn't pull away from him. I relished the way his hands felt on top of the fur of my coat, the way his mouth was so warm in contrast to the freezing air. I memorized how the snow fell around us, how, to the few passersby, we must have looked like reunited lovers in a romantic film.

And in some ways, we were. Only, this was a tale bound to end tragically, star-crossed lovers, missed fates, bad timing. Yes, when it came to timing, this was quite possibly the worst.

It was hard for me not to take it as a sign when I asked, "How did you know I would be here?" and he replied, "I didn't."

I laughed then. "You didn't know I was here?"

He brushed the snow off my hair. "No, I had no idea. I'm here for work."

"You're not serious?"

I remember then how he leaned forward, how he kissed the space under my eyes, first on the right side and then on the left. "How I have missed you, Ansley. I think of you every single day."

I smiled sadly. I'd never worked up the courage to pick up the phone to call Jack and tell him I was getting married. I knew I needed to tell him now, but the words wouldn't come.

"Walk with me?" he asked.

I nodded. I remember how warm I felt inside that mink, how I knew I shouldn't let Jack hold my hand inside his coat pocket, but I did anyway. The entire night was alive. I was swept away by its magic. It felt like a wonderful dream.

We walked for blocks and blocks before stepping inside a bar. We talked that night about politics and love, about work and family, about where life had taken us and where life would lead. And it wasn't until Jack said, "Come home with me, Ansley. Come back to Georgia," that I said, "I can't, Jack."

Then he had winked at me, setting his frosty mug on the table, and said, "Then at least come home with me tonight."

I hate to say that I thought about it, that I had a moment where I wondered what harm it would do. No one would know. We could have one last night together. But then I thought of

Carter and how I loved him so. I thought of how he had asked me to be his wife and I had said yes, how he had given me this whole life that I never would have dared to dream of, helped me to blossom into a woman who was fearless and forward-thinking. I wouldn't give that up. I wouldn't give him up. Not even for Jack.

That was when I took both of his hands in mine and said, "Jack, I don't know how to tell you this." I remember how his face fell even before I said, "I'm getting married tomorrow."

I braced myself, prepared for him to ask why I had let him hold my hand, why I hadn't mentioned a thing until that moment. But I think I had forgotten then how well this man knew me, how close he was to the very core of me. Because, for better or worse, it is those who love us when we're young who will always understand us best. The ones who remember how carefree we were, how we sang with abandon when we sipped PBR on the beach all day and danced by the light of the moon all night, our feet splashing in the ocean. The ones who knew us before the world got its hands on us and told us who we should be.

Jack knew the real me. He knew that girl I had been, that girl I had loved being. So he didn't ask me any of that. Instead, he asked simply, "Do you have to?"

We both laughed then, because how was I to answer that question? Did I have to? No. Would I? Yes.

"I'll be honest," I said. "I can't help but ask myself if this means something, if your showing up here isn't some sort of sign."

"It is most definitely a sign," he had said, taking a sip of his beer. "If you want to know my opinion, it's a sign that you should call off your wedding, come home with me, and never look back." When I didn't say anything, he added, "Or at least a sign that you should have one last night of single, mind-blowing sex before your life is over tomorrow."

I laughed so hard that my stomach began to hurt.

"Hey!" he said, feigning offense. Then he smiled. "Is there anything I could say to make you change your mind?"

I thought about that for a minute. Sitting across from me was a boy I had loved, one who had taught me what it was to feel happy, to feel that jolt of electricity when his hand touched mine, who was the very first person to ever put his lips on mine. Could I ever replace that? No. Was I sure we could have had a happy life together if I hadn't found Carter? Yes. But I *had* found Carter. And loving him had changed everything.

So I shook my head.

"Then I won't ask you." He smiled sadly. "And I won't make you think about poor, lonely Jack, who is utterly lost in the world now that his one true love is taken by another."

I knew he was partly joking, but that there was also a tinge of truth in those words. We shared another drink, another few moments in time—our last, as we thought then.

I let Jack put his arms inside my coat, around my waist. I let him pull me to him one last time. I let him kiss me good-bye. But I have to admit that it wasn't only for him; it was for me, too. I needed to know that I had closed this chapter of my life fully before I opened the next one. I needed to know that I would never look back and think I should have made a different decision.

Although it changed nothing, I still believed that Jack coming to me that night was a sign. Or maybe it was more like a gift. Because in those moments that we all inevitably have, when we wonder if we made the right choice, I knew, for sure, that I had actually chosen. I had stood on life's game-show floor, presented with door one and door two, and I had actively, consciously chosen door number two.

Still, I shed some tears that night as I told Jack good-bye in front of the Plaza. He kissed both of my hands and said, "Ansley, I love you forever and always. Anytime, anyplace, I will do absolutely anything for you. All you have to do is ask."

I wonder now if we hadn't had that last night together if my life would have unfolded differently, if I would have made different choices, if Carter and I would have risked IUI again, if we would have adopted, if we would have waited a few years and tried some of the fertility treatments that were trickling onto the market.

But the thought Jack had left me with, the one I was confident he wanted me to remember, was that he would do anything for me. All I had to do was ask. And ask I did. Twice.

And for that, I would never be sorry.

TWELVE

emerson: end scene

I had only assumed that the majority of the activity around the Murphy house would involve my wedding. I was wrong.

Mom hadn't been able to bring herself to go to Florida to dismantle Grammy's house after she lost her battle with breast cancer, and, much to all of our surprise, her brothers, Scott and John, had volunteered to go do it for her. It was only fair, really, since Mom had spent the last months of Grammy's life taking care of her. But what is fair is seldom what happens, especially when it comes to my uncle John, from whom we had all been estranged for years.

Before she left, Caroline had locked me in the guesthouse and wouldn't let me out until I called the doctor to get my test results.

"Please let me do it when I'm with Mark," I pleaded, feeling sweat gather on my brow.

"Nope," she said. "He's a bigger chicken than you are."

"Maybe I should tell Mom first, prepare her," I ventured.

"You can make excuses all day," Caroline said. "But I'm not letting you out of here under any circumstances until you've called."

Finally, I sighed and sat down on the bed. As soon as I dialed, Caroline sat down beside me and grabbed my free hand. She should be there for moral support. She was the one who had made me go to this doctor in New York, after all. She was the one who didn't trust my doctors here.

When the nurse answered, I hit the speaker button and said, "This is Emerson Murphy. I need to get some test results."

There was a long pause followed by some hold music, and a very apologetic nurse came back on the line.

"Ms. Murphy, I am so sorry. Dr. Thomas's head nurse is on vacation this week, the results seem to be locked in her computer, and Dr. Thomas is home with a sick child. I will get access and have someone call you back by tomorrow at the latest."

I breathed a sigh of relief. I didn't have to know. Not yet. "I'm actually coming to New York tomorrow with my family, so this can wait until next week."

"Oh, you're coming to the city? That's even better," she enthused. "Dr. Thomas always likes to deliver test results in person, so may I put you on his schedule for tomorrow?"

Before I could protest, Caroline said, "That would be ideal. We'll be there whenever you tell us to."

"Do you think that means it's bad news?" I asked quickly, my pulse racing. "And that's why he wants to deliver it in person?"

"No, no," the nurse said. "Just standard protocol." Then she added, "Good news or bad, you're in the best hands with Dr. Thomas."

Caroline took over the particulars, and as she hung up, I was saying, "Wonder what kind of job his wife has that is less important than an oncologist's so that he stays home with his sick kid?" I looked up and realized I had made the ultimate mistake, the thing I had been trying to avoid from the moment I first felt dizzy.

Mom was standing in the doorway, her mouth open, tears streaming down her face. "I knew there was something wrong with you!" she exclaimed. "And *you*," she said accusatorily, pointing at Caroline. "You lied to me. You both lied to me. How could you leave me in the dark like this?"

I put my hands up in the air. "Because of this, Mom. Because we don't even know if anything is wrong, and now you're all hysterical and sobbing and freaking out for no reason."

She took a deep breath. "You don't know if anything is wrong?"

"It could be aplastic anemia," I said cautiously. "But it isn't cancer, so that's good."

Mom swallowed. "Aunt Trudy had that."

That was when the lump settled in my stomach. I knew there was a good chance that I was absolutely fine, that all of this was just a bad couple of months that would pass. But knowing that there was a genetic component made me all the more sure that this inability to produce red blood cells, this life of uncontrolled bleeding and extreme fatigue, was going to be placed on me.

Mom sat down on the other side of me. "Whatever it is, we'll get through it together. It's going to be fine."

I knew logically that it wasn't her fault. We hadn't told her I was sick. She hadn't had the opportunity to be strong yet sympathetic yet. Still, I was annoyed. We had done this part already. Sloane and Caroline had made the offers of bone-marrow and child-carrying services. We were past all that. This was the real part, the part where we had to plunge forward and know the truth.

"We'll know tomorrow," Caroline said. "And once we know what we're fighting, we can win."

That was the difference between us. As long as I didn't know what I was fighting, I could pretend it didn't exist. Once we named it, I had to admit that it was happening. That was the part I liked the very least. Denial had always been my best friend. Honest to God, there was a part of me that still expected my dad to show up one day. They'd never found his body or his personal effects, like so many of the victims of the 9/11 tragedies. So in my mind, that meant that maybe he wasn't really dead. Maybe he had been in a coma for sixteen long-lost years, unidentifiable, and now he had made a miraculous recovery and would come walking through the front door one day like nothing had happened at all.

I heard a truck pulling into the gravel driveway, and Mom groaned. "What on earth are we going to do with all of Grammy's stuff?"

Seeing the havoc that had been wreaked when her own

mother had left Mom the house in Peachtree Bluff, Grammy had made precise, painstaking notes about who would be receiving each of her possessions—down to the contents of her fridge. Just as Grammy would have wanted it, the reading of her will had been an absolute riot.

We had all gone to the lawyer's office, weepy and dejected and—around the time he said, "Contents of my bathroom medicine cabinet I bequeath to my son Scott," and John piped up, "Are you kidding me? I wanted all those half-empty milk of magnesia bottles"—things had gotten pretty funny. I had seen the way death and dividing up possessions tore families apart. Mom and her brothers were lucky it hadn't happened to them—at least, not yet.

Our dad had died unexpectedly, of course, and I had always wondered if his affairs were in order when he went. He had always told my sisters and me that we would be taken care of, that he was leaving us a big enough nest egg that we would never have to worry. Honestly, it was one of the things that allowed me to be so brave, to take a chance on my acting. I knew I had something to fall back on.

"I'll go down and help unload," I said.

Before I could stand up, Mom and Caroline both shouted, "No!"

I rolled my eyes. "I feel wonderful today. I even went for a run this morning. Quit treating me like a patient." That wasn't totally true. It was more like a slow walk around the block, but I had kept up the running charade so Mom wouldn't get suspicious. Even Mark was in on it.

"You will rest and take care of yourself until tomorrow, when we know what this is," Mom said.

"Fine," I groaned. But I was secretly pleased. I hated manual labor, so I'd ride this illness out for another day.

Third children aren't made to be supervisors. They are made to be told what to do by their big sisters. Or I guess big brothers, maybe, but I can't really speak to that. So I didn't even try to stand out in the backyard by the truck. I went out to the front porch. Alone. Where I had plenty of space and time and quiet to think about all the things I didn't want to think about. Like the fact that I had to go to the doctor tomorrow and what that could mean. And the fact that Grammy's stuff coming back from Florida meant that she was really gone. And that I was getting married in a matter of weeks. And that I had to make some pretty big decisions between now and then.

Before I could ruminate too much, I heard the door open and Uncle Scott's voice saying, "I'm free!"

"Already? No way Mom let you out of her clutches that easily."

"It's amazing how when you aren't doing everything exactly how she wants it, you get finished much more quickly. She got some of her guys from the store to meet her at the rental storage place." He paused and handed me something. "Besides, I found something I thought my favorite niece would like."

I gasped. "I knew I was your favorite!"

We both laughed as I turned over the tarnished picture frame in my hand. It was a cheap birthday gift I had given Grammy during my first year in LA, when the only things that kept me from starving were big tips and a generous sister. Inside it was a picture of me in a Jaguar convertible, which, let's face it, was kind of an old-lady car but was perfect for feeling the LA sun on your face and letting it streak your long blond hair.

In our family, we didn't get cars when we were sixteen. We got cars when we got accepted to college. Well, Sloane did. Caroline refused to drive, and I refused to go to college. I don't know how I thought I was going to get to California with no car, but I trusted that the universe had laid this path out in front of me and that it would produce a way for me to get there. And produce it did.

Mom had been absolutely livid when Grammy gave me her car. That was actually the maddest I'd ever seen Mom be at Grammy—and she hadn't let us come live with her after Dad died, so that's really saying something. I think she honestly thought that if I couldn't get to California, I couldn't leave Peachtree. Then she'd have more time to talk me into the life she wanted for me.

I had overheard them arguing later about it. Mom had said, "I don't want her there. I don't want her jaded or corrupted or hurt. Can't you see that?"

Grammy had simply responded, "We all get hurt, darling. May as well get it over with, if you ask me." Then she paused. "And who knows? Maybe she'll be a star."

"Oh, I have no doubt she'll be a star," Mom had said. "That's exactly what I'm worried about."

She had never said anything like that to me, and although

my mom never knew I'd overheard that conversation, it was actually that very statement that kept me going through many a long, painful casting call and rejection after rejection after rejection.

"She was a crazy old bird, wasn't she?" I said now to my uncle, returning to the present.

Scott nodded. "When I remember her now, it's always with her Virginia Slims in her two-piece, flirting with the waiters at the club pool," Scott said. "And thank God. I was so afraid I'd only remember her dying."

I smiled, because I had been afraid of that, too. "She was so proud of you, you know."

My stomach tightened when I said it. Had she been proud of me? In the end, I mean? Had I been what she needed when times got tough, when the chips were down, when push came to shove? I'd like to think so. I'd never know for sure, of course. And I'd never forget. I'd never get over what had transpired during her last days.

Scott shook his head. "I don't know if I believe in heaven and eternal knowledge and all that, but if it exists and she gets there, she might not be too proud when she realizes what I really did."

"You saved Adam. What more could she want from you?"

Scott shook his head.

I was confused. "Am I wrong? Did you not rescue Adam?"

"Maybe. But at what cost?"

"What are you talking about?"

Scott put his head in his hands. "I have to get something

126

off my chest, Emerson," he said. "It has been eating me alive."

I knew what that felt like. I had bite marks, too.

I could see his eyes welling as he sucked his breath through his teeth. "I got a kid killed over there," he said. "I saved Adam, but I killed a kid."

I felt my eyes widen, but I was trying not to react too strongly. I didn't want to make him feel worse. "What do you mean?" I whispered.

"The man in the video? The one who fell? He wasn't a man. He was just a seventeen-year-old kid."

I cringed as I remembered that day, sitting in Caroline's beautiful, serene house in the Hamptons when I got the text from Kyle. He sent me a harrowing YouTube video of leaked drone footage. Logic told me that if the footage was current and it was legit, one of the men in that video was my brother-in-law. And I was going to have to be the one to show it to my sister.

"So what did that have to do with you?"

"He was the one who told me where Adam was. He was the one who helped him escape."

I gasped and put my hand to my mouth. "How did he know?"

Scott bit his lip. "He was one of the insurgent's sons. I appealed to him, made him feel guilty so that maybe he would tell me where Adam was. But I never thought I would have made him feel guilty enough that he would try to help Adam and his unit escape. I would never have done that."

I closed my eyes, knowing how this must weigh on Scott. In some ways, it put what I had done into perspective.

"I'm sorry, Scott," I said. "I really am. But it's not your fault. You didn't point the gun. You didn't pull the trigger."

I couldn't imagine a father killing his son, no matter what had happened, and I said so.

Scott shook his head. "His son had betrayed him in the worst possible way. He was dead to him anyway, I guess."

I nodded. "While we're airing our dirty laundry, I have something that I would love to get off my chest, too."

"Hit me with your best shot, kiddo," Scott said, leaning back in his chair.

I knew he was expecting something shiny and millennial, a fight with a friend, a social-media scandal. So maybe that was why such vast horror crossed his face when I said what I said.

"I killed Grammy."

End scene.

THIRTEEN

ansley: a wonderful surprise

Maybe I'd picked the fight with Jack. I couldn't really be sure. I mean, I was as on edge as I had ever been. We had Emerson's doctor's appointment, and, Caroline's surprise aside, any fool could see that coming back to Manhattan was beyond painful for me. I don't know why I had tried to dump this on top of everything else we had going on.

As we sat quietly in the back of the cab after having dropped the rest of the family off at Caroline's, I said, unable to let it go, "I still think it would be the perfect time."

I looked out the window, admiring the Fifth Avenue view. This had been my world. This had been my life. My life with Carter. It was impossible to come to Manhattan and not feel an ache for my husband. Because while, yes, things had been complicated, we had had years of unadulterated joy together.

I looked at Jack. Maybe now, sixteen years later, I was

getting a second chance at life. I was ruining it with this fight.

"I've always wanted to stay at the Viceroy," I said, changing the subject.

"I'm not ready to tell them," Jack said. "I'm sorry. I know this is your decision, and this was why you didn't want to be with me, but I want a little bit of time for them to get to know me, so maybe they won't cut me out of their lives when they do find out."

I took his hand, softening. "I don't think they'll cut you out of their lives, Jack."

"You don't know that."

"And they might already know," I added.

"That is vastly different from *knowing* knowing," he said.

The thought made my blood run cold.

The cab turned down Fifty-Eighth.

"Sir," I said, "you're going the wrong way."

"No, no," he replied in broken English. "Plaza is on corner."

"But we're not—"

"She's confused," Jack said.

I looked at him, and he winked at me, finally acquiescing. "I've wanted to stay with you at the Plaza ever since that night."

I smiled, remembering. "That was an amazing night."

"What if you hadn't gotten married that day?"

I shook my head. "It wouldn't have happened. I've thought about it a lot, but there is nothing you could have said that night that would have made me change my mind about Carter. When I saw you, I knew I still loved you, sure. But I also knew we wanted different things, and as much as I had always loved you, I wouldn't sacrifice the life I had dreamed of for so long."

"What if I had told you I wanted to have children?"

"I would have known you were lying."

I looked to my left, and there it was, the Manhattan icon, the home of Eloise, the place where I'd spent the night before my wedding, where I had taken my girls for birthday slumber parties when they were small. I had never felt like a New Yorker. Not really. So it surprised me when I got the slightest pang for my old life. We had had so many good times in this city; I had grown and changed so much here, had all of my children here. It was good to be back.

As Jack paid for the cab and got out our suitcases, I walked over and kissed him gently.

"You're right. This isn't the right time to tell them," I said, closing the wound from earlier. "But do you understand now why I never told them before?"

He nodded. He dropped the suitcases, and there we were, like we had been all those years ago, locked in an embrace in front of one of the world's most famous hotels. As we crowded into our bay of that revolving door with the double *P*s and entered the gilded lobby of the Plaza with its palm trees and beautiful sofas, I paused and kissed him again.

"This was a wonderful surprise," I said.

He rested his forehead on mine and said, "I know you have a lot of memories in this city, some good, some bad. I was hoping that maybe we could make a new one this weekend, a really good one."

All I could hope was that Jack's best attempts at a happy memory weren't thwarted by the results of Emerson's doctor appointment. There was no fancy hotel, no kiss, no memory, that could be strong enough, better enough, to heal the utter agony of my child being sick.

FOURTEEN

emerson: any excuse to eat a cheeseburger

I'm the only one in this family who has ever been able to keep a secret. My sisters and my mom think they can. But the thing about being the littlest sister is you learn at an early age that if you ever want to know anything, you have to sneak around to learn it.

Maybe that was why Grammy chose me to carry out her final wishes. Maybe she saw something in me the others didn't; maybe she was the only one who didn't see me as the baby, who didn't underestimate me.

In retrospect, it was the right choice. Caroline is outwardly the toughest, but that toughness works against her, in that sometimes she fights too long; sometimes she doesn't know when to leave well enough alone. Sloane is the sweetest. She has a quiet strength about her that allows her to persevere. She also has the strongest faith, which is terrific. But not for what Grammy needed.

Mom had been through enough, quite frankly.

Plus, they weren't who she chose. Grammy chose me.

We had all been out in the yard that day a few months earlier—Caroline, Sloane, Mom, and me. I was on the porch, telling Grammy a story about the worst first date I ever had in LA, about how this man was offensive and borderline sexist in every sense of the word. Determined to maintain my power and stand up for the good of the sisterhood, I had chewed him out and thrown the rest of my martini in his face. To be fair, it was only like two sips, so it wasn't that big a deal. But still, I marched out of the restaurant with a dramatic flourish. I even woke up the next morning feeling proud and vindicated—until I walked into an audition. And found out the director was my date from the night before.

"Oh, no!" Grammy said, laughing. "So you didn't get the part?"

I laughed then, too. "Oh, no. I got the part. In fact, I didn't even have to audition."

"What?"

I nodded. "As it turned out, the director had already told them about his lunatic date from the night before. And since the part was a crazy ex-girlfriend, they all knew I would be perfect for it."

That was when Grammy had lowered the boom. She had been fighting breast cancer, secretly, for more than a year. The treatments weren't working. The cancer had spread. She was going to stay on hormonal therapies and treatments as long as they worked, but when they quit, she would be ready to live out her final days in peace, however she pleased, not chained to a bag of chemo.

When the tears had subsided, when we had all agreed to Grammy's wishes to be happy and carefree and alive for as long as she could and, to that end, were all getting ready for lunch together, I walked into Grammy's room to see if she needed help.

She was sitting in a chair in the corner, looking at something in her hand. When I walked in, she smiled up at me. "Just the girl I wanted to see."

"Oh, yeah?" We all knew that Caroline was Grammy's favorite.

She put her hand in my hand, and I felt something in my palm.

When I opened it, there were several small pills in it.

"What is this?"

She cleared her throat and said a word I had never heard but would roll around in my head forever after: "Secobarbital." When no words escaped my suddenly dry mouth, she added, "I couldn't tell them all yet, but I'm going to be honest with you. The doctors have done all they can do to treat the metastasis to my brain. It's going to get ugly soon. And I'm afraid I won't be aware enough to make the decision."

I could feel myself going pale. "Grammy," I started, "what's—"

But she cut me off. "Darling," she said, "all I'm asking is that when I ask for these, you give them to me." She cleared her throat. "And if I can't ask for them, that means I'm asking for them."

I shook my head, feeling my heart race. "Grammy, I can't."

She cocked her head to the side. "Really? Because I think you can."

The way she looked at me was what convinced me. Because I knew she saw something in me that no one else did, that she believed in me in a way no one else ever had. But I still resisted. "What about Caroline? Or Mom?"

She shook her head and smiled. "Under all that pretty, you, my dear, have a spine of steel. I think we both know it has to be you."

"Where did you even get them?" I whispered, awed and suddenly paranoid.

She raised her eyebrow. "Do you really want to know?"

I looked at her warily.

"Mark," she whispered back.

I almost asked a follow-up question, but there was nothing to ask. Mark's father was a surgeon. A great surgeon. A revered one. He had access to anything he wanted. And it warmed my heart to think that Mark and his father would do this for my grandmother, that they would take this chance.

I looked into her face then: her kind, soft eyes, the lines around her mouth and nose from all the laughing she had done, her long eyelashes, even after all these years. She wasn't some dying woman who had lost her mind. She was still her. I took her hand in mine, if only to feel her warmth, the blood still running through her veins. God, I didn't want this. But it seemed as though it wasn't really a choice.

"Mark didn't tell me," I said, as though we were discussing

a dinner reservation, not the thing that would ultimately take my grandmother's life.

She squeezed my hand. "Well, darling, I asked him not to, of course."

"Of course."

I wondered what this meant, if it was one of Grammy's subtler signals. I couldn't imagine that she would ask for something so huge from someone she didn't trust and love, from someone she didn't want to be a part of her family. And I couldn't imagine that a man who would do all this for me, take a risk this big, wouldn't be the one for me.

Then I had another thought entirely.

I wasn't religious like Sloane, but in my mind, there were still a few guaranteed tickets to hell, and I was pretty sure that murder was one of them. "Gram," I said slowly, "I can't kill you. I can't have that black mark on my soul."

She nodded. "But you aren't murdering me," she said. "I'm *asking* you to do it. I'm asking you to help ease my way and put me out of pure misery. I'm asking you not to let me live when I don't know who my girls are, not to make me be one of those moaning women in so much pain she can't speak. That's not murder. That's mercy."

She had this look of pure determination, and truth be told, I knew I would do it the moment I saw how serious she was. In some ways, this would be one of the defining moments of my life, one of the things that would make me who I was, prove to me how strong I was, prepare me for the months to come.

"But you can't commit suicide," I said.

She smiled again. "It's not suicide if you give me the pills."

She couldn't possibly believe this. "Grammy, come on."

"Don't you see?" she said. "It's a loophole."

I laughed incredulously. "Grammy, I don't think God has loopholes."

Then she said something that would always remain with me: "Honey, we'd better hope that God has loopholes. Otherwise, we're all toast."

I wasn't sure what sat heavier on my heart, those words or those pills. But I slipped them into my pocket.

My mom, sisters, and uncles all marveled that my grandmother was so strong-willed she was able to fade off before things got really bad, disappear into the great unknown before she totally lost her mind, something that, with her brain metastasis, was almost guaranteed to happen.

If they had been paying attention, though, they would have noticed the way Grammy hugged me extra-long that night, after she had told us that she needed to sleep on the porch, that she needed to be alone with the wind and the sea and the stars. They would have seen how she whispered, "It's time, darling," in my ear. They would have seen me sneak onto the porch in the early hours of the morning to give my grandmother what she wanted.

Mom said it was OK that Grammy died alone, that she wouldn't have wanted us all there. But I was with her, holding her hand when she took her very last breath. I was the first one to cry over her.

Her last words on this earth had been, "The greatest blessing in my world has been this extraordinary family. Don't cry, darling. You are all going to be just fine."

When I confessed all this to Uncle Scott, when it all came pouring out after having been locked inside so tight for so long, I had never seen him that shocked or tongue-tied.

But then he did the strangest thing: he laughed.

"Um," I said, "that's not really a funny story."

He shook his head. "No, of course it isn't. It isn't funny at all. It's just that I'm so relieved."

Now I was really confused.

He cleared his throat and composed himself. "My mother was the most headstrong, resilient person I have ever met. She had the highest standards for herself and everyone around her. I'm relieved that her death was on her terms." He paused and looked me in the eye. "And, Em, I can't help but think that she knew this would help you see how strong you were, too."

It bolstered me when he said that. He wasn't mad. He didn't hate or condemn me for stealing what few precious extra days he might have gained with his mother.

"You did the right thing, Emerson. We all have the right to live life as we choose. That was her choice. You only helped her carry it out." Then he squeezed my hand and smiled supportively. "Mom was right, Em. Everything is going to be fine."

Today, in New York, I could only hope that Grammy's words held true, that as I went to meet my fate at Dr. Thomas's office, everything would be fine now, too.

I would have been an absolute mess about my appointment that day, but fortunately, Caroline always knew how to distract me. We spent the morning browsing in new boutiques in SoHo. She loved one of them so much that she took a selfie of us trying on dresses and posted it on her Instagram.

"I thought you only posted for people who paid you tons of money now," I said.

She shrugged. "Every now and then, I post something random." She paused. "It's my philanthropy."

We both laughed so hard that the mystified salesgirl came to check on us.

When it finally came time for my appointment, we ended up taking an UberXL, not exactly what I had envisioned for finding out my test results. But Mom insisted on coming. So did Caroline. And once Caroline said she was going, Sloane decided she was coming, too. And Mark said there was no way he was missing the appointment, either.

I was actually happy to be called back for labs so that I could have a little air to breathe. As I stuck my arm out for the nurse to swab, a little blond girl, who was probably seven or eight, in pink sparkly high-tops and a pink-and-white-striped dress, sat down at the station beside me.

"Hi," I said, smiling, trying not to flinch as the needle went in. She smiled back.

"Being at the doctor kind of stinks, doesn't it?"

She nodded. "But I'm not coming here anymore. My mom is here picking up my papers. I'm going to St. Jude's."

I looked away so she couldn't see the tears that had

sprung to my eyes without warning. Just like that, it was all in perspective. I might be sick, yeah. But I was a grown-up. This beautiful little girl hadn't even had a chance to live yet. And she could die.

"Oh, yeah?" I said lightly. I leaned toward her as the nurse put the Band-Aid on my arm. "St. Jude's is an awesome place. I've been there a few times."

She looked up at me with big, innocent blue eyes and said, as her mom approached, "Did you have cancer, too?"

I shook my head. "No," I said. "I'm an actress and—"

"I know who you are," she said cheerily. "You're Cinderella."

I laughed. "I sure am," I said. "I am Cinderella." I had played Cinderella recently in a series of TV fairy-tale remakes that had done shockingly well. I probably took more kid selfies these days than adult ones.

"And who are you?" I asked.

I smiled up at her mother, who was smiling with her mouth. Her eyes looked very, very tired—and terrified.

"I'm Maggie," she said. She paused and looked down at her swinging feet and then back up at me. "Could you come visit me when I'm at St. Jude's?"

I put my hand on my heart, and her mother interjected, "Maggie, I'm sure Ms. Murphy is very, very busy."

I stood up and looked her mother straight in the eye. "There is nothing on earth that could make me too busy to come visit Maggie when she is at St. Jude's."

Her eyes watered now, and she nodded.

I crouched down and said, "What about if I come as Cinderella, and I bring along Prince Charming and Snow White and Sleeping Beauty, too?"

Maggie nodded enthusiastically.

"But we'll have a secret, because you'll know it's really me." I winked at her.

She nodded again, and a nurse took her hand and said, "Want to come with me to get a sucker?"

Maggie said, "'Bye. See you soon."

"I can't wait, Maggie!" Then I called her back and said, "Hey, can you take a picture with me?" and snapped a selfie of the two of us.

I turned to her mom. "I'm so sorry," I said. "It's a dumb thing to say, but I am. What can I do for you? How can I help?"

She shrugged. "We're so lucky to get to go to St. Jude's. All their expertise and all their research and their success rates and . . . I have hope again, you know?"

I nodded and bit my lip.

"They have a ninety-percent cure rate for her kind of leukemia," she said. I could tell she was trying to bolster her own spirits.

"That's amazing," I said. "Absolutely amazing."

I didn't know what to say. What did you say to a mother who was getting ready to watch her child go through an ordeal that was nothing short of hellish even in the best of circumstances?

"We don't need anything," she said. "But anything you could do for them . . ." She trailed off.

I held up my phone. "Can I post this?"

"Oh, of course! Maggie will be thrilled."

I wrote down my contact information and gave Maggie's mom a hug. "Please promise me you'll get in touch. I'll get something amazing organized."

"Thank you," she said sincerely. "It means a lot."

I posted my picture on my Instastory and wrote: *My friend Maggie is headed to St. Jude's to show her leukemia who's boss. Let's show her some love by making a donation in her honor! Swipe up for more info.*

I walked back into the waiting room, knowing that no matter what happened to me today, I would get through it. If Maggie could, I could, too.

I motioned for my crazy brood to come on back and whispered to Caroline, "I tagged you in my story. Make sure you repost it."

She looked puzzled.

"It's *actual* philanthropy," I said.

Moments later, the five of us, one big happy family, were crammed into the doctor's tiny office. I was sitting in one of the chairs flanking the desk, Mom was in the other, Mark was standing beside me, and Caroline and Sloane were in the corner trying to make themselves smaller than they were.

When Dr. Thomas walked in, I was taken aback. I had forgotten how handsome he was. I wondered if it made the bad news he often delivered seem less harsh. I hoped I wouldn't find out.

"Wow," Dr. Thomas said. "I actually haven't ever had this many people at an appointment. At least, not a lab follow-up."

I smiled at him apologetically.

"You could say we're a close family," Caroline quipped.

I turned to Mom. She looked very pale.

"I'm *almost* family," Mark said jokingly. He was trying to keep his tone light, but the way he said it made me feel like he was looking for some kind of credit, like *I'm here and marrying her even though she might be defective*. But maybe I was being defensive. He was here, after all.

"Let's cut to the chase," Dr. Thomas said, and Mom squeezed her eyes shut like that would protect her if the news was bad.

"You're going to be fine."

There was a collective sigh, as if everyone in the room had been holding his or her breath.

"We could take this on the road," Dr. Thomas said, smiling.

He turned a sheet of paper around for me to see, one filled with lots of percentages and numbers that I didn't understand.

"Your iron, fibrinogen, and ferritin are all critically low. In fact . . ." He held his finger up to me, pressed a button on his phone, and said, "Karen, let's get Ms. Murphy started on an iron infusion now so she doesn't have to wait."

Then he looked back at me. "See this number?"

I nodded.

"This represents something in our bodies that scavenges for iron. You have twice the number that we normally see. Your body is working hard to keep up."

"So what's causing this?" Mark chimed in.

"I want to do some further testing to make sure there isn't an underlying infection, but my hunch is that with Emerson's history of heavy menstruation and the restrictive diet she has been on, her difficult travel schedule, the strain on her body . . ." He paused. "That's my fancy way of saying that iron-deficient anemia isn't uncommon in young women, and with a few iron infusions and some dietary changes, you should be as good as new."

Mom started crying right as the nurse walked into the room. I was so relieved I didn't even flinch as she swabbed my arm with alcohol and inserted the IV.

"Two bags," Dr. Thomas mouthed to her.

"Does she need a blood transfusion or anything?" Sloane asked.

"I'll give her one," Caroline and Sloane said at the same time.

Dr. Thomas looked back at me. "Are you on a vegan diet? Because if so, we can tailor this plan to fit your lifestyle, but I will warn you that some bodies simply respond better to heme sources of iron, which are the ones that come from animal products. We can try nonheme sources first and see—"

I put my hand up, dreaming of steak. "Any excuse to eat a cheeseburger is great with me."

He gave me a thumbs-up. "Then I'm going to give you this food list and several supplements that should help, and I'm going to ask you to come back here to see me in three weeks."

"But that's the week before the wedding," Mark said.

The trifecta of Murphys turned to glare at him.

"I can have Emerson's care transferred to—"

"No!" Caroline and Mom shouted at the same time.

He smiled. "I'd really like to check you out again this next visit, and then, if you're making the progress I think you'll be making, I can turn you over to a doctor closer to where you'll be living. Where is that?"

"LA," I said, as Mark said, "Georgia."

We looked at each other. Dr. Thomas looked at Mom. Then he looked back at me. "OK. Well, when you figure it out, let me know."

The nurse came in to give me a second bag, plugged in a heating pad, and placed it over my arm.

"Oh, I'm fine," I said.

"Trust me," she said. "As fast as you're sucking up that iron, you're going to need that heating pad."

I cringed.

"Any questions?" Dr. Thomas asked.

"Should she restrict her exercise?" Mom asked, as Caroline said, "Is it OK for her to drink alcohol?" and Sloane asked, "Are you sure this isn't aplastic anemia?" and Mark said, "Could travel be dangerous for her health?"

The doctor looked at me with a raised eyebrow.

"I know," I said, rolling my eyes. "But you might as well answer their questions now so they don't annoy me until I break down and call you later to ask."

"She is fine," Dr. Thomas said to the room with a smile. "Emerson may exercise as she feels able, may drink alcohol as she feels able, and her bone marrow looks beautiful, so no, this is not aplastic anemia." He turned to Mark. "And whatever argument you two are having about where you will live is not something that I can fix for you." He gave me a satisfied smile.

"Thank you so much for everything," I said. "We realize you have other, normal, non-high-maintenance patients waiting."

Dr. Thomas smiled. "Karen will be back in a few minutes to remove your IV." He handed me his card. "I take my celebrity patients very seriously." He cleared his throat. "I mean, I take *all* my patients seriously. But here is my private cell-phone number, so feel free to call me anytime, day or night."

He walked out the door and then turned, popping his head back through. "Oh, and Ms. Murphy?" Four of us turned to look. "I very much hope I'll be referring you to a doctor in LA. My wife absolutely adores you."

"His wife," Mark said under his breath. "Sure."

I tried to hide my smile. I squeezed Mark's hand encouragingly and braced myself for the hugs that I knew were about to engulf me. This was great news. Better than great. I expected to feel like the huge weight I had been carrying around for months had been lifted, like all my worries were floating away. I did feel better, sure. But now that I knew my health was going to be OK, now that I knew this was something I could fix, I had to admit that what had been gnawing at me wasn't these impending test results. It was something else. And now I was going to have to face what that was.

ansley: the queen of everything

Two hours later, Jack was zipping my red sleeveless dress. Caroline was right. I *had* needed to lose weight in my shoulders. I'd been sweating and grunting through arm exercises daily for the past few weeks, but my hard work was already beginning to pay off.

I felt free and alive, as if I were floating on air. That doctor's appointment, like life, could so easily have gone the other way. But my girl was OK. She was going to be OK. I'd had exactly, to a tee, the same issue in my twenties, and while it was something that had been monitored closely for the next several decades, it had never given me any major trouble.

"So what do you think Caroline's surprising us with?" Jack asked as he tied his black bow tie.

I walked to him, untied it, tied it again, and, pulling it tight, said, "With Caroline, you never know." Then I stood back to admire him. Jack was devastating in a tux. And he was all mine.

Jack smiled. "It's the best thing and the worst thing about her." Then he pulled me in, kissed me, and said, "You look sensational."

Twenty minutes later, a limo filled with my girls and practically overflowing with champagne pulled up outside the Plaza. James got out to let us in, in his tux, looking every part the movie-star husband, despite the fact that he was actually a lawyer. Adam looked the best I had seen him since he arrived home. But nothing could have been more gorgeous than my three girls, all in gold floor-length gowns of varying styles, their hair fixed and makeup on. I suddenly had the most glorious feeling that we were all going to be OK. Adam was holding Sloane's hand and smiling, Mark's arm was draped around Emerson's shoulder, and I realized that this was my family now. These daughters. These men. They would be in my life forever.

"You look like Oscar statuettes," Jack said, smiling.

"That's what we're channeling," Emerson said.

She was glowing. I could almost feel her relief. She had been handed a Get Out of Jail Free card today. And she knew it.

"Let's keep guessing," Sloane said.

"I think we're going to the opera," Emerson said, and Mark, James, and Adam groaned.

"I think we're going to a movie premiere," Adam said.

"You can quit guessing," Caroline interjected. "Because you will never guess. We could do this all night long, and you will never ever figure it out."

Two minutes later, the limo stopped. I tried to see out the window, but the car was so low and the buildings so tall that I wasn't sure where we were. Everyone shifted around, sitting on laps and leaning over on hips so that Caroline and James could get out first.

Then Emerson tied a silk scarf around my eyes, despite my protests. "Are you all in on this together?" I asked.

"I swear, Mom," Emerson said, "I have no idea what's going on."

Sloane got out first, and I heard her gasp, followed by Emerson's "Oh, my God."

I could feel the butterflies welling in my stomach.

Jack maneuvered me out onto the sidewalk, and I heard Caroline say, "Are you ready, Mom?" Even she seemed nervous.

"I'm as ready as I'll ever be, I guess."

She fiddled with the knot on the scarf and said, "OK. You can open your eyes."

It took me a moment to adjust to the dark sky and bright lights, and at first, I only saw huge glass picture windows. Gorgeous, enviable picture windows with stunning vignettes of furniture and accessories.

Then I looked up. And my gasp joined my daughters'. Right here, on Fifth Avenue in New York City, was a scrawling gold logo against a black granite façade. It read: *Sloane Emerson New York.*

"How?" I asked in amazement.

"I've been working on it for a while," Caroline said. "I just didn't want you to know until it was a done deal. That's why I asked if I could come work for you. I needed to open accounts with your vendors and learn more about your business. I wanted to get it right. I wanted it to be something you could be proud of."

Tears sprang to my eyes as I hugged my daughter. My beautiful, bold daughter.

"Well, for heaven's sake," Sloane said. "Let's go in!"

Caroline opened the door. She handed me a glass of Veuve Clicquot. I was utterly, totally speechless.

There was no arguing that Caroline had gorgeous taste. The ceiling was gold leaf, the floors dark wood, and the walls an off-white with the most beautiful moldings I had ever seen. In the center of the room, hanging over a round wooden entrance-hall table that was a bestseller in my store, was a tremendous beaded chandelier.

The "before" pictures blown up and scattered around the room displayed a bleak, cold, empty shell with studs for walls and concrete floors. I ran my hand along the marble counter that served as the checkout area.

"You weren't even here," I whispered. "I don't understand how you did all this."

She shrugged. "The week we came back for the Hamptons party, I picked everything, and then there was a lot of Skyping and pictures back and forth." She lowered her voice and said, "And James has been amazing. He did so much of it."

"I just can't believe you."

"You know, Mom, when your heart is really set on something, sometimes you move mountains to get it."

James came up from behind Caroline, put his arm around her, and kissed her cheek. "I am ridiculously proud of you."

I looked around again, finally noticing that every spare wall was covered with one of Sloane's paintings.

I walked over and hugged Sloane. She smiled. "I know. Pretty great, right?"

"Your sister did good."

"Want to look with me?"

We walked over to the first painting, and I peered down into the corner at the price tag.

I thought Sloane was going to spit out her champagne. "Caroline!" she scolded. "Have you lost your mind? I mean, you've always been insane, but this is a new level."

Adam squeezed her arm. "It's not insane, Sloane. You deserve this and so much more." He leaned down and kissed her, and warm, fuzzy feelings spread all through my body. Sloane's life had been ripped from stem to stern. I wasn't sure she would ever get back to a place where she could be happy. And now, tonight, everything in her life that had been hard or uncertain was culminating in this one glorious moment.

Caroline gestured out the window, where throngs of people had gathered. "These people," she said, "are not waiting for me. They are waiting for you."

Emerson cleared her throat and said, "OK. We've got to let this crowd in. But first, a toast." We all put our arms around one another and stood in a circle as she said, "Here's to taking risks and chasing dreams. May they all come true."

"Hear, hear!" Jack said, and we all clinked glasses. Jack

kissed me and said, "You are my dream come true. I need nothing else."

As the people flooded into Sloane Emerson New York, Emerson grabbed my arm and whispered, "It's amazing what all that beautiful Beaumont money can buy, isn't it?"

"Emerson!" I scolded, but, well, I'd been thinking the same thing. I had scrimped and saved to open my first tiny storefront. I had no doubt that James had thrown every cent he could at this project, just to see his wife happy. Despite his flaws, I'd give it to the man: when it came to Caroline, he was unfailingly generous with what seemed to be an endless well of money.

But the money wasn't the only thing flowing. The Veuve was, too, into the more than one thousand champagne coupes arranged in a tower underneath that giant light fixture, the string quartet was playing on the second-floor balcony, which was open to the first floor, and Caroline's salesgirls were ringing up merchandise as fast as their fingers could fly.

"This is unbelievable," Jack said.

I smiled and looked over at Sloane, whom people were swarming. Caroline floated over and whispered, "We've sold all the paintings."

I gasped. "You're kidding me."

She smiled. "I am not kidding you. She'd better get home and get painting so we can sell more. I have eleven names on a waiting list for her work."

I could feel pride swelling in my chest. Caroline, against all odds, had taken over the family business. Sloane, whose dream was to make a living as a painter, was able to do that. Emerson had succeeded as an actress and was beginning her journey with the man she loved, and I had Jack by my side. It was the best life had been in a long, long time. Maybe it was the champagne, and maybe it was the music, but I felt like I was walking on air that night. Caroline had made magic here in Manhattan. I vowed right then and there that I would visit her more often. I had avoided New York for too long, and now I couldn't deny that coming back here felt like coming home.

"There's nothing better than doing what you love and making a living off of it," Jack said.

"Exactly," Caroline said, gesturing toward Jack. "I mean, you love hot dogs, and look how well that worked out for you." Jack had started a chain of hot dog stands in college towns that he had later sold for a fortune.

We all laughed. One of her friends pulled her away as Jack slipped his arm around me and kissed me.

An extremely tall man walking through the door caught my eye, and I did a double take. Jack looked at the door and then looked back at me. "No," he said. "No way."

I cocked my head to the side as he came toward me, and said, "As I live and breathe, if it isn't my brother John."

He shrugged and smiled sheepishly. "I told you I was going to step it up."

I hugged him and said into his ear, "Thank you. Truly. This is a big deal."

When I pulled away, I could see that there were tears in his eyes. He sniffed and said, "If these past couple of months have taught me anything, it's that families have to stick together."

"Wait." I looked at Jack and then back at John. "Are you saying that we're your family?"

We laughed. I didn't have any grand expectations for my brother and our relationship. I didn't expect him to suddenly become the brother I had known growing up. But it touched me deeply that he was making the effort. I loved him, and I would take as much of him in my life as I could get, now and always. I had put my expectations to the side long ago. Now I could savor the moments for what they were.

Three hours later, the crowd had finally started to thin, the band was packing up, the champagne had nearly been drunk, and I was ready to get to work. Jack and I had moved to the immaculate storeroom, and I was trying to help a bit with inventory. This place might look like a million bucks, but there were still a lot of ins and outs that Caroline needed help with. With my clipboard in my hand, I was totally in my element.

Jack came up behind me and kissed my neck, wrapping his arms around my waist. I was still writing.

"You're right," Jack said.

I laughed, noting that my favorite L'Objet candles had completely sold out. "I so often am," I said. "What am I right about now?"

"You're right that we should tell the girls," Jack said. "You're their mother. You know best."

I laughed again, feeling sleepy and giddy and so happy I

never wanted the night to end. "OK," I said. "If you think we should tell the girls, then let's tell the girls."

"Tell the girls what?"

I turned to see the three of them crowded in the doorway. My mouth suddenly felt very dry.

"Tell the girls what?" Caroline repeated.

"Because we have something to tell you, too," Emerson said.

My heart was racing in my chest, because this was a perfect moment. They were all here, we were all happy. I could tell them all at once, rip the Band-Aid off. I would never again have to stay up nights worried about how they would react once I told them the truth. I would never again have to debate whether it was the perfect moment or not. No matter their reaction, it would finally be done.

"You first," I said.

"No," Sloane said warily. "You first."

I looked at Jack, my stomach muscles gripping. "Girls, there's something I've wanted to tell you for a long time." I sighed. "But I haven't because I wasn't sure how you'd react."

I could tell by the looks on their faces that I had killed their buzzes. Great. Now the night was ruined, no matter what. "You see, your father and I . . . Well, you already know that . . ." I trailed off. It felt like the words were stuck in my chest. I cleared my throat.

"Just spit it out, Mom," Caroline said. "Whatever it is, I'm sure it's fine." I could tell by her face that she knew. She logically knew. But that didn't mean it wasn't going to rock her world, rock all of their worlds, when I said it out loud, when I put it out there and we had to deal with it.

I nodded. Then, without even thinking about it, I blurted out, "The money. The money your father was going to leave for you is gone. He lost it in the market before he died, and we were left in the most horrible financial shape. That's why we had to move to Peachtree. I couldn't afford to stay in New York, but I didn't want any of you to know that was the real reason we left." I was sure I sounded manic.

Caroline gasped and put her hand up to her mouth. I, for one, felt somewhat cleansed. There was one major secret off my chest. I mean, it was the wrong secret, a far lesser secret. But one off my chest all the same.

"Oh, Mom," she said. "I'm so sorry I acted so horribly."

Emerson hugged me. "That is awful, Mom. You're amazing for getting us through like you did all on your own. I had no idea."

Sloane nodded. "You're our hero, Mom."

So this was a pleasant turn of events. Now I was the hero instead of the villain, which easily could have gone the other way if the other truth had been revealed. I couldn't bring myself to look at Jack.

"The good news is, I've been putting a little something away for all of you for when I'm gone."

Emerson waved her hand. "Clearly, Caroline doesn't need it, Sloane is going to be a gazillionaire by next year, and I . . ." She trailed off with a dramatic hand gesture. "I have decided to open Sloane Emerson LA!"

Sloane, Emerson, and Caroline squealed. I was shocked.

"But Emerson, your acting."

"Oh, I'll still act," she said. "But I want something to fall back on." She shrugged. "You know, I get on board and then let Caroline do everything. That's kind of my MO."

"Grand," Caroline said. But she was smiling ear to ear.

"This is terrific news," I said, meaning it. There had been some years when I couldn't give my girls things I really wanted to, some things I thought they really needed. But knowing that I had made something for us, I had made a living for us, and now they could use that business to make a life for themselves made me inexplicably proud—and more confident than ever that I had made some good choices along the way.

"Man," Sloane said. "I feel kind of left out. Where am *I* going to start a store?"

"Miami," Emerson said without a pause. "Then we can be like the Kardashians."

They all burst out laughing, and I rolled my eyes.

"You don't have time to start a shop, painter monkey," Caroline said.

"OK," I said, standing up straighter. "I'm feeling lighter. Been carrying that one around for sixteen years."

I saw tears starting to gather in Emerson's eyes. "What's the matter?" I whispered, drawing her in close to me.

"I just wish he could see us all now," she said. "I wish he could see us all grown-up."

I smiled and could feel tears in my eyes, too. "You can rest assured that your father would be beside himself. In fact, all he would do is brag to his friends about the three of you." I paused. "I'm not sure a father has ever loved three girls more."

"Well," Jack said, chiming in, "I know we don't all feel the same way about these things, but I think your father is watching over you. I think he knows how well you have all done."

I smiled up at him. I had to admit that I loved the idea that Carter could look down and see the four of us happy after all these years. I wondered if he would be bothered that part of the reason for my happiness was Jack, this man who had played such an incredibly complicated role in the story of our lives together. But I reasoned that all Carter had ever wanted for me was happiness. It was why he'd made some of the decisions he'd made.

A few minutes later, we were all filing out of the store into the warm New York night, the bright lights so different from the shining stars of Peachtree Bluff. It occurred to me that in a lot of ways, these skyscrapers and this traffic were as much a part of my story as the calming waters of Peachtree. There was something happy in that thought, something calming, too.

"You really nailed that confession," Jack whispered into my ear. I could hear the smile in his voice.

"I did, didn't I?" I whispered back wryly.

I hugged Sloane. "I'm so proud of you."

She smiled. "Thanks, Mom." Then she turned to Caroline. "I sort of hate you for doing it without my permission, but you gave me something back tonight that I had lost. I found a piece of myself again, and as much as I don't want to admit it, I found it because of you."

Caroline ventured a curtsy.

James said, "If Caroline is the queen of anything, it's pushing us all to be our best."

"The queen of *anything*?" Emerson said under her breath. "I thought she was the queen of *everything*."

They smiled at each other.

I hugged my eldest daughter. "Thank you for this. I never would have imagined that my vision for this store could turn into something so extraordinary."

"Oh, wait until you see Sloane Emerson LA," Emerson said. "It will really blow you away."

I kissed them all again and watched as Emerson took off with Mark, Caroline with James, and Sloane with Adam. It was right. It was perfect. I was so very much at peace.

Jack slipped his hand in mine and said, "Do you know that I think you are even more beautiful now than you were the night I inadvertently tried to stop your wedding?"

I blew air through my closed lips as if that was preposterous, which it was, and said, "That's just because I was covered in layers of fur, and you've always preferred me a little more scantily clad."

He winked at me and said, "Oh, I prefer you *much* more scantily clad."

We laughed, and as we made our way into the dark city, the honking horns and screeching brakes replacing the sounds of the wind and waves that I was used to, I felt down in the tips of my toes that while Peachtree was home, there was no city in the world quite as grand as New York.

emerson: compromise

Back at the Beaumont flat, we were all a little tipsy. The champagne was flowing, the sisters were laughing, the kids were sleeping—and the *Mark Loves Emerson* mix CD he had made my junior year was playing quietly over James's impressive sound system.

I was perhaps the tipsiest of all, but I was also the youngest and maybe the happiest. Even the news that the nest egg I had always imagined receiving one day no longer existed couldn't spoil my night.

Now that I knew the money from Dad was gone, my entire mind-set was different. I'll be honest, my first inkling had been to do what Mark wanted, move back to Peachtree Bluff and fall comfortably into the silk-pillow-cushy world he had created for me. But really, where would be the fun in that? Instead, I would throw myself headfirst into my acting and work on this new store project with Caroline. I knew that I would never be happy unless I was making my own way in the world.

"Caroline," Sloane said, "that was the best store opening in history."

"Until ours," I interrupted. "Because Caroline will have made all her mistakes on the first one."

James burst out laughing. "Mistakes?" He pulled Caroline close and said, "My girl doesn't make mistakes."

Yeah, that's only you, I wanted to interject. I would forever be watching him very, very carefully.

"Wait," Mark said. "You're not seriously thinking about opening a store in LA?"

I couldn't decide if his voice was accusatory or if it just sounded that way because I'd had too much to drink.

"Of course we are," Caroline said. "It's going to be amazing. Why wouldn't we open another store?"

Mark's cheeks were turning red, and I knew what was coming next. "Oh, gee. I don't know. Maybe because we just had a talk about how Emerson was going to spend as little time in LA as possible and that we were going to try to make this thing work in Peachtree Bluff. Did we not *just* have that conversation, Emerson?"

I saw Adam shift in his seat, and I could feel his big-brother protective instincts kicking in. "Dude, I don't like your tone."

Mark looked him up and down like he was pond scum. "I didn't ask your opinion, man."

Adam was silent and stock-still. Mark might not have

known it, but that was when he was at his scariest, his most primal, a predator about to attack prey that never saw it coming.

"It's not that big a deal," I said quickly, trying to ease the tension between the two men. "We're going to own it and spend time there, yeah. But we will also have a whole team of people in place running it."

Mark scoffed. "That shows how little you know about business. It's *your* business. No one is going to care about it like you do. And then it's going to be the day before our kid's second birthday, and the manager doesn't show up, and you're going to have to rush off to LA to check on your damn store." He paused. "First I have to compete with acting, and now this? You're such a selfish bitch, Emerson."

I didn't even have time to react. I almost didn't see it happening, it was so fast. In one swift motion, Adam was out of his chair and had Mark by the back of his neck, like a mother cat with a kitten. I heard the front door open and Adam say, "If you ever talk to my little sister like that again, she won't be crying over what you said to her. She'll be crying over whether to take you off life support."

Mark didn't say anything back, which might have been the first smart decision he had made in a while. I heard the door slam shut.

Everyone was silent as Adam walked back in, his limp seeming more pronounced. Sloane shot him a look, and I couldn't tell if it was one of approval or disapproval. I didn't know what to say. On the one hand, I felt proud that Adam thought of me as his little sister, that he had protected me like that. On the other, I felt sick to my stomach, because I knew he had humiliated Mark and I would be the one to pay for it later.

"Sorry," Adam said under his breath.

"There's nothing to be sorry for," Caroline said. "He shouldn't speak to her that way."

I felt glued to the floor. Part of me wanted to run after Mark. The bigger part of me wanted to sit here with my family.

"Emerson . . ." Sloane started.

I shook my head. "I can't, Sloane. It's fine. He just had too much to drink." I shrugged. "It's my fault. I knew this would make him mad, and I did it anyway."

I let his words sink in, roll around. Because he wasn't wrong. I was being selfish. Expecting him to agree with whatever I wanted wasn't compromise, and it wasn't a good way to start a marriage. I hated being wrong. But a part of me had to realize that I was.

It wasn't the first time I had made the wrong choice. I *had* played Edie Fitzgerald in that movie, and while, no, I hadn't known when I first took the part that James was having an affair with her, I'd found out in plenty of time to back out of the project, and I hadn't. That was selfish. Was this a pattern? It was more than I could process, and I didn't want to think about it anymore.

So to change the subject, I raised my glass. "To Caroline," I said, "who has always been able to make Sloane and me miserable or ecstatic. Thank you for using your powers for good."

We all clinked glasses, but my sisters eyed me warily.

"I just can't talk about it tonight, OK?" I said pleadingly.

Sloane rolled her eyes and turned to Caroline, silently obeying my wishes. "I can't believe you're doing this at all," Sloane said. "It's a lot of work. And if I know you, that hasn't always been your thing."

Caroline smiled that smile I knew very well, the one of self-satisfaction, of a job well done. "You know, I realized that work makes me happy. It really does." She shrugged. "Plus, it's like shopping, but instead of buying stuff for me, I get to buy lots and lots of stuff for other people."

"But not on my credit card," James interjected with a smile.

"I never really realized how hard Mom's job was," Caroline said. "I sort of thought she played around with fabric samples and went to High Point Market, but it's no joke."

"Let's talk about how I'm going to sell more paintings at the LA opening than Caroline did at the New York one," I chimed in.

"Oh, yeah?" Caroline said. "You're on."

"I like this," Sloane said. "It's excellent for my wallet. But I won't continue to do this unless you two take a cut of the earnings."

"No," Caroline said definitively.

"Not a chance," I seconded. "You are our sister. Making you famous is our top priority. You will eventually pay us back with exclusive dinner reservations."

"Exactly," Caroline said.

"It's a good thing I have a rental storage unit full of paintings," Sloane said. "Otherwise, I wouldn't even have time to eat over the next few months."

Caroline gave Sloane the up and down. "This might come as a shock to you, but I'll allow it."

We all laughed again, but my mind was somewhere else, out in this great, wide city, with Mark. Although I was thrilled about the store, I knew already that I might have to let it go. Marriage was a compromise, and I knew I wasn't holding up my end of the bargain by spending more time in LA. I could only hope that wherever he was, Mark could forgive me.

SEVENTEEN

ansley: the only answer

When I look back on the months of my life during and after conceiving Sloane, only one word comes to mind: *consumed*. Not by thoughts of my baby, of the person I wanted to create, but by thoughts of Jack. I counted down the moments until I could sneak away and call him, simply hear his voice. And those days we got to be together . . . well, there were never enough of those. Twenty times an hour, it seemed, I would decide, breathlessly, recklessly, that I couldn't live without Jack. I would leave Carter for him. I had to.

Then I would see my husband, really look at him, kiss him, watch the way he was with Caroline. And I would know that he was my family. He was the one I was meant to be with, and I would never leave him, never want to lose him. And so on and so forth, until I thought—no, assumed—that I was crazy.

For months, I convinced myself that what I was doing was

not having an affair. My husband knew about it, for heaven's sake. If I got caught, then this was what he had asked me to do. Well, maybe not *this* exactly. But if those months taught me something, it was that the human mind can rationalize absolutely anything. Even how it was OK to be in love with more than one person and to know that no matter what you did or how you tried, you would most likely be in love with both of them for the rest of your life.

As bad as it was for me, I knew it was worse for Jack. In some ways, I wondered why he didn't call the whole thing off. In other ways, I knew why. He, like me, felt addicted to this life. To the secret meetings, the sneaking around, the wanting to be together out in the open but knowing it could never be. But I'd like to think that it was more than that. The affair wasn't so hard because of the longing, the lust, the wanting something you may never fully have. It was hard because of the love.

If I thought it then, I knew it now. Because all these years later, sitting on the steps of the Plaza hotel, my heart still raced for Jack like it had all those years ago. I still couldn't bear to be away from his arms. I still longed to sneak away to him to share those particular moments of passion that I had never quite experienced with anyone else.

As I leaned into him that night, the hot summer day giving way to a warm, pleasant evening, he kissed my forehead. "Can I take you somewhere?" he asked.

It was only then that I realized how tired I was, how much I wanted to slip underneath the crisp, high-thread-count sheets upstairs and fall asleep beside the man I had waited to fall asleep beside for what seemed like a lifetime.

"Upstairs?" I replied.

He lifted my chin and kissed me. "No," he whispered. "Somewhere else. Somewhere I think you'll like."

I sat up and peered at him. "I told you, I am *not* going to have sex with you in Central Park. I'm sorry that's your lifelong fantasy, but you might have to put that one aside if you're going to be with me."

He laughed and stood up, reaching his hand out to me. "First of all, *you're* my lifelong fantasy. Second of all, we're not going to the park."

We walked hand in hand down the street. When Jack stopped and held open a door for me, I didn't recognize where we were at first. But then I walked in and gasped for the second time that night. Two things hit me right at the same time. One, this old wooden bar was completely empty, save for one bartender and the most beautiful arrangement of flowers and candles I had ever seen. Two, I hadn't been here in more than thirty-seven years.

"Jack!" I said. "This is the bar!"

"This is the bar," he repeated, kissing me.

I guess the flowers and the candles should have been a dead giveaway. But still, I heard yet another gasp escape my throat when Jack got down on his knee.

"Ans," he said, "I sat at that booth across from you thirty-seven years ago, and I asked you to come back to Georgia with me. I didn't get to say all that I wanted to say then, but I'm going to say it now. I love you, Ansley. I'm pretty sure that I have only ever loved you. I've wasted a lot of time in my life not saying what I meant or doing what I felt. I've spent a lot of time pushing aside what was right in front of me. What I wanted to say to you that night was that I wanted you to come back to Georgia with me as my wife. And that's what I want now. I want to marry you, Ansley. I want to spend every day and every night with you. I want to breathe every breath I have left in my body with you. So will you, Ansley? Will you marry me?"

My hands flew to my mouth, and I could barely see the ring he produced from his pocket because my eyes were so glazed over with tears. But, oh, it was beautiful. He was beautiful. I thought for a moment about all those years, all that time I'd had to fight to keep myself away from him, first because of my husband, then because of my daughters. I wouldn't have to fight that anymore. I would never again have to hold myself back. I could be with him the way I had wanted to be for all those long and confusing years. I could be with him in the dark of night or the light of day. I could be with him until I closed my eyes for the very last time.

It occurred to me to be scared or conflicted. But there was none of that now. Only the perfect clarity that on his knee before me was a man who had loved me for most of my life, who had been by far the most confusing and convoluted chapter of my life story but, in some ways, the simplest, too. Because when you sifted through the sins and the bad choices, the things we should have done and the things perhaps we shouldn't have, it came down to one thing: that man had always been there for me.

So it was obvious what I would say. I pulled him up off the floor, wrapped my arms around him, and kissed him long and hard, like maybe it was the first time or maybe the last. I broke away and looked him right in the eye so that he would be sure to hear me, sure to know how serious I was, that all the confusion and the games, the push and pull, the ebb and flow, that had been our relationship for all these years had been worth it, that they had led us back to this same bar in this same city but with a different conclusion.

"I want to make sure that you hear me when I say this," I said. "I love you with every ounce of who I am. I have loved you since the moment our hands met over that plate of brownies on the sandbar, and there hasn't been one day since then that I haven't thought of you. Sometimes I wish I could change the past, but I can't." I paused and took a deep breath. "You gave me everything, Jack. Even when we couldn't be together, you still gave me the life I had always wanted." I kissed him again and said, "There is some messiness for us to clean up along this road, but I want you to know that no matter what that looks like, no matter how it happens or how hard it is, I am going to be there by your side to make it right again. I am going to love you until the day I die, and then I will love you for an eternity after that. So yeah, Jack, I will. I will marry you any old time."

It reminded me of a song that Vivi played in her room a lot, by a young man named Jason Mraz, whose content was sometimes a touch suggestive for me but whose voice I was awfully fond of. One of his lines went, "It's like taking a guess when the only answer is yes." It finally made sense to me now. Yes was not an answer. It was the only answer.

Jack laughed and picked me up in the air and kissed me again. "You will not marry me any old time," he said. "We are going to have a celebration to remember. It is going to be epic. Nothing less."

I smiled and nodded. "OK, I can handle that."

Then he handed me the ring. It was a gorgeous round stone in an antique setting with sapphires and diamonds. "So do you want this old thing or what?"

"Hell, yeah, I do." We both laughed, and he slipped the ring on my finger. I held out my hand to admire it. "It is the most beautiful ring I've ever seen."

He nodded. "I saw it in a window today, and I knew you had to have it."

I could feel my mouth hanging open. "Are you serious? You just decided to propose to me today?"

"Oh, Ansley. I decided to propose to you forty-three years ago. It just wasn't until today that I was pretty sure you'd say yes."

We reminisced and drank champagne. I finally kissed him in that booth where we had sat all those years ago, where our story once had a different ending.

"I would like to show you my appreciation for this lovely piece of jewelry now adorning my left hand."

He grinned. "I would like that very much."

As we walked back out into the dark night, with fewer people on the street than there had been before, I said, "Don't you think it's kind of ironic that you didn't want children so we didn't get married, and then we had two children together anyway, and now we're getting married and you're going to have three daughters? And God only knows how many grandchildren?"

He stopped and pulled me close to him. "The biggest regret of my life is not wanting children back then. I spent years thinking that if I had decided to give you children, we could have been together all these years. We could have had this family and this life so long ago. I wasted so much time."

I shook my head. "No, Jack. That isn't it at all. This was how it was always meant to happen. I know that now."

I felt a bit guilty in that moment. I tried to push it away, but I didn't want this to diminish my life with Carter. Yes, I had loved Jack, and yes, there was a bad patch in there when I had contemplated throwing away my marriage for him. Aside from that, Carter and I had had a terrific life together. Before he died, I had been sure that he was all I would ever want in this world, that we would be together until our dying breath. But his dying breath had come sooner than I had anticipated.

But then I smiled again. Because this wasn't a time to feel sad or guilty. This was a time to feel happy. Elated. Life had given me a second chance.

When I saw Mark sitting on the steps of the Plaza, alone, I couldn't help but wonder if Emerson had rethought the second chance she had given him.

I rolled my eyes at Jack and mouthed, *Really?* We'd had, what, two hours of peace?

Jack sat down beside Mark, and I sat down beside him.

"Trouble in paradise?" Jack quipped.

Mark put his head in his hands, and that was when I realized he was crying. And I kind of felt sorry for him, even though in my heart of hearts, I thought he had been a touch obnoxious lately.

"I am never going to be enough for her," he said. I was sure my daughter was somewhere very upset right now, which worried me.

Jack and Mark were talking, but I wasn't even listening. I was just admiring the ring on my hand and feeling grateful.

Sitting on the steps of the Plaza that night, I felt like everything happened for a reason, like someone had put these puzzle pieces together in a very specific way to make sure that we ended up where we were supposed to be. For a moment, a beat of a beat, I couldn't help but feel like maybe God hadn't forgotten about us after all.

emerson: a little like love

The plane ride home was awkward, to say the least. Mark had apologized; I had apologized. But this wasn't our typical fight and make up. It was bigger than that, maybe because it was one of the first times that, instead of glossing over everything, we had both taken stock of what we had actually done wrong and what we needed to do to fix it. I had, anyway.

As we pulled onto Mark's street in Peachtree Bluff, I finally said, "Let's go inside and open a bottle of wine and really get it all out on the table. I have a lot to say, and I'm sure you do, too."

Mark took my hand and nodded. He seemed relieved. But as we made our way to the driveway, it became abundantly clear that it was not going to happen. Because *she* was here. In all her glory. In a Pucci caftan with marabou trim, a skinny belt accentuating her minute waist, a martini in one hand, Botoxed within an inch of her life, cigarette hand motioning to a mover to take her Louis Vuitton trunks upstairs.

"*This* is who is going to be taking care of our children?" I asked Mark under my breath as we stepped out of the car.

"Mom!" he called loudly, ignoring me as she scurried to him without spilling a drop of her martini. It was quite impressive.

"Darling, darling, darling," she said, kissing him three times. "Oh, you get more handsome every day. I absolutely swear you do. And Emerson," she said to me, giving me a critical eye. She smiled, and I almost thought she was going to compliment me. "Aren't you pinching yourself? You must be the luckiest girl in the world to have snagged my prince!"

I was thinking, *I can't, I absolutely cannot*, as Mark said, "I am the luckiest *man* in the world to be marrying Emerson Murphy. I can't believe it." He squeezed my hand supportively.

"I'm just back from the south of France with my new gentleman friend, and I think you two should have your honeymoon there," said Mark's mother. "It's absolutely fabulous. And I know everyone who's anyone there now, so I can fix it all up."

I looked at Mark. I couldn't imagine what his childhood must have been like. His mother was always gone, flitting off to Paris with this man, Provence with that one, being swept into the arms of a Saudi prince this week, an Israeli prime minister the next. It was shocking how many men this one had accrued. But she was beautiful and poised, and I could see why men liked her. I wasn't sure if they never kept her, but I believe it was that she never kept them. She had a collection of engagement rings that could rival the crown jewels. I wondered if the new ruby on her left hand was an addition to the set.

If I hadn't hated her so much for putting Mark through hell as a kid, I would have loved her. Despite her tendencies, she could be quite a bit of fun. But Mark carried scars so deep from a neglected childhood that even I couldn't heal them. And I felt a warm tenderness rise up for him then. All he had ever experienced was women leaving him. Of course he didn't want me to leave Peachtree for LA. At that thought, I snuggled into his side, wrapping my arm around his. He was like a stray dog. All he needed was someone to love him, someone to make him feel playful and fun, not so beaten down. That person was me. I was very lucky.

"Mrs. Becker," I began, ready to play nice and help her get settled in.

But then she said, "No, darling, it's Duchess now." And I knew then that I couldn't help her. No one could.

I looked up at Mark, and he looked down at me. And I wondered again how he could possibly have turned out normal at all.

MY UNCLE SCOTT WAS the one who made me wish I had a brother. He had always been super-protective of Mom.

When we got home from New York, Scott claimed he was coming to Peachtree Bluff straight from his latest humanitarian-aid-slash-reporting project in Puerto Rico because he wanted to help Mom go through the rest of Grammy's things. But we all knew better. He just wanted to check on his sister.

Our trip had given Mom an excuse to keep all of Grammy's things sitting in storage for a bit longer. She didn't have any use for them, but she also couldn't bear to part with the relics of Grammy's life. It made sense to me. It drove Caroline absolutely insane.

I was walking into the kitchen that morning when I overheard Caroline saying, "I mean, it's borderline hoarder behavior. She needs to hire one of those estate-sale companies and get it over with. People would be thrilled to have all that beautiful furniture."

I had rolled my eyes and turned to walk back upstairs, not interested in Caroline in *this* mood this early in the morning, when I heard Sloane say, "If Jack is any indication, Mom isn't great at cutting ties with the past."

"Lucky for us," Caroline whispered.

Sloane laughed. "Yeah. I guess it is."

Now my interest was piqued. On the one hand, the sneaky little sister in me didn't want them to know I had overheard their conversation. But the other part of me wanted to investigate, so I walked in, saying, "Why is that lucky for us?"

Sloane visibly winced, which was my first clue something was up. But Caroline, always quick on her feet, just said, "I mean, do you want to be looking after Mom forever?"

I pursed my lips and looked from one of them to the other. They were hiding something.

I crossed my arms. "That is not what you meant."

Before I could delve deeper, Scott burst through the door. "Favorite family member has arrived!"

Truth be told, Uncle Scott had always been our favorite, but after he helped find Adam and bring him home safely, we had all decided, definitively, that favorite-family-member status was his forever after. We even had a T-shirt made for him with his face on the front and *Favorite Uncle for Life* on the back, which he was currently wearing.

Scott was staying overnight, and I noticed he had only one backpack. I would never understand that man. Whatever packing gene he had, I did not get it.

"Em, you want to help me unpack?" he asked, totally distracting me from what my sisters had been saying before he walked in.

"Well, someone has to," I said lightly.

When we were out of earshot, walking toward the guest room, he asked, "How you holding up?"

After our dual confessions, we were partners in crime, with a bond that we didn't really share with anyone else. He was the only one who knew my secret, besides Mark. And I planned to keep it that way.

Instead of answering him, I shrugged. I thought about it ten times a day, that moment when Grammy was breathing and then she wasn't. And it was because of me. It was because of the glass of water I poured her. The pills I handed her.

"OK, I guess. I don't think about it as much. How about you?"

He nodded. "Doing mission work makes me feel like I'm atoning for my sins."

"Do you think it works like that?" I asked.

He shrugged. "Who knows? Can't hurt."

Scott set his backpack on a chair in the corner of the downstairs guest room. Grammy's room.

Before I could say anything, I heard Vivi screaming from the other room, "I'm not going to, and you can't make me!" Her voice was promptly followed by the sound of the front door slamming.

"What the hell?" I asked, walking into the entrance hall and finding a mystified Caroline.

"It's like the hormones have kidnapped her and taken her forever. I thought I had until she was a teenager before I had to deal with all this."

"What is she not doing and you can't make her?" I asked.

"Having a twelfth birthday party."

I burst out laughing, and so did Scott.

"You bitch," he said. "Why would you even *suggest* she have a birthday party? Of all the cruel and unforgiving things."

"I know," Caroline said, lightening now. "I am a total monster."

"I'll talk to her," I said. "She still seems to like me."

"So you say," Caroline said.

"Maybe she's having anxiety about getting older," Scott said. We all laughed again.

I walked out the front door to look for Vivi, but she was nowhere to be found. So I walked upstairs and out onto the second-floor deck, where she seemed to be spending quite a bit of time lately. I had been planning to head to the beach earlier, before all hell had broken loose, but I figured this was as good a place as any to admire the view. I took off my cover-up to catch a few rays while I waited for her.

I leaned back on the chaise and placed my sunglasses over my eyes, ready to relax. A few moments later, however, I heard voices downstairs. I opened one eye to peer through the slats in the railing and saw Mom and Jack, their backs to me on his downstairs porch next door, looking through old photo albums. The way the houses were built so close together and the way the wind was blowing, I could hear their voices almost better than if I had been sitting beside them, which was super-annoying. I was trying to sneak in a nap if I could. My doctor had said I needed rest, right?

I was feeling stronger every day. Every other week, I had an iron IV, and on the off weeks, I got what was known as a Myers' Cocktail, a fun little intravenous bag filled with vitamin C and other great goodies. I felt absolutely amazing. I was trying to eat regularly and exercise a normal amount and generally take care of myself. I would be on set again two days after the wedding, and I needed to feel my best.

"I wish I had been there," Jack was saying to Mom.

She laughed. "Yeah. That's because you've never done middle-of-the-night feedings and colic. It wasn't all fun and games." She pointed to another photo. "Oh, I love this one," Mom said. "Caroline wouldn't leave the house without that pink tutu."

"Whoa," Jack said.

"Oh, my gosh," Mom echoed. "Sloane looks exactly like your baby pictures in this one."

I shot up in my chaise, all the hairs on the back of my neck standing up, though I couldn't piece together what I was hearing just yet.

"Do you think now that we're engaged, it's the right time to tell them?" Jack asked.

My heart started pounding. I wanted to run inside at top speed, because I knew whatever I was overhearing was something I would wish I hadn't.

"I don't want to ruin Emerson's wedding," Mom said.

"Right," Jack said. "But it seems like she would care least of all."

Oh, my God. I felt frozen to my chair, my blood cold. My mind was catching up to my heart now.

"I don't think that's how she'll see it. I think she'll think it affects her most of all because then she'll be the only one without a living father."

I jumped up off the chaise before I could hear the rest and ran into my room and shut the door. I sat on the edge of my bed, catching my breath, and then decided that I had to go down there right now to confront them. I sat for a few minutes, trying to reason it out, trying to decide if this could possibly mean anything other than what I thought it did. *I would be the only one without a living father . . . which could only mean . . .*

"Oh, my God," I said out loud. "Oh, my God."

After what felt like an eternity of gathering myself, I swung the bedroom door open with conviction and then, looking down, realized I was wearing only my bikini. I stepped back out onto the porch to grab my cover-up, pulled it over my head, and saw Vivi and a friend there, on the floor of the porch, huddled around something that, when I got closer, I realized was a cigarette.

"Vivian Louise Beaumont!" I said sharply. "What on earth do you think you're doing?"

She and her friend both looked up, wide-eyed.

I held out my hand. "Give that to me right now."

I realized it was neither good for my health nor a good example when I put the cigarette to my mouth, cupped my hands around the flame, and inhaled. But if anyone had ever needed a cigarette, it was me now. I had just accidentally found out that Jack was Sloane and Caroline's biological father. A cigarette was in order.

"Smoking is the worst thing in the world for you," I said, as the two girls looked up at me. "You aren't even twelve years old."

"Actually, I am," the friend piped up.

I looked at her sternly. "Smoking stunts your growth, ruins your lungs, and keeps you from getting boobs." The last one wasn't true, per se, but I could tell from the looks on their faces that it was way more effective than any lung-cancer photos.

Their eyes went straight to my chest, and Vivi whispered, "Is that what happened to you?"

Bitches. I inhaled again and said, "Yes. Yes, it is." I exhaled slowly and said, "Your mother never smoked a cigarette in her life, which is why she's tall and her boobs are huge. Let that be a lesson to you."

It now occurred to me that Sloane and Caroline had boobs and I didn't because Jack was their father and Dad was mine. On the bright side, they would never be able to play boys on-stage with their C and D cups. My barely A cups were very versatile. I knew that Vivi's drama was helping me procrastinate about focusing on my own. But also, her health and safety would always come first, even above soul-shattering, life-changing revelations.

I sat down on the porch beside them, taking the last drag and then flicking it expertly so that the butt detached from the ash in one swift motion, the light going out and both pieces sailing into the bushes downstairs. You could say this wasn't the first time I had smoked a cigarette on this porch.

"What is going on with you and your mom?" I asked Vivi, realizing that something pretty major would be going on with my own mom and me in short order.

"I don't want to be who she wants me to be, and she can't get that through her head. I'm not her, and if I don't want to have the kind of party she wants to have, that doesn't make me crazy."

I nodded. "Look, no one understands being controlled by your mother better than I do. But she loves you more than anything, and she only wants to make you happy. Sometimes people only know how to make people happy the way they like to be made happy. Does that make sense?"

Vivi nodded sullenly.

"So what *do* you want for your birthday? If it's not having a party here, I mean," I asked.

"To stay in Peachtree Bluff and not go back to New York," she rolled off.

Yikes. This was going to be harder than I thought.

"Um," I said, looking out over the water, realizing that this parenting thing seemed pretty tough after all. "You know that's not realistic. Your dad works in New York, and your life is in New York. Peachtree Bluff is the best place in the world to visit, but it's not the kind of place you get to stay forever."

"Gransley gets to stay forever."

"I get to stay forever," the brunette friend said.

I glared at her. She wasn't helping my cause. Plus, she was trying to give my niece stale cigarettes. Not cool. Not cool at all.

"And I hate my dad," Vivi said. "I don't want to go back to live with him anyway."

"I hate your dad, too," I said before I could stop myself. I grinned sheepishly. "Look," I said, "I'm kidding. Take it from me, you only get one dad, and when he's gone, you're always going to wish you had him back. He made some mistakes, but you'll make some mistakes, too."

And then I realized that, yes, Vivi would only get one dad. I only got one dad. But it seemed my sisters got two.

I held up the lighter in my hand. "You almost ruined your boob chances, so you get what I mean."

She finally smiled, and I put my hand under her chin.

"So, besides staying in Peachtree Bluff forever, what would your second birthday wish be?"

"I don't want a big party," Vivi said. Then she lowered her

voice and said sheepishly, "I want to come to LA to see you film your new movie."

My heart felt like it would burst. That was the sweetest thing in the world. I tapped her on the head. "Wish granted. I heard the Francie Nolan character in the movie I'm filming, *A Tree Grows in Brooklyn*, needs a few friends. Do you think you could say a couple of lines and look dirty and disheveled?"

She nodded enthusiastically.

"Perfect," I said, feeling better about the whole day. "Read the book first. You'll love it." I got up but turned back to the girls before I headed into the house. "And don't forget: beer makes your hair fall out."

They both gasped, putting their hands up to their long, flat-ironed locks.

They'd probably only buy that one for another couple of years, but it was worth a shot.

"That must be why my dad is bald," Vivi's sidekick whispered.

I muffled my laugh as I walked inside, realizing that I was getting ready to do something very, very unpleasant. And I knew all at once that nobody in the Murphy family would be laughing again for a long, long time.

FAME IS A LITTLE like love. When it happens slowly, it's more likely to last. Sure, there are those overnight success stories, the ones who make it big right off the bat. But I like to think that they're one-hit wonders and that the way I've done it—or have been forced to do it, really—is better in the long run. That climbing the ladder slowly, one rung at a time, will eventually lead to something long and prosperous. I love the idea of being sixty years old and still being on the screen or the stage, being someone's idol.

So, despite how mixed up and frustrated and overwhelmed I felt about my career, I couldn't help but realize that there was the tiniest bit of joy mixed in there. Because while I didn't have that Oscar sitting on my shelf that I thought I would surely win before my thirtieth birthday, I did have fans, and I was someone's idol. Even if it was just my niece. And I couldn't believe my sweet Vivi would trade what I was sure would be the party of anyone's dreams for a chance to be with me on set. Despite all the bad that was going on, that was something to be grateful for.

After the Vivi cigarette fiasco, I had wanted to go straight over to confront Jack and Mom. But I decided against it. Maybe it was because I chickened out, but I told myself it was because I needed to tell Sloane and Caroline first. It seemed sort of like sisters' code.

I made my way very slowly toward Sloane Emerson, where I knew Caroline was working on my wedding. I had helped with all the big-picture items. I had picked the florist and the food and the band and the location and the photographer. But when it came to details, I was a mess. Caroline would come up with a whole list of ways we could transport the cake to Starlite Island, while I would nod and hum along, realizing I would never have thought of that. And she would figure out how many pieces of silverware we needed to rent and spend hours scouring the state for the right wineglasses, while I wouldn't even realize that choosing wineglasses was part of the wedding-planning process. I was beyond lucky. I had recommended hiring a wedding planner so Caroline wouldn't end up doing all the work, but she had looked at me like I had suggested we give vials of Ebola out as favors.

"I'm better than any wedding planner."

She was such a good sister. She loved me so much. Caroline and I had always been closer than Sloane and I, for whatever reason. I mean, Sloane and I were close, too, but we talked only once a week, whereas Caroline and I talked a highly dysfunctional, codependent three to five times a day.

I wouldn't say that Mom checked out after Dad died, but there were some long months in there when Caroline really looked after me. She let me sleep in her bed and made me breakfast when I got up really early and braided my hair in a crown across my head the way I liked it every day. We had always understood each other in a way that Sloane and I just hadn't. Caroline always joked that she was the glue that held the family together, and in this regard, she kind of was. I took a deep breath, my hand on the door of the store. And now I was going to make the glue's world come crashing down.

When I walked inside, Caroline was sitting on the stool behind the front glass counter, making notes in that ridiculously huge wedding-planning binder she had constructed for me. Well, for her. This was Caroline's wedding now. Besides the binder, the two of us were all alone.

I could pull her into the back storeroom and recount what I had heard. Then we could formulate how to tell Sloane. Together. Sloane was more sensitive than Caroline, and right now, with Adam so newly home and her wading through the waters of his trauma, I felt she had enough on her plate. I didn't want to heap one more thing on top of it all.

I started walking toward the counter, but before Caroline could even look up, Sloane walked out of the storeroom with a canvas in her paint-stained hands.

Great. What did I do now? I could tell them both and get it over with. Or I could walk out. Which I almost did, until they looked at me at almost the exact same time and said simultaneously, "Hi, Em."

Hi. Not *Hey.* Grammy always told us that *hey* was for horses, and it had stuck.

I felt a pang. How in sync they were at that moment made me realize how close they were, reminded me that they were whole, full-blood sisters. And I was only half. Did they talk about it when I wasn't there? Did they feel bad for me because I was less of a sister than they were? It made my heart hurt even to think that I was somehow less connected to either of these women whom I had looked up to since the day I was born.

Would the revelation that Jack was their biological father drive a wedge between us? That thought almost talked me out of telling them.

"What's up?" Caroline asked. "Did you sense that I was ordering those string lights you said you didn't want?"

I looked at her incredulously. "It's not that I don't like them. It's just too much trouble. All those poles and all those people you have to hire to put them up."

"It's your only wedding," Sloane said. "It should be perfect."

I cleared my throat, my heart racing. "Where's Leah?" I asked.

"She's supervising the installation at Kyle's," Caroline said, smiling.

As if my mouth were moving of its own volition, I heard it say, "Um, guys, can we talk?"

Sloane and Caroline shared a glance that let me know they somehow knew this was coming.

"Is this about Mark?" Caroline whispered.

I was taken aback. I crossed my arms. "Um, no. Why would it be about Mark?"

"No reason!" Sloane chimed in.

I looked warily from one sister to the other.

"I think we need to go to the conference room," I said after an awkward silence.

"Oh, wow," Sloane said. "So this is serious."

"Oh, my God," Caroline said, closing the binder and following me through the door as I led them to the other room. "Are you OK?"

I nodded gravely, closed the door behind us, and sat down in a woven navy-and-white Serena & Lily chair at the round marble Saarinen table, and Caroline and Sloane took their seats on either side of me.

I took a deep breath and took one of their hands in each of mine. "I don't know how to say this," I began.

Four eyes round as saucers were trained on my face, rapt with attention and dread. I felt nauseated for a million reasons at once. They were going to be upset. I didn't want to tell them. I didn't want this to be true. Mom, Jack, Caroline, and Sloane were family. Real, true family. Where did that leave me? But again, sisters' code. It was my responsibility to tell them.

"I think Jack is your biological father."

They both sat stock-still. I thought they were in shock until I realized that Sloane's hand suddenly felt sweaty in mine. Sloane sweated when she was lying.

Caroline glanced at Sloane. "What would make you think that?"

I pulled my hands away. "Why do you not look surprised?"

"No, we are surprised," Sloane said, speaking for both of them, which was my second clue that they definitely knew this already.

"We suspected," Caroline said. "But we didn't know for sure."

"You suspected, and you didn't even ask Mom about it?" I asked.

"Says the girl who wouldn't get her blood-test results for six weeks," Caroline shot back.

Touché, I thought. But I wouldn't give her the satisfaction of saying so.

"So that's what you were talking about," I said, the picture beginning to become clear in my mind. "It was lucky Mom couldn't let go of Jack even after she married Dad, because if she had, you wouldn't be here."

I could see that Sloane was starting to get worked up now. "When we only *suspected* he was our sperm donor, it was one thing . . ." she whispered. "But knowing for sure feels really different. Are you positive, Em?"

I nodded. "Mom and Jack were looking at photo albums, and I overheard their conversation. It's definitely true."

Caroline took a deep breath. She looked at Sloane. "So now it's real. Now we have to face it."

I could feel my heart racing. So many thoughts were running through my mind, but the one I spit out first was, "Oh, my God! Do you think Mom cheated on Dad?"

Sloane gave me an incredulous look. "Em, come on."

I got myself back together. Mom was our moral compass. She was the one always teaching us right from wrong. She was realistic about the world, but there were some things that were black and white. She might have lied to us, but she wouldn't have done that to Dad.

"Dad couldn't have known this," Sloane said, her face turning red. "There is no way that our father let Mom's ex-boyfriend be our sperm donor. Do you think?"

They might have suspected all of this earlier, but you could tell it was finally beginning to sink in, and now the emotions that my sisters had been holding back were flooding them.

Caroline shook her head, her expression now incredulous. "I didn't even think of that! Poor Dad. He would be furious if he knew. He would feel so betrayed."

I had opened this can of worms. We were in it now.

"This is so unfair to him," I said. "I can't believe Mom would do this. I mean, why not just pick a sperm donor like any other normal person?"

"I think the thing I'm maddest about is that you found out this way, right before your wedding," Caroline said. "I mean, how could Mom be so insensitive and careless?"

At that moment, the door opened, and Mom said nonchalantly, "What was I insensitive and careless about this time?"

Little did she know, she had just walked into a hornet's nest.

NINETEEN

ansley: insensitive

I had begged Caroline to come back to Peachtree Bluff. Pleaded with her. But the minute I walked into that conference room and saw her sitting with Sloane and Emerson at my table, I wished I hadn't.

Because as soon as the three of them looked up at me, I knew they knew. And when the three of them combined forces, nothing could overtake them.

Caroline looked at Sloane resolutely, and Sloane bit her lip. Oh, gosh. Here it was. They were finally going to confront me about Jack being their father. And I was terrified but also almost glad. We could get it out in the open, get it over with. We could deal with the emotions. I could tell the truth. It would be long and hard, but we would repair. We could finally move on.

I repeated, "What was I insensitive and careless about this time?"

Caroline gave me that steely look that is her most terrifying: unnaturally calm and unnerving to absolutely no end. "Sit down," she said, pointing to the empty chair at the table.

I stood up straighter—just in case I needed to run.

"We need to know, Mom," Sloane said. "Once and for all. Is Jack our sperm donor?"

I swallowed hard. Technically, no, he was not their sperm donor. He was much more than that. Jack had made love to me the way he had all those years ago in Peachtree Bluff when we first met. And it was as if time and reason simply slipped away. And suddenly, like I had always wanted, I had one daughter and then another. And they had been made out of so much love.

But that was something my girls would never know. Carter knew it. I knew it. Jack knew it. The rest of the world wouldn't understand what we had been through, couldn't imagine why I would do something so seemingly wrong.

I looked at each of my girls, memorizing their faces, not sure what was going to come next but knowing that the truth was out. And I had to face it head-on. How I said it didn't really matter now. All that mattered was that they forgave me. Because they were not only my daughters but also my best friends. And they deserved the truth.

So I said simply, "Yes. He is. Jack is your father."

We all sat in an unsettling silence.

"I do not understand," Sloane said slowly, "how you could live with a lie like that for all these years." She sounded more sad than angry.

"I never lied to you, Sloane," I said as calmly as possible, just wanting this to all go away. "I told the three of you from a time that most people would agree was way too early that you and Caroline had a sperm donor, that your father wasn't biologically your father. You have known this your entire life."

"Mom, come on," Caroline said. "You can't honestly believe that our knowing we had a sperm donor is the same thing as knowing that our sperm donor is our soon-to-be stepfather."

I took a deep breath to calm my nerves. "I don't expect you to understand," I said. "But when your father and I found out he couldn't have children, I couldn't stand the idea of half your genes coming from a total stranger. I wanted my babies to be made out of love. And Jack and I had loved each other. In another life, in another time, in another world, I could have had children with him. It made sense." I paused. "At the time, anyway."

It wasn't the whole truth, and it certainly left out the part that the insemination wasn't artificial. But it was all the truth they needed to know.

The door was standing half open, and from my vantage point, I could see Kyle's head peeking in at exactly the same time Emerson said, "Well, congratulations! Your dad is still alive, and you four get to be one big, happy family." She burst into tears and ran out the door, brushing past a stunned Kyle.

He stared at us, wide-eyed. "I have *got* to work on my timing." Then, without missing a beat, he followed Emerson out the door.

I had to consider that his timing couldn't possibly be better.

"How could you, Mom?" Caroline asked, seething now.

"Emerson heard you and Jack talking, Mom," Sloane interrupted. "She is the one who came and told us. She is the one who found out first. And you know how sensitive she is, especially right now."

"I hope you're happy," Caroline said. "You have officially ruined her wedding."

I had so many ways to defend myself, so many things to say. I wanted to tell them that I had done it for them. I wanted to tell them that I hadn't meant for any of them to find out this way, that we were going to tell them, that the timing never seemed to be right. But the two stone-cold faces looking back at me made me realize that whatever I said now would be falling on deaf ears.

"Did Dad even know, Mom?" Sloane asked. "Did he have any idea that two of his children were fathered by his wife's ex-boyfriend?" She crossed her arms.

Well, no, not at first. He hadn't wanted to know. But now I was glad he had found out eventually, so that I was telling the truth when I said, "Of course your father knew, Sloane. Of course he did. He was a part of every step of this process. In fact, a lot of it was his idea."

Caroline sighed and rolled her eyes.

"I can't change it," I said apologetically. "I wanted to tell you a million times, but you two are mothers. Surely you understand how it never seems like the right time to blow up your children's world."

"Sure, Mom," Sloane said. "But we aren't children. We're adults. You should have come to us with this the minute Jack was back in our lives. This was wrong on so many levels."

I wanted to retort that they sure as hell didn't act like adults when they were here, when they were back home with me. They relied on me for everything, just like they had as kids. They bickered with one another, they stayed out too late, and I would bet a million bucks none of them had folded a load of laundry in weeks. But I guessed that was really neither here nor there now.

Caroline added, "And now you've done it; you've blown up our world."

They both got up from the table and walked out of the room. I sat there, feeling dead inside.

My entire life revolved around my children. I hated fighting with them under any circumstances, but especially now, especially when I knew there was nothing to say, nothing to be done. The only thing that had a chance of healing this wound was the one thing we didn't have enough of: time.

Emerson was walking down the aisle in three weeks. And I knew that if I didn't figure out a way to fix this—and fast—I might not be there to see it.

emerson: a cereal box

I'd never been good at facing problems head-on. It was one of my worst qualities; I was nonconfrontational to the extreme. I was kind to people who didn't deserve it and let some things that were really important to me slip by because I didn't want to make a scene or cause a fuss.

Some might argue that walking out of a heated discussion like the one we were having was actually more dramatic than staying. But it was my defense mechanism. I couldn't take the heat, so I got out of the kitchen.

Only, when I walked out of Sloane Emerson, I didn't know where to go. I thought about going to Mark's, but I didn't want to risk running into the Duchess. That gave me an entirely new thing to be irritated about.

I didn't want to go home, because that was the first place Mom would look for me, and I couldn't go to Sloane's, because as much as I could have eaten my nephews up, they weren't what I needed right now.

So I picked up my pace and walked down to the dock. About the time I got to the *Miss Ansley*, floating on the water, I heard an out-of-breath voice calling, "Emerson, for God's sake, slow down."

It was only when I turned that I realized I was crying. I wasn't even sure why. Maybe because of the situation, but maybe because I hated fighting with my mom. I couldn't stand it. She was always my rock, and not having her on my side felt like too big a burden to bear.

I let Kyle catch up to me, climbed into the cockpit of Jack's boat, and retrieved the hidden key from the bottom drawer in the tackle center. I unlocked the cabin and slipped inside.

"Does he know we're here?" Kyle whispered, following close behind me.

I shrugged. "No. But he doesn't care." I paused. "Well, he wouldn't care if his daughters, Sloane and Caroline, were on it. But maybe he won't be thrilled if his mere soon-to-be-stepdaughter is."

Kyle moved very slowly and sat down on the navy-and-white-striped upholstered bench. "Um. I'm sorry. Could you repeat that, please?"

I raised my eyebrow and shook my head. "We always knew that Caroline and Sloane had a sperm donor."

"Yeah?" Kyle asked.

"But that sperm donor wasn't some random test tube." I took a deep breath before saying, "It was Jack."

Kyle's mouth hung open. "I'll be honest. I thought I knew every deep, dark secret around here. But I did *not* see that one coming."

"*You* didn't see it coming?" I asked under my breath. "Imagine how I feel."

I flopped dramatically beside him, even though there were plenty of other places I could sit. Kyle was a calming influence. I needed calm right now.

I checked my phone. Not so much as a text from my ungrateful mother. Ungrateful for what, I wasn't sure. It was just the first word that came to mind. But there was a text from one of my costars: *There go our Oscar nods.*

I felt all the blood rushing to my face. *What?* I unlocked my phone so I could see the whole thing.

We've been moved from full-length feature film to a limited-run series.

I looked up at Kyle incredulously and furiously started typing: *How is that even possible?*

The response: *That's showbiz, baby. The director dropped out.*

I let out a low, frustrated groan as she added, *I guess we're lucky it wasn't scrapped altogether, but still . . .*

Kyle squeezed my shoulder. "What's happening now?"

"As if it weren't enough to find out that my mom, my sisters, and *Jack* are going to be one big, happy family, I just found out that my movie is getting changed to a series, which I would usually be beyond thrilled about, but if ever there were a chance for a supporting actress Oscar, Sissy would be the character."

I leaned over and rested my head in my hands.

Kyle ran his finger down the length of my spine, leaving goose bumps in its wake. It actually distracted me so much that for a moment, I forgot my life was falling apart around me.

"Hey," Kyle said, and I looked up at him. He smiled and wiped away my tears, and for a second, a beat of a beat, I thought he was going to try to kiss me. But he didn't. He simply said, "Though she be but little . . ."

He trailed off and raised an eyebrow at me, and I finished for him, "She is fierce."

I was reminded again of that night in LA and that he hadn't forgotten, either. I wondered if it meant that maybe he remembered other things, too, and if that meant something. But then I looked down at my hand and wiped the thought away. I was engaged. I was Mark's. And that definitely meant something, something I wasn't willing to sacrifice, no matter how this moment with Kyle made me feel.

I nodded. "I don't feel fierce. I feel defeated."

Kyle stood up and began pacing around the cabin. I couldn't shake the feeling that I wanted to stand up, too, have him wrap his arms around me, and put my head on his chest. It occurred to me that was wrong, that I should want Mark to do that.

"Em," Kyle said, "it's none of my business. It's not my place to tell you how to run your life. I know you're frustrated, and I know it's hard, but sometimes, when it feels impossible, when it feels like you can't go on for one more moment, that's when the change is taking place; that's when the really big things are happening."

I sniffed and nodded. "Kind of like in a workout."

He laughed. "Exactly. Those last reps that you push through make all the difference."

"The weird thing is," I said, thinking back to all those nights alone in my apartment, "I would have sworn I never wanted to get married when I first moved to LA." I shrugged. "But I mean, that future is all I know. My mom got married and had babies, Caroline got married and had babies, Sloane got married and had babies. So I feel like I need to get married and have babies, too."

He stopped pacing. "Wait. I thought we were talking about acting and Jack."

I waved my hand and said, "We are, but I'm having a full-on existential life crisis right now, and I'm going to need you to keep up."

He sat down beside me again, his eyes locked on mine, and I saw something pass through them, like maybe he had a secret he wanted to tell me. But all he said was, "Em, you're you. You don't have to do what they do." He laughed under his breath. "And, I mean, I love your family, but I'm not sure storybook marriages are necessarily their forte."

Obviously, it didn't take a rocket scientist to realize that Caroline's marriage was far from a fairy tale. Everyone thought Sloane and Adam were this perfect couple, but their relationship was just so traditional. It wasn't what I wanted.

"I don't know," I said. "I mean, it's like even though their lives aren't perfect, at least they have someone fighting for them, you know? Someone to share in their successes and their failures? They aren't alone."

Something akin to incredulity passed over Kyle's face.

"What?" I asked.

"Nothing." He shook his head.

I picked three yellow buttercups from the vase on the table beside me, the one I was sure my mother had put there. I jammed my pinkie fingernail through one, feeling the water inside the stem ooze underneath my nail. I inserted the stem of the next flower into the tiny hole I had made. I grabbed a few more and kept stringing them together, like my sisters and I had done when we were little.

"You can't 'nothing' me, Kyle," I said. I looked up at him. "I know you. I can read you like a cereal box."

He laughed. "A cereal box?"

"Well, yeah. A cereal box."

"Why not a book?" he asked, studying my fingers as they worked. He picked up a few yellow flowers of his own, mimicking my actions.

"Because a book might be super-simple or terribly complex. A cereal box is always easy to read." I paused, watching as he struggled. "No, no. You're doing it too close to the bottom. The stems are going to break." I put my hand on his, just to stop him. But then I felt my fingers wrapping around his as if I hadn't been the one to do it. Kyle's eyes locked on mine.

I finally pulled away, feeling myself redden, and said, "Changing the subject isn't working on me."

"Sometimes it does," he almost whispered.

"Kyle," I persisted.

"Fine," he said, his fingers still stringing, not daring to look at me now, as if he were an ashamed child. "You may not see it this way, Emerson, but you *are* all alone. Mark may be chasing you, but he isn't what Adam is to Sloane or even what James is to Caroline. Because your success is his failure, and your failure is his success."

I gasped, tears coming to my eyes yet again. It felt so cruel, those harsh words coming from him. I started to stand, wanted to walk away, but Kyle grabbed my wrist before I could.

He stood now, too, and pulled me closer to him. Too close.

"No," he said, softening. "Don't be angry at me. I only say this because I have to, Em. I can't . . ." He trailed off. With the flowers he'd strung dangling from his arm, he pushed my hair behind my ears, sweeping it down my back, his fingertips grazing my shoulders. He took his flower chain and placed it on my head. "You are a princess," he said. "And you deserve to be treated like one."

It sounded silly, ridiculous, even. But Kyle had a way of saying these really corny things that had so much truth in them that you couldn't even roll your eyes, couldn't even mind, couldn't even feel embarrassed that he had said them.

"It's not his fault that he wants you to be all his, that he wants you to give up doing what you love," Kyle said. "And it's not your fault that you aren't willing to. But you have to go into this with open eyes. You have to know that what you want isn't what you're going to have. And if you're OK with that, then I wish you well. And if you're not OK with that, be the woman I know, Emerson. The strong, confident, fiery woman I met in the bar that night, the one I knew I would never forget."

It was then that I realized that Kyle loved me, that maybe he always had. He'd had a drink named for me at his favorite bar, for God's sake. That's romance.

I couldn't deny that I felt things for Kyle that I shouldn't—at least, not as a person engaged to another man. But with Kyle, there was uncertainty. I didn't know exactly what to expect with him, couldn't be positive that things would work out. I put my hand up to my flower crown and smiled just thinking of the way he would light up when he saw me, of the way I could tell him anything.

But despite everything, I loved Mark. And maybe he would never be able to love me the way that I wanted him to. Maybe he would never love me the way I had imagined. But he did love me. Maybe that was enough. Maybe enough was all that some of us ever got.

TWENTY-ONE

ansley: beautiful blond giraffe

When I woke up that morning, it took a moment for it all to come back to me, as it usually did. Some mornings, it began with 9/11, the phone call that Carter had made, the one where he said he was going to be OK but then he wasn't. Sometimes the realization that my mom was gone flooded back to me first. Today the first thought to steal my peace was that my daughters knew. Emerson storming out. Sloane's devastated eyes. Caroline's cold expression. It was all running through my mind now. The thing I had kept a secret for all these years. The thing I feared would absolutely wreck their lives if they found out.

Now none of them was speaking to me, which had wrecked my own. I had spent the night at Jack's house, and I still couldn't quite gather the courage to leave.

I took a moment now to gaze out through the double French doors on the front of the house that led out to the balcony off Jack's room. The water looked so peaceful. It was a perfect boat day. I knew that Jack and I would take a cocktail cruise that evening. Jack. Me. I stepped outside to inhale the salt air.

As I began to turn to walk inside, I noticed a car pulling into the driveway. The gate was closed, so the black Range Rover had to stop in front of it, giving me the perfect view. A woman stepped out of the car. Probably around Caroline's age. Even from upstairs, I could tell that she was extraordinarily tall, certainly nearly six feet if you included the snakeskin stilettos she had paired with a black sleeveless sheath that hugged her body perfectly. A single strand of baroque pearls hung around her neck, and her blond hair was long down her back.

She was striking, absolutely beautiful, the kind of girl you would expect to see on a runway, not a driveway. My interest was piqued. And then she rang the doorbell.

I looked down and instantly regretted wearing a pair of yoga pants and a top. With my hair unwashed and no makeup on, I did not look runway-ready like the girl downstairs. But for the first time in a long time, when I looked at myself, I didn't see all the flaws. I didn't see the wrinkles I should probably have attended to or the age spots on my forearms. I was still strong, still in great shape, and I had a man who loved me.

As I made my way downstairs, I heard the sound of muffled voices in the hallway. Jack, who'd been fixing us breakfast in the kitchen, must have beaten me to the door and the mystery woman. Maybe this was the new real estate agent who Georgia, Jack's former Realtor-turned-girlfriend, whom he had dated during the weeks we were apart, had sent to take her place since she and Jack had called it quits. Perhaps placing this woman with *my* man was her way of getting even with me. I smiled to myself. *Well played, Georgia. Well played.*

I tiptoed down the stairs. The way the walls were configured, I knew I could go into the entrance hall and the wall would block me from their view. It was stupid, I knew. I could have walked in. But despite how good I felt, I still didn't really want to meet this beautiful stranger in my exercise clothes.

Biscuit, who was happily living back in her old house with Jack, found me in the corner and whined at my feet. "I'll take you for a walk in just a minute," I whispered to her.

"I made a huge mistake," the woman was saying, in a voice that was at once strong and vulnerable—the voice of an opponent, I was coming to realize. "I've tried to move on, Jack, but nothing makes sense without you. I'd rather have you than a baby. I'd rather have you than anything else in the entire world."

I couldn't see them, but I could imagine her moving closer to him.

"Jack," she said softly, "I am more convinced than ever that you are my soul mate. I love you with everything I have in me."

I leaned against the wall, biting my lip to keep from crying, putting my hand on my heart to keep it from pounding out of my chest. I had no idea what to do. I couldn't burst in on this private moment and reveal that I had heard it all. I couldn't run in like a crazy woman and shout that I would fight for my man. But had he been cheating on me? I wouldn't stand for that.

"Lauren," he said, and sighed.

His ex-wife. Now I really was reeling. I had known she was younger, but Jack hadn't exactly let on that the woman he had been married to was practically a goddess. I was pretty sure every beautiful blonde born in the '80s was named Lauren. I thought of all the Laurens in Caroline's class. *Caroline's class.* I glimpsed myself in the mirror over the chest and suddenly saw myself again as I had for all those years. The lines around my mouth and eyes, the bit of gray starting to peek through at my part line where it needed to be colored. The way the tops of my arms weren't as defined and shapely as they'd once been.

This girl standing in there with Jack was young enough to be my daughter. It didn't matter how much I loved him or how much I fought for him or how much he acted like he loved me. He was a man. His future with her would be the breathtaking, uphill climb where you're full of excitement and anticipation. His life with me would be the screaming and terror on the way back down.

I was trying to figure out if I could sneak out the front door without them noticing me. They were so caught up in the melodrama happening in the living room, I could probably be stabbed to death upstairs, and no one would even hear my screams.

I turned and started toward the door, but when Jack said, "Lauren, I have given you everything you want. Just sign the papers," I stopped.

Sign the papers. The papers?

"But that's just it, Jack. I don't want your money. I want

you. I want the way you always took my hand when we walked and the way you held me close to you at night. I want the way you would look at me across a crowded room and I would know that I was yours. I want to make you poached eggs in the morning and read the paper together. I want—"

As if something from outside of me had taken over, I found myself in the doorway. Lauren's back was to me, but Jack was facing me, and when I cut her off, saying, "You aren't divorced?" they both turned to look at me.

"Who are you?" Lauren asked, as Jack was saying, "Ansley, it isn't like that."

"It isn't like what?" Lauren asked.

All these thoughts were streaming through my mind, fighting to get out. But all I could do was repeat, "You aren't divorced?" I could feel the blush in my face, and I knew I was practically purple by that point.

Before Jack could answer, Lauren said, "Wait a minute. This is *Ansley*?"

I wanted to defend myself in some way, maybe defend Jack. I wanted to say, *You should see me when I'm dressed with my makeup on.* I didn't, of course. I just stood there, mouth agape, like an idiot, trying to make sense of the fact that Jack was still married and that, even more shocking, he was married to this beautiful blond giraffe.

I couldn't stay here. I couldn't hear any more, couldn't process any more.

I turned to walk away, with Jack calling "Ansley!" behind me.

I heard Lauren say, "Jack, let her go."

And in that moment, as my feet hit the wooden front porch, the glass-paned storm door slamming behind me, I had the sinking feeling that since he was still married to her, it was possible that Jack could do exactly that.

emerson: wife material

The first few moments after waking up are always the best of the day. In the silence, the mind heavy with sleep, we can forget everything. We can forget that we helped end our grandmother's life or that our father is dead. We can forget that our mom's fiancé is our sisters' dad and that our entire lives have changed in an instant. We can forget we are fighting with our mother or that we had a moment with our barista the day before that was way too intense for an engaged girl.

I didn't often wake up in the morning with my head still on Mark's chest, but this morning, I did. I must have slept really hard, and he must have, too. It was quite the feat that we got to sleep together at all, but since I wasn't speaking to my mother, it didn't make much sense to go home. Since Mark's mother was sleeping in the room next door, I was going to have to climb out the window later. But it was really no big deal. I had perfected climbing out this window about a decade earlier.

"Only eighteen days until you're mine, all mine," Mark said.

I smiled and stretched, savoring the sight of the sliver of sun that peeked through the crack in the curtains. "Yay!" I said as quietly and enthusiastically as possible.

I didn't want to bring up bad things this early in the morning, but I also couldn't stand the thought of being apart from Mark the day after we got married. Filming started the day after that, so I had to go back to LA to get my ducks in a row.

"Will you please, please, come to LA for a few weeks? Please?"

He kissed my head. "Only if you promise me we can take a proper honeymoon as soon as you're finished filming."

I kissed him on the lips. "I positively promise."

He kissed me again, this time deeper, and I giggled. "Shhhh," he said. "You have to be really, really quiet."

"I can do that," I whispered back.

It was a perfect morning in every way—except, of course, that Mom and I weren't speaking. But I was an excellent compartmentalizer and kept pushing that thought away as soon as it came.

I put on the bikini and white crocheted cover-up I had left on the floor the night before and was getting ready to climb out the window when Mark said, "Meet me at the front door."

"Don't you have to go to work?"

He grinned. "I took the morning off. I thought we could go paddleboarding if you're feeling up to it."

I was feeling up to anything today. Mark and I had talked through the Jack situation, and he, as usual, was very level-headed, which made me feel levelheaded in turn. I hadn't even mentioned the movie, because why would I weigh him down with bad news if I didn't have to? I really felt like I was morphing into wife material.

A few minutes later, as I floated beside Mark on the water-way, making long, smooth strokes with my paddle, he said, "I was thinking it would be really cool if we left the wedding by paddleboard. Like if that was our going-away car."

I wanted to point out that this might be tricky considering I was going to be wearing a wedding gown. But Mark hadn't made one single decision about this wedding, so it seemed maybe it was his turn. Besides, I could change into a white bikini, and that would be really cool and sexy and very movie-star-esque.

"What else?" I asked.

"The only other thing I really want to do is cut the top off a magnum of champagne with a sword when we cut the cake."

I almost lost my balance, I laughed so hard.

"No, I'm serious," Mark said.

I wasn't a parent, but I always heard that you should fight the big fights. That sounded awful to me, but if it was Mark's dream, then so be it.

He nosed his board onto the sandy beach at Starlite Island, and I followed suit, pulling it up on the sand so it wouldn't float away.

I sat down, noting that I was probably the only person in

the world who loved the feel of sand on her rear end. But I did. It felt like summer. And exfoliant. Two for one.

Mark sat down beside me and took my hand. "I get to dance our first dance with you right here, babe," he said, kissing my hand.

"I'm so sorry to interrupt," a girl's voice said from beside me.

I smiled up at a pretty teenager with sun-bleached wavy hair and her friend who stood beside her. They both had on mismatched bikinis. I knew it was in style, but I just didn't get it. Who wanted to look like they had gotten dressed in the dark?

"Could we please get a picture with you?" the other girl asked.

I smiled. "Sure," I said, as Mark exhaled too loudly and too forcefully. I shot him a disapproving look.

"Thanks, girls," I said when they had taken a group selfie and a separate photo with each of them.

Mark stood up and shoved his board out into the water the moment the girls started walking away from us.

"Wait, are you ready to go back already?"

He threw his hands up in the air. "Well, the morning's ruined. Might as well."

I could feel my mouth open in amazement. His morning was ruined because two sweet little girls who were probably dreaming of becoming actresses wanted to take a picture? It took maybe thirty seconds. Probably less. But I didn't feel like getting into it with him. I wanted to rewind to the hand-kiss-on-the-beach part of the day. Was he right? Was it me? Had I ruined our day? Surely not. At least, I didn't think so. Seeing fans was the best part of my days.

We paddled back to the house in silence, and I was caught somewhere between guilt and anger and total and complete disinterest in this situation. But regardless of Mark's feelings about it, this was my life. It wasn't going to change. At least, I hoped it wasn't. I assumed it was only going to keep getting more frequent, God willing.

He held his hand up to help me onto the dock and then pulled my paddleboard up behind him. "I'm sorry," he finally said, while he was spraying off the boards. "I just want you all to myself."

I nodded slowly. "I get that, babe. I really do. But that's not reality."

"Reality is what we choose," he said. "It's what we make it."

Was it? Because I was sure as hell willing his mother to go away, and that hadn't happened yet. I didn't say that, of course.

I didn't want to keep feeling bad or guilty today. So I simply said, "I need to get back to the house. I need to talk to my sisters and figure out what we're going to do about Jack."

He nodded, and I hoped he noticed that I didn't kiss him good-bye.

It will get better once we're married and settled, I reassured myself. *It's all the uncertainty that's making him like this.*

I was good at convincing myself of the things I wished were true. I always had been. But even I had to wonder if that was as misguided as the people who have babies to fix their broken marriages. As I made my way up the front steps, I had to consider that maybe Mark wasn't the problem. Maybe everything else in my life that had gone wrong was clouding my feelings about our relationship, the one thing that I had always known to be right.

ansley: *the* thought

I guess I expected Jack to come after me. I wanted him to, I realized. I wanted him to come find me and tell me that I was the one and that girl meant nothing to him. But I was fifty-eight years old. And I knew that life was more complicated than all that. He loved her. Of course he did. He was married to the woman, for heaven's sake. If you could even call a "Lauren" a woman, that is.

I had had innumerable friends go through divorces that had dragged on for years, way past their love's expiration date. I had never had any reason to feel anything less than adored by Jack, and I knew he wasn't trying to pull a fast one on me. But we had planned a future together down to the nth degree. It seemed like something he should have at least mentioned.

I was standing in the kitchen, staring like a crazy person, trying to decide what to do now. Should I make a cup of coffee?

Go to work? Cry? I felt paralyzed. So I decided to make some pancakes. Pancakes helped everything.

As I was measuring and stirring, Sloane and Caroline walked into the kitchen. I felt my blood pressure rise. I knew they were angry with me, but quite frankly, I felt angry with them—or maybe I was more defensive. I didn't lie to them. They knew their entire lives that Carter wasn't their biological father. That Jack happened to be wasn't really pertinent. I should have told them, but I didn't. And damn, I wasn't perfect all the time. Weren't they old enough to know that?

I looked at them, licking batter off the back of my hand, and turned back to the griddle to ladle out several pancakes. For myself, I guess. I was hoping Vivi would come traipsing in and I could feed her, too.

"Why do I get the feeling that you're mad at us?" Sloane asked.

I didn't respond. If they could ice me out, I could ice them out, too. Let them see how it felt.

"I think she's giving us the silent treatment," Caroline said, "which is ridiculous, because if anyone has a right to be angry, it's us."

That did it. "But Caroline," I said sarcastically, "how can you be angry?"

"What do you mean, *how* can I be angry?" She crossed her arms, so indignant and self-righteous I honestly wanted to smack her. I mean, I would never actually hit her, of course. But I thought it would have felt good right about then.

"Well, if it weren't for Jack, you wouldn't be here," I said calmly and slowly. Then I added, "And then who would the world revolve around?"

Sloane burst out laughing, while Caroline's eyes widened and her mouth dropped.

I had taken her crap for thirty-five years. All the cards were on the table now. No more secrets, no more surprises. This was it, the good, the bad, and the ugly, and if she couldn't handle it, then she could take her moody self and her bad temper somewhere else. I didn't mean that, of course. One day without her had nearly killed me. But I was so worked up over the whole Lauren and Jack situation that I was feeling brazen. It was wildly uncharacteristic.

Even Caroline couldn't help but smile. "The world does revolve around me, doesn't it?" she said lightly.

There was a tap on the back door, and I realized that whoever it was had probably been standing there watching this all play out. I assumed it was Jack. But I caught a flash of blond hair out of the corner of my eye. And I wondered how it was remotely possible that this day could get any worse.

"Who is *that*?" Sloane asked.

"Oh," I said as I opened the door. "This is Lauren. This is Jack's wife."

Lauren raised her eyebrows. I had shocked her. I liked that.

"Ex-wife," Caroline corrected.

"Nope," I said, slamming the door behind Lauren. "Do you like pancakes?" I asked, realizing that my daughters had fled like cockroaches in a spotlight.

Lauren walked by me and into the living room, where she

sat down on the couch without my offering. How rude. Well, she might be a model-esque teenager who had the man I wanted, but at least I had manners.

"I guess we're sitting down," I said under my breath. I sat in a chair opposite her, where I had the water view. Another small victory for Ansley.

I wanted to be mad, but I noticed she had tears in her eyes. And this was her life falling apart here. She was so young I felt sort of maternal toward her, unfortunately. I hated my good nature.

"Do you know that Jack talks in his sleep?"

Before I could stop myself and be a little gentler, I spat out, "I was hearing Jack talk in his sleep before you were even born."

She sucked in her cheeks and closed her eyes, and I knew that had stung.

"I'm sorry," I said softly. "I truly apologize. He's your husband. He's not mine. You have more right to be upset here than I do."

She shrugged. "I let him go, Ansley. I pushed him away and brushed him aside. I wish I hadn't, but I did." She paused. "He never told me about you. Ever. Not once."

That sent actual pain shooting to the spot around my heart, but I supposed I understood it. Talking about exes was kind of childish, and even more than that, it could have opened the door for too much to come out. I had wondered, briefly, if he had told her about us, about the children we had made together, about the role he never got to hold in their lives. I knew now that he hadn't. That, at least, was a relief.

I stopped Lauren. "Look. I don't know what you're getting at—"

"You don't," she said. "You don't understand. Because what I'm trying to tell you is that he never mentioned you. But he talked about you in his sleep all the time."

"So?"

"So, I am lying beside this man in the home we share, studying my diamond, and he is muttering, 'Don't go, Ansley. I love you, Ansley.'" She paused. "I swear to God, the way he would talk about you, the things he would say, I thought you were dead."

I smiled ironically. "Just almost," I said. "You never asked him who he was dreaming about?" I was impressed with her maturity.

She shrugged. "No. I mean, I was over there having my fair share of sex dreams about our hot plumber. We can't control our subconscious mind. It didn't seem relevant at the time."

"So what are you doing in my living room, Lauren?" Part of me didn't want to know, but part of me wanted to get this over with.

"I wanted to tell you myself that I am signing the papers." She gave me a small smile. "I mean, I'm having Jack sign over that gorgeous house to me, and *then* I'm signing the papers."

I felt myself go pale. That was all I needed. Lauren strutting around in her bikini all day in the house next door.

"I'm kidding," she said. "I took the house in Aspen instead."

Great, I thought. *I hate to be cold, and if I never look at a pair of skis again, that is fine with me.*

"You're making the right decision," I said, and I didn't only mean it because her decision gave me what I wanted. "I know I don't know you from Adam's house cat, but what I do know is that if you give up having children for a man, you will resent him for the rest of your life."

I paused, swallowing the lump in my throat. His not wanting children had been the very reason I hadn't married Jack to begin with. It had been the reason I had walked away.

"There is nothing in all the world that is better than the love of your children. However they come to you, whether you birth them or adopt them or whatever it may be, if that's something you want, you shouldn't give up on it."

She cocked her head to the side. "Yeah." She sighed. "I mean, I know you're right. But it's hard—I still love him. I went back out there and started dating this Calvin Klein model, and even though he was so beautiful, I missed Jack anyway. That's really saying something."

I laughed. Jack was a very handsome man, but I would venture to say he could no longer appear on a billboard. "Ah," I said.

"He chose you, Ansley," she said, her shoulders slumping the tiniest bit in defeat.

I put my hands up. "There is no logical reason why he would choose me."

She stood up, rubbed her hands down the length of her dress, and said, "Logic never matters. You know that. Logic tells me to keep fighting, but my gut tells me I've lost."

"I'm sorry," I said. "I honestly am. I don't want to break up a marriage. I don't want to take your husband."

She smiled at me sadly. "Oh, Ansley. You know as well as anyone that he was never really mine."

I shrugged.

"OK, then. I'm off to meet someone with willing sperm."

"Keep in touch," I said, half meaning it, closing the door behind Lauren.

When I turned, I gasped. Jack was right behind me, on his knees. For a split second, I thought he was proposing, but I realized, one, he was on two knees, two, he had already proposed to me, and three, I had made him promise never to propose when my hair and makeup weren't done. Which they now most definitely were not.

"Please don't leave me, Ansley," he said. "I swear I will die. I won't survive. I didn't tell you I wasn't divorced yet because it didn't matter. We had been separated for almost two years, and we weren't divorced because she wouldn't sign the damn papers. It wasn't my lingering feelings for her or because we were trying to work it out. I promise you."

I moved closer to him, and he hugged me around my thighs, which were, I might add, about twice the size and half the tone of Lauren's. Still, I couldn't help but run my fingers through his thick hair.

"I'm sorry," he said. "I am so sorry."

This reminded me of years earlier, when Carter and I had passed Jack on the dock, when Jack's shock at my Emerson-pregnant belly had unwittingly told Carter that Jack was Caroline and Sloane's father. Carter had been so angry at me, and I had been the one, like Jack, on my knees, begging for forgiveness.

So I said what Carter had said to me all those years ago. "Get up. You're too beautiful for the floor."

Jack swept me up in his arms and kissed me, and it felt so right that I couldn't imagine that only a few minutes earlier, I had even momentarily entertained the idea that he could choose someone else.

He carried me up the stairs, and though I never wanted to think about Lauren again, I knew why she loved him. I knew why she wanted him back. He was a passionate man who seemed almost immortal. To be loved by him, truly loved, was more than a woman could wish for, as I was remembering now.

Lying beside him later, in the silence, I asked, "Jack, did you ever think about me?"

"What?" he asked, lazily trailing his fingers up and down my arm.

"All those years we were apart, when you were married to Lauren, when our lives were going in different directions, did you think about me?"

He laughed and rolled over onto his side. I pulled the covers up over my chest, and he pulled them back down. "Ansley, you have been my every thought, my only thought, *the* thought, for most of my life."

I rolled over, facing him. "So why didn't you at least call me? Why didn't you tell me you were getting married?"

"You were very clear about my role in your life. You made it plain that I was to leave you and your family alone and that I was never to contact you again."

"But that's when the girls were young," I whispered. "When Carter was alive. You scared me so badly, Jack. You have to understand that."

"And you have to understand, my beautiful Ansley," he said, as he pushed a strand of hair out of my face and tucked it behind my ear, "that your being afraid of me broke me. Not just a little bit of me. All of me."

I nodded. Of course it had. I understood that. It had broken me, too. I knew the way I acted would make Jack stay away from me, from the girls he wanted to know. I had to get him out of our lives in order to keep our secret. I didn't want to hurt Jack then, and I didn't want to hurt him now. But if I had to do it over again, I would do that same thing.

"So that's why you didn't find me before you got married?" I asked. "Because I had hurt you?"

"No," he said, shaking his head. "Because I was happy—or as happy as I believed I could be without you. And I knew if I even so much as heard the sound of your voice, that would be over."

I smiled and kissed him softly. He pulled me close to him, and I laid my head on his chest.

"Did you really think that I would even for a minute consider going back to her?"

I propped myself up on my elbow and looked at him. "I mean, I won't lie. If Ryan Gosling walked in right now and declared his everlasting love for me, I would still choose you, but it would give me pause."

"It would not," he said, laughing.

"Yeah. You're right. It wouldn't."

"When can we get married?" he whispered.

I thought, *When things are right with the girls*, but I didn't want to spoil the moment.

So, instead, I said, "I love you."

"I love you more."

Sometimes there isn't any more to say.

emerson: a nice tie

You never think of your mother as a real person. I mean, obviously, you know she's a *person*. But it's hard to think of your mother as a human being who has a life and interactions that don't involve the orbit she has always taken around you.

So when Caroline told me about Lauren before our walk that morning—and everything she had heard from eavesdropping on their conversation—it was a bit of a shock to me. It was hard enough to wrap my mind around the fact that my mother could actually be in love with and marrying a man who wasn't my father. To wrap my mind around the idea that she was involved in some sort of seedy love triangle was almost more than I could take.

Caroline whispered, "She was Gigi Hadid gorgeous."

I widened my eyes. That wasn't a term Caroline and I threw around. We had a lot of levels of beautiful in our repertoire. But Gigi Hadid was the highest level a woman could attain.

"And he chose Mom anyway?"

She looked at me, never slowing her pace or the furious swinging of her arms. "I have to think that, really, he chose us. All of us."

I laughed ironically. "You, maybe. And Sloane. His daughters. And Mom, the mother of his children. But he sure as hell didn't choose me. I'm just some poor orphan kid next door."

Even though I could only see her side profile as we walked down the street, I could tell that Caroline was rolling her eyes.

"You're so damn dramatic about everything. He's a sperm donor, Em. It's not like we spent every other weekend and Wednesdays with him and now he's here to reclaim us. We're Mom's grown kids. We're part of the very large package that comes with marrying her."

"Is that your nice way of saying that we're baggage?"

"We are, aren't we?"

"Maybe you are," I said under my breath.

It was a perfect eighty-three degrees, the sun was shining, the birds were chirping, newborn foals were roaming Starlite Island, and I was in such a foul mood I couldn't enjoy any of it. The logical, adult part of me knew that it was stupid to feel like Sloane and Caroline had gotten a replacement father while mine was still dead. But the silly, childish part of me felt like I was an outsider in the real family that Mom, Jack, Sloane, and Caroline had found. Like I was a goose being raised by a family of swans.

When I'd said that to Mark, he had said, "Em, trust me. If

anyone's the swan, it's you." It was the perfect thing to say. I was lucky I was marrying him, despite the fact that his mother refused to leave the living room because the humidity outside "absolutely ruined" her hair. People would kill to spend one day in a place like Peachtree Bluff, and she and her martini wouldn't get off the damn couch.

The day before, I had tried to talk to her, had tried to have a civil moment in time with her, make some small talk. In the midst of my telling her all the details about the cast of *A Tree Grows in Brooklyn*, she had looked at me, as if we had been talking about it the entire time, and said, "Are you pregnant?"

I'm sure I looked at her like she was insane, because she *was* insane. "Um, no. Definitely not."

"Oh, OK," she said, the feathers on today's pale-pink caftan blowing as she whisked her arm like *c'est la vie*.

"Why?" I asked.

"I suppose I assumed that's why you and Mark were getting married."

Fortunately, Mark came in to intervene. "Mom, you should get out of the house today. Go take a walk. Call a friend for lunch. Anything."

She gave him a death stare. "I am absolutely exhausted from my trip. I'll do no such thing."

"A little fresh air might make you feel better," I chimed in.

She looked at me with daggers in her eyes and said, "Is that why you insist on going back to LA? For the fresh air?"

At that point, I stood up, saluted to Mark, and mouthed, *I'm out. Godspeed.*

Just thinking about it now irritated me all over again, making me even more unpleasant on my walk with Caroline.

She broke me out of my thoughts, saying, "We're still sisters, Em. We're still family. Nothing has changed between us."

"Maybe not for *you*," I practically spat.

"We have got to get you acting again," she said. "Give you somewhere to channel all this energy."

I stopped and crossed my arms. Caroline walked a few more paces before she even noticed. Then she turned and crossed her arms back at me.

"What? I'm not being a bitch. You need your creative outlet. It's not a bad thing. It's just reality."

"First," I said, not caring about all the tourists walking down the street, whispering and pointing. They knew who I was, so I definitely should have been behaving better. But sometimes I get to this point where I don't care, and I can't control it. "You are *always* being a bitch, so that's not true. And second, you have been so incredibly insensitive to me about this whole thing. You sit up there on your high horse with your perfect self and your perfect life and look down and judge us all and deem our little problems insignificant. My problems are real, and they are significant."

I stormed off, and after a few minutes, I finally got the nerve to turn around. Caroline wasn't following me. Instead, she was continuing to walk ahead without me. Sisters are important to Caroline, but steps are more important. My anger at her was already burning off. It had been a stupid thing to say. Her life was far from perfect.

But it probably was true that she couldn't understand what I was feeling right now. I had always been the little sister, always been the one who wasn't big enough, wasn't old enough. The one who didn't understand the inside jokes and was left out of the talks about boys. And now I was left out in the worst possible way.

By the time I got home, I had cooled down. I had talked myself down off the ledge. I saw AJ and Taylor out on the dock, in their tiny life jackets, fishing. They were both blond from all the sun and so tan. If anything could make me feel better, it was those two.

"What you doing, dudes?" I asked.

Taylor was scooping minnows with a tiny net and putting them into a bucket. Poor minnows.

"Just fishin'," AJ said. He looked up at me, and I realized he had his goggles on. I made my most serious face to keep from laughing. "Aunt Emmy," he said, as I sat down on the dock, cross-legged. "Do fish love one another?"

I smiled. Taylor was looking at me now, too, rapt with attention.

"Well, sure," I said. "Why do you ask?"

He shrugged.

"Do you love someone?" I asked, putting the pieces together.

Taylor threw his arms around my neck and said, "I love you!" giving me a slobbery kiss right on the lips. I pulled him into my lap and wrapped my arms around him, resting my head on his. He was so adorable.

"I love Caitlyn in my class," AJ said.

I had to bite my lip to keep from laughing. "Why do you love her?"

He cast his line again, thinking, and said, "I love her because she always runs as fast as she can."

"That is a great reason, bud," a deep voice from underneath me said.

"Oh, my gosh!" I gasped. "Adam, you scared me to death."

I looked down and saw that he was sitting in the kayak, almost under the dock because the tide was so low. "I wondered why the boys were out here alone."

"Oh, you know," he said, "they're two and four now, so we just slap a life jacket on them and let them have at it."

We both laughed.

I fished with the boys for a little longer and then walked straight to the guesthouse to avoid seeing Mom. But as I turned down the street, I saw someone even worse walking toward me: Jack. I had been avoiding him, too, because heaven knew he wasn't going to know what to say to me. I thought about turning around, but after a few seconds of rationality, it seemed immature.

I waved and kept looking straight ahead as I passed him.

"Emerson," he said softly.

I had to stop, didn't I?

"I just can't," I said.

He nodded. "I understand. You don't have to do anything. I don't want anything from you."

Well, that sounded nice. Everyone always wanted something from me: to put in a good word with my agent, to critique their audition tape, to appear at their fund-raiser, to endorse their product. The only people who never really wanted anything from me were my sisters and my mom. They let me be myself, and they loved me anyway. And I was shutting them out and acting like an infant because of some perceived slight that, really, none of them could help. I bit my lip to keep from crying. Not because I was sad but because, suddenly, I was all filled up. I wasn't half of Caroline or Sloane's sister. I wasn't less of Mom's child. I wasn't less a part of my own family.

Jack said, "Well, maybe you could come find me when you are ready?"

He was walking away when I said, "Say what you need to say, Jack."

He turned and smiled at me. "Oh, God. I didn't expect that. I have nothing prepared."

I couldn't help but half-smile.

He put his hands in his pockets, jangling his change nervously. "I guess I just need you to know that I wanted to be in their lives, Emerson. I wanted to know my daughters."

If this was supposed to make me feel better, it didn't. It was only accentuating the fact that *they* were his daughters. I was not.

"I approached your mom one day on Starlite Island, when you and your sisters were little. I had planned it all out. But that day, when I approached your mom, I saw you. And I realized that by being a part of their lives, I would mess up yours."

I bit my lip. It was hard to explain how I felt, how this was such a slap in the face, like I was on the outside looking in. I wanted Jack to understand that, but for once, I found myself at a total loss for words.

Jack put his hand on my arm. "This is an impossible situation for me, Em. I don't know how to act or what to do. I know it's too much too soon, but I love you just as much as your sisters, Emerson. In my heart, you have always been a little bit mine because you are your mother's. And in my heart, she has always been all mine. That's how I've always seen it."

It seemed ridiculous when he said it, but to stand there and look at his face, to see in his eyes how fervently he meant what he said, changed something in me that day. I didn't just see Jack, the man in the yard, the one who was marrying my mom. I saw the Jack from thirty-five years ago, the one who sacrificed the most important part of himself for the woman he loved, even though he would never get anything in return.

I've always known in my heart that what makes me a good actress is my empathy, my ability to feel other people's pain and to internalize it. I didn't want to feel Jack's pain right now. I couldn't, and yet I couldn't not. His whole life had been defined by this one big loss. But we both knew that Ansley Murphy chose her daughters over all else. If I didn't get on board, he was in danger of losing everything he almost had all over again. He knew it, I knew it, the trees rustling in the yard knew it. And I had borne enough burdens this summer. I had taken responsibility for one huge thing I could never take back. Was I willing to do that again?

Jack cleared his throat. "I will never be your father. Carter is your father. Carter is Caroline and Sloane's father. I'm just the guy marrying your mom. If you want me to be more, I can. If you don't, I won't."

I nodded. I knew in that moment that I would always, in some ways, feel like a stranger in my own family now that I knew the truth. But this was the hand I had been dealt, and I had to choose how to play it. Did I want to be the one responsible for taking happiness away from Jack, for denying my mother the future that she so desperately wanted, even knowing that neither of them would ever do the same to me?

I cleared my throat and swallowed my tears, making a decision. It was one I knew I would have to continue to make over and over again, every day, until it really felt like it stuck. "Jack," I said quietly. I looked up at him, that face so full of anticipation and worry. I could almost feel how badly he wanted to please me, to make something right that never could be.

"Yes?" he replied.

"Do you think you could walk me down the aisle?"

He put his hand over his heart, and I could see his eyes pooling with tears as he said, "Emerson, it would be the thrill of my lifetime."

I hugged him, and he hugged me back, and I felt his worry dissipate. I felt him relax in the knowledge that he was going to get this second chance after all. I had granted him that. I had given him life when I didn't have to. And I wondered if maybe that would be enough to atone for the death I had caused not twenty feet from the spot where we were standing.

I wondered if when Caroline and Sloane were close to him, Jack smelled like their father, if his scent, that of coffee and Brooks Brothers aftershave, made them feel some certain way, like they shared DNA, like he was half the reason they were on the earth. When I pulled away and saw how he was looking at me, like I was all he had ever wanted in all the world, I wondered if maybe it was possible that one day, Jack would smell like my father, too.

———

IN SOME WAYS, IT wasn't the perfect time for the dresses to arrive. In other ways, it was the absolute perfect time. Sloane and Caroline were waiting for me in the guesthouse when I'd finished talking to Jack, wearing their beautiful couture gowns, standing at full attention on either side of the bed, holding pale-blue hydrangeas cut from Jack's yard that matched the dresses perfectly. They were the same blue hydrangeas from the same bush that Mr. Solomon, Mom's former neighbor, had left for her on the back porch as a peace offering.

In some ways, they were a peace offering now, too.

I smiled when I saw them. I knew they were trying to cheer me up. I put my hand on my heart. "You two look absolutely beautiful."

That wasn't exactly true. Sloane had no makeup on, and Caroline's hair was in this slouchy, messy bun she wore when she hadn't had time to do her hair yet that day. And they were both barefoot, not exactly ready to walk down the aisle. But the dresses were exquisite. They were the perfect shade of pale blue, with the tiniest hint of aqua that would mimic the water without making the whole effect go green.

"Try yours on!" Sloane said enthusiastically. She pointed to my closet, where the gown was hanging in a garment bag. It felt really, really wrong to try on my wedding gown without my mom. But then again, I remembered, I was mad at my mom. Why wait?

Plus, Caroline had already made the decision and started unzipping the garment bag.

"Be careful," Sloane said. "Don't snag the lace."

Mom's dress was hanging conspicuously beside mine. I wanted to see it, but I also wasn't quite ready to part with my anger.

My sisters helped me step into the gown. Sloane zipped me up, and we all stood back from the mirror and admired it. It was made completely of lace and fit my body perfectly. It flowed out starting at about my knees so that I could walk, and it had a small train—which was impractical for a beach wedding, I had to admit. But I didn't care. This was my one wedding, and I wanted a train.

I heard a gasp from behind me, and I turned to see my mom staring at me, her hand over her mouth. When I saw the tears in her eyes, my own started flowing silently down my cheeks like they hadn't since I was a child. She walked toward me and, cautiously, took my hands in hers like Mark would do in just a few weeks.

"I recognize this," she whispered.

"You should," I said, not bothering to wipe my eyes. "It's yours."

Mom's wedding gown had been simple and beautiful but too full for my tastes. Caroline, Sloane, and I had agreed that Mom wouldn't mind if I had her dress remade. It would make her happy that one of her girls wore it, and knowing what I knew now, it actually made the most sense that I would be the one, since she had worn it in her wedding to *my* father.

"I hope it's OK that I had it remade," I said.

She smiled. "It's perfect, Emerson. You look beautiful." She took a deep breath and said, "I know you're upset, and I understand why. I honestly, truly do."

"Mom, it's fine," I said. "Let's please not do this in front of the dress."

She rolled her eyes and kept talking. "I'm not saying I made the right decision or that I did the right thing. But one day, you might feel like you're backed into a corner and that no decision is the right one, that you just have to do the best you can. And on that day, maybe you'll think of me. And maybe you'll try to understand why I did what I did."

I saw Caroline and Sloane exchange a glance in the mirror.

It was like Grammy came to me in that moment. I was back in her bedroom with her that day when she asked me to do the unthinkable. My heart was racing, sweat gathering on my brow.

Because I didn't want to have any part in my grandmother's death. But if I didn't have a part in her death, wasn't I playing a role in her suffering? And wasn't that worse? I knew what Mom meant. I knew what it felt like for your back to be up against the wall, because mine certainly had been that day. I hadn't had any good options. So I chose as best I could and hoped against hope that if there were a God, he would understand, that he wouldn't punish me for choosing my grandmother's comfort, her desire to leave a world that held nothing else for her but pain.

Mom took me away from my thoughts as she continued. "I swear with everything in me, I did it out of love. I didn't even know or have any of you yet, and I already loved you more than anything else in the world. I loved you so much that I was willing to risk everything I had—my marriage, my family, my life, and my world as I knew it—to get you."

"I just want to point out," Caroline interrupted, "that Emerson gets this sweet, mushy talk, and I was snarkily asked what the world would revolve around if I weren't here."

I couldn't help but smile, and Mom smiled back at me.

"I asked Jack to walk me down the aisle," I said. It wasn't forgiving her, exactly. But it was a start.

"I know," Mom said, tears in her eyes again. "I don't think anything has ever meant more to anyone."

I finally dropped her hands. "Well, do you want to see your dress?"

When Caroline unzipped the garment bag, Mom gasped for the second time in only a few minutes. She ran one finger along the lace. "How did you do this?" she whispered.

"It was all Ramon's idea. I took him Grammy's wedding dress, and he said he couldn't make the aged lace white again but that he could dye it and use the best pieces to make your dress. So my lace is old, my dress is new, the family veil is my something borrowed, and you're my something blue," I said.

Mom was crying in earnest now. "Sloane, get me a tissue. I don't want to get makeup on Grammy's dress."

She slipped it on. She looked perfect. Elegant, beautiful. She looked like the mother of the bride. My mother. The one who hadn't always been honest with me, who hadn't always told the truth, but who had loved us before she even knew us. I thought of Grammy again, of how she told me that her biggest regret was the time she'd spent fighting with Mom. "Life is too short to fight with family," she'd said. "Because no matter what happens between you, you will always come back to one another; like the tide returns to the shore. It is the same blood running through your veins. You were chosen to be together."

She didn't know yet that this was going to happen. Or, I had to think, maybe she did know. And maybe that was why this was one of the last pearls of wisdom that she gave me as she got closer to the end. "I'm not the kind of woman to have regrets," she had said, "but I have the gift of perspective. Life is so short, Emerson. It's so very short. Don't waste any of it fretting over things you can't change."

I couldn't change that Jack was Caroline and Sloane's biological father. I couldn't change that Jack was marrying Mom, that the four of them were going to be this whole family that I wasn't a part of. And most of all, I couldn't change that my own dad was gone. He couldn't be there to walk me down the aisle.

But then it hit me that of the three of us, I was the only one who would have any dad to walk her down the aisle. Sloane and Caroline didn't get that, but I had this man right next door who, despite not being my blood relative, loved and cared about me and wanted me to be happy. He wanted to give me away because my real dad couldn't do that. It was a gift, I realized. One that a lot of people didn't get, one that my own sisters didn't get.

And I would take it.

Caroline shrugged at me, and I shrugged back. "We should probably get Jack a Father's Day gift," she said in mock seriousness.

I nodded, giving her a small smile. "Maybe a nice tie."

She caught my eye in the mirror and then Sloane's. And I looked at Mom, her blue eyes locking with my identical ones. "You can't lie to me," she used to say. "You have my eyes." As I looked back at my sisters, something occurred to me for the first time. Their eyes were exactly the same. Brown eyes. Almond eyes. Jack's eyes.

TWENTY-FIVE

ansley: very clean hair

It's funny how we change as we get older, how the things that once mattered to us—like appearances and outside opinions—seem to float away. When I had gotten engaged to Carter, I had been so enamored with his life. As a girl from Georgia, Manhattan had always seemed so glamorous when I visited, and the fact that Carter had really made it there, and that we were going to make our life there, seemed like pure magic. I was as swept away by the idea of our big-city life as I had been by Carter's proposal.

And a reception at the Plaza, in the Grand Ballroom, no less? It was something out of a storybook. I wanted everyone to be there, to see me in my gown. Weddings then weren't like they are now. They were fun and festive, but they weren't over the top. People didn't take out second mortgages on their houses to pay for them. It wasn't a contest to see who could

249

have the most flowers and the biggest bands and the most famous photographers. It was a simple celebration of love. And our simple celebration of love was going to be at one of the world's most iconic hotels. Which, looking back now, I had to admit wasn't simple at all.

Carter and I wanted a black-and-white wedding, a nod to Truman Capote's fabulous balls that were held in that very same venue. And as Carter and I swayed in time to the orchestra for our first dance, I looked around at the hundreds of people who had gathered, swathed in finery, champagne in hand, to celebrate us. And when I looked up, I could have sworn that I saw Eloise herself hiding out in one of the room's massive circular lights, like she did in *Eloise at the Plaza*.

Bathed in lace and held by the man of my dreams, as handsome in his tux as any leading man I had ever seen, I wanted the moment to last forever, wished that the leading man in my life and I could always be so happy. Still, despite my glee, I had to realize that in a lot of ways, nothing about this celebration that I had planned every inch of was actually a reflection of me.

I would be a New York woman now, but in so many more ways, I was still that little girl from Georgia who spent her summers hunting for sand dollars with her toes in the surf.

Now, almost forty years later, I was planning a wedding that I hoped would reflect my daughter and the man of her dreams.

Despite my joy over her upcoming nuptials, my heart couldn't help but feel heavy. Things with my daughters were better, but they were still very strained. And with only one week until Emerson's wedding, I knew I had to fix them fast.

A light rap on my door and an urgent "Mom! Mom!" broke me out of my thoughts.

"Come in," I called, delighted that my sweet Sloane was looking for me. Sloane had mostly been keeping to her house for the past few days.

"Mom," Sloane said, her face pure white. "We have an emergency."

My heart sank. I couldn't handle another emergency. Not now.

I shot up in bed. "What's wrong?"

"It's the boys," she said.

I flung the covers back and had my shoes on before she could even whisper, "They have lice."

I shook my head. "Sloane, for heaven's sake. You had me panicked."

The color was rising up her cheeks now. "Mom, they have *lice.* And Vivi and Emerson babysat for them all day yesterday."

Oh, Lord. This *was* a problem. I sat down on the edge of the bed. "OK. Let's not panic."

What did you even do for lice? None of my kids ever had lice. I was horrified, and if I was honest, I wanted Sloane out of my clean, un-liced house. But then again, if Vivi and Emerson had it, we were all goners.

I heard a shriek from down the hall, and I went running. I burst into Vivi's room, where she was holding her hair out like she had stuck her finger in an electrical socket.

Sloane and I shared a glance.

"Gransley, help me!" she cried.

"It's OK," I said. "Calm down. It's just lice."

"Just lice?" she asked. And then, her voice louder, "Just *lice*? Are you kidding me with this? That is the nastiest thing ever!"

"Well, actually," Sloane chimed in, "lice only infest very clean hair."

Vivi glared at her. "From now on, I will only babysit while wearing a shower cap."

Sloane looked sheepish. "I'm so sorry, Viv. If I had known about the outbreak at Mother's Morning Out, I never would have asked you to babysit."

"Emerson," Vivi whispered now, as if she were saying the name of an apparition.

"Just pray," Sloane said. "It's our only hope now."

Vivi nodded.

Emerson was, um, how should I put this nicely? Worked up about her impending wedding. This might put her over the edge.

"Look," I said. "I'm going downstairs to call Sandra. She told me about this lice service that comes to your house and treats you and makes it safe to come back home."

Sloane scrunched her nose. "You know, Mom, I read that you really don't even need to treat the house, that all that is an expensive racket."

I glared at her. "Sloane, your sister is getting married in one week. One week. Would you like to take the chance that the house is still infested, or would you like to do everything we can to ensure that her entire wedding party isn't scratching their heads down the aisle?"

At that exact moment, another piercing scream came from down the hall. Vivi, Sloane, and I whispered simultaneously, "Emerson."

Good luck, I mouthed to Sloane as I beelined downstairs for my phone. I hadn't been the one to start this, but I knew I'd better fix it—and fast. As I picked up the phone and dialed Sandra, I had a feeling that at least for today, Jack's role in her life and in our family would be the last thing on Emerson's mind.

emerson: prom queen

The wedding was a week away. And the mothers were driving me crazy. Mom was freaking out about every detail. I knew she wanted it to be perfect, but honestly, I just wanted them to handle it and leave me out of it. I needed to look beautiful and relaxed on my wedding day, not stressed and exhausted.

The Duchess had thrown a fit about everything you could imagine—including not being listed on the wedding invitation. Mark had calmly explained, "Mom, you know that the bride's parents are the ones listed on the wedding invitation because they are the ones who are throwing it. You get to be listed on the rehearsal dinner invitation."

She'd rolled her eyes, put her sunglasses down to cover them, dramatically thrown her silk scarf around her neck, and said, "I guess being the mother of the groom means nothing to these people. It's all about the bride, bride, bride."

Mark had put his arm around me and said, "I'm sorry. My mother has trouble not being the center of attention."

"You don't say. Perhaps we should put her picture in the paper instead of my bridal portrait with the wedding announcement."

"Oh, sweetie, you are so selfless," Mark said, before noticing my incredulous look. "Right," he said. "You're kidding. That would be insane."

"Yes," I agreed. "Completely and utterly insane."

But the bright side of all the family drama was that it had brought Mark and me together as a united front more than I could have imagined. And I had no doubt left in my mind that we were meant to be together. We were as solid as they came. And Mark was the sweetest human on earth.

The night before, he had taken me to the ballroom at the Peachtree Bluff Inn, which was almost always empty except for a few special occasions a year, so we were the only people there. He had pulled out his phone to play a song, resting it on a nearby table before grabbing my hand. As he pulled me to him, Jason Mraz started crooning from the speaker, "So I won't hesitate no more, no more."

I had smiled and pulled him closer, kissing him. We had danced to this same song, in this same place, after being crowned prom king and queen.

"It doesn't seem like it was even that long ago, does it?"

Mark shook his head as he led me around the carpeted room like he had eight years earlier. I remembered thinking then that we would be together forever, that this was the first of a lifetime of dances, that one day people would be crowded around watching us do this at our wedding. And now it was almost here. I hadn't been wrong.

It couldn't help but make me think of Grammy. Mom had signed up to chaperone the prom, and I had been horrified. *Horrified*. Ever the patient mother, she hadn't wanted to shirk her responsibilities to the school but also didn't want to add to the long list of potential items I could complain to my theoretical therapist about in my later life. So she had let Grammy chaperone instead. It made me sad to think that Grammy wouldn't see my first dance at my wedding. But she had gotten to see me dance with Mark that night. So maybe that was almost as good.

We hadn't talked about what happened with Grammy, not ever. But this seemed like the right time.

"Mark?"

"Hmmmm?"

"I want to thank you for everything with Grammy, for, um, you know, the pills."

He leaned back and smiled and kissed me. "You know I would do anything for you, Emerson."

I nodded. "If I didn't know it before, then that definitely proved it. That was above and beyond, Mark."

He shrugged. "Well, I would never let someone so special suffer if I could help it. And I could help it, so I did."

I kissed him, and we kept dancing, silently.

I had gone to sleep that night feeling so content. So it startled me how unsettled I felt waking up. *Seven days*, I thought.

A distinct nausea welled up in me. I tried to push it away, but I couldn't help but wonder why I felt so anxious—and itchy. I reached up to scratch my head. When I did, I realized that it was itchy all over. And when I pulled my hand away, there was a bug on my finger.

It took me a moment to realize what was going on. I had lice. I HAD LICE. I didn't know what to do. My heart was racing, my mouth went dry, and I jumped out of my bed like it was what had infected me. I was trying to decide whether I should get into the shower or not when I heard myself screaming at the top of my lungs, "There are bugs in my hair!"

Vivi opened the door and said, very calmly, "It's OK, Aunt Emmy. It's just lice. Gransley is calling someone now to come treat us all."

I peered at her, trying to stay calm. "Did you give me lice?"

A terrified look passed over her face. "No! Of course not!" She glanced from one side to the other and whispered, hand over her mouth, "It was AJ and Taylor."

Of course it was, those little rats. I mean, I loved them. But this was my *wedding*. My wedding was a week away, and I was being attacked by parasites.

I noticed some movement in my bed, which was when I remembered that Biscuit had slept with me. That was great. Just great. I was sure the dog had lice now, too.

Vivi's phone beeped, and she looked at the screen. "The Lice Doctors are going to be here in an hour to get us all fixed up," she said, "but we have to spend the night at the Peachtree Bluff Inn."

"Who said that?" I asked.

"Gransley."

"Why wouldn't Gransley come up here and tell me herself?" I asked.

"Because Gransley is terrified of you," Sloane said, walking through the doorway, looking sheepish.

"You're the one who should be terrified, not her. How could you?" I shouted at Sloane.

She rolled her eyes, which made me even madder.

"How could I what?" she asked, as if she didn't know.

"How could you give me lice the week before my wedding?"

Sloane put her hands on her hips. "Oh, yeah," she said. "This is exactly what I wanted. I was *dying* for there to be a lice outbreak at Mother's Morning Out so that the boys could get lice and I would have to deal with that on top of my husband's physical therapy, becoming my family's breadwinner, and planning *your* wedding. That was not annoying at all and totally in my life plan."

Mom walked in. "Girls, let's calm down. What's the problem?"

I pointed at Sloane and then crossed my arms as she pointed at me.

"She thinks I gave her lice on purpose," Sloane said.

I could feel myself getting choked up for no good reason. Even I couldn't figure out why I was so emotional lately. "You are all trying to sabotage my wedding," I said, turning and walking downstairs.

"Don't touch anything!" Mom called. "The Lice Doctors will be here in less than an hour, and we have to go stay at the Peachtree Bluff Inn posttreatment."

"So I hear," I said.

I texted Mark: *Murphy family lice infestation. Truth time: I have it, so you probably have it, too. Someone has to come fumigate your house. Meet me at PBI in thirty.*

He texted back: *How am I going to get to the Palm Beach airport in thirty minutes?*

Then: *Ohhhhh . . . The Peachtree Bluff Inn.*

Then: *Shit. Is that why my head is so itchy?*

Me: *You might want to warn Her Royal Highness.*

Mark: *Maybe it will go to her brain . . .*

Me: *Wishful thinking . . .*

I went out to my classic childhood cooling-off spot—the dock—to try to put things in perspective. There was something about the breeze and the open water that made everything seem right again. When I heard footsteps behind me, I expected to see Mom or maybe Sloane, though I had the feeling she had had it with me.

But it was Caroline who sat down beside me. She tapped my temple. "What's going on in there?"

I shrugged. "I have lice, and you just touched it."

"Oh, my God," she said, jumping up and moving far, far away from me. She leaned way over, so far that I was afraid she would fall in, to cleanse her hand with salt water.

I smiled sweetly at her. "Vivi has it, too. The whole family has to be treated."

"Special," she said. "What a great start to the day."

"A great start to your day? I have bugs crawling around in my head because my sister is trying to sabotage my wedding."

Caroline cocked her head to the side. "You don't actually think Sloane tried to give you lice to sabotage your wedding? I mean, what is going on with you lately? You're a disaster."

I knew that was true. I knew I hadn't been myself. There were so many emotions swirling around inside me about all that had happened recently. I had always had a hard time facing my emotions, sorting them out. It seemed to be even more difficult for me lately.

I sighed. "There's just so much going on. I'm overwhelmed, and I don't know why."

Caroline laughed. "You're overwhelmed because our life right now is overwhelming. It's crazy. And you're getting married. That's a lot to take in." She paused. "Em, don't get mad . . ."

I looked at her expectantly.

"But are you sure you want to go through with this wedding? Are you sure that Mark's the one?"

I looked out over the horizon. "It's just hard because when I was in LA, all those guys I dated there made me feel like the me I was moving into, the future Emerson, who was living the life she had always wanted. But then Mark makes me feel like the girl I used to be. He makes me feel young and free and alive and happy."

Caroline squinted at me. "And that's how you want to feel?"

"Who wouldn't want to feel like her younger self?"

A smile played on Caroline's lips as she said, "And what about Kyle? How does Kyle make you feel?"

I rolled my eyes. My mouth said, "Kyle makes me feel like I enjoy superfood lattes."

But my heart thought, *The men in LA made me feel like my future. Mark makes me feel like my past. But Kyle? Kyle makes me feel like both.*

⁓⁓⁓

ansley: there she is

I wouldn't wish a lice epidemic—and the bill that comes with it—on my worst enemy. Still, I think it might have been one of the best things to ever happen to my family. After we had all been heat-treated, combed out, coated with an extra-precautionary dose of antilice cream, our hair all up in shower caps and wrapped in towel turbans, we took our lice-free selves out of our lice-infested houses and camped out at the Peachtree Bluff Inn. I warned Tim and Mary Lou, the owners, because I sure didn't want them having a lice problem, but they seemed excited about the entire thing, probably because they would be able to tell future guests that Emerson Murphy had stayed there—and Emerson had been asked by *Town & Country* to take readers on a tour of Peachtree, and she was planning to include the inn in her recommendations. That was probably worth a possible fumigation. Having Emerson back home, and the flurry of street selfies that came along with it, made me realize how well known she was becoming.

As we all sat around the living room of the inn in our shower caps, laughing and reminiscing, I realized that we would be able to get back to this place eventually. My daughters would forgive me one day, because we were stronger than anything life could throw our way.

I looked over at Emerson, snuggled up beside Mark. They were grinning at each other, and I thought maybe this was the right decision. But we don't ever truly know, do we? Sometimes the marriages we think were fated in the stars are annulled the next week, and the ones we think won't last a year end up being the happiest. And I knew that no matter what, whether Emerson's marriage soared or failed, we would make it through that together, too.

Emerson had insisted that everyone get treated, symptomatic or not. So Hippie Hal, who was doing some work for Sloane and Adam the day before was there, reminiscing right along with us.

"My first memory of you two together is when your boat battery died out past the sandbar," he was saying, "and when I drove past and you flagged me down, you were sunburned and beer-drunk and—"

"Hey!" I interrupted. "Don't spread rumors about my perfect Emmy. She would never have been drinking before she was twenty-one."

Everyone laughed heartily, because Emerson had not exactly been an easy child. Her behavior was fair at best.

Hal continued, "But I knew you two were going to make it, because most couples would have been ornery and fighting with each other, but you two took it all in stride."

"We have always been good together," Mark said, kissing the tip of Emerson's nose.

"Speaking of rumors . . ." Caroline said.

"Should Mrs. McClasky be treated for lice, too?" Sloane interjected.

I glared at them. I had specifically told them not to ask him about that.

He smiled sneakily. "Oh, I never kiss and tell."

My girls burst out laughing.

All the kids had been asleep for hours that night when I finally insisted that everyone get some rest. I didn't want this wonderful spell to be broken, but, because Emerson didn't want a bridesmaid's luncheon or a shower, my friends had insisted on throwing a party for her the next night with our fifty favorite friends. And before that, James was throwing a birthday brunch for Caroline.

I didn't want anyone exhausted or hungover. And fortunately, if the signed guarantee I held from the company was to be believed, we were all lice-free now. I had never had lice to begin with, of course. But I wasn't one to argue with a nervous bride the week before her wedding.

I barely slept at all that night, feeling as unsettled about the party that would transpire the next night as I was by the summer storm that had begun brewing after dinner and set in around midnight.

When I heard a key in my door, I wasn't even concerned. I looked over at my clock, which read 3:11 a.m. I figured Jack couldn't sleep, either.

But when I flipped the bedside lamp on and reached for my glasses, I realized it wasn't Jack at all. It was Kyle.

"Um, hi," I said. "Do you realize this is my room?"

He sat down in the small upholstered armchair across from my bed and sighed. "She's really going to do it, isn't she?" he asked, which was when I realized that Kyle, whom I had never seen with a cocktail, was a little drunk.

"Kyle, how did you get my room key?"

"Tim and Mary Lou were asleep, so I made myself one."

"Ah," I said, disturbed that pretty much anyone could figure out how to do that.

I got up, resigning myself to the fact that I was not going to sleep tonight. Wouldn't be the first time, wouldn't be the last.

As I sat down in the other upholstered club chair, I heard, "Mom, for heaven's sake. Anyone could walk right into your room," as Caroline pushed through the doorway, Sloane behind her.

Caroline stopped so quickly when she saw Kyle that Sloane ran right into her. She looked from Kyle to me and said, "What is going on here?"

I couldn't help but laugh. "Kyle and I are having a torrid love affair. Didn't you know?"

"I sure as hell didn't know," I heard Jack's voice call from the hardwood-floored vestibule that served as an entrance hall for the suite.

He sauntered in, in his white undershirt and Johnnie-O pajama pants. He pointed at Kyle. "You'd better keep your hands off my girl."

Kyle put his hands up in defense. Sloane and Caroline were already perched in my bed, under the covers. Sloane was crunching on some sort of cracker. Those crumbs were going to feel great—if I ever got to get back in the bed, that is.

Jack was rustling around the minibar and came back with coffee mugs full of wine for everyone.

He sat in one of two small chairs that accompanied the tiny dining table on the other side of the bed. Then he said, "So what's going on?"

"I think Kyle and I were having a private talk."

Kyle shook his head. "There's no such thing as a private talk with a Murphy. If I tell one, you all know anyway."

That was true.

He took a sip of wine and hiccupped. Oh, God. Now we really were in trouble.

"I'm sorry," he mumbled. "Too many Starlite Starlets."

"I'm sorry. What?" Caroline inquired.

"I guess Emerson never told you I named a cocktail after her in LA."

Sloane sat straight up. "Back the hell up. You knew Emerson in LA?"

"Sloane, language," I said half-heartedly.

Kyle nodded sadly. "Yeah. She walked into my coffee shop in LA one morning, and I saw her, and I was like, *There she is.*"

I think we were all speechless.

"Not *There she is, Emerson Murphy*, because no one knew who she was then anyway. I was like, *There she is, the girl I've been waiting to spend my life with.*"

"And now she's marrying someone else," Jack said, nodding. "Yup. Been there, man."

I smiled sadly at Jack but immediately turned my gaze back to Kyle. This news had me reeling.

"So how did you name a drink after her?" Sloane asked.

"We had drinks, I thought of it, and the bartender put it on the menu. I was so sad, because I had just met her, and I knew that I was moving the next day, but when she mentioned Starlite Island, I knew that fate would somehow bring us back together. When I walked out of Ansley's guesthouse at the beginning of the summer, and there she was, I knew this was the universe giving me a second chance. Finally."

"Only that's what Mark thought, too," Sloane said.

Jack got up and poured more wine into Kyle's cup.

"I think he's had enough," I said, giving Jack a look.

Jack shook his head. "That's what you don't understand, Ansley. There isn't enough."

"Have you told her how you feel?" Sloane asked.

Kyle shook his head sadly. "It doesn't matter. I love her, but she loves Mark."

"Wait," Caroline said, as thunder crashed so loudly it sounded like it was inside the room. "You *love* her?"

"Are you sure?" I asked, my heart racing. "Because if you really mean it, that's a big deal."

"Of course I'm sure. Do you think I would be this upset if I weren't sure?" He smiled off into the distance and said, "As my main man AJ says, she always runs as fast as she can."

I laughed. That was so cute. Then I nodded. "She does, doesn't she?"

"That's why I'm here," Kyle said. "I need your advice."

"It's too late," Jack said. "You can't tell her now."

"What?" Caroline practically spat.

"You tell her," Sloane said, almost frantically. "This is your last chance. This is it. She's going to be married next week, and she needs to have all the information before she makes that commitment."

Everyone turned to look at me. I was the mother, so my vote carried the most weight. The part of me that had paid for a wedding, most of which was nonrefundable, would rather Kyle not tell Emerson. The part of me that always felt this weird electricity between them, that had always felt like she smiled more when he was around, thought she ought to know. Although, to be honest, I didn't think it would matter. Her heart seemed pretty set on Mark.

I shrugged. "All I can say is follow your heart."

Kyle shot up.

"No, no, no!" I shouted.

He sat back down.

"Follow your heart when you're *sober*. You only get one chance. It better be sincere."

"Just please let me be the one to decide," Kyle said. "Please don't tell her."

Caroline laughed. "I'm pretty sure none of us would touch that with a ten-foot pole."

Kyle nodded. "OK," he said, sighing. "I'm going to go home now and pray your treatment worked and I don't get lice."

Sloane held up two crossed fingers as Kyle left the room.

"Caroline, you had to have known about Kyle and Emerson," Sloane said, once the door had shut behind him.

Her eyes widened. "Hand to God, I had no idea. She never said a word about it."

"Why is she so tight-lipped about everything?" I wondered aloud.

Jack laughed incredulously. "Gosh, what a mystery . . ." He got up from his chair. "I came over here because I couldn't sleep, but I feel like this might be a Murphy woman kind of thing."

"No," I whined. "Don't go."

"You should stay," Caroline said. "Honestly."

Sloane added quietly, "You're family, too."

Caroline had said that same thing when we were spreading my mother's ashes on Starlite Island. But now those words carried a totally different weight.

Jack smiled and sat back down, and I could tell his heart was about to burst in two. So was mine.

We talked for hours, until the sun began peeking through the curtains, and I crawled back into bed with Sloane and Caroline, and Jack lay down on the couch, all of us hoping for a couple of hours of sleep. That would be enough to get us through.

If only Emerson were here right now, I thought as I drifted off, *everything would be perfect.*

emerson: fly

I woke up slowly, Mark beside me, and the first thing I did was frantically ruffle my hair. No itch. No lice. Thank God. And then I remembered. Our first party of our wedding week was happening today! And despite how conflicted I'd been lately, I felt nothing but pure joy. I kissed Mark's chest and sprang out of bed to look out the window. The thunderstorms of the previous night had burned off into a beautiful, sunny morning.

I grabbed my phone and sank lazily back into bed, realizing that I had four whole hours to catch up on social media and email until Caroline's birthday brunch. I didn't blame her, because James had planned it, but, I mean, really? She always had to have a little bit of the spotlight. Well, I *was* having a party on her birthday. But whatever. You could really see both sides of that one.

My first email was from my agent. The subject line said, *Entertainment Now is stupid.*

I felt my stomach drop. The Edie Fitzgerald movie was coming out next month, and the first reviews were starting to come in. I opened the review link my agent had sent, scanning the article until I saw my name and then the words that stuck: *very little substance.*

My heart sank. Sometimes I felt angry or mad or wanted to throw my phone across the room. Today I felt defeated.

I closed my eyes and nudged the man sleeping beside me. "Mark," I said, "I just got the worst review."

He opened one eye. "If you would quit, you wouldn't have to deal with that anymore." I swear he was snoring heavily again before he'd even finished the sentence. He'd had enough beers the night before that he'd probably be out for a while.

I fished my bikini and a cover-up out of my bag, now fuming not only about the review but also about the fact that Mark couldn't be supportive for one damn minute.

Things had been so bad with my mom lately that I thought I might ask her to come with me. I knew she'd be awake. And I knew she was feeling guilty about everything, so she'd be extra-supportive, too. I got the key to her room out of the pocket of the shorts I'd been wearing the day before. I walked the two doors down, slid the key into the lock, and tiptoed in. Maybe it was because of the review or maybe it was because of what I was seeing, but I felt like I had been punched in the stomach. Mom, Sloane, and Caroline were asleep in her bed, with Jack on the couch beside them. The four of them. The little family.

I swallowed and closed the door silently behind me.

A few minutes later, I was sitting on the dock, ruminating. Bad reviews. No family. The mother-in-law from hell. A totally unsupportive fiancé. I was trying to focus on the positive, but I couldn't help but feel my life was falling apart. I had to wonder if maybe I was making all the wrong decisions, if I shouldn't scrap the life I had and figure out something else. Maybe Mark was right. Maybe it was time to come back to Peachtree Bluff for good. Although here, every other second was a reminder of Jack and Mom.

I heard footsteps behind me, and I didn't turn. If it was Mom, I didn't want to talk to her. It occurred to me that many of the most important moments of my life had happened on a dock—bad ones like this, sure, but mostly great ones. I learned to swim, learned to smoke a joint, took my first sip of beer, had Mark propose to me.

I couldn't see him, but all of a sudden, I knew who was there.

"They make it look so easy," I said, looking out at the dozens of birds in front of me. They all clumped together, periodically diving down for fish, and then, in one smooth motion, flying away.

He sat down beside me, his bare feet trailing in the water. Mine wouldn't be able to do that until high tide. I looked at him, at the line of sweat around the bottom of his brown hair, which was slightly curled from the humidity. He was wearing an oxford with the sleeves rolled up to the elbows, paper-thin from being washed a million times, so soft that you could only dream about having it to sleep in every night. He pulled it off over his head and threw it behind him on the dock, revealing a tan, toned abdomen. The way he did it was totally unselfconscious.

I envied that, how sure of himself Kyle was, how he always seemed to know right where he was going.

"It's a wonder, isn't it?" he said. "There's so little effort there. They just fly."

That's how I'd thought it would be for me, when I first decided to leave Peachtree to become an actress. I know it sounds so naive, but I was eighteen and beautiful and free-spirited, and I thought I would go to LA and become a star and it would be perfect. It would be easy. It was my destiny.

"I have worked so hard, Kyle," I said. "I mean, I still am. I feel like I'm begging for every scrap of food they'll throw me under the table. And yet somehow it doesn't feel like it amounts to all that much."

Kyle studied my face, like he did so often. Again, totally unselfconsciously. I could never hold someone's stare for that long without looking away, without feeling like I was invading his personal space.

"What are we really talking about here, Em? Because the woman I've watched on that screen is alive. She is in her element. She isn't clawing or scraping." We both looked up as another one of those birds took off and flew high into the sky. Kyle pointed. "That. That was you."

I bit my lip to keep from smiling. He wasn't wrong. Acting, becoming someone else, playing a part, was where I felt most alive. It was the other stuff that was hard. But I had to admit that it was exponentially easier than a couple of years ago. And there was no telling where this new part would lead. I knew it would be big. Even so, there was a lot of bad that came along with the good in this job, as there was with most things in life.

"I got a bad review today, and they always throw me."

"Here's a good one for you," he said. "I think you are the most amazing woman I have ever known, and I think you act beautifully."

I smiled and bit my lip, looking down at my feet, trying to keep the tears from coming down my cheeks. Why was the wrong person always saying the right words?

"You can tell me," he said. He took my hand and put it on his chest, on his heart, making mine beat faster. It was so warm and the tiniest bit damp from the heat. "You have to feel the power in saying your truth out loud."

"You were right," I whispered. "A few weeks ago. You were right. Mark and I will never have what Sloane and Adam have or what Caroline and James have or what Mom and Jack have." I felt the tears welling up in my eyes. "He wants something I can't give him," I said, my voice breaking. "He wants me to be someone I'm not."

Kyle scooted close to me and put his arms around me until my tears were mingling with the layer of perspiration on his chest. And though it was hard not to feel attracted to someone so hot holding you so close and resting his head on yours, really, what I felt was safe.

My heart was pounding, and I realized I wasn't crying anymore. Instead, I was only thinking about what might happen if I moved my head up an inch, if I put my mouth on Kyle's. I had done it before. What if I did it again? I knew I was engaged. I knew it was wrong. But I had this feeling deep inside like this kiss would solve all my problems, be the answer to all my prayers. It wouldn't, of course. But I was a pro at making these mistakes.

Kyle squirmed, slipping his arm underneath my legs and standing up like I weighed nothing. My arms were around his neck, he was holding me like he was going to carry me over the threshold, and our faces were so close that I knew this was it. This was the moment. I knew it, and he knew it, and I couldn't hold myself back any longer. I had to kiss him. But as I leaned in, I felt myself flying through the air, and right before I hit the water, I realized it: he had thrown me in, that bastard. The water felt cold and refreshing and just salty enough. I felt a splash beside me, and as we both came up for air, Kyle and I were laughing.

Laughing like children. Laughing like I hadn't laughed in a long time.

I treaded water with my feet and leaned my head back to make my hair trail perfectly down my back in one long, straight line. When I was little, it used to make me feel like a mermaid.

"You are perfect, Kyle," I said. "Why haven't you found someone to settle down with?"

Kyle shrugged. "Oh, you know . . ." He trailed off.

"Just waiting to find the right one?" I filled in for him.

He shook his head. "No, Em. I'm waiting for her to find me."

TWENTY-NINE

ansley: starlite sisters

When I woke up that morning, the first thing I did was the same thing I did every morning: I looked out the window and thought about how incredibly lucky I was to live in such a beautiful place. I was so distracted by the sun and the glittering sea, which is always most beautiful after a storm, if you ask me, that it took me a few moments to realize that the person I was watching hug Emerson on the dock wasn't Mark. It was Kyle.

I held my breath as he picked her up and threw her in the water. Had he told her? They were both laughing, but that was all I could see. Not that I thought she would call things off with Mark under any circumstances. But honestly, this was Emerson. She was impulsive. Who knew what she would do? I couldn't wait to test the waters at Caroline's brunch.

She was so sullen when we all gathered to celebrate my firstborn's birthday that I had to assume he had told her, that she was grappling with a major life decision. I wanted to help, but I presumed if she wanted my help, she would have told me.

James had set up a gorgeous bar on the huge lawn of the house that he technically owned, even though Sloane and Adam were currently living in it. Ellie Mae the goat, who had become a treasured family pet, had to be tied up in the yard to keep her from eating the provisions at the Bloody Mary bar.

I did wonder why there was only a bar. But then he said, "Actually, guys, we won't be eating here."

The twelve of us dutifully followed James like baby ducklings behind a mother duck. We started down to the docks, and I looked at Jack, assuming that we were going to the boat, but he shrugged.

But as James led Caroline aboard a pristine Hinckley Picnic Boat, I realized that we weren't boarding Jack's boat after all. Three girls in matching white dresses were fussing over a huge spread of food on a table that had been set up across the stern, and as I stepped over onto the boat's deck, James pulled Caroline to him and kissed her head. "Happy birthday, baby."

She smiled up at him. "Brunch looks amazing. Thank you for going to all this trouble."

"No, no," he said, laughing. "The brunch isn't the present. The boat is."

Caroline and I gasped in unison.

"We can keep it here or in the Hamptons. Wherever you want. I thought it was high time you had a boat of your very own."

Caroline kissed him and smiled. "James, that is the most thoughtful thing you've ever done for me."

I agreed. It was extravagant, sure. But it wasn't really about that. It was more that James had put so much thought into getting something that Caroline would really enjoy. It wasn't another piece of jewelry to adorn her; it was something she would truly use.

As a mother, that meant a lot to me, but not nearly as much as when I heard Caroline say, "Oh, my God. The *name.*"

"The name?" I asked.

"*Starlite Sisters,*" Caroline said quietly, pointing to where it was painted in beautiful script on the boat's stern.

James kissed her again. "I figured this boat would really be yours, Sloane's, and Emerson's, so it seemed like the right choice."

Caroline put her hand to her heart. "Honest to God, James, I've never loved a present more."

I was close enough to hear him say in her ear, "I've never loved a person more."

They weren't all good moments between these two. The damage that had been done cut deep. But this was one of the sweetest things I'd seen in a long, long time.

I put my arm around Emerson and said, "I am so excited for tonight."

In typical mother fashion, I was worried that my eldest daughter's extravagant birthday would take some of the shine away from my baby girl's prewedding celebration. It was too late to call it an engagement party, really. But in essence, that was what it was.

She pursed her lips and said, "Your sleepover with your real family looked fun last night," and pulled away from me.

Great. "Emerson," I called behind her, but she was already on the other side of the boat, cuddled up to Mark. At this point, I figured it had to mostly be for show. She couldn't honestly think they were my real family and she wasn't. But oh, my Em. She had always had a flair for the dramatic. It actually surprised me that she didn't have a whole mantel full of statuettes. There was no point in forcing her to talk about it. She was my child who had to work things out in her own time.

Sloane was scolding Taylor and AJ as they chased each other around the table, and for a heartbeat, I couldn't help but understand how Emerson felt. These grandchildren were biologically mine and Jack's. That had to hurt.

Jack handed me a plate overflowing with crepes and eggs Benedict; thick, crispy bacon; and a salad of dragonfruit, strawberries, and kiwi.

"Thank you, sweetheart," I said. "But you know I'll never be able to eat all of this."

"Oh, I know," he said, his mouth full. "This one is mine. But I thought I would look like less of a pig if I pretended we were sharing it."

Caroline was sitting in the captain's chair with Preston on her lap, who was pretending to steer. It took my breath away to think that seven entire months had gone by since these girls had first come home to me, since my Caroline had been as hurt as I had ever seen her. It made me think that maybe time could heal this latest wound. It had healed all the others.

It also reminded me that next month, Carter, my husband and my love, would have been gone for sixteen years. Sixteen years since the world had changed. We had moved forward—my family, the country. We would never be whole in the same way we were before those towers fell, and I knew that didn't only mean me or my family or those who knew the victims. It meant all of us, the citizens of this country, who, when it really mattered, when our backs were to the wall, could join together in one united pulse, a voice singing a song that broke all of our hearts and yet, at the same time, put us back together again.

I walked into the cabin to find Sloane alone.

"AJ had to use the bathroom," she said, making air quotes. Toddlers were endlessly fascinated by new bathrooms, and I could imagine that this one was pretty novel and exciting.

I could see Adam outside, laughing with Jack. "He seems like himself again," I said quietly.

Sloane nodded and smiled, and for the first time in a long time, I sensed that it was an actual smile, a real one. "He's so strong, Mom. He's getting better every day." Tears gathered in her eyes. "I am so blessed to have him here. I can't believe it."

I smiled at her, and she continued. "He thinks he's ready to start talking about the future. For a while, he said he wanted to stay in the Army, that he would serve in some other way. But now he says he can't bear to be behind some military desk if he can't be in the action. He thinks it would kill him."

"And you?"

Her eyes locked with mine. "I know it would kill him. And I just got him back."

I felt that lurch in my stomach that this was really none of my business, but it worried me anyway. Adam had planned a career in the military, and I was fine with him now choosing a different path. But he had gone to only one year of college. What would his future hold? Of course, between her art sales at Sloane Emerson and Sloane Emerson New York, Sloane could support her family—and certainly while she was living for free in Caroline's house.

"I can see something starting to shift in him," Sloane said. "I know when he was finally rescued and going through the worst days of his treatment and PT, he felt trapped, but now, in Peachtree, it seems like he's starting to feel free." She paused. "I know it seems weird, but I remember that feeling."

I nodded. Growing up in a small Southern town, I used to feel a bit under a microscope. It wasn't all bad. I was a good girl who made good grades, so there was a bright light that shone on me, for sure. But there was also that keen awareness that people were always watching me.

For me, moving to New York was freedom. No one knew me. No one was watching. I could succeed or fail as I saw fit, and no one was commenting on it or even noticing. But I realized in raising my girls there that their story would be quite the opposite. By the time they were born, we had friends and a church, schools, and sports. We had a community who was watching their every move, waiting to talk about what they did right or wrong.

But when we moved to Peachtree Bluff, life became different for them. Their Peachtree Bluff was my New York, a clean slate where no one knew who they were or what they had done. No one had seen them take their first steps or heard stories about how they refused to eat mashed peaches or washed their hair with finger paint. No one knew the exact time and place of Sloane's first kiss or knew the name of Caroline's homecoming date or had seen Emerson in her first stage production.

So I understood what Sloane meant about a clean slate for Adam and for her family. Sometimes it's too hard to go back to an old life that will be forever altered.

I told Sloane all of that and said, "You know, in a lot of ways, places are just places. The South and the North aren't really all that different."

"Well," she replied, "Georgia is the Empire State of the South, after all."

I raised my eyebrows. "Really? That's a thing?"

She nodded. "It is indeed."

Jack walked in and looked around. "I really need to upgrade," he said. "This makes my boat look like it's ready for the burn pile." Then his eyes widened. "Speaking of boats, I have a present for Vivi. I didn't want to steal anybody's thunder, but it is her twelfth birthday tomorrow, and I thought she deserved something special."

I leaned into his side, and he put his arm around me. He was the best man.

"Emerson saw us all asleep in my room this morning," I said.

"Uh-oh," Sloane said. "That couldn't have gone well."

I shook my head. Jack and I had been going through our

calendars earlier that morning, trying to pin down a date for our own nuptials. Since Emerson was basically having the wedding we had talked about, we decided to get married just the two of us and then have a nice dinner with our families afterward.

"Jack," I said now, "I'm so sorry. I know we were planning earlier, but I think we need to put off setting a date until I can make things right with her. I don't want our marriage to be the source of this unhappiness."

For the first time in a long time, I couldn't read his expression. "Ansley, look," he said, "I'm fine with being fourth. I get it. I will always come after your girls, and I am good with that. But if we are going to be together, you have to be willing to fight for me the way I have always fought for you. And if you can't do that, then I'd rather know now."

As he turned around and walked out the door, I thought about what I had put him through over these past six months. Not wanting to be together because of the girls. Then not wanting to introduce him to the girls. Then, when we were finally giving this thing a shot, breaking up with him because Adam was MIA and Sloane needed all my attention. He took the backseat to them regularly, and he handled it with ease. I guessed this was the tipping point for him.

I sighed and turned to say something to Sloane and realized that Emerson was standing there, too, holding AJ's hand, looking white and not in the bridal way.

I bit my lip. "I didn't know you were there."

She didn't say anything but walked past me, too. "Great," I said to Sloane. "That's just great."

"Gransley!" AJ said, with so much excitement that it took my mind off what was going on. "I got to go potty on a boat! It was so fun!"

I scooped him up onto my hip and kissed his round cheek, as ripe and juicy as a fresh peach. "I love you so much," I said.

"I love you, too, Gransley."

Finally, someone who wasn't mad at me.

Vivi ran into the cabin. "Gransley, Gransley, you have to come see what Jack got me for my birthday!"

I couldn't even imagine, but as soon as I walked outside, I saw it. I gasped for the second time that morning and put my hand over my mouth, scrambling onto the dock.

"Jack," I said, "is this the one?" The night Jack and I had met, we kissed for the first time standing in his tiny thirteen-foot Boston Whaler.

He nodded, reaching his hand out to me. As I stepped into the boat, now perfectly restored with new teak and a new engine, I let myself, for a moment, be that fifteen-year-old girl again, the one who had met Jack at the sandbar party, who had stayed late with her friends, who had been so swept away by that boy from the second her eyes met his.

"I'm sorry," he whispered. "I know you want everything to be perfect. It's just that I only want *you*. Under any circumstances."

It wasn't a moon tide. And it wasn't the sandbar party, but I leaned into Jack and kissed him right there, in the broad daylight, where everyone could see, even my own family. The birds were chirping instead of the cicadas humming, but either way, this man, this kiss, these sounds, this had become, for me, the cadence of summertime. And I vowed right then and there to make sure that no matter what else happened, Jack knew he was my priority. What he wanted mattered.

"September 22," I whispered, as I pulled away from him.

Jack smiled and nodded.

"That's the day I want to marry you," I said. "September 22 is the harvest moon, and I think we should get married underneath it."

Jack teared up as he kissed me again. "September 22," he said. "The day I've been waiting for since I kissed you on this boat for the very first time."

I heard a screech from the *Starlite Sisters*. I looked up to see Caroline wrestling a magnum of Veuve from James.

"But we have to christen the boat," he was saying.

"You are not smashing that bottle and ruining the finish on this perfect boat."

"Forget the boat," Emerson said. "You're not wasting all that Veuve."

She hoisted it onto her hip and handed it to Mark. "There, honey," she said.

He kissed her softly. "You're going to let me do it? Spear the magnum with the sword?"

She nodded. "I was hoping you would do it tonight instead of at the wedding, since this is sort of our kickoff."

That clever, clever girl.

"September 22 is going to be the best day of my life," Jack said in my ear.

I would drink to that.

THIRTY

emerson: a love like that

I still remembered the morning of September 11, 2001, like it was yesterday. I was a bundle of excitement, prancing around the house in my angel costume. For some unknown reason, Mom had finally decided to let me act, even though she had been so against it for years. I had gotten the starring role of the littlest angel in the school play. I straightened my halo one more time before I walked into the kitchen, where, as usual, it felt like more was happening than on all the streets of Manhattan combined.

I thought Caroline looked so cool in her lace-up jeans and popcorn shirt that were all the rage. Mom was saying, "Take the eyeliner off, right now," and Sloane was saying, "Mom, I totally forgot that I have to take two dozen cookies for the field trip today, and I told them you would chaperone."

She sighed. "After Emmy's play. We're all going to Emmy's play first."

That was when my dad came in and swept me up off the ground and said, "We sure are." I gave him a big kiss on the lips and threw my arms around his neck. "I love you, my little angel," he said. "And I'm so proud of you."

"I love you, too, Daddy."

Then he kissed Caroline's cheek and said, "I love you, too, even if you're wearing too much makeup."

And he kissed Sloane's cheek and said, "And I love you, and I will bring the cookies for your field trip to the play so Mom doesn't have to do that."

Mom put her hand over her heart and said, "My real-life Prince Charming."

He winked at her, pulled her close, and kissed her on the lips. "You, my darling . . . I may love you best of all."

"Hey!" I protested.

"Not as much as I love you," Mom said. She kissed him one more time and then went back to making sandwiches and packing backpacks and cleaning up breakfast. I remember thinking then that I wanted to be just like my parents when I grew up. I wanted to find a love like that, a marriage like that. I wanted to have a home and kids and a family who loved one another, who created mass chaos in the mornings.

"See you in a couple of hours," Daddy said. "Break a leg, Em!"

Those were the last words my father ever said to me. That had to mean something, didn't it? At least, it did to me. It was those last words I heard echoing in my mind when I boarded a plane to LA instead of going to UGA. It was what I heard when

I spent all my tips on acting lessons and endured the humiliation of the worst parts imaginable because I believed that they might lead to something bigger. I always believed that my dad was leading me, that he was guiding me down the right path. He had wanted me to act, hadn't he? Could there possibly be any other reason those had been his last words to me?

It was almost as if I could hear my late father's voice in my ear now, saying, "Break a leg, Em!" as I stood in the guesthouse bathroom getting ready for my engagement party.

I had thought that after years of auditions and getting parts and really putting myself out there, I was beyond jitters. But my hands were shaking so badly I could barely get my earring in. Caroline had surprised me that morning with a huge pair of mother-of-pearl flower earrings, which were the only accessory I needed with my loose bun and white maxi dress.

"I'll help you," Caroline whispered, putting the earring in my ear.

"Did you feel like this?" I asked.

She shrugged. "Honestly, no, but look where that got me. I don't think nerves are a bad thing."

"It's like it's real now, you know? We're going out there in front of all our family and friends, and there's no turning back. This is actually happening."

Caroline smiled. "Hon, I've spent the past two months doing nothing but work on this wedding. There's no turning back now, for more reasons than one."

"Speaking of," I said, "were you able to get that flower crown that Vivi wanted?"

Caroline zipped my dress. "Em, it's all under control." She raised her eyebrow. "Also, I don't know where she ever got the idea that smoking would keep her from getting boobs and drinking would make her hair fall out, but I totally love it."

I smiled, feeling calmer now. "Aunt extraordinaire and Grade-A liar."

"Thanks for doing that for me," she said. "I owe you."

My eyes widened in surprise as I applied my pink lip gloss. "Wow. You owe me? That's pretty major."

She laughed. "OK, how about you owe me a little less for all the years I paid for you to live in LA?"

"Ah," I said. "That's more like it."

Caroline held her hand out, and I gave her the lip gloss. As she applied it, she cut her eyes at me in the mirror. "Could you please do one more thing for me?"

"Maybe."

"Cut Mom some slack. She's doing the best she can."

"Is she?"

Later that night, a display from another mother would lend me an entirely new respect for mine.

IT WAS THE PERFECT night for an engagement party at the Yacht House. The humidity had broken, the storm the night before had cooled things off a few degrees, and the sun was making its radiant descent. The huge barn doors were open to reveal an unobstructed view of the creek and Starlite Island across the waterway. As if they had been hired out for the party, the new foals on the island were frolicking merrily.

The exterior of the Yacht House was white clapboard like many of the houses around town, with a steeply pitched roof. The interior of the space was made completely of raw wood and exposed beams—a little bit rustic and austerely beautiful. Mom's friends had had three huge chandeliers brought in to hang from the ceilings, and tall cocktail tables were adorned with arrangements of the largest pink and white peonies I'd ever seen. Light from the votive candles around them flickered in the reflection of the vases. The glamour juxtaposed with the rustic vibe was stunning. And though I was intent on holding a grudge, I had to realize that my mom had done this. It had her mark all over it. And I realized that Caroline was right. She had done her best. I felt myself soften toward her.

The band was set up off to the side, so as not to obstruct the view of the space, and as we smiled and laughed and said our thank-yous, Mark didn't let go of my hand even once. He must have sensed how nervous I was.

We snuck out onto the deck for a moment to steal a kiss and a sip of a cocktail. "Do you think they'd let us dance?" he asked.

I laughed. "It's our party, and we'll dance if we want to." I smiled at him, and for the first time in a while, I really saw him. No, Mark might not have totally understood me or the life I wanted. And I might not have totally understood why he couldn't give in and give that life to me. But he loved me. And I loved him. It had always been so. And after next week, it would continue to be so forever.

The band abruptly stopped in the middle of a song, and as I heard a slurred "Excuse me, excuse me," I could feel Mark's body tense beside mine.

"Oh, God," he said. "We have got to get her off that stage."

As I walked back through the door, I felt my stomach sink. There was the Duchess, in all her glory, in a form-fitting white gown. She looked amazing, if not terribly overdressed and like she was trying to take focus away from the bride—which, let's face it, she was. At least that was one fewer white gown she could potentially wear to the wedding. When she and Mom had been coordinating outfits for the ceremony, she told her she was wearing pale pink.

"So pale pink that it's actually white?" I had asked.

Mom had laughed. "We should be prepared for that."

Now the Duchess was swaying in time to, I guessed, the music in her head, saying, "I am so happy for my little Mark that he has finally managed to capture his one true love, the girl who dropped him like a bad habit and ran off to LA all those years ago." Then she put her hand up around her mouth and fake-whispered into the microphone, "Let's just hope history doesn't repeat itself, right?"

That did it. Mark made his way to the stage and grabbed his mother by the top of the arm, like my mom used to do when we were toddlers.

"What?" she said, still into the mic. "It was a joke. It was funny."

Mark glared at her.

"No, no," the Duchess said. "I'm done. I'm done."

Mark looked at me helplessly, and I honestly didn't know what to do. I shrugged and motioned for him to come back to me, because he couldn't very well just drag her off the stage like an old vaudeville act.

I put my arms around his waist and rested my head on his chest. "You can't stop the train wreck, babe. You have to let the collision happen."

He rested his ear on my head. "If you can love me through this, then you really love me."

"I really love you," I repeated. And I did.

That feeling intensified when the Duchess said, "My only regret is that I won't get to be here to see these two walk down the aisle. As many of you know, I have been betrothed to a Saudi prince, and he insists that I come with him on business to the Greek isles immediately."

"What?" Mark said.

"That can't be true. She came back here for this."

She raised her martini glass. "To my great love, my Mark. I hope this marriage is everything you've dreamed of for all these years and that you do it a little better than your dear old mum."

Mum? Really? The woman was born and raised in south Georgia. She was no one's "Mum."

Mark shook his head and rolled his eyes. He was trying to act nonchalant, but I could tell he was rattled.

His mother walked out the door, and I followed her. "Connie!" I shouted.

She was drunk enough that she actually turned, even though "Duchess" was all she responded to these days.

"You have one son. You cannot leave him the week before his wedding."

I felt Mark's hand on my back. I knew he was trying to calm me, but I was way past calm.

"Oh, you don't understand. It's a monthlong cruise of the Greek isles on a two-hundred-fifty-foot yacht with its own helicopter pad. It's a once-in-a-lifetime opportunity."

"No!" I shouted at her. "No, it isn't. Seeing your only son get married is a once-in-a-lifetime opportunity. A cruise to the Greek isles is something you can do anytime. This is abandoning your child."

She glared at me, teetering on her heels. "Don't you talk to me about abandoning my son. It seems like that's something you know plenty about." She turned haughtily toward home. It would have felt more like the stomping out she wanted it to be if she hadn't been so wobbly. Then she turned and shot back, "Plus, I'd be willing to bet that this isn't his only wedding."

Mark sat down on the sidewalk, head in his hands. I sat down beside him and rubbed his back, feeling like the world's worst person. I was marrying Mark, yes, but I wasn't giving him what he wanted. In some ways, in the back of my mind, I had been incensed this whole time that he wouldn't drop everything and do what I wanted. But that wasn't fair. He had a whole life that he had worked really hard for, just like I did. He had totally reinvented a company—a family company, at that—for a new millennium and had become massively successful in his own right, all from the comfort of the one-stoplight town where he wanted to live. He took care of his mother despite her clear lunacy, and he took care of me. He made me feel beautiful and wanted and safe and adored. And all I ever did was keep him at arm's length.

"I don't know why I did this to myself," he said, "why I let myself get so far along in this fantasy."

I took his hand in mine and kissed it. "What do you mean, sweetheart?"

"This," he said, pointing to me and then to himself. "She's a crazy drunk, but my mother isn't wrong. I'm here again, trying to tether you to me and to this town, and you don't want any of it, not really."

There was so much hurt in his eyes. I wanted to argue with him. I wanted to tell him I would stay, I would do anything. I felt so desperate in that moment.

"Why can't I be enough?" he asked. He put his head in his hands. "Why can't I be enough for someone to stay?"

I picked his head up and looked him straight in the eye. "Don't ever say that again, Mark Becker. You are enough. You are more than enough. Your mother leaving isn't about you, it's about her." God, I hated to put myself in the same category with that horrid, horrid woman. But I guess I was, when you got right down to it. "And Mark, I'm not leaving you, sweetheart. I'm not. I'm here. I'm yours. I'm going to go off and work, and sometimes you'll come with me, and sometimes you won't. But that's not me leaving you. I swear it isn't."

He looked so pitiful and so forlorn that I wanted to tell

him that I would stay forever, that I would give it all up. I felt in my heart that even though he hadn't said it, he was offering me an ultimatum. And I wanted to pick him. I wanted more than anything to tell him that I would give it up, that I would be all his. But it wasn't my truth. And I knew that. So I tried to level with him.

"I just don't know if I can give it up, Mark. I love becoming absorbed by a totally different world of playing someone else . . ."

I trailed off. His eyes were so sad. I hated that I was hurting him, but I knew now that giving yourself up to please another person never works. You spend your entire life unhappy and resentful. I didn't want to do that.

Mark sighed, and when he looked back up at me, he said, "So what's so wrong with being here and being you?"

I took Mark's hand, and instead of getting angry that he couldn't understand me, I became drenched in an unmistakable sadness, drowning in his hurt. Because I knew, although I was the one sitting in front of him now, that was a question he actually wanted to ask his mother.

THIRTY-ONE

ansley: what mothers do

"Well," Sloane was saying, as we sat around in our PJs. "That was a dramatic ending to an engagement party."

"It has been a dramatic all-around day," Caroline said. "I still can't believe Jack gave Vivi that boat."

He had even had it named *T/T Starlite Sisters* (*Tender To Starlite Sisters*). It was so sweet. My heart surged with love for him, and even though I was enjoying this moment, I was ready for them to get out of here so I could get back to him.

"I don't want to tell Emerson until after her wedding," I said, looking around to make sure she was out of earshot. "She is so upset with me that I don't want to add fuel to the fire. But Jack and I have set our wedding date."

Caroline said, "Well, Mom, it's now or never," as Emerson walked up to the front gate, her hair disheveled, shoes in her hands.

I nodded and decided then and there that I knew she was mad, and I knew things were tough, but Jack was right. I had to choose him every now and then. I was going to marry him. No tantrum from my youngest daughter was going to change that.

So I said, as she reached the top step of the porch, "I want you all to know that Jack and I are getting married September 22. It's the harvest moon, and it's going to be simple and small and nothing to speak of. I want you there, but I understand if it's too hard."

"Did you even love Daddy?" Emerson asked me, her voice already high and worked up.

"Emerson!" Sloane scolded.

God, it cut me when she said that. Carter and I had had an imperfect marriage. We had both made some pretty big mistakes, and I had gotten some tough surprises in the wake of his death. But I had loved him through it all, and I hadn't so much as looked at or thought about another man for sixteen years after he passed away.

I stood up and crossed my arms. I had been nice, and I had acquiesced to the four hundred fits she'd had up till now. I had soothed, and I had coddled. But she had crossed the line. I was done.

"How about *Thank you, Mom, for planning my dream wedding*? Or maybe *Thanks, Mom, for paying for every ridiculous thing I wanted to try to make this day perfect for me*? Or maybe even *Thanks for always putting us first, Mom*?" I threw my hands up in the air. "I loved your father. Don't you ever, ever doubt that. But you have no idea what it was like for me. To lose my husband, to lose my money and my life and everything I had worked for and have to drag all of you back here because it was all we had left. To never tell you. To go back to work and keep this family together and raise you all alone. It wasn't easy, Emerson. It wasn't. I'm sorry if you don't approve of my decisions. I'm sorry if you don't want me to marry Jack. But I sacrificed everything for all of you for my entire life. It's my turn now."

She crossed her arms, too. "You can't even remember if you told him you loved him on September 11. I always hear you say that. Maybe you wanted this to happen the whole time so that you could be with Jack."

I nodded. I was so over this. I had to consider that maybe she would always carry this grudge. "Fine," I said. "That's fine."

And I walked off the porch, down the steps, and down the sidewalk to Jack's house. I didn't want to unload all of this onto him. I honestly didn't. But I couldn't help myself. I was fuming and pacing, and the whole story came tumbling out.

"All I know is that you will work it out, Ans. The Murphy girls are a package deal. You can't have one without the other three. That's how it has always been. It's how it will always be."

I nodded. That *was* true. Or at least, it had been, I realized sadly.

Jack got up and pulled me to him and whispered in my ear, "You looked so beautiful tonight. All I could think about was getting you back home." As he led me up the stairs, I honestly forgot all about my fight with Emerson, the guilt I felt over Carter, the pain that had risen so sharply to the surface I could have reached out and held it in my hand.

It was just Jack and me in our bedroom, in our house, the one he had bought for us, in this life that we had made together.

As we lay there, bathing in the moonlight, I whispered something to him that I'd never thought I would ever utter. "Maybe we should move."

It was a stupid thing to say. I knew even then that I didn't mean it, but I felt so ripped open that night. I thought back to the conversation I'd had with Sloane earlier about fresh starts. Maybe that was what Jack and I needed.

He shot up in bed. "I'm sorry. What?"

I shrugged. "We don't have to. It's just a thought. A clean slate. All that. But if you don't want to—"

He kissed me, cutting me off. "Ansley, I came to Peachtree Bluff for you. I'd follow you anywhere."

I smiled. I felt exactly the same way.

There was a light rap at the back door. Jack and I shared a glance. I got up and put my robe on, knowing it was probably Emerson and that, really, I was too tired and too old to fight it out tonight.

"I should go down and make sure it isn't a serial killer," Jack said. "I need to protect you." He flexed his muscles as he said it, making me laugh.

I nodded seriously as I tied my robe and followed him down the stairs. As I had suspected, it was Emerson. When Jack opened the door, she practically fell into me, sobbing.

"He called it off. Mark and I aren't getting married."

Just like that, I forgave her. Because that's what mothers do.

THIRTY-TWO

emerson: too much for the man

I kept it hidden between the pages of my contract for the Edie Fitzgerald movie. No one wanted to see that thing ever again, least of all me. But I knew I would want to see the letter, that I would want to have it despite the fact that it could incriminate me in a big way. And I had to admit that Grammy's words were the ones I thought of as I talked to Mark that night. Hers were the words that suddenly made everything seem so clear.

Dear Emerson,

Thank you, my love. I wouldn't be here now without you, and I thank you for setting me free, for allowing me back to a place where I could be with my husband again, where I could be out of pain and at peace. Do not spend one single day thinking about this, worrying about it, fretting over it. It was my choice and my decision. The only part of this that is on you is my eternal gratitude.

I have studied you since you were a child, Emerson, seen the way your struggle is so visible to the outside world, the way you wear your heart on your sleeve. As you have gotten older, I have seen you withdraw into yourself more, and while I don't think that's a bad thing, I want to tell you that it's OK to show people how you feel. Being vulnerable is how we grow and change; it's how we let others see us. Sometimes it's how we come to understand ourselves.

Darling girl, if I had to guess, you are going to have a lot of big decisions to make this year. How I wish I could be here to witness them, to guide you in a way that only someone with more than eighty years of life experience can. A lot of grandmothers would tell you to follow your heart, but I have to think that advice is a bit simplistic. My advice would be to find out what it is that you really, truly want. And then don't let anything get in the way of that. Life is too short to settle, my girl. Or, actually, maybe it's too long to settle. It certainly must seem that way to those who choose an inauthentic path.

No matter what happens, please remember that you are always my star. And when you look into the sky at night and see another star twinkling extra bright, know that that is me, shining down on you, helping to illuminate your path. Until we meet again . . .

All my love forever,
Grammy

As we sat on the sidewalk after our engagement party, which was supposed to be one of the happiest nights of our life together, Mark took my hand and said, "Tonight made it all seem real. It's like I realized this was actually happening, that this thing I have dreamed about for so long was coming to fruition."

My stomach felt very unsettled, but I smiled encouragingly and said, "It is, Mark. It's finally happening, and it's going to be amazing."

He smiled sadly at me, and I knew what he was going to say next. "Em, I love you. I have wanted only you for my entire life. But I'm not going to beg you to stay here for me. I spent my childhood doing it to my mother, and I can't spend my adulthood doing it to you."

I exhaled slowly, tears springing to my eyes. "Mark," I whispered, "please don't do this." But I truly didn't know what to say next.

"It's OK," he said. "I know you love me, too. But we want different things." He scooted closer to me and put his arm around me, pulling me into him. "As much as I *want* to marry you—and as much as I think you really want to marry me, too—I think we also both know that marriage isn't going to fix our problems."

"It might," I said, more to the wind than to Mark. They were just words. We both knew they weren't true.

I rested my head on his shoulder for what I knew would be one of the last times, inhaling the scent of him that was as familiar as my own. I put my hand on his leg, feeling the rough fabric of his khaki pants, balling it in my hands like that would make him stay, like it would make all of this different. I could taste my tears now, the lights of the museum across the street blurring in front of me. This part of my life was finally over— but even in that devastating moment, I had to admit that it had really ended when I was still the head cheerleader.

We sat there like that for a long time, neither of us saying a word. I finally leaned back and put my hand on Mark's cheek. "Look at me," I said. "It breaks me that you think you're not good enough for someone to stay. I can't leave here tonight having you think that, Mark. You are, hands down, one of the very best people I know, and you are worthy of everything wonderful life has to offer. Please, please, don't ever forget that."

He kissed me then. There were tears in his eyes as he said, "And Emerson, you deserve to have your dreams. You deserve not to have them taken away from you. I want everything for you, too."

I kissed him one last time, and it took all I had to stand up and walk away, because, even though it was clearly the right decision, sometimes you want the wrong decision. Quite often, actually. I couldn't turn or look back because I knew if I saw him sitting on that sidewalk all alone like a forgotten child, I would run back to him and beg him to change his mind. And while I knew I could be happy with him, I also knew I would never be happy feeling constantly torn between two worlds, always feeling guilty for doing the one thing that made me feel most alive. As Grammy had written to me, that would make life feel terribly long.

I still don't know what made me take it all out on my

mother a few minutes later on my front porch, what made me say the worst thing to her that a child could possibly say, when I asked if she had ever even loved my father.

I honestly think, in some twisted way, I had been pushing her all this time, just like I did when I was a kid, seeing how long she would maintain her composure until she absolutely snapped. As I watched her walk to Jack's house, I felt suddenly so empty. She didn't know about Mark and me. I hadn't told her. She was the only one who could make it better. And I had pushed her away—probably because I didn't *want* to feel better. I didn't feel like I deserved to. Not yet.

"Wow," Sloane said, opening the front door for us to go inside.

"I'm still a little mad at her," Caroline said, "but that was evil."

Sloane nodded, and I crossed my arms, looking from one sister to the other.

"Mark and I aren't getting married," I said, sobbing, as if that was some sort of excuse for why I had accused our mother of something so vicious.

My sisters exchanged a knowing glace, which annoyed the hell out of me.

I threw my arms up in the air. "Fine," I said. "Fine. Just say it. You don't like Mark. You're glad I'm not marrying him."

"No, no, no, no," Sloane said, pulling me in close to her.

Caroline stroked my hair and said soothingly, "We love Mark. We adore him."

"We only want you to be happy," Sloane said. "We want you to have everything you want."

"I know," I said, wiping my eyes, pulling away from Sloane. "But I do love him." I sniffed, feeling a little better.

"Baby, sometimes love just ain't enough," Caroline said.

I rolled my eyes, my tears beginning to subside. This wasn't the time to be quoting country songs. Or maybe it was. I probably wasn't an expert on that.

"LA proved too much for the man," Caroline said, winking at Sloane.

But I didn't find it funny, not at all. I sniffed and wiped my eyes and said, "Caroline, what is wrong with you? I'm having a real life crisis, and you're having karaoke night."

"He's leavin'," Sloane crooned.

"On that midnight train to Georgia," Caroline chimed in.

"Leavin' on that midnight train," they both added together.

They'd had too much wine. That was certain. I was beginning to get warm, fuzzy feelings, remembering all those good moments with my sisters when we were growing up, as Caroline sang, "I'd rather live in his world," and Sloane chimed in, "Than live without him in mine."

But I realized something all at once. It hit me so hard that it took my breath away. As my sisters inhaled, I interrupted them, tears streaming down my face. "I'd rather live in *my* world."

Sloane took my hand. "Oh, honey. Don't cry. It's OK."

Caroline put her arm around me and pulled me close to her, as I put my head in my hands. "What is wrong with me?" I sobbed. "You should pick true love. I feel like the most selfish person in the world."

Sloane gently took my hands off my face. "That's the thing, sweet Emmy. When it's true love, you make a different choice."

I wasn't sure I believed that then. But either way, despite my sadness, I knew Mark and I had done the right thing. I looked out the window, where I could see the light on at Jack's house. I knew that the one person who could make me feel better, the one I had been so horrible to, was over there. I had always done this, pushed her away when I needed her the most. I had to go over there. I had to apologize. And it made me wish I could get on the midnight train, not to Georgia, but going absolutely anywhere else.

THIRTY-THREE

ansley: the far corners of siberia

After Emerson had told me about her canceled engagement, she said something that shocked me: "I'm so sorry, Mom."

It was an apology I hadn't expected, honestly. But it was one I felt I deserved.

Once she stopped crying, once she calmed down, I said, "Honey, I am so sorry about Mark. And I am so sorry about everything these past few months. I think you know that." I cleared my throat, trying not to cry. "But to think you could even consider that I didn't love your father is just . . ."

I trailed off, and she shook her head. "I shouldn't have said that, Mom. I was just trying to hurt you."

I nodded. "You did an excellent job." Then I smiled sadly. "Is it time for the more-fish-in-the-sea conversation?"

Emerson laughed sadly and took a deep breath. "I'll find

my fish. I just really wanted it to be Mark, you know? I wanted us to want the same things."

"Oh, honey," I said. "I wanted it to be Mark, too."

Even once Emerson stopped crying, I couldn't sleep. I was so worried about her. She hadn't been herself at all lately, and between her health and this tumultuous engagement, I couldn't possibly close my eyes and drift off. I just sat there stroking her long hair, wanting more than anything to wash the dried mascara off her face.

The small-town mother in me wanted my child to move home, marry Mark, have babies, and go to lunch with me. I wouldn't have to worry about her anymore. She wouldn't be facing the world alone with Mark there to take care of her, wouldn't be living her life as a series of triumphs and failures, oftentimes ones that the entire world was there to see. But I knew that was what she loved about her life in LA—the rush, the full-throttle sense of living right on the edge, an ever-exhilarating day-to-day existence. It was a love affair that never ended, one that she loved more fiercely than she loved Mark. And I understood.

In the middle of the night, Jack came and sat beside me on the couch. He held my hand, and I laid my head on his shoulder until we both drifted off. When I woke up the next morning, Emerson was gone.

"Why in God's holy name do you keep me around?" I asked Jack.

All he said was, "Ans, I don't get to walk her down the aisle."

I smiled sadly and squeezed his shoulder. "Oh, honey. I'm so sorry."

"I thought it would help," he said. "Maybe give us a bond that I don't have with Caroline and Sloane, even the score in her mind a little."

I shrugged. "Maybe. But I think you'll get there with her anyway. I have to believe that it will all work out."

He kissed me and said, "Yeah. You're right. And I'll settle for walking down the aisle with you."

"You are too kind, sir. Every woman wants to be settled for." We both laughed. No man settling for a woman would ever endure all this.

He smirked and shifted to the other end of the sofa, looking at me intently. "Still want to move?"

I sighed and smiled. "Well . . ."

"I can't imagine my girl leaving Peachtree Bluff."

I shrugged. "For better or worse, even when it's hard, it's home."

"It's such a part of your story, of our story, really," Jack said. "I want to go different places and do different things, build a life with you, but I can't imagine home plate being anywhere but right here."

I heard a knock at the back door, followed by it swinging open. I smelled the coffee before I saw Kyle hand the cups to Jack and me right at the downstairs couch where we had spent a sleepless night that had led to a very stiff neck—at least for me.

"I got the feeling you might need these."

He sat down in a wing chair flanking the sofa.

"Is it true?" he whispered.

I nodded.

He looked down at his feet. I would have thought he would be happy, but he looked distraught. "How is she?"

"She'll be OK," I said, smiling encouragingly.

"I don't want her to be sad ever," Kyle said. Then he shot me a small smile. "Even though it was pretty clear that her wedding day was my funeral."

I shook my head. "You can't tell her now, Kyle," I blurted out. "She's very sensitive at the moment."

"Ansley, I'm not a masochist. And I have some sense of propriety." He stood up. "I'm just off to take the girls their coffee and juice."

Jack saluted him. "Godspeed, my man. I wouldn't go into that house, and if you haven't heard, two of the three of them are mine."

Kyle laughed. "People in the far corners of Siberia have heard, Jack."

I got up. "I'd better go, too."

Kyle and I walked across the backyard between Jack's house and mine and opened my back door. Caroline and Sloane were sitting in the kitchen, but Emerson was nowhere to be found. I had a horrifying thought. Emerson had woken up, found Mark, and changed his mind, trading the future we all knew she really wanted for him. I sighed. Well, if she had, I guessed that was OK. And I was glad I hadn't said anything critical about him.

"Hi, Kyle," Sloane said at the same time as Caroline said, "Mom, have a seat."

I sat down at one of the woven barstools, feeling exhausted. She slid something across the island. I picked it up and did a double take.

It was an engraved Crane invitation with our family crest at the top. It read:

Mrs. Caroline Murphy Beaumont, Mrs. Sloane Murphy Andrews, and Miss Emerson Virginia Murphy

Request the Honor of Your Presence at the Marriage of Their Mother

Mrs. Ansley Morgan Murphy

To Mr. John Stanley Richards III

Saturday, September 2, 2017, at half past six o'clock in the evening

At the Sandbar

And at the Reception to Follow on Starlite Island

Black Tie and Bare Feet

In lieu of gifts, donations may be made to the Wounded Warrior Fund

I was wide-eyed, but I didn't even know what to say. "How did you get an engraved invitation overnight?" I started.

"Even *I* can't get an engraved invitation overnight," Caroline said. "I've had these for three months." She paused. "Along with the ones that say *We regret to inform you . . .*"

I shuddered. No one wanted to send the wedding cancellation cards, especially this close to the date. But we didn't have much of a choice.

"But this is Emerson's wedding day."

"Right." She drew out the word like I was slow. "She was

never going to marry him. Not in high school, not now. He's darling, and she loves him, but he isn't her soul mate. He doesn't understand her."

The flash in her eye and the almost imperceptible glance she shared with Kyle made me know that she had someone else in mind when she mentioned Emerson's soul mate, and I had to consider that I might have known who that someone was.

"Mom, honestly," Caroline said, "the wedding on the sandbar, the reception on Starlite Island, the bouquets of peonies and hydrangeas, leaving by boat, that dress that would be totally ridiculous for a mother of the bride . . . Don't you think I have your back by now? I planned this wedding for *you*." She paused. "And I knew the date would work, because it wasn't like any of us could be anywhere else. And all your friends would be planning to come to Emerson's wedding, so they'd have the date saved, too."

I was stunned and teary-eyed. I had no idea that my daughter knew me this well, and I certainly didn't know that she knew Jack and me as a couple this well. "I don't know. I guess when you were making all those plans, I did think they sounded quite a bit like Jack and me."

I shook my head and slid the invitation back across the island. "It is a ridiculous mother-of-the-bride dress," I said. "And I absolutely love that you thought of this, but I can't do that to Emerson. I would never, ever hurt her like that."

"You have to," Emerson said, appearing from the dining room.

"You have *got* to quit being so sneaky," I said. "I feel like everywhere I am now, you just pop in."

"You and Jack take the wedding, Mom. You won't get any of the money back now, and it really is your perfect wedding. It's a fairy tale. You deserve it."

"Em—" I started, protesting.

"Mom," she said, "you waited sixteen years to move on. You and Jack deserve a really special wedding."

I looked down at the ring on my right hand. Carter's ring. Even though I was remarrying, I would wear that ring, as a symbol of my love for my first husband, forever.

Then I looked up to see Kyle looking at Emerson.

"And Mom," she said, exhaling deeply. "I know you loved Daddy. You told him you loved him on September 11. And you kissed him good-bye. Twice."

"What?" I asked, my heart racing. It was the thing I had wondered about for sixteen years, one that had haunted me. Had I kissed my husband good-bye? Had I told him I loved him on that last day? Did he wonder as the towers fell?

"I remember," she went on. "He said he loved you best of all, and you said you loved him more, and you kissed. Twice." Her eyes filled with tears. "And his last words to me as he left were 'Break a leg, Em.'"

I wanted to hug her then, but it was Kyle who got that privilege. She put her head on his chest, and he wrapped her up in his arms, and I heard him whisper, "You are going to be fine. You're the Starlite starlet, remember?"

And it occurred to me that there was no reason for Kyle to tell Emerson how he felt. She already knew.

emerson: a cookie smile

There is something surreal about rushing around and putting the perfect finishing touches on a wedding that was supposed to be yours.

With five days until the big day, the first question had to do with invitations. They were all stuffed and sealed and stamped already, which irritated me at first. But there was no time to be irritated.

"So how do we get all these out?" I asked.

"Oh, Vivi!" Caroline called.

Vivi paraded through the door wearing a flower crown. Seven other twelve-year-old girls, also in flower crowns, came in behind her.

Caroline cleared her throat and said, "Presenting the Ansley and Jack Wedding Invitation Delivery Team." Vivi grinned. "It's so much more personal than the mail."

I smiled. They looked much more innocent when they were wearing flower crowns than when they were smoking cigarettes. "Do you really think you can pull this off?"

"It's only twenty-five invitations," Vivi said, shrugging. "I'd say we can handle it."

I winked at her. The newfound bit of freedom with the boat Jack had given her had done wonders for Vivi. I liked to think that I had played a role in that, too.

I peeked out through the kitchen window and saw Jack. He caught my eye and motioned for me to come outside.

As I walked to meet him, I wondered what this was going to be about. I was on board with Mom and Jack taking my wedding. I mean, it was only practical. Mom had spent all this money, and when I really thought about it, it did seem more like them than Mark and me. They were the ones who had met on the sandbar, who had fallen in love on Starlite Island.

"Could you come to my house for a minute?" Jack asked once I reached him. He seemed nervous.

I shrugged and followed him into the kitchen. He motioned toward the barstool at his island and poured us each a cup of milk and pulled out a bag of Oreos once I sat down. I could have told him that I didn't want any—I had to watch my figure, after all—but I found myself dipping the cookies into the milk anyway. They seemed to soothe the butterflies in my stomach.

He looked at me for a second and took a deep breath, looking down into his cup. "Kyle told me what you said about your mom, Sloane, Caroline, and me being a family," he said slowly.

Snitches get stitches ran through my mind. Kyle was going to get an earful from me later.

"That's not how I feel," he said. "I don't feel like we're our own family and you aren't—"

I cut him off, saying, "But you aren't me, Jack."

"Right," he said. "That's where I was going with this. I'm not you. And even though I don't feel any differently about you from how I feel about Caroline and Sloane, I can see how you would feel that way." He took a bite of Oreo and grinned at me—without teeth, thank goodness. A cookie smile is not cute over the age of five. "I want to fix that. And I might know how."

I was going to tell him that there was no way to fix it. No matter what, I was never going to be one of them, not like they would be to one another. But I was intrigued. So I cocked my head to the side and let him continue.

"I want to adopt you," Jack said.

I burst out laughing. "That is literally the most ridiculous thing I have ever heard."

I felt a little bad when I saw how crestfallen he looked. But only a little. It was a laughable idea.

"Jack, I'm a legal adult. You can't adopt me."

"Well, that's where you're wrong," he said. He took a sip of his milk. "I've looked into it, and you can adopt a person of any age. And I'd like to adopt you."

I felt very flustered by all of this. I mean, my dad was my

dad. This man, no matter how cute my mom thought he was, was never going to be my father. My father was my father, and that was that. I was almost offended that he would suggest something so insensitive. But then I was also a little bit flattered.

"You are absolutely insane," I said. "You and Mark's mom could be friends." But I smiled when I said it.

Jack smiled, too. "Just think about it," he said.

"It's so sweet, Jack, but I don't know what it would change."

"It would change a lot."

I patted Jack's hand. "Again," I said, "I'm twenty-six. I had a father, and he died. I'm fine. I don't need a new one now."

Jack nodded, and I ate my final bite of Oreo and got up off the stool.

"Hey, Em," he said. I turned to look at him. "Just think about it, OK?"

I was surprised to find that I was. But ultimately, I felt like maybe it would be a betrayal of my father. And, really, I didn't need a piece of paper or a legal document to change what I already knew in my heart. Jack wanted to adopt me. He wanted me to be his. He wanted to fix this so it didn't hurt me anymore.

I realized as I walked through the yard and back to my house that just knowing that was enough. It meant more to me than any piece of paper ever could.

ansley: jump

The old drawbridge that led from Peachtree Bluff to Pecan Beach had a very large *No Jumping* sign when I was a kid. And all I can say is that it was a waste of taxpayer dollars, because no one ever obeyed it. Jumping off the Peachtree Bridge was a rite of passage, something that all us kids did at one point or another. But I, being the rule-following teenager I was, would never have even considered it. It was too scary, too risky, and there was a *sign*, for heaven's sake.

But one night, the summer I was sixteen and Jack was seventeen, Sandra, Emily, Jack, three of his friends, and I were on his Boston Whaler. It was past curfew, but there wasn't really all that much trouble we could get into around Peachtree Bluff, and our parents never waited up, so we thought of our curfews as more of a suggestion than a rule.

I wasn't much of a drinker, but sipping lukewarm beer out

of red Solo cups was a summer tradition, so that's what we were doing that night.

"We have a surprise for you," Sandra said.

I raised my eyebrow at her.

"You're not going to like it!" Emily sang.

I was sitting beside Jack, who was captaining the tiny vessel. He squeezed my shoulder. "Oh, yes, she is. She is going to absolutely love it."

I was very, very wary then. And when he nosed the boat onto a tiny spot of sand right beside the Peachtree Bridge and pulled it up onto the beach, I got the sickening feeling that I knew exactly what this surprise was going to be.

"No," I said, before we had even gotten out of the boat. "No, no, no, no."

"Oh, come on, Ans," Jack's friend George said. "We've all done it. It's fine."

Jack took my hand and pulled me toward the bridge. I was trying to stand firm. We were all still in our bathing suits, and the night had turned chilly. The water would be freezing.

"Yeah, Ansley," Peter chimed in. "It's just a fifteen-foot jump. It's no big deal."

"Summer is for making memories," Emily said, pushing me from behind, while Jack pulled.

Jack turned and winked at me, and I finally smiled. I didn't want to seem like a wimp in front of him. I wanted to be brave and strong and independent. I could make my own rules, bridge sign or not.

The seven of us lined up on the edge of the bridge, Jack and me in the middle.

"We're all going to do it together on the count of three," Jack's friend Marshall said, as Jack took my hand.

My heart was pounding, and my mouth was dry. But Jack was there. My best friends were there. It was summer. I was in my favorite bikini. I was invincible.

"Let's do a cannonball!" Jack shouted.

Our friends counted. "One, two, three, jump!"

And then I did it, the thing I hadn't thought I could ever do: I jumped. I screamed as I hit the water, and then I came back up. We were all shouting and laughing, and it felt absolutely amazing. I had faced my fear, and it had been fun.

Today, now, with my three grown daughters crowded around me in the guesthouse that had been dubbed "wedding central," I realized that Jack was making me face my fear again. When Carter had died, I didn't think I would ever be able to move on. There was no way. And now, here I was, in my white silky robe, Caroline putting flowers in my bun, Emerson swiping blush on my cheeks, and Sloane steaming all our dresses one final time.

"You look beautiful, Mom," Emerson said.

I mouthed *Are you OK?* to her.

"I promise," she said out loud.

Still, I knew today was hard for her. I knew she was trying to pretend it wasn't. And honestly, that made me feel proud. I would always put my daughters first, but I liked to be reminded that sometimes they could put other people first, too, even just their old mother.

"Of course you look beautiful," Caroline said. "No one has to promise that."

When they were finished, I stood up and motioned for my girls to come to me. "Thank you for giving me the gift of this amazing day," I said. "I am so grateful to all of you for your love and your friendship and your maturity. I wouldn't be here without you." I cleared my throat. "And I want you to remember that, with me, you always come first. Always."

"See?" Caroline said, pulling away from us. "This is why you need champagne in the bridal suite. There needs to be toasts now, and there is nothing to toast with."

It was a very hot day, and I was afraid that if everyone had champagne, someone would faint.

"No toasts," I said. "They would ruin my beautiful makeup."

Vivi came running up the stairs, her voice ahead of her. "Gransley!" she shouted. "It's time, it's time!"

I slipped into my beautiful pale-blue lace gown, and with a zip and three final kisses, we were off.

Twenty minutes later, I stood beside Jack on the sandbar where we had met, up at a makeshift altar of two wooden crosses covered with peonies. As I was about to pledge my life to him, I noticed the scar above his right eyebrow. And for just a second, I was back in that teenage night when we had jumped off the bridge, when I had felt so alive. It hadn't been until we got back to shore that I'd realized there was blood pouring out of Jack's right eyebrow. When he'd grabbed his legs, his knee had jerked up, his head went down, and the force had given him a cut that resulted in three stitches at the emergency room and a scar forever.

That was the moment I knew, the moment I knew I was in love with him, the moment I knew that everything else I would ever do would pale in comparison to this love I felt for him. He had helped me face my fear—and had gotten hurt in the process. But he didn't care. All he cared about was me. And when I saw that scar over his eyebrow now, it was a reminder of that fact. I had never felt so sure about anything as I did about this.

Today, on this makeshift altar with the sun shining and the water sparkling around us, his eyes filled with tears, and mine did, too. My one hope was that I would be able to hold it together through my vows, but I knew now that wasn't a possibility. Because, as I stood there, I didn't really see Jack the fifty-nine-year-old man. I saw Jack the teenager who had changed me, who had made me believe that life was full of wonder and possibility, that what we lived through and the things that changed us were beautiful no matter what. I saw the twenty-something Jack I had asked an unaskable favor, the one who had willingly given me the one thing Carter and I couldn't have—children—without asking me for anything in return. Not even my love.

It hadn't all been easy between us. There had been fights and disagreements, heartbreaks and pain. But through it all, from that very first day, there had been love. I looked out all around us at the water surrounding our strip of sand. Jack and me on our own little island. Only, as I winked at my brother Scott, who was standing behind Jack, I realized that we weren't an island. We were surrounded by our best friends, our precious family members. And now, finally, after all these years, we were going to be family, too.

Hal stood between us, officiating, and over his shoulder the sun was beginning to set, making its way through the sky and into the marsh grass. And when Hal said, "Ansley, do you take Jack to be your lawfully wedded husband?" I said, "I do," so quickly that everyone laughed. Jack squeezed my hands.

With the birds chirping and the fish jumping and the boats of the people who had known us as long as we had been us anchored all around, Jack and I promised to love each other forever.

Our vows seemed almost redundant at this point, because I knew that whether Jack and I had ever gotten together again, whether we had ever gotten married, I would have loved him forever anyway. And I liked to believe that no matter what, he would have loved me forever, too. Still, I felt the tears pouring down my face as he said, "Ansley, the first time I ever saw you, right here in this spot, I knew that you were going to be a part of me for the rest of my life. There have been times over the past forty-three years when I felt like you were everything. You were my purpose. As you well know, life can be cruel, and it can be unforgiving, and it can often be unexpected. For that reason, there's not a whole lot I can promise. But I can promise you that I will love you until my dying breath."

The sand felt cool and moist beneath my feet. I felt so grounded to this place, to this moment in time, like the past and the future were converging here on this same strip of sand where I had first seen that sandy-haired boy who had stolen my heart at fifteen.

I can't say whether it was right or wrong, but I couldn't help but think of Carter then, and I knew that some of those tears I was shedding were for him, too. Because I had stood in front of him this same way, and I had vowed to love him until death parted us. And death had parted us. But even though he might be gone, I knew that I would love him forever and for always, just as I would love Jack. And somehow that made this moment seem even bigger.

"Jack," I began, "you have proven your devotion to me time after time in all the years we have been a part of each other's lives. And now I promise that I will love you with that same devotion, that same tenderness, and that same forgiveness with which you have always loved me. I will love you until death parts us, and then I will love you for an eternity after that, because this one life we have is simply not enough. But you, Jack, are always enough. And today I promise that you always will be."

Jack kissed me then to seal our vows, and it really did feel like the first time. And in so many ways, it was. For Jack and me, this was a fresh start, a new day. It was the beginning of a time in our lives that represented freedom. No secrets, no lies, no hiding. Jack and I and our life together, the one we had dreamed of for so many years. I kissed him back, wholeheartedly, and I felt the tears coming down my cheeks again, because we were here. After so many years of heartache and uncertainty, so many years when things hadn't been right or good between us, we had made it to the other side. And it was going to be perfect.

I grinned at each of my daughters, and they grinned back at me. They were radiant in their pale-blue gowns. I noticed that Vivi was feeding Preston, AJ, and Taylor marshmallows to keep them quiet, and I laughed.

It occurred to me how Emerson must be feeling right now, watching her mother get married in what was supposed to be *her* ceremony. But when I looked over at her, my Emmy looked as happy as I had seen her in a long time.

Jack and I walked back down the aisle, grinning from ear to ear and pausing to stop in the middle of the aisle to kiss to thunderous applause from the crowd. Hal and Mrs. McClasky gathered everyone into the boats. My brothers congratulated me.

"Mom would be so happy right now," Scott said, laughing.

John nodded in agreement. "Wherever they are, Ans, I know Mom and Dad are so proud." He squeezed my hand. "Thanks for letting me walk you down the aisle. I can't tell you what that meant."

As he wiped his eyes, Scott said, "OK. We'll leave you two lovebirds alone."

And then there were two. We sat down in the chairs that had previously held our guests and drank the champagne that had been left for us.

"To my wife," Jack said.

"To my husband."

We clinked our glasses, as the sun sank farther in the sky.

"I honestly cannot believe it," Jack said. "I wanted to trap you in a closet somewhere yesterday so that nothing could go wrong and make you change your mind again." He paused. "Or, you know, something less creepy and kidnapper-ish."

I leaned over and kissed him. "I still can't believe you sacrificed that hot young blonde for me."

Jack laughed. "You are way hotter," he lied. "Plus, youth is overrated. I'll take middle age any day—especially now."

"I will, too," I agreed.

"How do you think Emerson's doing?" he asked.

"I think she's doing OK. She's sad, but she knows she did the right thing." And I said something that was so uncharacteristic his jaw dropped. "Today I'm going to focus on having the time of my life with you, and I'm going to worry about all our real-life problems tomorrow."

"Well, actually," he said, "we won't have much time to worry about them tomorrow."

I raised an eyebrow questioningly.

"I thought Connie was really onto something with that Greek isles thing, so you and I are going to take a three-week break and see it all."

I opened my mouth to ask all the questions I needed to ask. Who would take care of my store? What about the client projects that needed to be finished? Who would feed Biscuit? Who would see Caroline back to New York and Emerson back to LA?

But before I could ask them, Jack said, "Sloane has it all covered, Ansley. I know you forget sometimes, but they are grown-ups. She is going to take over all your responsibilities while you're gone, so don't worry about a thing."

I sighed and leaned into Jack, who put his arm around me.

"You are the most amazing man ever," I said.

"I really am," he agreed, kissing my temple.

We both laughed. A few minutes later, I was holding up the very sandy bottom of my dress while Jack helped me onto the boat he had borrowed back from Vivi for the day. What better way for the bride and groom to arrive at their wedding reception than in the boat where they had kissed for the very first time?

"I have dreamed about this day," Jack said, "for forty-three years. And now, finally, you are all mine."

As we drove away toward Starlite Island, I realized that I, too, had been dreaming of this day for forty-three years. But as my mind skipped to Emerson and her heartache and Sloane and how she would manage while I was away and Caroline and how she would settle back into her life in Manhattan with James, I realized that once a woman became a mother, she was never really all of anyone's again—not even her own.

emerson: a family of secrets

I was sitting in one of the gold Chiavari chairs Caroline had rented for the reception, which were arranged around round tables adorned with white tablecloths and more of those astonishingly large peonies and hydrangeas in vases that were about half as tall as I was. Starlite Island at this time of night was beautiful no matter how you sliced it, but under a tent with twinkle lights, it was breathtaking.

The sun had almost set when Mom and Jack pulled up to rousing applause from the now semi-tipsy guests, who had made the most of the open bar at cocktail hour. Mom had insisted on using Kimmy for the food, which consisted of fresh fish and vegetables. It was amazing, but it didn't soak up the alcohol quite like a cheeseburger.

I'd had a respectable three glasses of champagne that were making me feel light and buzzy but not drunk-drunk, which, let's face it, I easily could have been. Hell, I probably should have been.

But I felt so much peace about the day, about Jack. When Scott and John had walked Mom down the aisle earlier, Jack had taken both of Mom's hands in his and leaned down to kiss her on the cheek.

"Hey!" said Hal, who was officiating. "We're not at that point yet."

"Then hurry up!" Jack scolded, making the friends gathered laugh.

It was my favorite part of the day. That man absolutely could not wait to marry my mother. And I had to think that he couldn't wait to be our stepfather, either.

In a lot of ways, I had thought our relationships were parallel: young loves that translated into grown-up ones. Mark and I had had young love. That was certain. But I could already see that we relied way too much on the past to help us create our future. Mom and Jack didn't. Their relationship in the here and now was as dreamy as it had been when they were teenagers. And that was the difference.

Mom and Jack hugged a few people as they made their way into the reception, but the lead singer of the band interrupted their slow walk by saying, "Mr. and Mrs. Jack Richards, you are needed on the dance floor." Jack put his finger up to the singer and, instead, motioned for Sloane, Caroline, and me to come over to him and Mom.

The bandleader was calling again. "The happy couple is wanted on the dance floor."

Jack reached into his pocket and handed something to each of us. Three pieces of staurolite, one for each of the Starlite sisters.

Caroline held her piece up to her chest and smiled at me.

"I think these belong to you," Jack said. "I used to pull them out and look at them almost every day to remind me of the girls out there somewhere who, even though they didn't know me, were the most important part of my heart. And I used to dream that one day, I would get to know them. And I think it's safe to say that is happening." Mom leaned into him as he said, "I'm sorry I've had them for all this time, but, to be honest, I don't think I could have made it through without them."

Not a dry eye in the family.

It was a weird and wonderful moment, and I had to think that as we navigated this new life with our mother married to someone who wasn't Carter Murphy, there would be a lot of moments like this.

None of us said a word as Mom and Jack made their way to the dance floor.

Mom hadn't really wanted to do all the typical wedding things, claiming that she had done all that once before. But this was her wedding. We really thought she needed a first dance. And we had done some digging to find out what song that dance should be done to.

As the first few bars of the song played, I saw Mom put her hand over her heart as Jack reached for her other one. As the band was singing "Come a little bit closer," he pulled her to him. It really was kind of sweet. And I had a feeling they were dreaming this night away.

As the singer reached the refrain, I saw Mom and Jack both mouth to each other, *Because I'm still in love with you.*

It wasn't quite a harvest moon, like they had planned, but it was a moon tide. And that was close enough.

I smiled, thinking that Grammy would have loved this. She had wanted Mom and Jack together forever. And in some small way, she was here, on this island, where her ashes were scattered along with Grandpop's. I had felt my fair share of consternation over the past few months about my contribution to her death. But tonight, surrounded by people I loved, I realized that she wasn't gone. Not really. She lived on through all of us. And I finally felt at peace with my decision to give my grandmother the dignified end she deserved.

Mom started motioning people onto the dance floor. We were such opposites. I would have wanted all eyes on me for as long as possible.

"May I have this dance?" I heard a voice from behind me say.

It sent shivers up my spine.

I turned, and I was so tall in my heels that my eyes met Kyle's directly. God, he was gorgeous. Leading-man material. The pitter-pat in my heart felt dangerous as Kyle led me to the dance floor. It was even more dangerous when he pulled me close and led me through those satin dance moves of his.

An hour later, we were still dancing when he leaned over and whispered, "I want to show you something."

I raised my eyebrow. Sounded like a proposition to me. I was up for it.

We snuck out behind the band, and Kyle took my shoes off and put them in his back pockets, which I found irresistible for some reason. He held my hand as we walked into the depths of Starlite Island.

"Are there snakes out here?"

"Nah," he lied.

"Will the horses stampede us?"

Kyle laughed. "I don't think stampeding is something horses do to humans. It's something they do in general."

"That's not an answer," I pointed out, slapping at a mosquito.

I had never been back into the woods of Starlite Island, where Kyle was leading me. After a few more minutes of walking, Kyle stopped and said, "OK."

I looked around. It just looked like trees to me.

He laughed. "You have to look up, Emmy."

I did. And I gasped. There, right in front of me, was a tree house. Not just any tree house—an epic one. It had a roof and doors and windows and a rope ladder.

"What is this?"

"It's my tree house," Kyle said. "Well, I mean, it *was* my tree house, when I was a kid."

"This is the coolest thing I've ever seen."

He grinned. "Want to go up there?"

I nodded enthusiastically.

I went first, but Kyle was right behind me. He wasn't going

to let me fall. But with him so close and so warm, I had to admit to myself that as much as I had tried to deny it, I had fallen a little already.

It was sandy inside but not as bad as I would have thought. There were still three beanbag chairs on the floor and assorted shells and nature paraphernalia scattered around.

I walked out the door onto the balcony and leaned on the railing, looking out at the moon over the water. "This is absolutely spectacular," I said. "The best piece of real estate in Peachtree Bluff."

"You can play in it anytime," Kyle said, winking at me.

I cocked my head to the side, and he took a step closer to me.

"I bet you were a cute kid," I said, trying to defuse some of the very real tension between us.

"I know *you* were," he said. "One day, Ansley showed me all the family photo albums."

I groaned. Those family photo albums had gotten us into enough trouble already this year.

"I used to come up here, and my friends and I would pretend we were pirates on a lost island, defending our buried treasure."

I finally looked up into his eyes. I'd been trying not to, because I knew what I would see in them. I knew what I would find. But I couldn't help myself.

"Kyle," I whispered.

I didn't know what I even wanted to say. Maybe that I couldn't do this now. Maybe that I could. Maybe that I had thought about him for years and that I knew it was stupid, but that one night we had spent together had been more than all the nights combined I'd had with anyone else. Or maybe that I didn't feel what I thought he felt, and I was flattered, but this wasn't going to happen. I didn't know. I wasn't sure. So I didn't say anything.

We shared a long silence before Kyle filled it for me, saying maybe the same thing I wanted to say. "I swore to myself I wouldn't do this, Em. I promised. I know it's bad timing, and you're vulnerable, but you are all I think about. I live for the next moment when I'm going to be beside you." He took another step forward and put his hand on my cheek, cautiously.

There was more for him to say, more for me to say. But then, also, there was nothing left to say, not now, not ever, not from that first moment. Instead of responding, I stood up on my tiptoes, wrapped my arms around him, and kissed him long and slow and deep, just like I had that night in LA all those years ago. I pulled away from him, unzipped my dress, and in one fluid motion, the heavy fabric fell to the floor.

I took his hand and led him back inside to those beanbags.

"Em," he whispered, "are you sure?"

I put my hand on his beautiful cheekbone and said, "Kyle, remember the night we met, when you traced my favorite quote with your finger on my arm?"

He nodded. "Of course."

"I have thought about this moment pretty much every day since that one."

He grinned. "That is a lot of thoughts."

I nodded and pulled him down to the floor with me. As he kissed me, Kyle said, "I love you, Emerson. I'm sorry, but I need you to know that."

It seemed insane, and I didn't say it back. But wrapped in his arms in his childhood tree house, I knew that I was falling in love with Kyle, too.

———

WHEN I WOKE UP a few hours later, it took me a minute to figure out where I was. In a tree house, with Kyle, who loved me, on an island. I panicked. What had I done? I couldn't stay here. I was repeating the same mistake all over again. Peachtree Bluff was a deep black hole, and no matter how hard I tried to get away, it kept pulling me in. I started filming in two days. I had to be back in LA, not in love in Peachtree Bluff. I thought my heart would break in two, but I scooted out from underneath Kyle's arm and leg, found my heavy raw-silk dress on the balcony, and, against all odds, found my way back to the site of the wedding with my cell-phone flashlight.

There were two paddleboards with Kyle's initials on them pulled up on the beach probably ten yards from the tent. I wouldn't have stranded him there—though I was more convinced than ever after last night that, if need be, that man could swim all the way to shore and barely break a sweat—but there was an extra. I wish I could have seen myself, how ridiculous I looked paddling to shore in a floor-length couture gown. My heart actually physically hurt as I pulled the paddleboard up onto the dock, not from exertion but from the pain of leaving him behind.

But I wouldn't go through what I had gone through with Mark again. I refused to do it. My bags were already packed, so I scrawled a quick note to Mom, turned off my cell phone, and got into my car. I needed to cut all ties with this place and get home. I needed to get back to LA before I made another mistake.

SIX WEEKS OF FILMING, and I was beginning to *feel* like Sissy. I had put on the tiniest bit of weight, and my boobs were even a little bigger, like I was slowly becoming her. Usually, weight gain would have been a bad thing, but with this role, it was actually a bonus. I knew that this was by far the most important role I had ever played, that big-screen or miniseries or whatever it was didn't matter. I had been too wrapped up in the appearance of it, of what it sounded like to say it, of what people would think. This was a story that would resonate with audiences, would stand the test of time.

Being back in LA had been the best medicine. It was like the time I'd spent in Peachtree Bluff was a hazy apparition, and I had, for all intents and purposes, morphed into the moody teenager who had lived there so many years ago. The space had given me the clarity to see that what Mark and I had was better left in the past and that my mother deserved a blissful future. Jack would always be a part of our lives now, moving forward— a happy part.

I unfortunately hadn't been feeling as well now that I was back in LA and back to long hours and late nights. But I had

IVs scheduled for the next day, and I knew they would perk me right up.

What it all boiled down to was that Caroline had been right: I needed to get back to acting. I needed a place to put all my pent-up energy.

Vivi had started school again, so Caroline was back in New York spending way too much time curating Sloane Emerson. But, as we had promised, Caroline was bringing Vivi to the set today for her birthday gift. The star of the show, Hazel Bennett, was Vivi's age, and I really thought they'd hit it off. Plus, Vivi was going to get to play one of the little girls in Francie Nolan's class. She had only one line, but I knew she would be so excited.

Vivi practically floated onto the set, and Caroline looked as happy as I'd seen her in a long time. I gave Vivi, who was only a few inches shorter than I was now, a big hug and kiss and said, "Go, go! Hair and makeup need you now."

She scurried off, and I squeezed my sister. I pulled back from her. "What have you had done? You look radiant."

"I haven't had anything done," she said. "I'm just happy."

I put my hand over my mouth in mock shock. "Well, that's news."

"I got an apartment," Caroline said.

"Like a new one?"

She nodded, and I felt my stomach sink. "For your family?"

She shook her head, and I understood.

"You're leaving him?" I whispered.

"Not necessarily," she said. "But I need to know that I can."

I felt like I should ask her more, but I really didn't have to. I understood. No one wants to feel trapped in her marriage. It made me think of Mark, whom, I'm embarrassed to say, I hadn't thought of much. We had talked on the phone a few times, and we were both still mourning the end of our relationship, but the reality was that I was happy here. This work fulfilled me. I was where I needed to be.

"Emerson!" the director called.

I squeezed Caroline again and scampered off. We were doing one of my favorite scenes, the one where Johnny, my sister's husband, came home drunk, and I locked myself in a room with him and got him off the bottle, with nothing more than whisky and my raw sexuality to keep the tremors at bay. This was the second take, and I had to admit that this scene—and every scene I shot with one of my husbands or lovers—made me think about Kyle. Not in a fleeting, wistful way but in an obsessive, can't-go-another-minute-without-your-kiss kind of way.

As I walked over to the set's fake bedroom, adorned with a stark Victorian bed and a night table with a worn Bible on it, I started to feel a little light-headed. I went to reach for a chair that was close by, but before I could, I felt my legs go out from under me, and I knew that I was fainting. Before I hit the floor, I had the sickening feeling that the doctor in New York had been too nonchalant. Something was very, very wrong.

———

IT SHOCKED ME WHEN I woke up in the backseat of a car that Caroline was driving. "Oh, God," I said. "Did I pee?"

"Shockingly, no."

I had a cold compress over my head. Well, that was a relief, at least. I usually peed when I fainted. "Where are we going?"

"The ER, obviously."

I was super-glad she hadn't, but I had to ask anyway. "You didn't call an ambulance?"

"Too much traffic," she said. She almost seemed mad at me.

"Where's Vivi?" I asked, suddenly remembering my niece.

"Hazel's mom is taking them to dinner. Sorry, Emerson. Your present just got beat."

I laughed. "I think I'm fine," I said. "I probably didn't eat enough today."

"You are not fine," Caroline said, her voice cracking. "That quack in New York was wrong, and you are sick, and it's all my fault because I made you go there."

"It's not your fault, and I'm fine," I repeated, not totally believing it.

Caroline, who hates hospitals with a vengeance, pulled into the emergency lane, took a deep breath, and hoisted me out of the backseat. "I'm being brave," she said, "but I'd sooner die than touch one of those hospital wheelchairs."

I was still dizzy, but I was fine to walk with Caroline's assistance. As soon as the double doors opened, a gurney appeared, and I was immediately swept back to triage and hooked to an IV of fluids and iron, on my New York doctor's insistence. It was only then that I said, "Caroline, your car."

"I don't give a shit about the car," Caroline snapped. "They can impound it for all I care."

Caroline very rarely cussed, so it made me nervous.

A very kind doctor who looked a few years older than I was said, "Ms. Murphy, we're going to run a few tests to see what's going on here. I've talked to your doctor in New York, so I'm all up to speed there."

A nurse came in to take blood, and Caroline looked like she was trying not to cry, vomit, or touch anything.

"You can go," I said. "I know this is killing you."

She looked horrified. "I'm not going to go. I'm going to stay right here with my baby sister. Do we think Hazel is well behaved?"

I nodded. "Totally. She's very serious about her work. Plus, her mom is stricter than you."

Caroline looked slightly more relaxed.

"How's Mom?" I asked, trying to change the subject.

"Amazing. In love. She and Jack came to New York last week on their way home from the Greek isles, and it's funny, because it's like they've been together forever."

I nodded. "She said they had the best time in New York."

"You can ask me," Caroline said.

I thought she meant about James. "No, I mean, you can talk about it when you're ready. This is your deal, and I'm not going to push you on it."

"That's not what I mean," she said, and I could feel the blush rising to my cheeks. It was then that I knew what she was talking about, so I asked the question that had been on my mind since the moment Caroline got to the set.

"How's Kyle?" I whispered.

"Potentially more brokenhearted than Mark," Caroline said. "And I don't say that to make you feel guilty. I say that because anyone with eyes can see that you love him."

"I just can't right now, OK? It's too soon after Mark, and I don't feel like dealing with another fight about a long-distance relationship."

"Kyle isn't Mark."

"Maybe not," I started, as the doctor reentered the room with a grave expression on her face.

"I have your test results," she said. She looked at Caroline.

"Oh, it's fine," I said. "She's my sister. Anything you say to me you can say to her."

Caroline actually sat down in the chair beside me, which was completely shocking. Now she would have to burn her outfit as well as her shoes.

When the doctor told us the news, I think my heart stopped beating.

Caroline took my hand and said, "Oh, my God, Emerson."

I couldn't breathe, couldn't respond. When I finally got my wits about me, I said, "I need you to call my director, and then I need you to take me home."

"Right," she said, grabbing her car keys.

"No," I said. "Home to Peachtree Bluff."

THIRTY-SEVEN

ansley: a better investment

As I sat on Jack's front porch that morning—actually, my front porch—I still couldn't believe it. Every morning for the past six weeks, I had woken up beside Jack and thought, *Wow. My husband.* Today was no exception. The normalcy of our life was extraordinary.

I gazed out at Starlite Island and could almost relive our incredible wedding, the moments we had shared, how astoundingly perfect it all was. And when I looked over there, I could see another moment with Jack on that island, one that had happened years ago. One that wasn't quite as perfect.

I could still remember that morning, how trying it had been. Emerson was right in the thick of the terrible twos, while Caroline was a shockingly teenage-acting eleven, and Sloane, right in the middle, was trying to make peace but, that morning, in a whiny and grating way that was driving me crazy.

I was grateful for them always. I loved them constantly. But those children were going to send me to a mental institution. I had to get them out of the house and into the fresh air, and as soon as we piled into the boat that Daddy had kept tied at the dock for when they came down for visits, their moods shifted. There's something about the salt air that can do that. I'm absolutely sure of it.

By the time we got to Starlite, they were all best friends again, Sloane and Caroline making sand castles and letting Emmy help. It was one of those golden moments, one of the ones that we really don't get to have enough as parents, that make us feel whole, as though everything we have toiled for all these years has been worth it. For this one magical moment, all seems right with the world, and you feel pretty sure that your kids are not, in fact, going to grow up to be serial killers.

I felt so relaxed then that I actually let myself do something that took a monk's level of devotion and concentration to avoid: I slipped back into a memory of Jack. It was nothing earthshaking, just one of the many days that we spent over at this island in our youth, him throwing a football with his friends, the way the tan of his skin and the blond of his hair made it seem like he would be young forever.

I turned my head to the right, to let the wind shift the hair out of my face, and when I did, I saw a man walking toward me. I scolded myself for thinking he looked like Jack. But when he threw me a small wave and a half smile, I realized that, as so often happens in life, I had been thinking about Jack, and now he had appeared.

"Caroline!" I called. "Watch your sisters, please, and no one get in the water."

"OK," she called back in a tone that was downright cheery, one I hadn't heard in a long time.

I had loved Jack for years, had trusted him so much that I had children with him. But for some reason, my mom antennae were on high alert that day. For whatever reason, I didn't want him near my girls, so I walked a few yards down the beach to meet him.

"Ans," he said. "It's you."

I remember hugging him in my mint-green-and-pink bikini, him in his blue swim trunks, and wanting to pretend that I didn't feel that same zip of electricity for him that I always had. But I had to consider that he might not have felt that same zip for me anymore.

"I didn't know you were in town," he said breezily. So breezily that it led me to believe he had known I was in town.

"Yup. Family vacation," I said. I wanted to say something about Carter and that he had to run home to take care of something for work. But I couldn't, for some reason.

Jack pushed his sunglasses up on top of his head and, squinting in the bright sun, asked, "Could I talk to you for a minute?"

That was when I knew for sure that Jack had known I was here and that, somehow, he had planned this.

"OK," I said hesitantly. Maybe it made me foolish or high on myself, but I honestly thought this was going to be a conversation about us, how he missed us and wanted us together again. And as tempted as I would be, I knew I would say no. But nothing could have prepared me for what he said next.

"I know the situation with Carter might be tricky, but I was wondering how you might feel about letting me spend a little bit of time with Caroline and Sloane." I felt my throat constrict. "They don't have to know the truth or anything like that, but I would love to get to know them."

I felt breathless. "What?" I whispered.

He was smiling at me, all happy, like this was the best idea he had ever had and that surely I was going to jump right on board. "Ansley," he said. "Why do you look like I stole your puppy?"

I shook my head. "No, Jack," I said. "No."

He looked crestfallen. "Again, I'm not saying I want them to know I'm their biological father or anything like that. But I'd love to just take them out for ice cream or something. Anything." He whispered, "They're my children."

That was when I felt strong. That was when my mama bear instincts kicked in at full force. "You can't flip the script on me now, Jack. You agreed to this. This is what you asked for. You didn't want children. I did. We couldn't be together. Remember? I have Carter. I'm happy. I have a whole life. I won't let you ruin it."

Now it was his turn to look at me like I'd stolen his puppy. But honestly, did he think I was going to agree to this? It was too preposterous to even consider.

"I'm not going to ruin your life, Ansley," he said, emotion lacing his voice. "I love you far too much to ever hurt you."

That was it. Those were the last words Jack and I shared until our fateful meeting on his boat many years later. All I could say was what a difference a few years could make. Whereas that day on the beach, he had made me feel trapped and terrified, now, sitting beside me as my new husband, he couldn't have made me feel safer.

I looked up at him now and said, "It feels weird with them all gone. It's like those first few days when they would all be back in school and the house was quiet." I paused and smiled up at him. "But now you're here. And that's pretty great, too."

Jack leaned down and kissed me. "Well, my darling, I hate to leave you, but I'm going to go look at a building with Adam."

"What?" I asked in surprise.

"Yeah. With the store downtown gone, we were thinking that someone should start a new one. Drinks, simple groceries, yacht provisions, a small deli. I think it would be a terrific business, and I've been looking for something to invest in."

I laughed. "You've been looking to invest in Adam is what you've been looking to do," I said.

"Can't really think of a better investment," Jack said. He stood up and patted my knee. "Family first."

I stood up, stretched, and realized that I needed to be at work—it was almost ten, after all. I kissed my husband (my husband!) and walked down the street to my store.

I knew when I got there that Sloane would be in the window painting, enjoying her alone time, while my grandsons were safely at their preschool down the street. Vivi was loving sixth grade in Manhattan. Preston was accompanying his mommy in the mornings on her trips to Sloane Emerson New York. Emerson was as effusive as I had ever heard her over her new role as Sissy—and more than a little relieved that she hadn't, in the end, married Mark.

Life was so good right now. I bit my lip, as if even thinking that was tempting fate. But we had been through our fair share of surprises this year. For now, I had to assume, we were sailing as calmly ahead as the boats beside me, making their way through the glass-slick channel.

emerson: the status quo

In my life, things had always had an order. For good or bad news, I always called Caroline first. Then Sloane. Then Mom. Then, the past few months, Mark. Mark was no longer a part of my life, but still, I felt like this was news he needed to hear from me.

James had flown to LA to pick up Vivi, and Caroline and I were crammed like sardines in the back of coach. We had booked first class, but our first flight was delayed, causing us to be bumped off our second flight. We were lucky to be in seats 27D and E, by the bathroom, actually. I was wearing my cashmere travel mask Mom had gotten us all for Christmas, trying to sleep, which had been impossible the past two days. Every time I closed my eyes, I tried to picture how I was going to tell Mom the news. It was not something I ever thought I would have to face, not something I had even envisioned. I knew I wanted Jack there. She was stronger when Jack was there. And I had to admit that maybe I was, too.

Caroline was flipping through French *Vogue*. She had become fluent in French over the past ten years, when she decided to get Vivi French lessons and sat in on them as well. She thought French was very chic and that everyone should know how to speak it. It would come in handy now that she was going to Paris and Morocco every few months to buy items for the store.

"Have you decided about your new apartment?" I asked. I felt Caroline jump beside me. She must have thought I was asleep. But who could possibly sleep at a time like this?

"Um," she said. "You know, Em, I think now is a time for the status quo."

I pulled my mask up and looked at her. "Because of me, you mean? Because everyone will have enough to deal with, with me?"

She shook her head and said softly, "No, sweetie. I don't mean that at all." She flipped her magazine closed and handed it to me.

"I can't read that," I said. I, the uncivilized sister, did not speak French.

"I assure you, you can. There's not a lot of translation. It's basically interviews with beautiful actresses whom you know talking about how many Oscars they've won. You can figure it out."

I rolled my eyes. "James," I said. "Why are you trying to change the subject?"

"It's not important right now, Em," she snapped.

"Of course it's important."

Caroline sighed.

I wanted to say that even I knew that living with one foot out the door was no way to live. But frankly, I probably wasn't the best person to give love advice right now, since I'd been jilted by my fiancé and then slept with my best friend and ignored the nine phone calls and seven text messages he had attempted since.

"Hey!" Caroline said. "You can come live in my apartment when you're finished filming. Mount Sinai is amazing. You can even have a room with a view of the park."

That did sound kind of nice, if you could consider any hospital anywhere kind of nice. It wasn't exactly a place people wanted to visit.

"So what do I even say?" I asked.

Caroline shook her head. "I have no idea, sweetie. This is a tough one. I think you practice on Sloane." She paused. "I mean, I can tell them if you want."

I squeezed her hand. "Thanks. That would be really great."

She went white, and I laughed.

"I'm kidding. I'm kidding. This should definitely come from me."

Two hours later, the driver James had arranged to pick us up from the airport was dropping us at Sloane's house. Well, Caroline's house. Whatever. Real estate was very confusing these days.

I probably should have knocked, but I just walked in the front door, calling, "Sloane!"

"Em?" she called from upstairs.

"And Caroline!" Caroline called.

Sloane ran down the stairs. "Oh, my gosh!" she said, engulfing us in a hug as though it had been a year since she had seen us, not six weeks. "I am so excited!"

She must have seen the grave looks on our faces, because she sat down on the step. "OK, I'm not excited. What's wrong? I feel like I can't breathe."

"Well . . ." I said, not knowing where to start. "I fainted on set. Fortunately, Caroline was there to take me to the emergency room."

Sloane gasped. "Oh, my God. What is it? What's wrong?"

"Actually," I said, blowing all my breath out. Caroline and I had lots of secrets, but once I said this out loud to anyone else, it was real. Like really, really real.

But Sloane was starting to cry, and I didn't want to keep her in suspense any longer, so I just said, "I'm pregnant."

She jumped up off the step. "What?"

"That was really good," Caroline said. "Play up that hospital part to Mom, because she'll be so relieved you aren't dying she'll be less mad that you're pregnant."

Sloane threw her arms around my neck and almost knocked me down. "I know it isn't probably the best news to you, but oh, my God, Em, this is the *best* news."

I actually hadn't expected her to react this way, but you never knew with Sloane. These days, she was all about the moment and living life and doing what felt good and throwing caution to the wind. Adam wasn't the only one who had gotten a second chance at life.

"What did Mark say?" she asked.

"I haven't told him," I said truthfully.

"Emerson . . ." Caroline started.

I bit my lip and said quietly, "I haven't told him because he's not the father."

"Emerson," Sloane scolded. "Please tell me this isn't a Maury Povich paternity-test situation."

I shook my head and crossed my arms. "It isn't *that* bad."

"It's worse," Caroline said under her breath, and I slapped her arm with the back of my hand.

"It's not worse." There was a knock at the door, and Caroline stood to open it. I heard the front door creak behind me right as I said, "It's Kyle."

"Wow," a voice from behind me said. "You must have eyes in the back of your head." He had a very sarcastic tone. I didn't blame him. I turned slowly and, looking down at my feet, contritely said, "Hi."

Kyle handed Sloane a cup and said, "I'll be on my way now."

"Wait," Caroline said before he could turn around. She pushed me toward him and said, "Emerson needs to tell you something."

I glared at her, and she and Sloane scampered out of the room.

"What?" Kyle asked, crossing his arms.

"Um," I started, looking around for anyone who could save me. "Maybe you should sit down."

My phone beeped in my pocket. "Wow," he said, as I sat down on the sofa beside him. "Your phone *does* work."

"Kyle," I said. "It's not like that."

"Then what's it like?" he asked. "I wake up in the tree house to find you gone, my paddleboard gone, and myself completely humiliated."

I knew I couldn't defend myself. There was nothing I could say to make this right, so I just blurted it out. "I'm pregnant."

"Great," he said, crossing his arms. "That's great. That's fine if you and Mark are having a baby and getting back together and living happily ever after." He stood up. "But you could have at least had the decency to shoot me a text."

He was out the door before I could say anything else.

"You have got to work on your delivery," Sloane said, peeking her head from around the doorframe.

"Yeah, Em, really," Caroline said, her head on top of Sloane's. They looked like a comedy skit in an old black-and-white movie. "You ruined his day. He might have been happy. You don't know."

I had heard it my whole life, so my sisters were only reiterating what I already knew: everyone, and I do mean everyone, is a critic.

THIRTY-NINE

ansley: the four horsemen
of the apocalypse

Ordinarily, I would have screamed with joy when I saw my three girls walking up the front steps of Jack's house. But it wasn't my birthday. There was no reason for them to be surprising me. So that could only mean that these daughters were three of the four Horsemen of the Apocalypse.

They weren't even in the house yet before I was opening the door and saying, frantically, "What's wrong?"

"Why do you always go there, Mom?" Caroline groaned.

"Because the three of you don't show up together unannounced unless something terrible has happened."

It was true, whether they wanted to admit it or not. When Caroline was suspended for smoking in the bathroom? The three of them. When Sloane ran her car into the telephone pole? The three of them. When Emerson announced that she wasn't going to college after all? The three of them.

"Just tell me," I said. "Put me out of my misery." Their little-girl problems had seemed big at the time. Their grown-up problems, I was learning, were much, much worse.

"Mom, inside, please," Emerson said.

My heart sank. So it was Emerson. I knew it. I knew she was still sick. I knew that damn doctor was wrong. A mother's intuition is always right. I glanced her up and down. But wow. She looked incredible. She looked the healthiest I had seen her look in years. I guess you never can tell what's lurking underneath.

"Well, Mom," she started nervously, "I fainted on set with Caroline yesterday."

When she said she fainted, I almost fainted, because I knew this wasn't good. I was absolutely beside myself, wracked with grief.

My breath was getting shallow as she said, "Caroline took me to the hospital, and they were in contact with my New York doctor all along the way . . ."

Tears were running down my face, and sobs were caught in my throat, as she said, "And, well, it turns out that I'm pregnant."

"Wait," I said, my brain trying to catch up. I had been so sure that she was going to hit me with some sort of death sentence or life-threatening illness. I was already jumping into mother mode, making mental lists of doctors I needed to call, friends I needed to consult. "You're pregnant and you're dying?"

She looked at me like I was dense. "No, Mom. I'm great. I'm not dying. I'm not even sick. My blood work was amazing. I'm just pregnant. Only pregnant."

There was a knock on the front door. "Not now," I said, but obviously not loud enough, because Kyle's voice called, "Emerson!"

I put my finger up to my mouth, but Caroline called, "In here."

I gave her a look. Well, this was great. I had so many questions. Did Mark know? Were they going to get married now? Was she coming back home? How many weeks was she? Could she still work?

"I'm so sorry, Emerson," he said. "I shouldn't have flown off the handle like that. I'm happy for you and Mark; I really am. I had forty-six days to really work myself up, and it came at you all at once."

Now I was really confused.

Emerson looked at Caroline and then at Sloane. Sloane just shrugged, and I knew something else was coming.

"Kyle, I need you to sit down," Emerson said.

He crossed his arms. "I will not sit down."

She touched his arm gently and said, very slowly, "The baby isn't Mark's."

Oh, this was great. Just great. Now I was going to be on *Jerry Springer*. I had never used this expression in my whole life, but I was going to wring that child's neck. I absolutely was.

This look of realization came over Kyle's face that was totally lost on me. "Oh, my God," he said. "Are you saying what I think you're saying?"

Emerson nodded. I was so confused. "Look," she said, "I don't expect anything from you. You deserve to know, but this doesn't have to change your life in any way—"

I was finally catching on. "What?" I practically spat. "You and *Kyle* are having a baby?"

"Well—I mean—" Emerson stammered. "I am having a baby. It's up to Kyle how involved he wants to be."

"Oh, my Lord," Sloane said. "That is going to be the world's most beautiful baby."

"What?" I asked again. "How?"

Caroline was saying, "Well, Mom, a boy and a girl meet, and they fall in love," as Emerson said, "You took my wedding, Mom. I was sad. It's a legitimate thing."

"Oh, so this is my fault?"

"Hold up," Kyle said, raising his voice above the chatter just as Jack walked in and said, "What is going on?"

Kyle took Emerson's hand and said, "Would it be all right with you if we maybe discussed this privately?"

"It would save so much time if you would discuss it with all of us," Caroline said.

"Yeah," Sloane agreed. "Plus, things always get lost in translation."

Emerson glared at them and followed Kyle out the door.

Jack repeated, "What is going on?"

"Let's see," I said. "Emerson is pregnant, and Kyle is, apparently, the father." Then I turned to Caroline. "Did you know about this?"

Jack opened the fridge and poured half a bottle of wine into a glass and handed it to me.

"Thank you, love."

"Well, I mean, I knew yesterday. Yeah."

"But did you know about the two of them?"

Sloane and Caroline shared a glance. Sometimes it drove me insane how they all seemed to be talking to one another without saying anything, like they had some secret language that they used to decide what poor, crazy Mom was privy to.

"Yes," they said simultaneously.

"But Ansley, come on," Jack said. "You can't be surprised. I mean, the guys at coffee have been talking about how those two belong together since the day Emerson came back to town."

I rolled my eyes. "Really, Jack? The guys at coffee? I think I know my daughter a little better than the guys at coffee."

"Well . . ." Caroline said. "The guys at coffee know it all, Mom. It's not something against you. No one can compete with their wealth of knowledge."

"And you," I said, pointing at Caroline.

"Whoa," she said, putting her hands up. "Emerson is pregnant and you're mad at me?"

"Can you explain why every time I ask my car voice control to 'Call Caroline,' it responds, 'Finding nearest fitness center'?" I crossed my arms for emphasis.

Caroline bit her lip to try to hide her smile. "Gosh, Mom. I don't know. All I can say is that the universe is always sending us signals if we take the time to listen."

Sloane laughed and scolded, "Caroline! You are the worst." Then she said, "Mom, how do you feel?"

"She'd feel better if she found the nearest fitness center a little more," Caroline said under her breath.

I gave her my best *you're in trouble* look.

I didn't know how I felt. Overwhelmed. Terrified. Excited. But when I narrowed it down to one overarching emotion, it was one that surprised me. "I feel . . . relieved."

"Relieved? Emerson is pregnant, with Coffee Kyle's baby, out of wedlock," Sloane said. "I mean, I'm thrilled. But you're Ansley Murphy, classic Southern, conservative mother. How can you feel relieved?"

"She's actually Ansley Richards now," Caroline interjected. "And no one says 'wedlock' ever."

"When you have three daughters, the idea that one of them could get pregnant at any moment is always on your mind. She's almost twenty-seven. She can support herself and her child. It could be much, much worse. So I'm relieved."

And now I could only hope that Emerson felt the same way. I looked at Jack, and I realized that we, like my girls, shared a language. And he was almost as excited about seeing this grandchild come into the world as I was.

emerson: the seed

"We can't just stand here in the yard," I said. "Everyone will hear us. The entire town will know in like five minutes."

Kyle nodded, looking dazed. He started walking next door, to the back of Mom's house, and I followed him. He pulled the hide-a-key out of the lantern and unlocked the back door. It was kind of hot in her kitchen, since no one had been living here since she and Jack got married. Maybe it was in my head, but my ankles already felt a little swollen in all this Georgia humidity.

I sat down on one of the barstools, and Kyle sat down beside me. He turned his stool to me and then reached over and slid me around to face him. I didn't know why it was so hot, but it totally was. That was not what I should have been thinking about in that moment that could really determine the rest of my life. But it was what I was usually thinking when Kyle was around.

"First," he said, "are you sure? Because I can't get my hopes all up like this and then be let down."

I was a little offended, but I could see his point. And also really surprised. If he was getting his hopes up, did that mean he was excited?

"I am one hundred percent, totally positive," I began cautiously. "Mark and I had made a no-sex pact before our wedding, and I have been so utterly destroyed since our night in the tree house that I haven't even looked at anyone else."

Kyle looked at me for a long minute, as if he couldn't quite digest what I was saying. "Em!" he said, so loudly it startled me. "We're having a baby!"

I was afraid he was losing his mind. "Yes," I said slowly. "I am aware of that."

"So why aren't you more excited?" he asked, grinning like his face might break in two.

"I mean, I am excited. I'm just overwhelmed and trying to figure out how you're going to react."

He jumped off his stool so quickly it toppled over and wrapped me up and kissed me. It was exactly what I needed. "That's how I'm feeling," he said. "It's the best damn news ever."

I laughed. I was so relieved. This really could have gone a different way.

"Well, we have a lot of details to work out," I said.

The back door opened, and the entire family trailed in, as Kyle, with his hands on my belly, which was, I might add, still perfectly flat, said, "What's to work out?"

"Like where are you going to live?" Sloane asked.

"LA, of course," Kyle said. He motioned with his hands like he was saying, *Keep 'em coming.*

"Really?" I asked. "You would move to LA?"

He walked over, put his arm around me, and kissed my head. "Em, I saw you on that set when you were filming the movie of which we do not speak. That's your home. That's where you belong."

"But now with the baby . . ."

"The baby?" he said. "Everyone in Hollywood has like a half-dozen of them. And I am great with kids. I mean, I can change a diaper like you've never seen."

"You can?" I was surprised.

He shrugged. "I've never actually done it, but theoretically."

"SJP filmed *Sex and the City* while she was pregnant," Caroline interjected.

"Yeah," Sloane said. "Reese Witherspoon filmed *Cruel Intentions* while she was pregnant."

"Well, actually," Mom said, "I think she got pregnant while filming *Cruel Intentions.*"

"OK, guys," Kyle interjected. "We're getting a little off topic here."

I sighed. This was all too much. "I mean, you could move and pack up your life, and I might never really do anything good, and then we would have wasted all this time and energy." I paused. "It's too much pressure for one person."

"It's OK," Kyle said. "Whatever it is, it's OK. Whether you win an Oscar or film commercials for adult diapers, it's all OK. Changing course doesn't mean you failed. But don't change course because you're scared. Change course because your heart is leading you in a different direction."

"Damn," Caroline said. "I feel so inspired."

"And so what if in a few years, I realize the acting thing isn't going to work out?"

Kyle looked confused. "I feel like you know me better than anyone, but this line of questioning is leading me to believe differently." He paused and took my hand. "Emerson, I honestly believe the best part of life is the surprises, the reinvention of yourself. This is the best one I can think of. And when the next surprise comes, we'll roll with it. It's not a big deal."

"It's kind of a big deal," Sloane said under her breath.

"What will that look like?" I asked.

"I'll move into your place, and we'll raise the baby together. Pretty simple." He grinned at me. He was probably the most beautiful man I had ever seen in real life. I could only hope this baby looked just like him. He shrugged. "Or we get a new place. It doesn't matter. I honestly don't care." He looked so excited that I felt certain he was going to burst into song.

I knew, looking at him then, that he was what I wanted, maybe what I had wanted for a long, long time. "But Kyle, I can't be back in the same situation, with someone who doesn't understand what I do."

He laughed. "And that's where you're wrong, Em. Because I've lived in Hollywood, and I do understand. I know why Hollywood relationships never work out."

"I would love to know why," Caroline said. "I mean, I know I should be prepared, but it still breaks my heart every time."

Sloane patted her arm in mock support.

"Because what draws you together initially is your love of the same thing, that you speak the same language, that you understand how it feels to become someone else, to become totally absorbed in another world," Kyle said. "But the reality is that it can never work, because you both want the same thing, so there's an underlying level of competition, not to mention that being famous doesn't allow time for a real life. Someone has to grocery shop, someone has to take care of the kids. Someone has to be the seed, and someone has to water it."

He pointed at me and said, "Seed." Then he pointed back at himself. "Water."

That was actually the most brilliant thing I'd ever heard.

"So what will you do?" Sloane asked, ever the practical one.

"I already own a coffee shop in LA. Of course, I'm going to rebrand. I won't call it a coffee shop. I'll call it, like, Kyle's organic, gluten-free, non-GMO, fair trade, grass-fed, slimming, shiny hair, better skin magic tonics."

Caroline nodded seriously. "That will do very, very well in LA." She paused. "If you'd like to franchise to New York, I'll be your first investor."

"You're too late," he said. "I already have. And Phoenix, Atlanta, and Charlotte, too."

"What?" I asked. "You didn't mention any of that to me."

Kyle shrugged. "It never came up."

Mom put up her hand to stop everyone. "Hold on just one fat second."

Ah, yes. This was what I had been waiting for. It was sinking in. The freak-out was coming.

"Kyle, you may not leave Peachtree Bluff."

"Whoa," I said. "He can't leave, but I can?"

"I don't care what you do. He has the coffee."

We all laughed.

"I'm not closing down the shop. My cousin Keith and I can switch places." Kyle shrugged. "He'd be up for it."

Mom shook her head. "It's not the same."

"So?" Kyle turned and asked me.

I couldn't help myself. I threw my arms around his neck and kissed him.

"Emerson," Mom said. "For heaven's sake. Control yourself."

"You're cool as a cucumber that she's pregnant but don't want her to kiss him?" Caroline asked.

"Yeah, Mom," Sloane said. "How do you think she got this way?"

Mom sighed, and I finally pulled away from Kyle.

"Living in sin with a baby," Mom said. "It's a new day. Im getting too old for this."

Jack walked through the back door, cautiously. "Is it safe to come in now?"

Mom motioned for him to come in and said, "I'll get the guesthouse ready."

"It's OK," Kyle said. "Em can stay with me."

I shook my head. "No way. I have to get back to set tomorrow. I want us all together, one big, happy family. Let's spend the night at Jack's!"

"Yay!" Caroline cheered.

Mom looked up at Jack. "You wanted them, remember? You wanted to know them and be in their lives. This is what you get."

"Yeah, Grack," Sloane said, patting Jack on the back.

We all laughed hysterically.

And I realized that this was one of the many, many reasons that I loved the movies. Things working out like they should. Everything being OK. Happily ever afters. And now, finally, it looked like I might just get mine.

FORTY-ONE

ansley: everything you never wanted

I was on Kimmy's farm with Taylor, AJ, and Jack when I got the call. Emerson, who was three days past her due date, would be induced in two days. There was so much to do. We were already packed, but I needed to call Caroline and Sloane, book a flight, get a hotel room . . . But before I rushed off to tend to the to-dos, I looked over at Kimmy, the produce girl who, little by little, had wormed her way into my heart and finally, after all these years, had broken down and let me give her an alliterated nickname like everyone else in town had: Kohlrabi Kimmy. The town still preferred Kale Kimmy, but she had insisted that kale was too trendy for her. Kohlrabi, her favorite root vegetable, evidently was a classic.

Taylor and AJ were running after the chickens while she showed them her crops. It was a little-boy paradise, and it made me realize that I should bring them out here more often,

I leaned against Jack, the hot midday sun beating down on my face as we sat on the dusty ground, and I was glad I had remembered my SPF that morning.

He kissed my head. "My grandchildren are a miracle," he said. Then he looked at me. "Am I allowed to say that now? My grandchildren?"

I laughed. He had accidentally said that several months earlier while helping me with the boys when Sloane was out for the night, and I had nearly panicked. Inside, I mean. Externally, I thought I had done a fairly good job of keeping it together. Obviously not.

Kimmy was kneeling in front of Taylor, showing him one of her namesake kohlrabis. She was one of those rare people who was a bit awkward with grown-ups but an absolute genius with kids. It was a gift to be that way, I believed. I smiled at them before turning back to my husband.

"Yes, Jack. I'd say that you can legitimately call them your grandchildren now."

"I get to be there when one of them is born," Jack said excitedly. I looked up and kissed him softly. My kids were lucky to have him. So were my grandkids.

"Funny how sometimes getting everything you never wanted can make you so happy," he added.

We both laughed. "It's peaceful out here, isn't it?" I asked.

He nodded. "Maybe we should get some land."

I shrugged. "Maybe we should just borrow Kimmy's. I think she likes it when we come out here." Judging from the glow on her face, I think she loved it, actually.

"Speaking of that, what do we do about the houses?"

I jerked my head up off his shoulder. "What do you mean, what do we do about the houses?" I could feel that I was glaring.

He put his hands up in surrender. "Hey, calm down. I'm just asking. Do we keep two houses right next door to each other?"

"I can't possibly part with Grandmother's house," I said. "All of my best memories are in that house. My mother died in that house." That was something I always thought I would consider a black mark against a place. Instead, I still loved walking onto that calm, peaceful porch and remembering that was where my mother took her last breath, that we were all under the same roof when it happened. It felt special, not creepy.

"Can you part with my house?"

I shook my head. "Oh, no. Never. I decorated that house for us. That's *our* house."

He nodded. "Great. Then we'll keep them both. Got it."

I smiled. "What would you think about my letting Sloane and Adam live in my house? They can't stay at Caroline and James's forever."

Jack nodded slowly. "That's a great idea. But I think you should let them pay you rent. Adam won't like it if you don't, and the store is doing really well. We're finally in the black."

Jack leaned over and picked up a half-rotten crab apple from the ground. Then, running away from me, he called, "Hey, AJ. Catch!"

I walked to Kimmy, where she was fussing over a patch of

kale. Greens grew well in our soil. It was one of the few things she didn't grow hydroponically.

"You should keep bringing the boys out here," Kimmy said. "I let them plant some seeds today, and I want to let them watch them grow." She paused. "It's the best way I know of to teach kids about God."

I was shocked, and I was sure my face didn't disguise that well. I couldn't imagine that Kimmy, who barely smiled and grew weed in her spare time, was religious.

"Wow," I said. "That's not what I expected from you."

"Ansley," she said, flashing me a rare smile, "you can't do what I do day after day—watch beautiful things come from the earth—and not believe in God. It's impossible. You know?"

I nodded, though I didn't know. Well, I mean, I had known before, at one time or another. I could remember those days in the church pew, feeling like God's favor must be on me. Three little heads adorned with bows. One handsome husband. We hadn't gotten to that place in the conventional way, but we had gotten there. And then that life imploded. Or maybe it exploded, in grand fashion. I had spent years thinking that maybe I had gotten what I deserved, that maybe this was God's way of punishing me for what I had done.

But maybe it wasn't a punishment, not really. Maybe it was just life, one of those classic cases where bad things happen. Maybe, I had to consider, watching Jack chase after our grandsons, listening to Taylor's happy squeals as Jack threw him over his shoulder, I had focused so much on the bad that I had forgotten to see all the good.

Carter had died tragically, yes. But I had found love again. Adam was MIA, but he had come home. James had cheated on Caroline, but I'd dare to say they were perhaps getting along better than ever.

So maybe the good was the thing to look for; maybe I didn't have to spend so much energy focusing on the bad. Because maybe it was like my mom always said, that it was all being woven together in the perfect way.

Two days later, standing in a delivery room for the birth of my fifth grandchild, I couldn't help but believe that was true. I had never seen my daughter happier. I had never seen Kyle happier. And I was pretty sure I had never been happier, either. As Kyle handed my new perfect granddaughter to me, I gasped. Her full lips, her brow line, the shape of her eyes—she looked like her grandfather. She looked like Carter.

I was trying to keep it together, but then Emerson said, "Mom, we're going to name her Carter Ansley."

With that, I could feel the tears streaming down my face. Because although Carter was gone and would never know his grandchildren, this little girl—this perfect angel—was his legacy. She was one-fourth of him, and he would live on in her forever.

"Oh, honey," I said. "That is the greatest thing I've ever heard."

As Jack walked into the room, he smiled but didn't say a word. "This is Carter," I whispered as I handed her to him.

He looked down at her and whispered, "Hi, Carter," as Kyle walked over and put his arm around me and kissed my cheek.

"She's more than I deserve," Kyle said.

"Carter?" I asked.

"I meant Emerson, but yes, of course, Carter, too." He paused. "I know you hate surprises, but you have to admit that this was a damn good one."

I had to admit that it was.

Jack looked up at me and smiled. "Now I see what all the fuss is about. Do they all smell this good?"

I laughed as Sloane and Caroline walked through the door along with AJ, Taylor, Vivi, and Preston to introduce them to their new cousin. I thought I might burst with pride. Here they were. All of them. My family. The only person missing was my first husband, the one who would have loved this moment perhaps more than anyone else. But I had to think that maybe he was here, too, that maybe he was even the one who'd sent baby Carter to us in the first place. I knew already that her birth would help to heal us all.

My relationships with my girls still weren't perfect after the tumult of the year we had been through together. But they were almost back to normal. No, not just normal. Better than before, stronger than before. And I understood now that the things I thought would break me didn't break me at all. In fact, they made me who I am.

As Jack handed baby Carter back to Emerson, he took my hand and squeezed it. And I realized that despite what I had believed, sometimes life gives you a second chance. It might take sixteen years, but it does. And when it does, don't do what I did. Don't drag your feet; don't give it the opportunity to slip away. Grab it. And then hold on for dear life.

FORTY-TWO

emerson: hope

Sloane, Caroline, and I stepped out of the limo onto the LA street, leaving a crew of rowdy men and even rowdier children inside. It was something to see the kids in our family like that, all lined up in car seats, with the exception of Vivi, who was sitting, arms crossed, beside James, sulking because she didn't get to walk the red carpet with us. James was trying to make her smile any way he knew how—namely, by bribing her with a new necklace—but he was learning that jewelry didn't work as well on her as it did on her mother.

Caroline was still living in the New York apartment she'd rented down the block from James to take some time for herself, time that we all agreed she really needed and deserved. But she loved her family, and she realized she wanted to fight for them more than she wanted to make everyone else's opinions go away. And we were all at a place where we knew that—

no matter what she ultimately decided about James—Caroline, Vivi, and Preston were going to be OK.

What was most amazing about those babies in those car seats was that one of them was mine, that she, with my bright blue eyes and Kyle's Maybelline-long eyelashes, had been mine for almost three entire months. We hadn't found out what we were having, and for months Kyle had predicted, "It's a girl, and I hope she's exactly like her mommy."

So far, he was right. I could already tell that she was going to be as strong-willed as they come.

I posed for the cameras as I stepped out, smiling at each photographer who yelled, "Emerson, over here!"

I took my sisters' hands, one on each side. They were beautiful, both of them, and I wondered if those children sleeping in the back would turn out to be little versions of the three of us. They wouldn't be siblings, of course. But they would have a bond, one of shared summers, of sleepovers and sneaking out and long months by the shore. They would have what we had—only, I hoped and prayed, with less adversity than we had faced.

I squeezed their hands and then turned to pull my mom out of the limo. She had complained that her dress was too fitted, but she looked as beautiful as I'd ever seen her, right up there with her second wedding day.

Part of me wanted Kyle on my arm that night, wanted him there to see me if I actually, like everyone was predicting, won the Emmy for my role in *A Tree Grows in Brooklyn*. It made me think of that first night with him at Limelight, all those years ago, when I had known that my life was about to change. Kyle had been a part of it then, and he was a part of it now.

But this seemed more fitting in a lot of ways. These women were the reason I was who I was, the reason I did the things I did. And Kyle, God bless him, understood that better than anyone.

"So, Emerson," one reporter said as he stuck a microphone in my face, "are the rumors true? Are you marrying the owner of the Peachtree Perk empire?"

It made me smile. It made my heart race. It made me think that despite my ambivalence about marriage, maybe I could actually take that plunge with Kyle, that I could commit to forever because he was the forever I wanted. I had, after all, suggested he put a Peachtree Perk right inside Sloane Emerson LA, which was opening next month. If that wasn't commitment, what was? I got butterflies just thinking of it. It was what Kyle had always done for me, combined my past and my present in that seamless, perfect way.

Caroline raised her eyebrow like that was news to her and held up my left hand. "No ring, no wedding," she said.

We lined up against the black-and-gold Emmy backdrop on the red carpet to have our photo taken, and I took my sisters' hands again. My stomach flipped. I knew that whether I won the Emmy or not, I was already on the path where I ultimately saw myself going. It might not be the move that would change my career forever, but it was the right direction, no doubt.

What I had learned this year was that work wasn't everything—that who I was to the outside world didn't really mean that much. It was the other stuff that counted: the way

Kyle had held a washcloth to my forehead so gently when our little girl was born, the way I knew he would always hold my heart just the same way. The way my family rallied around one another no matter what, dropped anything and everything to be together when it mattered. The way my mom marrying Jack had, against all odds, ended up repairing a fracture in my family that had been there for so long I couldn't even see it.

Their love made me want to be the best of the best in everything I did. But nothing had ever meant more to me than being in a place where I knew that I was whole either way.

I couldn't change the past, couldn't predict the future, couldn't know where I would end up. But for now, as my sisters and my mom stood beside me, I had something I hadn't had in a while: hope. And sometimes that's all a girl can really ask for. For today, that was good enough for me.

I reached into my bag then and handed Caroline and Sloane the surprise I had brought with me all the way from Peachtree Bluff: our staurolite. I had heard the story so many times it was almost as if I remembered it, despite the fact that I was two years old when Caroline had found it. Grandpop had told Caroline that these stones were rare and precious, that she had been chosen by the fairies to find them. These stones would keep us safe. As I clasped my fist around my piece, I could almost hear Grandpop telling us the most important thing that any girl could hear: we could grow up to be anything we wanted. And we had.

But Grandpop had been wrong, too, because it hadn't taken growing up to become what we wanted to be. Tonight, despite the evening gowns and the Emmy backdrop, we were what we had always been, what we would forever be, until our ashes, too, were spread among the sea oats and the wind and the gentle waves lapping the shore on the island that had raised us. Forever and always, the women flanking me and I would be those little girls building castles on the southern side of paradise. We would always be the Starlite sisters.

As we walked away, a reporter shouted to me, "New baby, hot mogul boyfriend, blossoming career . . . Emerson, you have it all!"

When I was younger, I thought having it all meant an Oscar, an eight-figure yearly salary, a star on the Hollywood Walk of Fame. I didn't have all that. But I had Carter. And Kyle. And Mom, Caroline, and Sloane.

We walked inside the theater, and Caroline grabbed four glasses of champagne and handed one to each of us.

Mom raised her glass and said, "To my girls, my Starlite sisters. May you have it all."

I smiled at each of them as we clinked glasses. And I knew, deep in my heart, that we already did.

acknowledgments

In 2017, Peachtree Bluff, Georgia, and its indomitable Murphy women were born, with *Slightly South of Simple*. This was my first series, and I was terrified at how it would be received, but you, my wonderful readers, were there, encouraging me every step of the way. I wrote Peachtree Bluff for you, and nothing has ever meant more to me than your kind comments, emails, notes, and reviews, that you have attended signings and followed me on Instagram and signed up for my newsletter . . . Basically, I have the best readers in the world, and I hope you know how much you mean to me!

My editor, Lauren McKenna, is the one who took this leap of faith with me, who told me it was time to write a series and that, yes, I could. Lauren, you, as usual, were right. Thank you for being such a huge part of this story—and maybe most of all for spending a whole week with me in the real Peachtree.

My team at Gallery Books is beyond incredible, and I wouldn't get to do what I do without each of you! Thanks especially to Jen Bergstrom for all your encouragement, Michelle Podberezniak for your tireless efforts to spread the word about my work, and Maggie Loughran for handling a million details with grace. I appreciate you so much.

Kathie Bennett, thank you for giving me the opportunity to share my stories with readers all over the country. There is no one else like you, and I am so grateful not only for your expertise but also for your friendship.

Thank you to Elisabeth Weed and The Book Group for your big, beautiful vision for my career and for all you have already done to implement it.

Tamara Welch, your expertise means everything to me, and I am so grateful for everything you do every day. You amaze me!

Absolutely no one has supported my career more than my husband, Will, despite the fact that my long tours and weekends spent writing probably affected him most of all. Thank you for being my biggest fan and for answering my incessant boating and fishing questions that I had to ask to make this series work. And thank you to my son, Will, for being all-around awesome, my very best buddy—and for occasionally listening to a chapter or two as a bedtime story.

Thanks, as always, to my amazing parents, Beth and Paul Woodson, who have always gotten behind every dream I've ever had, even the crazy ones (like this!). Thank you for all your love, enthusiasm, and everything you do behind the scenes.

acknowledgments

I am eternally grateful to the bloggers, reporters, reviewers, and book angels in my life. Andrea Katz, thanks for your amazing advice and endless support. Susan Roberts, Michele Collard, Karen Means, Jenny Belk, Donna Cimorelli, Gina Heron, and Rose Goforth, thank you so much for always going above and beyond for me, not only online but also by going out of your way to make it to events. I love seeing your smiling faces! Kristy Barrett, you are a true gem, and I am so grateful you are in my life! Linda Zagon, Nicole McManus, Leigh Davis, Susan Schleicher, Stephanie Gray, Megan Wessell, Monica Ramirez, Kristin Thorvaldsen, Bethany Clark, Heather Finley, Marlene Engel, Jessica Porter, Erin Bass, Kinah Lindsay, Beth Ann Chiles, Amy Sullivan, Mary Ann Miller, Jennifer O'Regan, Jessica Padula, Judith Collins, Kate Tilton, Kristin Jones, Jennifer Vida, Margie Durham, Annie Mendez, and Stephanie Burns, I can't thank you enough for taking the time to review my books and share them with your readers since the very beginning.

I absolutely would not be here without my amazing design blogger friends I have met through my blog, *Design Chic*, who have opened their homes, their shops, and their corners of the internet to my books and me. I am so grateful to each and every one of you. There are too many to name, but a special heaping helping of love to: Kathie Perdue from *Good Life of Design*, Tina Yaraghi from *The Enchanted Home*, Patty Day from *Patty's Epiphanies*, Katie Clooney from *Preppy Empty Nester*, Danielle Driscoll from *Finding Silver Pennies*, Debra Phillips from *Scentimental Gardens*, Patricia van Essche from

PVE Designs, Marty Oravetz from *A Stroll Thru Life*, Shelley Molineux from *Calypso in the Country*, Cindy Hattersley from *Cindy Hattersley Design*, Cynthia James Matrullo and Carolyn James McDonough from *The Buzz*, Carrie Waller from *Dream Green DIY*, Kim Montero from *Exquisitely Unremarkable*, Lidy Baars from *French Garden House*, Lissy Parker from *Lissy Parker*, Cindy Barganier from *Cindy Barganier Interiors*, Elizabeth Moles from *Pinecones and Acorns*, Nancy Powell from *Powell Brower Home*, Kelly Bernier from *Kelly Bernier Designs*, Teresa Hatfield from *Splendid Sass*, Karolyn Stephenson from *Town and Country Home*, Luciane from *Home Bunch*, Vel Baricuatro-Criste from *Life and Home at 2102*, René Zieg from *Cottage and Vine*, Grace Atwood of *The Stripe*, Sandy Grodsky from *You May Be Wandering*, artist Jeanne McKay Hartmann, and Paloma Contreras from *La Dolce Vita*.

To everyone who has hosted events, invited me to his or her book club, in person or via Skype, shared my books with friends, asked a local bookstore to stock them, or sold them in a store, I am eternally grateful to you. I get to do what I do because of you. There aren't enough thank-yous. A special thanks to Marshall Watson, Michelle Black White, Leslie Sinclair, Cindy Burnett, and Patricia Suggs and everyone at Beaufort Historical Association for putting together such amazing events for *The Southern Side of Paradise* tour.

I want to thank all the amazing independent bookstores who open up their homes away from home to me and hand sell my books, especially my beloved SIBA stores and the ultimate champion for indie bookstores and authors everywhere, Wanda Jewell.

Thank you again to you, my incredible reader. I hope you love taking this last trip to Peachtree Bluff as much as I enjoyed writing it.